Evil is a breed . . .

KISS OF EVIL

Other Titles by Richard Montanari

THE VIOLET HOUR
DEVIANT WAY

KISS OF EVIL

RICHARD MONTANARI

HarperTorch

An Imprint of HarperCollins*Publishers*

This is a work of fiction. Names, characters, places, and incidents are products of the author's imagination or are used fictitiously and are not to be construed as real. Any resemblance to actual events, locales, organizations, or persons, living or dead, is entirely coincidental.

HARPERTORCH
An Imprint of HarperCollins*Publishers*
10 East 53rd Street
New York, New York 10022-5299

Copyright © 2001 by Richard Montanari
ISBN: 0-380-79534-5

First HarperTorch paperback printing: March 2002
First William Morrow hardcover printing: April 2001

HarperCollins ®, HarperTorch™, and ◆ are trademarks of HarperCollins Publishers Inc.

Printed in the United States of America

Visit HarperTorch on the World Wide Web at www.harpercollins.com

10 9 8 7 6 5 4 3 2 1

For my mother,
who first gave me a spoon.

Kes lusigaga alustab, see kulbiga lobetab,
Kes kulbiga alustab, see lusigaga lobetab.

—ESTONIAN PROVERB

If there are demons, there must,
of course, be demonesses.

—VOLTAIRE

KISS
OF
EVIL

Two years earlier . . .

MICHAEL RYAN SITS in a gray leatherette swivel chair, in a dimly lit hotel room, tapping his right foot to some unheard song from the seventies, thinking, This is so much better than sex, it doesn't even show up on the radar; thinking:

This moment, *this lunatic moment,* is why he became a cop in the first place.

His pulse rages.

The Beretta 9000 holstered under his left arm feels as long as a cannon and twice as heavy.

The young woman sitting on the edge of the bed in front of him is a tall, graceful beauty, uptown in a manner of fashion and speech and poise that had always driven Mike Ryan around the bend, even when he was just a cocksure, working-class kid from the wrong side of the Cuyahoga. Tonight the woman is wearing a teal blue dress, sexy heels, diamond earrings. Try as he had, he had not been able to evict her from his thoughts for more than fifteen minutes during the past two weeks; he had seen her face in every movie, every magazine, every catalog.

She is not a classic beauty, but to Michael Ryan she is perfect: long, shapely legs; porcelain skin; dusky, almost-Asian eyes. It had taken four meetings to get her and this amount of money in the same room, and at each of those meetings she had looked better—sweats to jeans to slacks to this damned *dress*.

In the back of Michael's mind, Dolores Alessio Ryan, his Sicilian-tempered wife of fifteen years, threatens castration. This woman had gotten *way* under his skin.

He wants this over.

"I'm happy," Michael says. "You?"

"Yes," she replies softly.

He had just handed her the envelope. She, in turn, had just handed *him* the four stacks of cash. Ten thousand dollars, small bills, well worn. Invisible. Except for the twenty-dollar bill on top of one of the stacks. The twenty on top had some kind of red mark on it, a strange little drawing of a bow and arrow.

After handing him the money, she had grabbed the slender sterling flask that had been sitting on the nightstand between them, smiled, unscrewed the top, brought it to her lips. She had handed the flask to Michael and Michael had known—known as fully and completely as any lesson he had learned in his forty-six years—that he shouldn't. But he did anyway. Two big swallows to steady his hands. It was Cuban rum, top-shelf. It warmed him.

And now it is showtime.

In the instant before Michael can make his move, the woman stands, then reaches into her big leather bag. Michael is sure that, when she withdraws her hand, it will be holding a pistol. This is a certainty. He freezes, the breath catching in his throat, his muscles tightening.

It is not a gun.

It is instead . . . a Montecristo? Yes. Michael goes cool for a moment, dimpled with relief. He can smell the sweet tobacco, even from five feet away. "What's this?" he asks, his face risking a half-smile.

The woman doesn't answer but rather begins to wordlessly perform the cigar smoker's ritual—sniffing, rolling, end-cutting, gently spinning the cigar as it is being lit with a wooden kitchen match. After a few puffs, she kneels in front of him, rests her hands on his knees. Her touch electrifies him. Michael, a two-pack-a-day man, doesn't cough, isn't bothered by the smoke in the least.

It's just . . . *weird*, right?

A woman like this smoking a Cristo?

Then, for the first time since they'd met, through the silvery haze of smoke made blue by the muted hotel TV, through the sudden, heady miasma of her perfume, Michael notices the pristine blackness of this woman's eyes, the cruelty that lives there, and he is frightened.

Something is *wrong*.

He tries to stand, but whatever hallucinogenic drug was in the rum seizes his world and makes it stutter and weave and lurch in front of him. He reaches for his gun. Gone, somehow. His heart races to burst, his legs feel thick and useless. He falls back into the chair.

"Here comes the dark, officer," the woman says, flipping off the safety of the Beretta, jacking a round into the firing chamber. "Here comes the night."

Before the darkness, in a breathtaking panorama behind his eyes, Detective First Grade Michael Patrick Ryan of the Cleveland Police Department observes a thousand dazzling visions at once. Some are so brutal in their majesty, so radiant, that tears come to his eyes. Most are terribly sad: Carrie, his young daughter, forever waiting for him on the front porch, her wheelchair gleaming in the late-afternoon sun. Dolores, mad as hell. Dolores's father had died in the line of duty, you see. Every morning, for fifteen years, Michael had promised her he would not die in the line of duty.

But this isn't really duty, is it, Mike?

Michael Ryan glances up at the barrel of his own weapon, at the delicate white finger on the trigger, the bloodred fingernail. He closes his eyes one last time, thinking:

It was all for my girls.

All of it.

And no one will ever know.

PART ONE

❖ ❖

ALTAR

❖ 1 ❖

I STEP INTO the white room at precisely eleven o'clock. White walls, thick white carpeting, white stippled ceiling. The lights are on and it is very bright, very warm. Aside from the blue-screened computer on the desk in the corner, the only color in the room is the plum velvet wing chair, dead center, facing the computer's small video camera, facing the lights.

I am dressed in charcoal trousers, pleated, and a powder blue shirt with French cuffs. I am also wearing a pair of black Ray-Ban Wayfarer sunglasses. I am barefoot and the shirt is open at the top.

I received the e-mail from Dante at eight-thirty and that gave me just enough time to get to the dry cleaner, just enough time to flirt with a waitress and pick up some dinner at Sfuzzi. I can still taste the garlic from the veal piccata and feel like I might be cheating this woman, even though she is going to be light-years away, figuratively speaking. But I understand what compels the person on the other side of the session to call, to arrange, to pay. I respect that.

So I take out my Binaca and freshen my breath.

I sit down.

At eleven-ten the computer speakers sizzle with static, the small window in the upper right of the computer monitor flickers once, twice, but does not yield an image. I do not expect it to. Although the connection allows for two-way video transmission, I have yet to see anyone appear in that frame. Watchers *watch*.

Soon, from the speakers, there comes a synthesized voice, robotic, yet unmistakably female.

"Hello," the voice says.

"Hello," I answer, knowing she can see me now.

"Are you the police officer?"

The game. Eternally the game. First the game, then the guilt. But always, in the middle, the come. "Yes."

"Just home from a tough day at work?"

"Just walked through the door," I say. "Just kicked off my shoes."

"Shoot anyone today?"

"Not today."

"Arrest anyone?"

"Yes."

"Who?"

"Just a girl. A very wicked girl."

She laughs, pauses for a few moments, then says: "Fix yourself a drink."

I stand, walk out of the frame. There is no bar in this room, but there is a desk with some of the items I anticipated needing. She cannot see these things, these props I will use to produce this chimera for her. Nor, of course, can she see the cauldron, the long-rusted hooks.

Those are in the black room.

As I pick up the tumbler containing a few inches of rum, I hear an increase in the pace of the woman's electronic breathing. Watchers like to anticipate, too. Watchers like it even when they can't watch.

I play her for a few moments, then reenter the frame and sit down.

"Drink," she says, a little breathless now.

I drink. The liquid is pleasant amber fire in my stomach.

"Stand up."

A strong, authoritative command. I obey.

"Now . . ." the voice continues, "I want you to take your shirt off. Slowly."

I turn my right wrist, look again at my silver cuff links, at the ancient symbol engraved into the smooth matte surface. I take the cuff links out with great drama, then unbutton my shirt slowly, one mother-of-pearl button at a time, and let it slip over my shoulders to the floor.

"Good," says the voice. "Very good. You are a *very* beautiful young man."

"Thank you."

"Now your trousers. Belt first, then the button, then the zipper."

I do as I am told. Soon I am naked. I sit down on the chair. My penis looks thick and heavily veined against the purple velvet.

"Do you know who I am?" asks the voice.

I do not. I say so.

"Do you *want* to know who I am?"

I remain silent.

"I can't tell you anyway," the voice says. "But I do know what I want you to do now."

"What is that?"

"I want you to think about the woman you saw today. At the whorehouse."

"Okay."

"Do you remember her?"

"Yes. I haven't been able to forget her."

The voice continues, a little faster. "The woman you saw on the top floor. Did you like her?"

"Yes," I say, my erection beginning to amass. This was the easy part. "Very much."

"Did it turn you on to watch her?"

"Yes." Up a few more degrees. Then a few more.

"That was me, you know. I was the whore."

"I see."

"Do you like to watch me do that to other men?"

"Yes. I love it."

"Spread your legs," she says, the transmission breaking up a bit.

"Like this?"

A few more moments of static, then: "Meet me."

"No."

"Meet me tonight."

It is a plea, now. The power has shifted, as it always does. "No," I reply.

"Meet me and *fuck* me."

I wait a few beats. My heart begins to race. *Is she going to be the one?* "If I say yes, what will you do for me?"

"I . . . I'll *pay* you," she says. "I have cash."

"I don't want your money."

"Then what do you want?"

I pause. For effect. "Obedience."

"Obedience?"

"If we meet, you will do as I say?"

"Yes."

"You will do *exactly* as I say?"

"I . . . *yes* . . . *please*."

"Are you alone now?"

"Yes."

"Then listen to me carefully, because I will tell you this once."

She remains silent. I shift in the chair, continue.

"There is an abandoned building on the southeast corner of East Fortieth and Central," I say. "There is a doorway on the East Fortieth side. I want you to stand there, facing the door. Understand?"

"Yes."

"Do you truly have the courage to go there? To *do* this?"

The slightest hesitation, then: "Yes."

"Do you understand that I am going to fuck you in that doorway? Do you understand that I am going to walk up behind you and fuck you in that filthy doorway?"

"I . . . *God.* Yes."

"You will wear a short white skirt."

"Yes."

"You will wear nothing underneath it."

"Nothing."

"You will wear nothing on top either, just a short jacket of some sort. Leather. Do you have one?"

"Yes."

"And your highest heels."

"I'm wearing them now."

"You will not turn around. You will not look at me. Do you understand?"

"Yes."

"*Say it.*"

"I will not look at you."

"You will not speak."

"I will not."

"You will submit to me totally."

"*Yes.*"

"Can you be there in one hour?"

"Yes."

"If you are one minute late, I will leave."

"I won't be late."

I stand, my erection now a huge bowsprit in front of me. "Then *go.*"

And so it begins, this casting of the spell. My very first. I had made a promise, *un beso sangre*, and now I must make good.

I cross the room, turn off the computer's camera. But before I can shut down the speakers I hear the woman sigh, loud and long. It is an animal sound of base pleasure, a human sound of great pain.

Soon after, as I grab my keys and lock the door to the white room, I realize that for me it is the latter, not the former, that has now become the need.

❖ 2 ❖

TINA HAS HIM. He knows it, she knows it.

She produces a Gitane from her silver case with a grand, Garbo flourish, then pauses, waiting. He grabs a pack of matches off the bar, lights the cigarette, and, as she blows out the match, she holds his hand gently, looks into his eyes, and can almost see the shudder run through his body, down to his crotch, back up: a thick electrical charge that seems to backlight his eyes for a moment.

"Thanks," she says.

And has him.

The Cobalt Club is mobbed; the scent of a hundred different perfumes seems to languish beneath the smoke and noise and perspiration like a gutter full of dying flowers, like the dizzying effluence of a hundred blind cats in season. The man slides onto the stool next to Tina, raises his hand to the bartender. Oyster Rolex, custom shirt. His suit—ventless, notched lapels—looks like a Cerruti. His shoulders say that he played contact sports in his younger days.

Tina is wearing her Michael Kors dress, Ferragamo heels, a thin strand of pearls.

"What's a nice girl like you, blah, blah, blah," the man says, smiling. Tina figures him to be in his late fifties, a prime candidate. He dresses well, she thinks, if not a little young for his age. He has an earring, for God's sake. She glances at his hands. Manicured. A good sign.

12

"I got stood up," Tina says. "Can you believe that?"

The man recoils in mock horror while Tina tries to see if he is wearing a rug. The light at this end of the bar is very subdued—mostly Christmas lights, some blues and reds and yellows from the dance floor—and it is hard to tell. She thinks his hair looks a little dark for a man pushing sixty, and there appears to be a slightly unnatural ridge over his ears, but, if it *is* a rug, at least it is a good one. It is not a place to skimp, she had always thought, and she had had a lot of interaction with men who wore toupees.

She is wearing a wig herself, one of a dozen she owns. Tonight, the red pageboy. She also has on green contact lenses, false eyelashes, fake nails, a ridiculous amount of makeup. Her own mother wouldn't recognize her.

And that, after all, was the point.

"Someone stood *you* up?" the man says, dramatically. "What is he, blind? Stupid? All of the above?"

Tina laughs, fawning at the compliment. The man raises his hand again, his sugar-daddy cool imperiled by a lack of bartender interest. Tina notices the ring, the discreet setting, the big diamond.

"My name's Elton, by the way. Like the singer." He deliberately drops his key chain on the bar, a set of three keys held together by a gold ring and a fob bearing the unmistakable Ferrari logo. Unmistakable, that is, to women like Tina. "What's yours?"

"Tina," she says, smiling, arching her back slightly. "Tina Falcone. Like the bird of prey."

Tina props the Polaroid camera on the bar, sets the timer for sixty seconds. They are in Elton Merryweather's paneled recreation room, the lower level of his huge split-level house in Westlake, a house most assuredly decorated (in a faux-southwestern motif) by his trophy wife, who is curiously absent from the downstairs activities, which included a "tequila kiss," one of Tina's specialties. A tequila kiss heavily laced with Rohypnol, that is.

Elton, like the others, is a music-industry executive, specifically, an entertainment lawyer. He had wanted to go to a motel, even though his wife—whom he freely admitted existed, whom he freely confessed understood him not—was out of town. But Tina had insisted that they go to his house. By the time they were in the elevator, heading to the nightclub's parking lot, and Tina had managed to unzip Elton's fly and slip her hand inside for a quick *pas de deux*, Elton was convinced.

But now, in his masculinely appointed rec room, at just after midnight, Elton Merryweather is baby-naked, save for his knee-high executive black hose, and snoring like a Louisiana sawmill.

Tina steps over to the couch, slips out of her dress. She reaches behind her, unsnaps her bra, sits down on the couch next to Elton, crosses her legs. She puts Elton's fleshy pink arm around her, looks away from the lens. Ten seconds go by. Twenty. Thirty. Elton stirs, Tina's muscles go rigid. She is sure he has ingested enough of the drug to topple a moose. He raises his arm for a moment, as if to make a point, then drops it, his wrist brushing her right breast. In spite of herself, her nipple stiffens. She looks at the top of his head and, in this light, sees the seam. It is a rug. Then she looks at the camera.

Come on, come *on*.

She is just about to get up when the flashbulb pops and the mechanical whine of the camera fills the room. The sound rouses Elton, but before he can move, Tina slips out from under his arm, sets the timer again—this time for twenty seconds—and sits back down.

Whoosh goes the flashbulb, and Tina's work is done.

Within moments she has her dress on, and both of the now-developed Polaroid pictures in her hand. Perfect. In both photographs you can clearly see Elton's naked body, his face. Her face is turned away from the lens, of course, but her breasts and legs are visible. As is the glass crack pipe she placed in Elton's hand. She is tempted to turn on the lights over the bar and see how good her body really does look, but she resists.

God she was vain.

It would be her downfall yet.

She checks her bag, making sure she has everything. The Rolex and the ring, along with the pair of diamond tennis bracelets she found in the upstairs bedroom. Expensive little baubles she is certain Elton is going to have a devil of a time replacing by the time Tiffany or Ashley or Courtney or whatever the hell her name is gets back.

Tina retrieves her champagne glass, dropping it in her bag, along with the crack pipe.

Number thirteen.

Done . . . *yes?*

Handling it by the edges, she places one of the photos on Elton Merryweather's lap, then makes another quick scan of the room.

Number thirteen. Yes.

Done.

❖ 3 ❖

IT IS JUST after midnight and I am standing in the shadows of a vacant lot on the west side of East Fortieth Street, my heart jackhammering in my chest. There are no streetlights for three blocks in each direction. There is no traffic, no commerce. Across from me sits the Reginald Building, a slanty, clapboard hovel that once housed Weeza's Corner Café, a rib-and-shoulder-sandwich joint. Before that, the Shante House of Style.

Now it is long-forsaken, save for the woman standing in the deep violet darkness of the doorway, a little girl punished, her feet spread slightly apart, her shoulders hunched against the chill. In the moonlight that slices through the tortured trees along East Fortieth Street I can see the ivory glow of her calves, her thighs.

I am dressed in a black suede duster, black jeans, no shirt, boots.

I cross the street, silently, and step up behind her.

She is wearing a leather motorcycle jacket, studded and zippered, a short white cheerleader skirt with accordion pleats, high white heels. She is thirty, blond, petite, fit. Within moments I am fully erect again.

I pull down my zipper and free myself as I lift the back of her skirt and tuck it into her waistband. She is violently trembling with anticipation, softly crying with the deep degradation of this moment. But in spite of her penitence, in

16

spite of the chill in the air, I can see the glistening rivulet of fluid trickling down her leg. Without a word I trace my finger up her inner thigh, taste her brine. I then take a fistful of her hair in my right hand and slip my left hand around her waist, under the front of her skirt, to the warm oasis of her abdomen. I step closer, and enter her slowly.

She bites her hand as I fill her, the tears flowing freely now. My face is inches away from hers. I can see her in profile: a child's nose, a small cleft in her chin, long lashes.

She pushes against me, hard, increasing the rhythm, allowing me ever deeper, her descent now complete. I pull her jacket off roughly and put my full weight against her, pressing her smooth white breasts against the filth of decades of grime.

In my hand now: a single-edged razor blade. Without warning, I scratch a very shallow inch-long cut between her shoulders—quickly, sparing her any undue suffering. Her body becomes rigid for a moment as the tip of the razor slides across her flesh. But I can smell the alcohol on her vaporous breath and know that she has medicated herself against all manner of fear. She will accept *this* level of pain, it seems.

And so I continue, my much-practiced hand engaged, for the first time, in marking a human being.

I drop the blade, pull her close, blotting her blood with my chest. I bury myself deep inside her and, within moments, I feel the electricity building, and know that she is coming.

A soft snow begins to whisper down as she embraces the throes of her orgasm, submitting to the dirtiest realities of her darkest fantasy fulfilled. She plants her hands firmly on the door and pushes back into me with all of her strength.

I reach over my left shoulder and remove the much bigger blade from the scabbard strapped to my back as the woman comes in a long steady flow, spiraling her warmth around her legs onto the frozen ground, shedding her final tears.

The machete flutters above us: a saber-sharp wing in the moonlight.

Then, like a sleek silver peregrine, it descends.

❖ 4 ❖

IT IS FOUR days until Christmas, and Public Square is sparkling with displays, robust with early-morning shoppers. This year, the city-center quadrant is decked with strands of silver garland, dotted with white and gold lights. The streetlamps have been refitted to look like gas lamps. This season's theme: A Dickens Christmas in Cleveland.

Yet homicide detective John Salvatore Paris knows that there is no amount of candlepower that can begin to illuminate the dark corners of his heart, the lightless chambers of his memory. It is the third Christmas since his divorce, the third time he has shopped alone, celebrated alone, wrapped his daughter's gifts alone—absolutely certain he had purchased the queerest, goofiest, *hokiest* presents an eleven-year-old girl could imagine. Sure, the therapist said that the average healing time for these things is two years or so, but it was common knowledge that therapists don't know what the fuck they're talking about. It was three full years and still his heart sank with every carol, every clang of the Salvation Army bell, every rum-pum-pum-pum.

How had it all slipped away? Hadn't he been certain that all his Christmases and birthdays and Thanksgiving dinners, for the rest of his life, were guaranteed to be joyous?

As the light turns green at Euclid Avenue and East Fourth Street, Jack Paris edges his old Oldsmobile forward, realizing the answer to that question is a heart-clamping

18

no. Then, as always, the other realizations begin to scrimmage in his mind: he is on the Centrum Silver side of forty, he lives with a Jack Russell terrier named Manfred in a crumbling walk-up on Carnegie, and he cannot remember the last time he walked down the street without his 9 mm, without looking over his shoulder every ten seconds.

But still Jack Paris knows exactly what it is that keeps him on the fifty-yard line of the zone, what has so far prevented him from quitting the force, taking a job in security somewhere, and moving to Lakewood or Lyndhurst or Linndale.

He likes the inner city.

No, God save him, he *loves* it.

For the past eighteen years he has climbed the city's darkest stairways, descended into its dankest cellars, ventured down its most threatening alleyways, walked among its neediest denizens of the night. From Fairfax to Collinwood to Hough to Old Brooklyn. It had cost him his marriage and a few billion alcohol-sotted brain cells, but the rush was still there, his heart still leapt in his chest when the case-making piece of evidence presented itself to him. The body might not respond the way it did when he was a rookie, it might take a few extra steps to run down a suspect, but he still brought a young man's fervor to this game of crime and punishment.

And thus—if for no other reason than to keep that body from collapsing with a myocardial infarction from climbing three flights of stairs every day—it is time for a change. At least in his living arrangements. He had appointments all over the east side during the week after New Year's. He would find new digs. Maybe it would vanquish the malaise that had settled over him of late.

The last real advance in his career was the task force he had headed during the Pharaoh murders, a series of killings in Cleveland, courtesy of a pair of psychopaths named Saila and Pharaoh and their bloody game of voyeurism, seduction, and murder.

Since that time there had been scores of homicides in Cleveland. The figures were mercifully down from even a year earlier, but still the bloodshed continued. Bar shootings, armed carjackings, convenience-store holdups, the ever escalating carnage of domestic disputes.

He is busy enough. Yet there is nothing on his plate that compares to that night when he had been run all over town in a maniacal race against time, back when his heart nearly broke forever in an alleyway off St. Clair Avenue.

Back when his daughter had been in the hands of a madwoman.

"She'll be twelve in February," Paris says. "Valentine's Day."

The woman at the perfume counter at Dillard's is wearing a long white coat and a name tag that identifies her as "Oksana." Paris looks at the lab coat and wonders if Oksana is indeed the chemist responsible for the perfume she is selling and might be summoned back to the lab for some crucial research at any minute. He thinks about making a joke, but Oksana sounds Russian, and a lousy joke in English is probably a lot worse when translated into broken English.

Paris had gone through the women's clothes sections, his mind dizzied, as always, by the categories: Missy, Teen, Junior, Petite, Plus Size. Eventually he got to what appeared to be the hip-hop section but, after looking at the mannequins in their baggy jeans and huge shirts, he decided that he didn't want to be responsible for his daughter looking like a bag lady. If he bought Melissa perfume, she would only have to wear it when he was around, and it wouldn't take up precious closet space.

"This is very popular with the younger girls," Oksana says. She looks about forty or so and has on more makeup than Marilyn Manson. Paris wonders what "younger" means to her.

Oksana spritzes a little of the perfume onto a small white card bearing a Lancôme logo. She waves the card around a bit, then hands it to Paris.

Paris sniffs the card, but, in such close proximity to all the other fragrances in the air, can't really tell too much. It all smells good to him, because Jack Paris is, and always has been, a sucker for women's perfume. Even the cheap stuff. Which, if he sees the price tag accurately, this stuff is not.

"I'll take it," he says.

The Homicide Unit of the Cleveland Police Department occupies part of the sixth floor of the Justice Center in the heart of downtown Cleveland. On the twelfth floor is the Grand Jury; on the ninth, the communications center and the chief's office. The building might not look as daunting as it did when it was built in the seventies, back when the glass and steel facade made it an imposing watchdog over the city's criminal element, but it is still functional, and the self-contained, bag-'em-book-'em-and-bolt-'em method of justice still maintains a certain efficient symbiosis.

At just after ten A.M. Paris crosses the underground garage, punches the button, steps into the elevator car. But before the doors can close fully, they open again.

A shadow appears. A deep male voice says:

"Well, well. Detective John S. Paris."

The voice has a Texas seasoning, an arrogant southern cadence that Paris had come to abhor over a recent five-week period. The owner, the man entering the elevator, is in his late twenties or early thirties, dressed in a well-tailored pinstriped suit. Dark-haired, impeccably groomed and accessorized, he carries both the de rigeur Louis Vuitton leather briefcase and the vainglorious bearing of a young criminal defense attorney.

"Counselor," Paris replies curtly.

Although Paris knows many of the defense attorneys in Cleveland fairly well, he had never heard of Jeremiah Cross, Esq., before the Sarah Lynn Weiss trial a year and a half or so earlier, nor had anyone else in the prosecutor's office for that matter. Sarah Weiss was a former fashion model who stood accused of shooting a cop named Michael Ryan to death.

Paris had been at the Hard Rock Café, within a block of the Renaissance Hotel, when the call of shots fired on the twelfth floor came in. Within minutes, the hotel was sealed, and within minutes of *that* Sarah Weiss had been found alone in the ladies' room on the mezzanine level, a bloodied bag of money—just under ten thousand in small bills—at her feet, although technically in the next stall.

Other things were detected, too. Michael Ryan's brains, for instance. They were discovered on the brocade curtains in room 1206. The investigation also found a small pile of ashes in the bathroom sink, ashes that were thought to be, although never proven to be, the remnants of an official city document. There were also fibers from a burned twenty-dollar bill. The murder weapon, Mike Ryan's Beretta, had been found, wiped clean, beneath the hotel bed.

The homicide was Paris's case and he had pushed hard for first-degree murder, even for the death penalty, but he knew it would never fly, knew it was rooted more in emotion and anger than anything resembling clear thinking. The idea didn't even make it out of the prosecutor's office. No one could put Sarah Weiss in the room at the time of the shooting, or even on the twelfth floor.

Sarah had scrubbed her hands and forearms with soap and hot water in the ladies' room, so there was no trace evidence of gunpowder to be found, no blowback of blood or tissue from the force of the point-blank impact. Not enough to stand up to a savvy defense expert witness, that is.

The defense painted Michael Ryan as a rogue cop, a man with no shortage of violent acquaintances who may have wanted him dead. Michael was not officially on duty at the time of his killing. Plus, he had been under investigation by Internal Affairs for alleged strong-arm extortion—none of which was ever proven.

The jury deliberated for three days.

Without testifying, without ever saying a single word, Sarah Lynn Weiss was acquitted.

Paris hits the button for six; Jeremiah Cross, the lobby.

The doors take their sweet time closing. Paris extracts the *USA Today* from under his arm and very deliberately opens it, halves it, and begins reading, hoping that the word *counselor* would be the breadth and depth of this conversation.

No such luck.

"I'm assuming you've heard the news, detective?" asks Cross.

Paris looks up. "Trying to *read* the news."

"Oh, you won't find it in there. Not the news I'm talking about. The news I'm talking about doesn't make national headlines. In fact, it's already ancient history as far as the real world is concerned."

Paris locks eyes with Cross, recalling the last time he had seen the man. It was just after the trial. It was also just after a snoutful of Jim Beam and soda at Wilbert's Bar. The two men had to be separated. Paris replies: "Is this the part where I feign interest?"

"Sarah Weiss is dead."

Although the information is not really shocking—the oldest, truest axiom regarding the swords by which we live and die applying here—Paris is taken aback slightly by the news. "Is that a fact?"

"Very much so."

Paris remains silent for a moment, then says: "Funny thing, that karma business."

"It seems she got dressed to the nines one night, then drove to a remote spot in Russell Township. It appears she then doused the inside of the car with gasoline, chugged a fifth of whiskey, and lit a match."

Paris is more than a little stunned at the visual. In addition to being a cold-blooded killer, Sarah Lynn Weiss had been a rather exotic-looking young woman. He glances back at his newspaper as the elevator mercifully starts upward, not really seeing the words now, then back at Jeremiah Cross. Cross is staring at him, dark eyebrows aloft, as if some sort of response to this news is mandatory.

Paris obliges. "What do you want me to say?"

"You have no thoughts on the matter?"

"She murdered a friend of mine. I'm not going to place a wreath."

"She was innocent, detective."

Paris almost laughs. "From your mouth, right?"

"And now she is *dead*."

"Mike Ryan is dead, too," Paris says, up a decibel. "And as worm fodder goes, Michael has a pretty good head start."

"If it makes you feel better, Sarah Weiss was in hell for those two years. And your office put her there."

"Let me ask you something, pal," Paris says, up another few decibels. He is glad they are in the elevator. "Do you remember Carrie Ryan? Michael's daughter? Do you? The girl in the wheelchair? Do you remember that sweet little face at the back of the courtroom the day your client walked? She's *eleven* now. And do you know what she'll be in five years? *Sixteen*. Michael gets to see none of it."

"Your friend was dirty."

"My friend made a difference. What the fuck do *you* do for a living?"

The elevator stops and chimes the lobby, like a time-keeper at a boxing match. The doors shudder once, then open. Cross says: "I just want to know how it feels, Detective Paris."

"How *what* feels?" Paris answers, turning his body the slightest degree toward Jeremiah Cross, who stands an inch or so taller. Defense, not offense. At least for the moment.

"How does it feel to have finally gotten the death penalty for Sarah Weiss?"

"Have a nice day, counselor."

The doors begin to close. Paris catches them, clearing Jeremiah Cross's path.

Paris watches Cross glide across the huge lobby at the Justice Center. He remembers the chaotic five-week trial of Sarah Weiss. At that time, a busybody friend in the prosecutor's office had told Paris that Jeremiah Cross was a bit of an enigma. She had done her standard snooping, then doubled her efforts when she had seen: (1) Jeremiah Cross's good looks and (2) an empty computer screen when she had tried to dig up something on him.

In the end, all she could find out is that he subscribed to a telephone-answering service, and his letterheads had a post-office box return address on them, a 44118 zip code, which meant he picked up his mail in Cleveland Heights.

Of the twenty detectives in the Homicide Unit, eighteen are men, all are sergeants. Three men are under consideration for lieutenant: Jack Paris, Greg Ebersole, and Robert Dietricht. Paris isn't interested, Ebersole doesn't have the administrative personality, and Dietricht is one of the most officiously obnoxious pricks in the department, which means he's a natural for the position. He's also a brilliant detective.

At the moment, Bobby Dietricht is sitting on the edge of Paris's desk, picking at an imaginary ball of lint on his perfectly creased pantleg, pumping one of his sources on Paris's telephone. Bobby is thirty-nine years old, a few inches shorter than Paris's five-eleven but in far better shape. Bobby, who never touches a drop of alcohol or a bite of red meat during the week, is in the gym every other day. Where Paris's hair is thick and chestnut in color, constantly creeping over his collar, Bobby's hair is an almost white blond, trimmed Marine Corps close on the sides and back, thinning in the front. Since Tommy Raposo's passing, Bobby Dietricht had assumed the mantle of the Homicide Unit's fashion plate. And he never rolls up his sleeves, even on the hottest days of the year.

"Okay," Bobby says, "here's what we're going to do, Ahmed. I'm going to ask you one question, you're going to give me one answer. Okay? Not your usual six. Just one. Got it?"

Paris, sitting behind the desk, only half-listening, knows the case Dietricht is working on. Muslim woman raped and murdered at Lakeview Terrace.

"Here it comes, Ahmed. Simple question requiring a one-word answer. Ready? Did you, or did you not, see Terrance Muhammad in the lobby of 8160 that night?" With this, Bobby reaches over and hits the speakerphone button, making Paris privy to the conversation, and to what Bobby obviously believes will be a classic piece-of-shit answer.

He is right.

"It is not so simple," Ahmed says. "As you know, the CMHA is way behind on their repairs. We have taken them to court many, many times over this. Leaking ceilings, peeling plaster, unsafe balcony railings. And not to mention the rats, the vermin. Add to this the low wattage of the singular lamp in the lobby of 8160 and the certainty of such an identification becomes suspect at best. I would like to say that I saw Mr. Muhammad with some degree of certitude, but I cannot. And to think, a few extra watts, a few extra pennies a year might have made all the difference in a criminal investigation."

"Ahmed, I've got you on the speakerphone now. I'm sitting here with Special Agent Johnny Rivers of the Federal Bureau of Investigation. Say hello to him."

Paris buries his head in his hands. Johnny Rivers. Bobby Dietricht is famous for the pop culture mixed reference. Johnny Rivers recorded "Secret Agent Man," not "Special Agent Man." But it was close enough for Ahmed, and that's all that matters.

"The FBI is there?" Ahmed asks, a little sheepishly. "I don't . . . why is this, please?"

"Because the Justice Department is looking into the Nation of Islam and the contracts they have with Housing and Urban Development," Bobby says. "Seems there's been some allegations of corruption, extortion, things like that."

Silence. Bobby has him.

"Could you take me off the speakerphone, please?" Ahmed asks.

Bobby and Paris perform a silent high five. Bobby picks up the handset. "Buy me coffee, Ahmed. When? No . . . how about now? *Now* is good for me. Twenty minutes. Hatton's."

Bobby hangs up the phone, stands, shoots his cuffs, turns to leave, then suddenly stops, sniffs the air. "Jack?"

"Yeah."

"Question for you."

"Yeah," Paris answers, annoyed. He has just read the same sentence for the fifth time.

"Why do you smell like one of the Spice Girls?"

The phone. Of all the possibilities that exist when a homicide detective's phone rings at work—from his long list of lowlife informants, to the coroner's office calling with bad news, to the unit commander ringing with the cheery tidings that another body has been found and you get to go poke it with things—the one call that invariably changes his day completely is the one that begins:

"Hi, Daddy!"

It is always springtime in his daughter's voice.

"*Hi,* Missy."

"Merry Christmas!"

"Merry Christmas to you, honey," Paris says. "How's school?"

"Good. We got out last Friday for the holidays."

Of course, Paris realizes. Why doesn't he ever stop and think before asking questions like that? "So what's cookin'?"

"Well," she says, taking a big swallow. "You know that we haven't seen each other in a week and a half, right?"

"*Okay,*" Paris says, his heart aching with love for this little girl. She is so much like her mother. The Setup. The Flattery. The Kill. He lets her play it out.

"And I miss you," Melissa adds.

"I miss you, too."

Swallow number two. "Did Mom tell you that she has her office Christmas party tonight?"

"She may have mentioned something about it."

"And do you remember if she told you that I was thinking about having a few of my friends over tonight, too?"

"No, honey. But it sounds like fun."

"Well . . . it turns out that Darla has a cold."

"Is that right?"

"Uh-huh. She can't baby-sit."

"I see," Paris says, thinking about what a brilliant tactic this is, having Melissa call.

"So, do you think you could do it?" Melissa asks, then outdoes even her mother in the charm department. "I really *miss* you, Daddy."

God, she's going to be a dangerous woman, Paris thinks. He had planned to rent *Sea of Love* again, toss a turkey dinner in the microwave, maybe do a few loads of laundry. Why on *earth* would he give all that up to spend a few hours with his daughter? "Sure."

"Thanks, Daddy. Mom says eight o'clock."

"Eight o'clock it is."

"*Oh!* I almost forgot!"

"What, sweetie?"

"Did Mom tell you what she got for me as an early Christmas present?"

"No, she didn't," Paris says, fully prepared to have been outspent, outhipped. What he is not prepared for is outhustled.

"It's the coolest," Melissa says. "The absolute coolest."

"What'd you get?"

"Lancôme *perfume*."

On the way back to the store to return the perfume—having already dumped the Lancôme sample card after Bobby Dietricht's smart-ass comment—Paris finds his thoughts returning to Sarah Weiss, a name he had tried very hard to put out of his mind for the past eighteen months. Although he had never partnered with Mike Ryan, Paris had considered him a friend, had known him to be a solid, stand-up cop, a family man with a terrific wife and a little girl in a wheelchair whom he loved to the heavens.

It was Mike Ryan who had given Paris the station-house

nickname of Fingers, referring to Paris's penchant for the impromptu card trick, complete with scatalogical patter, a habit stemming from a lifelong interest in close-up magic. Paris could remember at least a dozen times when a grinning Mike Ryan had staggered across a crowded downtown bar on a Friday night, a quartet of people in tow, a deck of cards in hand, shouting: *"Hey, Fingers! Show 'em the one where all the kings lose their nuts in a hunting accident."* Or, *"Hey, Fingers! Do the one with the four jacks, the queen, and the circle jerk."*

Or, how about *this*, Paris thinks as he rounds the corner onto Ontario Street:

Hey, Fingers! I'm gonna get my fuckin' brains blown out in a hotel room one of these days. Do me a favor, okay? Cop to cop. With my blessing, please return the favor to the bitch who pulled the trigger.

Sarah Lynn Weiss.

Dead.

Paris recalls Sarah Weiss's willowy figure, her clear obsidian eyes. Sarah's story was that she had found the leather satchel in the ladies' room and was about to look inside for identification when the police searched the rest rooms. The only physical evidence tying her to the shooting had been traces of Michael Ryan's blood on the big leather purse lying near her feet.

But Paris had seen it in her eyes. He had looked into her eyes not twenty minutes after she had killed a man and the madness still raged there.

He thinks about the drunken Sarah Weiss sitting in a burning car, her lungs filling with smoke, the heat blistering the skin from her flesh. He thinks about Mike Ryan's lifeless body slumped in that hotel chair.

Detective John Salvatore Paris finds the symmetry he wants in this sad and violent diorama, the balance he *needs*, and thinks:

It's finally over, Mikey.

We close the book today.

Paris steps onto Euclid Avenue, the aroma of diesel fumes and roasting cashews divining its very own recess of city smells in his memory, a scent that leads him down a long arcade of recollection to Higbee's, Halle's, and Sterling Lindner's—the magnificent, glimmering department stores of his youth—and the deep promise of Christmas morning.

As he enters Dillard's, a momentarily contented man, he has no way of knowing that within one hour his phone will ring again.

He will answer.

And, on the city of his birth, an ancient darkness will fall.

❖ 5 ❖

THE TWENTY-SUITE Cain Manor apartment building is a blocky blond sandstone on Lee Road near Cain Park, always fully occupied due to its reasonable rents, always offering new faces due to the generally rapid turnover of rental property in Cleveland Heights. To the building's right sits its identical twenty-suite twin, called Cain Towers, also a blocky blond sandstone.

In the two years she had called her one bedroom apartment on the fourth floor at the Cain Manor home, she had yet to determine exactly what it is that makes one characterless yellow building a manor, and the other a tower.

This morning she sits at the small dinette table overlooking Lee Road. The slushy hum of winter traffic is heard beneath WCPN's morning show, floating up from the boom box on the floor. She is barefoot, bundled into a lavender silk robe, smoking a French cigarette, sipping coffee. Moses, her ancient Siamese, guards the sill.

At five minutes to eleven she straightens her hair, smooths her cheeks, adjusts the front of her robe. These gestures are, of course, as automatic as they are unnecessary, because she had never come within a hundred yards of actually *meeting* Jesse Ray Carpenter, and doubted if she ever would. Still, the notion that this man of small mystery will be pulling into the parking lot across the street in a few minutes never fails to engage her basic vanities.

31

Jesse Ray is always prompt.

She stands, crosses the kitchen, retrieves the coffeepot from the counter. She returns, fills her cup, considers the sky over the city, the melancholy clouds, thick with snow. If life were perfect, at about eight o'clock that morning, she would have stood on the corner of Lee Road and East Overlook, waiting for the Mayfair preschool van with her daughter, Isabella. Bella, with cheeks the color of winter raspberries and Tiffany blue eyes to change the cold December sky, would have been stuffed into her pink jacket and thick matching mittens. If life were perfect, Isabella's mom would then have been off to some job—health club twice a week, happy hour Fridays, rent a couple of movies for Saturday night. One for Bella. One for her.

Instead, at eleven o'clock in the morning, on a weekday, she is waiting for a pair of criminals.

Glancing across the street, she sees the top of Jesse Ray's black luxury sedan as it pulls into the Dairy Barn lot and comes to a halt next to the drive-up phone booth. She sees the window roll down, sees his dark coat sleeve emerge, his bright white shirt cuff, his gold watch. It is practically all she has ever seen of him, although, once, she thought she had seen his car pulling out from behind the Borders at La Place and had followed him for ten minutes or so before losing him somewhere around Green Road and Shaker Boulevard.

Soon, she will see Celeste, tall and full of nervous energy, emerge from the passenger side.

She had met Celeste quite by accident one night, having idiotically stepped in when a rather inebriated man was threatening Celeste in the lobby of the Beachwood Marriott. Big guy, long hair, Harley T-shirt, a huge tattoo of an orange rattlesnake wrapped around his right forearm. A few sheets to the wind herself, she had gotten between them and flashed the man the Buck knife she carried. The man had mockingly skulked away. Celeste had thanked her with a round of cocktails and margarita led to margarita led to confession and Celeste had told her a few larcenous details regarding her life. A little grifting, a little insurance fraud, a little petty theft. Two weeks later they met for drinks again and she had asked Celeste if she knew anyone to whom she could sell some jewelry. Celeste had said yes.

That night was two years and nearly forty-five thousand dollars ago. The night she struck the devil's deal with herself.

Fifty thousand, not a penny less.

Celeste's knock on the door is, as always, a little too loud.

"Hi, honey," Celeste says, bounding into the apartment with a teenager's enthusiasm, hugging her briefly. They had taken to hugging at some point recently. Celeste is regal and slender, smooth-complected, just this side of runway-model pretty. Today she is wearing red ski slacks, a black faux-fur bomber jacket, a red scarf. Her dark hair is loose, wind-blown. She wears a pair of long silver earrings shaped like icicles.

"Is it cold?"

"Freezing," Celeste answers. "Coffee?"

"Help yourself," she says, bolting and chaining the door. "Thanks."

Celeste unwraps her thick red scarf, retrieves a cup from a cabinet. She pours herself coffee as Bird's version of "Bloomdido" bops from the box. She sits down at the table.

"How's Jesse Ray?" She always asked, although Celeste had never really been all that forthcoming about Jesse Ray Carpenter, having only told her the man's name after they had done more than ten thousand dollars in business. They look out the window in unison. A ribbon of silvery smoke winds its way skyward from Jesse Ray's car window. Jesse Ray the control freak. Whenever she wants to see Celeste, it is Jesse Ray she pages.

"He's okay. Actually . . . he's kind of pissed at me," Celeste says.

"Why? What happened?" She isn't really sure what the nature of Celeste's relationship with Jesse Ray is, except that she had seen Celeste moon a few times when she talked about the man. In Celeste's opinion, Jesse Ray is the grifter's grifter. A magician. "Oh, nothing. You know how he gets."

"Actually, I *don't* know how he gets. Never met the man."

"Well, let's just say I missed a cue in a very important situation." Celeste falls silent, reddening slightly as if she had been scolded all over again, sipping her coffee with a somewhat unsteady hand.

She regards Celeste for a few moments, then reaches into the kitchen drawer behind her, removes the paper bag, tosses it to Celeste, officially changing the subject, as she always does when their small talk turns to business.

Celeste looks inside the bag, brightens. "So . . . who was it this time?"

"Tina."

"The *falcon*," Celeste says ominously, forming her hands into talons.

Tina Falcone is one of a dozen aliases she uses, each one corresponding to a different physical look, a different style. She is fairly good at accents, too. When she plays the Latina, she is flawlessly Hispanic. Her confused Brit isn't half bad either. Her favorite alias, though, is Rachel Anne O'Malley. Sounds like a child film star from the twenties.

But, of all her names, her real name is the simplest. Mary. Plain-old vanilla-flavored-nobody-notices Mary.

Celeste asks, "Did the falcon swoop?"

Mary laughs. "Yeah. Old Elton was dead in his tracks."

"Elton?"

"Yep. That was a first."

Celeste shakes her head, smiling, taking it all in. "Elton," she repeats, reverentially, as if a mark never sounded quite so ripe. She stands, finishes her coffee, wraps her scarf around her neck. "I'm gonna get going, hon. Jesse Ray's got somewhere to be. I'll call you tomorrow."

"Okay," she says, but her voice sounds distant and sad.

"You all right, girl?" Celeste asks.

"I'm gonna bring her home, you know. Soon."

"I know," Celeste replies, her stock answer. "You will. It won't be long."

"All I need is six thousand dollars. That's all. A lousy six Gs. A little less, even."

Celeste lifts the jewelry bag into the air, shakes it, rattles the contents. "Cake."

Celeste is virtually the only person she can talk to about Isabella, and how much this money means to the two of them.

Mary had never married Isabella's father, Donny, a rock-drumming miscreant from Zanesville, Ohio. But she *had* lived the rock-and-roll life for two years with Donny Kilgore and his band, Android Beach, a motley assemblage of career potheads who played a nearly unlistenable mix of technodance music and seventies stadium rock. For almost two years she had toured with Donny and the boys, washing the band's clothes, cooking a ton of pasta on a hot plate, bailing them out of the drunk tank more times than she could count, puking in her share of motel lobbies.

When Isabella was born, Donny had made her a solemn, tearful promise that the drinking and the drugs were a thing of his past. Donny told her it was all going to change, that he was hooked up with a new circle. *Real* record people who were going to make it happen for the band.

What Donny had failed to mention was that these record people had certain needs, and that one morning, around five, the door would come crashing in and a German shepherd named Quincy would find 2.2 pounds of cocaine in the basement.

She had suspected Donny of dealing for a while, had torn their small Bedford Heights house and garage apart a number of times looking for his stash, never finding it. But what she *had* found was a list of forty or so music-business bigwigs—addresses, phone numbers, cell phone numbers, e-mail addresses, wives' names. Favorite cocktails, even. Donny's schmooze list. Most were lawyers and accountants, pillars of their communities. A few owned record labels. But most were men in very conservative suits with second wives and no prenuptial agreements. She was absolutely certain that these were the people to whom Donny had been dealing in an attempt to launch Android Beach.

From the day she had found it in Donny's van, she had taken *very* good care of the list.

After cooperating with the DEA, Donny had drawn a five-year sentence and she was given two years' probation and two hundred hours of community service. She had known nothing about the coke, but she *had* known Donny Kilgore and that should have tipped her.

But the worst was yet to come. Within three weeks of the hearing, her father had pulled every string he had—and he had many, reaching to the highest levels of the Cuyahoga County political machine—and taken Isabella away.

That was two and a half years ago. She had already missed more than half of Isabella's life so far. Her two legal attempts to get her daughter back had failed miserably, had cost her thousands of dollars, had created such acrimony in her family that it had now been more than ten months since she had spoken to her father.

Two and a half years. Two and a half years of wigs and makeup and wandering hands and sour, boozy tongues. Two and a half years of working her way down a list of boring record-company men with their tales of cold wives and industry pressure.

Two and a half years without Bella.

She stands in the phone booth near the corner of Taylor Road and Fairmount Boulevard, her huge sunglasses in place, in deference to the sudden winter sun streaking through the clouds, in support of her disguise. Her hair is tucked up under a wool beret, her baggy ski parka conceals everything else. In spite of the restraining order, she still finds herself in this phone booth twice a week, struggling to catch a glimpse of Bella from afar—a fog-shrouded film of a boisterous playground, cast with women her age, hugging the children, drying their tears, herding them into groups, protecting them.

She looks at her watch. Although she is late for one of her two legitimate part-time jobs, she can't leave. Even though she needs to pick up spiral notepads, buy panty hose, fill the car with gas, and stop at the dry cleaner, she can't walk away.

She never can.

The bell claps and clamors, calling the preschoolers from the Mayfair School outside.

And the film, blurred by a mother's tears, unspools anew.

❖ 6 ❖

"HOMICIDE, DETECTIVE PARIS."

At first, the telephone line sounds dead, as if the caller had hung up while they were on hold. Which, if Paris is correct, had been no more than sixty seconds or so. Then, the troubled breath on the other end tells him that someone is indeed there. It also tells him that some sort of information—true, false, or, most likely, a barely recognizable hybrid of the two—is coming his way. He had heard that deep breath a million and one times.

A man says: "Detective, my name is Mr. Church."

Paris closes his eyes, as he often does when speaking to a total stranger on the phone for the first time. He tries to put a physical description to the voice. A little cop game of his. "What can I do for you, Mr. Church?"

"I think I might have some information for you."

"Regarding?"

"A woman."

What a *shock*, Paris thinks. "I'll need a little more information, sir."

The man says: "She may be missing."

Cool. *Handoff.* "Ah. Okay," Paris begins, making a mental note to talk to the dispatcher for the ten thousandth time. "That's a completely different department altogether. If you'll hang on, I can transfer you to—"

"I fear for her. She may no longer be among the living."

38

"I'm sure she's just fine, sir," Paris says, wondering who, outside of Christopher Lee, perhaps, ever uses a phrase like *among the living*. "But I'm afraid the Homicide Unit doesn't get involved with missing persons."

"Although it *is* necessary, I suppose," the man continues. "Like deadheading a flower. Orchids, lilies, roses."

Somehow, Paris had known this conversation was blasting off-planet. After nearly twenty years, you begin to hear the launch take place in real time. "Like deadheading a flower?"

"Yes. You know something about that, don't you, officer?"

"I'm afraid not, sir. Look, if there is something the Homicide Unit can do for you, I'll be more than happy to—"

"You will take her place in *ofún*."

I will take her place in no fun? "I'm sorry?"

"White chalk, detective," the man says. Almost a whisper now.

Right.

"Okay, Mr. Church. Thanks for calling. I'll be on the look-out for a—"

But the line is dead. Seconds later comes the dial tone.

Like deadheading a flower . . .

For some reason, Paris keeps the phone to his ear for the moment.

"Jack?"

Orchids, lilies, roses . . .

"Jack?"

Paris suddenly realizes that the unit commander, Captain Randall Elliott, and a woman he does not recognize are standing in the doorway to his office.

Paris rises to his feet, sensing an introduction. He also senses a bullshit assignment coming down the pike. He is right on both counts.

"Got a minute, Jack?" Elliott asks.

"For you, captain?"

"This is Ms. Cruz. She's with *Mondo Latino*," Elliott

says, his lips drawn into a tight, phony smile, the one that screams political pitchout. Elliott is in his early fifties, white-haired, bulky in his blues, ruddied by a half-century of Cleveland winters. "She's going to be spending a week here, watching how the unit operates. I figured you'd be the most likely candidate to show her around. She said she wanted to work with the best."

The look Paris gives Elliott at that moment could slice concrete. Thin.

Paris hates these my-week-with-the-cops things that local reporters do to demonstrate how gosh-awful tough it can be at times for the city's finest, leaving them free to trash the department the other fifty-one weeks of the year. *Mondo Latino* is a small west-side newspaper serving the city's Cuban, Mexican, and Puerto Rican communities. In spite of the fact that the paper always seems to be relatively fair with its coverage of the department, the last thing Paris really wants is to carry around a reporter for a week.

Ms. Cruz is afloat somewhere in her twenties, plain to an excruciating fault, wearing thick drugstore glasses, nylon hiking boots, a bulky burnt-orange sweater set. Her hair, the color of wet tobacco, hangs lifelessly to her shoulders. She seems to be a somewhat attractive young woman who goes way out of her way to subvert any chance of appearing so.

"Mercedes F. Cruz," the woman says, almost grabbing Paris's hand from his pocket and shaking it with royal enthusiasm. "Nice to meet you."

"Nice to meet *you*," Paris replies, noticing that Mercedes F. Cruz is wearing what looks like a temporary metal retainer on her teeth and a plastic barrette in the shape of a yawning kitten in her hair. "Victor Sandoval still the editor over there?"

"*Oh* yes," she says.

"Still hide his Sambuca in a Fresca bottle?"

"Is that what's in there?" she asks, smiling.

"Just a rumor," Paris says, winking at Elliott, resigning

himself to the task at hand. "Welcome to the Homicide Unit."

"Thank you." She looks at her notebook. "You were involved in that incident next to The Good Egg Restaurant, weren't you?"

"Yes," Paris says, already impressed with Ms. Cruz and her homework, flattered, as always, to be the subject of a young woman's scrutiny. Even a young woman wearing a bright yellow kitty-cat barrette.

"I followed the Pharaoh case pretty closely," Mercedes says. "Young single woman alone and all."

"Of course."

The conversation stalls long enough for Elliott to make his move. "Well," he says, "I'll leave you two to iron out the details. Once again, nice to meet you, Ms. Cruz. Always a pleasure to work with our friends in the Hispanic community."

Elliott departs, leaving Paris and Ms. Cruz awkwardly standing face-to-face.

"So," Paris says, leading Mercedes Cruz into his office. "When would you like to get started?"

"How about right now?"

"Well, I've got a lot of reading to do at the moment. Nothing too exciting, I'm afraid."

"That's okay," she says. "I'm interested in every aspect of a homicide investigation."

Paris thinks: Is she going to watch me *read*?

It appears so.

Mercedes Cruz drops her bag on the floor, positions her chair in the corner of Paris's paper-besieged office, and sits down, her spiral-bound stenographer's notebook on her lap, her pen at the ready. Paris notices that the cover of the notebook is festooned with an elaborate rendering of blue and red concentric hearts drawn with a ballpoint pen. A schoolgirl's daydream.

And it's only Day One, Paris thinks.

"Just go about your business, detective," Mercedes says,

adjusting the kitten on her head. "You won't even know I'm here."

The noise level is *astonishing*.

As a veteran of an urban police force, he has, of course, been privy to a great many scenarios of audio overload. From automatic weapon fire on the range, to the sound of a dozen crackheads in a two-bedroom house all yelling at the same time, to the tremendous thunder of a five-unit pursuit up an alley, code three. He had even chased a suspect through the crowd at a ZZ Top concert at Public Hall once. There were moments during that madhouse scene when it sounded like he was on a runway at Hopkins airport, standing under the wing of a 747.

But there is nothing, Paris has to admit as he steps into his ex-wife's apartment on Shaker Square, nothing in the world quite as loud as the wall of noise produced by a half-dozen eleven-year-old girls at a pajama party.

"What's all this?" Paris asks. They are in one of Beth's two spare bedrooms, thankfully past their small-talk threshold, having already fulfilled their conversational quota of job-related woes. For brief moments, at times like these, it was as if nothing ever happened to their marriage. Except that Beth is wearing a green velvet cocktail dress. And that she is going out without him.

"Wild, huh?" Beth answers, clipping an earring in place. Her hair is butterscotch, falling softly to her shoulders; her lips, tonight, a deep claret. Her figure, Paris would swear under oath, even now, in her mid-thirties, had not changed from that of the young woman he had fallen in love with more than a dozen years earlier. For Jack Paris, Elizabeth Shefler was, and is, the very criterion of beauty.

He studies her for that moment, a little unstuck in time, knowing in his heart that he will never fall in love again. Not like he had with Beth.

"Welcome to command and control," Beth adds with a

smile, clearly recalling the years of cop-talk, mercifully de-railing his train of thought.

On the corner desk sits a large computer monitor, ringed with yellow Post-it notes. Beneath the desk Paris can see a mini-tower computer, its two green lights glowing like some electronic tomcat on sentry.

"The company paid for it," Beth continues. "I can do half my work from here now."

"You're that good with a computer?"

"They paid for the three-day training, too. I can get around."

On top of the monitor is something that looks like a small plastic tennis ball with a shiny black dot in the middle. Paris walks over, fiddles with it. He notices that the object is stuck to the top of the monitor with a suction cup.

"Isn't that neat?" Beth says. "It's a video camera. We use it for conferencing."

"Conferencing?"

"Videoconferencing."

"Sorry," Paris says. "You know what a Luddite I am."

Beth joins him at the desk. She hits a few keys, starting a software program called Video Director. Then, suddenly, the two of them appear on the monitor screen.

Crazily, Paris feels as if he is walking through Sears, on one of those forays through the electronics department where you stroll by the camcorder display and they let you see how shitty you really look. Except, this was in the privacy of your own, well, wherever you had your computer. Beth's computer is in her spare bedroom. And thus a million prurient scenarios jog through Jack Paris's mind. He banishes them. "Wow" is all he can manage.

For a moment, on the screen—a poorly lit shot of the two of them from the waist up—Paris sees his ex-wife as another woman for some peculiar reason, a very attractive stranger standing inches away. He is fascinated by the way the light plays over her breasts, her shoulders, her hair. But he cannot see her face.

And, for some equally peculiar reason, that fact stirs him even more.

"By the way," Beth says, punching a few keys, killing the image on the screen. "Have you had a chance to get to the safety deposit box?"

Shit, Paris thinks. He was hoping to milk this one for a while. If she hadn't asked him this time, it would mean another between-visitation liaison. "This week. I promise."

"I wouldn't want anything to happen to it," Beth adds, speaking of her mother's wedding ring, a mostly sentimental piece of jewelry that was part of the ever-dwindling residue of their marriage. It had sat in a box at Republic Bank at Severance since the divorce.

"This week," Paris repeats.

"Thanks." Beth smiles a smile that reaches Paris's knees, the one that won his heart. She kisses him on the cheek. "I'll be back by one."

A little late for an office Christmas party, isn't it? Paris thinks. But he says nothing about it. "They'll all be asleep by then, right?"

Beth laughs. "Sure, Jack."

"How old are your friends, Missy?" They are in the kitchen, making what has to be their fifth pitcher of iced tea. The noise in the living room has abated for a while, save for the occasional barrage of laughter. Somehow, for Paris, as the father of a near-teenager, the silence was worse.

"My age," Melissa says. "Jennifer's twelve, Jessica's eleven, Mindy's twelve."

Twelve, Paris thinks, retrieving a not-quite-frozen tray of ice cubes from the freezer. One of them looked at least sixteen. Was this how teenage boys saw his daughter? "They're all in your class at school?"

"Yep," Melissa replies.

"Some of them look so . . . I don't know . . ."

"Mature?"

"Yeah. I guess that's what I mean. Mature."

"I *know*," Melissa says. "Jessica's getting boobs."

The word hangs in the air for a moment, immobilizing Jack Paris, freezing all ability to function, to think. Boobs. His daughter said *boobs*. What the hell was next? Paris attempts speech. "I hadn't . . . I mean . . . I didn't . . . y'know—"

"Can we get pizza?" Melissa asks, sparing him. "Mom says the new guy who delivers for Domino's is really cute. Everybody wants to see him."

My God, Paris thinks. *Cute. Boobs. Guys.* One conversation. He feels as if the floor beneath him has suddenly spit out a few nails. He looks at his daughter, at her long mahogany hair, her bright eyes, her still-girlish figure, and wonders how the hell he is going to survive the next ten years of her life.

Luckily, at that moment, somebody's favorite song comes on the radio in the living room, and Jessica/Jennifer/Mindy turns it up. It is one of the reasons Paris does not hear the phone ring.

The other reason is that the call is coming in on Beth's second line, the one in the spare bedroom, the one dedicated to the computer's modem.

As Paris brings the pitcher of iced tea into the living room and looks up the number for Domino's Pizza, the computer in the bedroom makes that noise two computers make when they link, then settles back into a stillness marred only by the occasional *skrit-skrit-skrit* of the hard drive as it downloads a file: silent, dutiful, discreet.

Click here.

Paris looks at the two words on the computer monitor's screen, written in bold red letters drop-shadowed in gray. They are centered on a black background and seem to float in space.

He is in the spare bedroom, standing in front of the computer. He knows he is prying, of course, and he hates himself for it. But that doesn't stop him. Beth is due any minute and still he can't resist the temptation. Was it the detective in him? Or just the asshole?

Paris votes for the asshole.

Click here.

Next to the words, just to the right, is the mouse cursor—a small white arrow angling inward, to the left. What little actual computing Paris had done in the past was all done with a keyboard, but he had wielded a mouse once or twice in his short cyber career.

He sits in the office chair, distributes his weight, takes the mouse in hand. After circling *Click here* a few times, he manages to hover the white arrow over the second *c* in *Click*.

He presses the left mouse button.

And although he wasn't sure *what* he expected to see when he clicked on the word (perhaps a spreadsheet of some sort, perhaps a database of Beth's realty clients), what he actually sees confuses the hell out of him.

It is a chair.

A velvet wing chair.

The image is a little fuzzy, fading in and out a bit like bad TV reception. It is also black and white. But for some reason Paris can tell it is not a still photograph he is looking at, but rather a live shot of some sort. A live shot of a *chair*.

The Internet, Paris muses. Big friggin' deal. He is almost proud of his resistance to computers. He squints, trying to see if there is an impression on the chair, trying to determine if someone had just recently been sitting there, but the angle is too head-on.

The image reverts back to its *Click here* screen.

Paris feels safe that he has not violated any trust here, although he knows he doesn't have the right to click *anywhere* in Beth's life anymore. It wasn't his business what she had on her computer. What was he expecting to find? Love letters? Beth isn't the kind of woman who would type a love letter anyway. Beth is the kind of woman who would find just the right stationery, just the right ink, just the right sentiment. In fact, Beth is—

Standing in the bedroom doorway.

Watching him.

Somehow she had entered the apartment, no doubt checked on Melissa and her friends, and made it all the way up the hallway without making a sound.

What a cop *I* am, Paris thinks. Ever vigilant.

"I, uh . . ." Paris manages, rising to his feet. "I was just . . ."

She has seen him at the computer, of course. Paris looks at the floor, waits for the lecture that will surely include the f-word and end with something about him never being left alone in any dwelling of hers for the rest of everyone's life.

But that doesn't happen. Beth greets him instead with a huge, eggnog-sodden smile. And a *hug*. "Merry Christmas, Jack," she says.

Paris can smell the booze. He hugs back, instantly aroused at her soft, perfumed nearness. "Merry Christmas. How was the party?"

"Same as always," Beth says, flopping onto the bed. "But drunker. A little more obnoxious than usual."

Seeing as she wasn't going to yell at him, Paris decides to push his luck. Like always. "What is this?" He sits back down at the desk and positions the mouse cursor over the big red *Click*. He clicks. After a few turns of the hard drive, the image appears.

"What is what?" Beth asks, sitting up.

"This." Paris turns and points to the velvet wing chair on the screen. Except the chair is gone. It has been replaced by a picture of the space shuttle making a perfect three-point landing at Andrews Air Force Base.

"*Uh* . . ." Paris says. He looks at the top of the screen. CNN.com

"That's called the news, Jack," Beth says, unzipping the back of her dress, as if they were still married and about to hit the sack. "The national news. Stuff that doesn't happen in Cleveland. You may have heard of it."

"But there was just some kind of, I don't know, performance-art thing on for a minute or so. Nothing but a chair. The all-chair channel or something."

"Right," Beth says, rising from the bed, a little unsteadily, then kicking off her shoes. "Master Bedroom Theater." She laughs at her joke, leans in front of Paris, grabs the mouse, and clicks on an icon. The Video Director icon. "No peeking."

It is a familiar, sexy taunt. An early marriage-game for the two of them that began on their wedding night. Paris, tipsy outside the window. Beth, a terry-cloth blur inside their motel room.

In a few seconds, the room behind Paris appears on the screen, courtesy of the small digital camera suction-cupped to the top of the monitor. The woman on the screen lets her velvet cocktail dress slip to the floor as she moves, in a series of still shots, to the closet.

At that moment, to Jack Paris, the woman on the screen is somebody else's wife, somebody else's girlfriend, somebody else's mistress. A movie-sexy total stranger within his reach.

But . . . *should* he reach? Was Beth actually trying to *seduce* him? Was the moment he had longed for and dreamed about for years finally happening?

He is as unsure of the answers to those questions as he is unable to tear his eyes from the computer monitor. The stranger on the screen slips her bra over her shoulders, her back prudently to the camera.

And, in spite of his explicit instructions, Jack Paris peeks.

❖ 7 ❖

SHE IS GINGER tonight; blond and demure. Grace Kelly with a leopard clutch purse.

The mark is black, in his late forties.

She has never gone out twice in one week. Far too risky, far too much wear and tear on her nerves. She usually prefers at least a one-month span between hits, preferably two, but something terrible happened when she watched Isabella from the phone booth that morning. For a few minutes, she had thought another child was her daughter, a little girl about the size Isabella had been six months earlier. When she realized her mistake she searched the playground, frantic for a few moments, then finally burst into tears when she saw Isabella, sitting on a bench, her shoes untied as always, waiting for someone to help. Isabella had been the girl in the navy blue coat and matching tam-o'-shanter. The first girl out of the building when the bell rang.

She had seen her daughter and not recognized her.

There was no longer any time to waste. Every day she doesn't hold her daughter is a day she will never get back. She is not going to live up to her father's low expectations.

She closes her eyes, finds her center, finds *Ginger*, takes a deep breath, exhales.

When she opens her eyes, she glances over at the table in the corner and draws Willis Walker to the bar with a smile that yields the rumblings of his very first erection of the night.

"I've never seen you here before," Willis says.

"Oh, but I've seen *you*," Ginger answers.

"Is that right?"

"It is."

Willis Walker leans against the bar, a huge slab of black man in a mauve three-piece suit, matching tie and socks. The president of Black Alley Records, a small hip-hop label run out of a warehouse on Kinsman Road, Willis smells of Lagerfeld cologne, dance-floor sweat, and Vidalia onions tonight, the lattermost courtesy of Vernelle's special blend of barbecue sauce. The clientele at Vernelle's Party Center on St. Clair Avenue is mostly black, mostly monied, mostly on the hustle in some manner or another. A beautiful young white woman, alone at the bar, usually means one of two things, both trouble. Everyone knows that.

But, this night, the woman is *that* fine, and Willis Walker is far too loaded to care.

Ginger lights a cigarette, moves a little to the music—a raucous version of "Climbing Up the Ladder" by The Isley Brothers. She squares herself in front of Willis Walker, reels him gently in. "So . . . you gonna do a tequila kiss with me?"

"A tequila kiss?" Willis answers. "What's that?"

"I'd prefer to show you," Ginger says. "But it has something to do with an ounce or two of Cuervo."

"Oh yeah?" Willis asks, his white-girl rap now fully engaged. "What else?"

Ginger arches her back slightly. Willis's eyes stray to her breasts, back up to her lips. She waits. "A lemon, of course."

"*Gotta* have that lemon." Another smile. Big, pearly shark. He moves a little closer. "Anything else?"

Ginger parts her lips slightly, her eyes roaming Willis Walker's considerable bulk. She whispers, "My *mouth*."

Willis's eyes light up. "Your mouth?"

"*Sí.*"

Willis calls the bartender.

"Not here," Ginger says.

Willis looks dismayed for a moment. Then snaps the golden hook. "Okay," he says. "Where?"

Ginger removes what looks like eight hundred dollars in cash from the inside of Willis's suit coat, along with his watch, his rings, the sapphire stickpin in his tie. There is no need for photo insurance this time. Willis Walker is not exactly the kind of man you threaten with blackmail.

Willis is spread out over one of the two beds in Room 116 of the Dream-A-Dream Motel on East Seventy-ninth Street. His shirt is unbuttoned, his pants unzipped. At the moment, he is snoring loudly, spreading a small pond of drool on the stained pillowcase.

In the background, Conan O'Brien chats with an emaciated blonde in a too-short dress.

Ginger shoves the cash into her oversized purse. An extraordinary haul for twenty-five minutes' work, she thinks. As per her routine, she will now put on the dark knit cap she carries, along with the calf-length plastic raincoat that folds into a bundle no larger than a pack of Marlboros. At night, from even ten feet away, she would look like a bag lady. She would walk the five blocks back to Vernelle's, and her car, pepper spray at the ready.

She peeks through the curtains as she slips on her raincoat. Dark parking lot. Fewer than five cars. Safe. She opens the door.

And knows that he is behind her.

Even before his fingers dig into her neck.

"Goddamn *bitch*," Willis Walker screams, pulling her roughly back into the room. "Goddamn fuggin' *bitch*!"

He bangs shut the door as Ginger crashes to the floor, rolls to her right, gets up, snaps off a heel. She stumbles into the wall, her heart racing. How had he survived that much Rohypnol? She had increased the dose because of his size, but here he was wide awake. How could he—

She does not finish the thought. Willis Walker interrupts the process with a right cross that smashes into her jaw, stunning her, showing her mind a galaxy of stars. Bile sours her throat as she hits the floor again—knees first, then hips, shoulders, head. The room tumbles like a crazy red clothes dryer.

"Fuggin' *kill* you, bitch," Willis chants, stumbling toward the nightstand between the beds, plowing into the table lamp, exploding the bulb against the wall.

Ginger finds her way to her feet, her head a shrieking carousel of noise and pain. She holds onto the wall, kicks off her shoes, finds her balance. For a moment, she thinks she is hallucinating. But there it is, rising into the shaft of moonlight streaming through the window, swinging her way.

A nickel-plated twenty-five.

Ginger dives into the bathroom, slams the door. She barely gets the knob on the lock turned before Willis pummels the door, rattling the hinges, splintering the jamb. "*Biiiiiiiiitch!*"

She looks around, her mind reeling. No windows. Nothing even remotely resembling a weapon. She grabs the doorknob, attempting to help herself to her feet, but the lock explodes in her hand. Bits of hot metal and smoldering wood fly through the air as the bullet clinks off the side of the toilet and falls to the floor, inches from her feet. The smell of gunpowder and burned sawdust fills her nostrils.

This is it, she thinks. My life is over. He is going to shoot me. I am going to die in a twenty-dollar motel room.

But it is Isabella who helps her to her feet, then guides her over to the toilet where she removes the heavy cover off the tank. It is her daughter's tiny hand that closes the shower curtain behind her as she steps into the tub, waiting, her pulse pounding in her ears.

With a crack of thunder, Willis Walker kicks the door in with a size-thirteen shoe, then lurches into the bathroom. "Where *y'at,* bitch?" he screams. "You *want* some? I *got* some for ya. Willis Walker *got* some for ya."

He raises the gun, fires it drunkenly into the mirror—shattering it into a dozen pieces—then stumbles back, his ears momentarily stuffed from the gun blast, his central nervous system besieged by the drug.

It is Ginger's moment to act.

Before Willis can recover, she shoves open the shower curtain and, with all of her strength, brings the lid down on the back of his head, twice, the sickening thuds mingling with the smell of discharged gunpowder, converging with her revulsion. Willis Walker slumps to the tile, rolls onto his back. She drops the lid. It bounces off his huge stomach and slides to the floor.

And, suddenly, as quickly as it had begun, it is over.

A linen silence fills the room. She looks down. Willis Walker is lying on the bathroom floor, still and quiet, a small puddle of blood beneath his head. She takes a mildewed towel from the rack, replaces the lid on the back of the toilet, wiping the blood and her fingerprints from it.

And, for the next few minutes, as nausea grows within her, she continues to wipe down the motel room—everything, whether she remembers touching it or not.

A short time later, as she stands on the berm of I-90 East, retching into the culvert, she is certain—as certain as she is that she will see the death mask of Willis Walker every night for the rest of her life—that she has left something behind.

❖ 8 ❖

THE DREAM-A-DREAM MOTEL on East Seventy-ninth Street and St. Clair Avenue is a U-shaped, single story building, an inner-city cathouse patched with imitation-stucco board to cover the bullet holes, the graffiti, the long streaks of dried vomit under the windowsills.

I watched her enter Room 116 at about one o'clock. A blonde this time. Not really her color. I like her best as a brunette. I always have, ever since the day I first followed her to see where she went so mysteriously incognito all the time, to see how she peddled her charms. Even then I could feel her pull, that raw dynamism that says *you can't have me unless you step into* my *world.*

A short time after she entered the motel room I heard the gunshots, the whipcrack of a small-caliber weapon fired in a confined space. Within minutes she emerged, frantic, dressed in a dark cap, dark raincoat.

I ran off a full roll of film, my finger depressed on the shutter release as she sprinted from the room, across the lot, down St. Clair Avenue. I am sure I got her face. How recognizable it will be is yet to be determined, although my SP-7901 Starscope night-vision lens has yet to let me down.

I step inside Room 116, my sidearm drawn. The room is in disarray, but I immediately see the body on the floor, smell the metal of just-spent blood, the carbon of just-flashed powder.

The body is half in, half out of the bathroom.

I holster my weapon, place the shoulder bag on the bed, cock my head to the night. No sirens. I set about the tasks at hand. I place the knives on the floor at my feet, open the pint bottle of Matusalem rum laced with the magic mushroom, and swallow deeply. Then I slowly, carefully, light the cigar.

La madrina mia.

Why did she begin her own madness this night?

The man on the floor begins to move.

I think about her as I set about my business. It has been so long since I have said the words *I love you* to a woman that it seems I might hesitate when I tell her. This is a fear. Another fear is that she will resist me. And although romance is as important to me as it is to the next man, I do not have time to court her properly. Not now.

There will be time for romance.

The man on the floor groans.

Now I must gather.

Now I must take my hands from my ears and willfully let in the discord, the shrill fury of my father's violence. Now I must be strong and urgent and bestial. Now I must go to work.

The volume in my head soars as the *Amanita muscaria* takes me in its dark embrace.

I select my sharpest knife.

And set upon the body.

❖ 9 ❖

"WHERE *Y'AT,* JACKIE?" the man behind the counter asks. *"Comment ça va?"*

"I'm good, Ronnie," Paris says. "As good as can be expected from a man my age, on a day such as this."

The big man winks, hands Paris a red thermos, takes the empty. "It is all *bon, oui?"*

It is a rhetorical question. An old, comfortable routine. Paris studies the man, again marveling at Ronnie Boudreaux's grace at more than three hundred pounds. "You are definitely the hardest-working man in show business, Ronnie. When are you going to take a vacation?"

Ronnie Boudreaux laughs, pulls a rack from the glass display case. "I get a vacation when my two ex-wives get married or die, *mec.*" He bags a pair of beignets, hands the bag to Paris. "Or my *chouchou* love me six feet under."

This draws a laugh from the regulars at the five-stool counter.

Paris had been in a zone car one sweltering night, years earlier, and had helped to foil an armed robbery at Ronnie's Famous Louisiana Fry Cakes on Hough Avenue. Most likely a rape, too. When Paris and Vince Stella had answered the call they found Ronnie unconscious behind the counter. They also found the robber and Ronnie's terrified, half-dressed daughter in the back room. Lucia Boudreaux was ten years old at the time.

56

Jack Paris and Vince Stella brought the suspect down that night. *Hard*.

Since then, there has been a thermos of fresh coffee waiting for Paris at Ronnie's Famous, right next to the register, no matter when he stops by. They are currently on a two-thermos rotation since Paris decided to make a science out of obtaining Ronnie's fresh beignets at precisely seven A.M. or seven P.M., the two times of day when you can get the delicately sweet, square little doughnuts right out of the oil.

It has been this way for many years.

"Gotta roll," Paris says, grabbing the bag and his freshly filled thermos. "See you, Ronnie."

"Laissez les bon *temps roulet,"* Ronnie replies, on cue.

Let the *good* times roll, he says.

Paris drops a couple of dollars into the tip jar—he had stopped trying to pay for the coffee and doughnuts a long time ago—and steps out into the frigid morning. He opens the white bag, removes a warm beignet and sinks his teeth into it, eyes shut, chewing slowly, enraptured by the light dusting of powdered sugar, by the extraordinary little pockets of air. He pauses, lost in the present, until that sound destroys the moment again, as it always does. The sound of his pager.

The sound of another body falling to the earth.

Jack Paris slips behind the wheel of his car, pours himself a cup of Hough Avenue blend, and rolls.

There are a few things for which homicide detectives, even veteran homicide detectives, are never fully braced. One is dead children. Another—or perhaps it is a horror that dwells exclusively in the minds of *male* police officers—is castration. Paris had seen it only once before, a Mafia payback hit. That time, like this time, he was stupefied at the amount of blood.

The forensic activity in Room 116 of the Dream-A-Dream Motel on East Seventy-ninth Street, a stone's throw from Rockefeller Park, moves along briskly, not necessarily because the victim, a small-time hustler named Willis Walker, is deserving of such rapid progress in the investigation of his death, but rather because there is not a man in the room who can bear to look at the corpse for too long. More than once, Paris had noticed someone from the Special Investigation Unit subconsciously shield his crotch as he moved swiftly past the body, as if the murderer might still be lurking behind the damp, nicotine-grimed curtains, teeth bared, razor poised.

The blood from Willis Walker's groin had spread on the bathroom floor into a huge, tormented circle of blackish grue. The blood behind his head is another story—this, a dark-purple paste, flecked with bits of skull, rootlets of hair.

Next to the body is a .25 caliber pistol, recently discharged.

Paris snaps on a pair of gloves, crouches by the body. He carefully explores the man's front pants pockets. Empty, save for a blood-soaked pack of matches from Vernelle's Party Center, a cheat spot located a few blocks west of the motel on St. Clair.

Paris pokes about Willis Walker's body, probing here and there, putting off the inevitable. Finally, he can avoid it no longer. He hears a brief salvo of stifled laughter from behind him and turns around to see Reuben Ocasio, one of Cuyahoga County's deputy coroners, looking grim and serious and thoroughly guilty of the laughter.

"*You* want to do it?" Paris asks.

"Not a chance," answers Reuben. "I'm confident in my sexuality and all. But you're the fuckin' detective."

Paris takes a deep breath of air curiously redolent with cigar smoke. Curious, because there were no cigar ashes in either of the room's two ashtrays, no cigar butts in or near Room 116. The other smell was more explainable—rum. It seemed to be everywhere. A tart, acidic scent that probes some catacomb of Paris's memory, a place webbed in shadows at the moment, just beyond recall.

Shit, Paris thinks.

It is time.

He reaches into Reuben's black bag, removes a long, narrow tongue depressor. He then leans forward with supreme reluctance, glacial speed, and begins to separate the two sides of the unzipped fly on Willis Walker's blood-drenched pants with the sole intention of verifying the obvious—that Willis Walker not only had his head bashed in but also had been violently separated from his penis and/or testicles sometime within the past twelve hours.

Paris grits his teeth, looks inside.

They are truly gone.

The whole set.

And they hadn't been found in the motel room or, so far, on the grounds of the Dream-A-Dream Motel.

"Well," Paris says, jumping to his feet, dropping the wooden stick into the wastebasket as if it were radioactive. "Nothing *there*. All yours, Reuben."

Reuben shakes his head. "There goes that myth, eh?"

Paris laughs, but it is more from nervous relief than Reuben's bon mot.

"Move aside, rook," Reuben says. "Let a detached professional do his job."

Paris steps into the December morning, grateful for the frigid air. He lights a cigarette and looks down the walk at the scarred and battered doors of the Dream-A-Dream Motel. All the same. A million mournful dramas behind each. A million more to come.

He flicks his cigarette onto the asphalt, disgusted with himself for lighting it, bone-weary from the previous night's lack of rest. He hadn't had the courage to stay and see if Beth's intentions were romantic in nature, having all but sprinted from the apartment, knowing that his heart couldn't have taken the disappointment if he had miscalculated the signals. He hadn't slept more than twenty minutes since leaving Shaker Square.

"Get in here, Jack," Reuben says, that all-business tone now in his voice.

Paris steps back into Room 116, across to the bathroom. Reuben is leaning over the body, his skin ashen, the good humor gone.

Reuben has seen a ghost.

"What do you have?" Paris asks.

Reuben looks at the floor, at the ceiling, at the walls, anywhere but at the corpse. He is Cuban American, a fairly big man at six feet, two-forty, but at the moment he looks small and troubled. He points to Willis Walker's mouth, specifically to the man's tongue, which lolls to the side, lifeless and gray. He presses on the tip of the tongue with a depressor, flattening it out. "Look."

Paris leans in. At first he cannot see anything, but, as he moves closer, it appears as if there is something drawn on Walker's tongue. "What is it, a scar?"

"No scar, amigo. It's fresh."

Paris squints, and the shape comes into focus. "It's a bow and arrow?" As odd as it sounds to Paris, the shallow carving on Willis Walker's tongue *does* look like a small, stylized bow and arrow. Crosshatches, sharp angles, curved lines—all made of drying blood.

"I'm no expert, but it looks like some kind of voodoo symbol. Or something similar," Reuben says. "Palo Mayombe, maybe."

"I'm sorry?"

"Palo Mayombe is a very dark side of Santeria," Reuben replies, making a quick sign of the cross with a not-so-steady hand. "I think this is one of their marks."

"I'm lost, Reuben."

"You've heard of Santeria?"

"Yes. But I'm not at all familiar with it."

"Most of the people who follow Santeria are good people, Jack. Ordinary folks practicing a religion with some odd-seeming rituals attached. But Palo Mayombe? That kind of shit?" Reuben crosses himself again, touching his fingers to his lips. He finds Paris with wet, frightened eyes. "It's about torture. Mutilation. Black ceremony."

"You're saying this was a religious sacrifice?"

"I don't know," Reuben says. "I'm just saying that there may be something worse coming, *padrone*. Something *very* bad."

❖ 10 ❖

THE SNOWSTORM STARTS at noon. Five inches by rush hour, the radio says. More on the way. As always, whenever the city of Cleveland is pummeled for the first time of the season, a general traffic-psychosis descends upon the town and everyone seems to forget how to drive on ice. On his drive to the westside restaurant, Paris had seen a trio of rear-enders, had heard a half-dozen accident calls go out on the police radio.

He is sitting in a back booth at Mom's Family Restaurant on Clark Avenue and West Sixty-fifth Street, waiting for Mercedes Cruz, whom he fully expects to be late.

On the table, next to his coffee cup, sits his leather hand-cuff case. He had never gotten used to sitting in a booth with it at the bottom of his spine. Next to the case: a small but daunting pile of material on the religion called Santeria, courtesy of a quick stop at the main library.

He has learned that Santeria originated in the Caribbean and means, literally, "way of the saints." It is a religion that combines the beliefs of the Yoruba and Bantu people in southern Nigeria, Senegal, and the Guinea coast with the god, saints, and beliefs of Roman Catholicism.

Raised in the sixties, Paris is a long-lapsed Catholic, spir-itually afloat between the Latin mass and the English mass, between the austere dictates of Vatican I and the somewhat looser views of Vatican II. It was a time when the church was

62

beginning to get bombarded with issues it had not had to deal with in two thousand years: birth control, abortion, open homosexuality, women in the priesthood.

But long before the reforms of Vatican II, when Catholicism was forced on African slaves, native practices were suppressed. The slaves developed a unique way of keeping their old beliefs alive by equating the gods and goddesses of their traditional religions with the Christian saints. Slaves would pray openly to St. Lazarus over a suffering child, but the offering was really to Balbalz Ayi, the Bantu patron of the sick.

Since that time, the religion, and its many offshoots, has continued to flourish in a number of Latin countries. Mexican Santeria favors its Catholic beginnings; Cuban Santeria leans toward African origins. In Brazil, the followers of Candomblé and Macumba are said to number one million.

Like many Catholics, Paris was scared shitless by movies like *The Exorcist*. And his own mystic vision of hell. But the liturgy of *being* a Catholic—especially the rites of confession and communion—had long since dissolved into Jack Paris's past. He has borne witness to too much inhumanity to bank on a benevolent God these days.

Just as Paris is about to try and reconcile all of this with his strict Catholic upbringing for the millionth time, a shadow darkens his table.

It is Jeremiah Cross.

Again.

Behind Cross stands a woman—a brunette with a long, swanlike neck, round oversized sunglasses, short black jacket. Paris sees her only in profile for a moment before she proceeds to the register to pay the check. Cross, wearing a dark overcoat and paisley silk scarf, approaches. "We meet again, detective."

"Lucky us," Paris replies.

Cross deliberately puts on his leather gloves, stalling, clearly as misdirection, as prelude to something. After the ritual, he says, "I was wondering if you were aware of the fact that the Geauga County prosecutor's office is looking into new evidence regarding the Sarah Weiss so-called suicide."

Paris sips his coffee. "Well, as you know, counselor, Cleveland is in Cuyahoga County. I'm not at all certain why this would concern me."

"It seems there may have been a second car on the hill where Sarah Weiss burned to death that night."

"Is that right?"

"It is. A little *yellow* car. You don't drive a little yellow car, do you, detective?"

"No, I'm afraid not. You?"

"No," Cross replies. "I drive a black Lexus, as a matter of fact."

"I'm stunned."

Cross takes a step forward. "But it gets one to thinking, you know?"

"Thinking, too?" Paris asks. "Thinking's extra in your line of work, isn't it?"

Cross ignores the shot, places his hands, knuckles down, on Paris's table. One glance from Paris apparently makes him rethink and withdraw.

"Consider this scenario," Cross begins, lowering his voice. "A veteran cop eats a bullet doing a dirty deal. The innocent woman the cops try to hang the murder on is acquitted. A year and a half or so pass, the press and public move on. But not the cops. One Friday night, a couple of the boys from the unit start slamming the Buds back at the Caprice, then the Wild Turkey. Around midnight they decide to take a drive out to Russell Township—off a street called Hemlock Point no less—and pay back the woman who dusted their pal. What do you think?"

"I think it'd make a great movie of the week," Paris says. "I'm seeing Judd Nelson in your part."

"It *is* a compelling story, isn't it?"

"I see it a little differently."

"How's that?"

"I see a peacock defense attorney who falls hard for his sexy client, gets her off by smearing the victim. After the trial, the sexy client rebuffs the advances of this perfumed rustic and, on the aforementioned Friday night, he downs a bottle of absinthe or Campari or aquavit or whatever perfumed rustics drink these days, drives out to Russell Township, flicks his Bic, et cetera, et cetera. Compelling, yes?"

Jeremiah Cross stares at Paris, trumped for the moment, then notices that Paris has begun to tap his coffee spoon on something sitting on the table. A police-issue handcuff case. Cross smiles, holding up his hands, wrists together, arrestee-style, revealing a gold Patek Philippe watch, white French cuffs. "I never mix stainless steel and gold, myself, detective." He turns to leave, stops, adds: "Only a rustic would do that."

With this, Cross lingers for the proper amount of time, exchanging resolve with Paris, then heads to the door. Without a final glance, he and the woman exit.

It takes Paris a few moments to return his blood pressure to normal. Why does this guy bug the *shit* out of him? But he knows the answer to that, a basic premise that has driven him for years. The belief—the conviction—that you do not have to destroy someone's family to exact justice.

Jeremiah Cross had all but destroyed Michael Ryan's family.

Paris tries to return to the information on Santeria but finds his mind drifting to a hill in Russell Township, to the image of a burning automobile carcass lighting the night sky. His cop-mind now adds a small yellow car to the scene—lights off, engine humming, two unseen eyes behind a dark windshield, watching the manic ballet of red and orange flames, the thick black smoke curling skyward.

Before he can let the scene take hold of his mood, Paris sees Mercedes Cruz loping toward the back of the restaurant, smiling broadly, dressed, it appears, for arctic exploration.

"Good *afternoon*, Detective Paris," she says brightly, removing her huge parka, ski vest, wool cardigan, scarf, gloves, muffler, earmuffs, and hat. Today, Paris notices, the barrette keeping her sweat-dampened hair to the side is a red reindeer. Her dress is blue denim, shapeless. Her glasses are completely fogged over.

"Good afternoon," Paris says. He motions to the waitress.

Mercedes wipes her glasses with a napkin, looks at some of the material on the table. "Santeria, eh?" she asks, rolling the *r* perfectly. She slips into the booth, orders coffee, sunny-side-up eggs and cinnamon toast. She takes out her spiral notebook and pen. "What is your interest in Santeria?"

"Off the record?"

"Off the record," Mercedes repeats, hand over heart. She drops her pen into her bag.

Paris studies her earnest face for a few moments. He couldn't give her too many details of the investigation into Willis Walker's murder but decides he will trust her about the record. "It may be involved in a homicide I'm working on."

"I see."

"Are you a . . . um . . ."

"Am I a follower?"

"Okay. Are you?" Paris asks.

Mercedes laughs. "No, far from it. I'm a Catholic girl, detective. Twelve years of nuns at St. Augustine's, four more with the Jesuits at Marquette. Skirts an inch from the floor when kneeling, confession every Saturday, catechism every Wednesday."

Paris smiles with the recollection of his own youth and the dreaded confessional. Father Fitzgerald and his booming baritone, bellowing Paris's sins for half the church to hear. "Catholic Youth Organization, too?"

"*Oh* yeah. I was the talent coordinator for CYO dances for three years. Got Flock of Seagulls once."

"Impressive."

Mercedes's food arrives. She begins a ritual of making two half-sandwiches of the cinnamon toast and eggs—including a carefully placed dollop of ketchup on each slice—then meticulously stacking them on top of each other. A fried-egg-ketchup-and-cinnamon club sandwich, Paris thinks. That's a new one. She tucks into the drippy yellow-and-red concoction like a long-haul trucker after a three-day speed run.

"Anyway," Mercedes continues, wiping her lips, "with that résumé, I guess I'm about as far from a *santero* as a gal can be, eh?"

A *santero*, Paris had learned no more than a few minutes earlier, is a type of Santerian priest. "I'd say so."

"But I do know that there is a popular botanica on Fulton Road," Mercedes says. "Right near St. Rocco's."

"A botanica?"

"A botanica is a place to buy charms, herbs, potions. Most of the items are for followers of Santeria, but sometimes I think they get—how shall I say—more *diverse* requests for materials."

"Such as?"

"I'm not really sure. Like I said, I still carry a St. Christopher medal, okay? That's how Catholic *I* am. I have a few friends in the old neighborhood who dabble in Santeria. What I've told you is about all I know about it."

"Have you ever heard of Palo Mayombe?"

"No. Sorry."

Paris thinks for a moment. "So, if somebody was into the darker ends of Santeria, they might frequent this botanica?"

"Or one like it. Like Catholicism, Santeria is full of ceremony. Ceremony needs props. There's always an ad or two for botanicas in my newspaper."

Mercedes rummages in her bag, produces a copy of *Mondo Latino*. She opens it to the center, then taps a small display ad in the lower right-hand corner of the page.

Paris takes it from her and—suddenly self-conscious for some reason—puts his glasses on. The ad is for La Botanica Macumba on Fulton Road and trumpets some of the shop's exotic wares: brimstone, lodestone, black salt, quills, palm oil, rose water. The botanica also offers custom gift baskets that include spirit-calling sticks, dream pillows, magnetic sand, dove's blood ink. To Paris, two of the stranger-sounding products in the ad are the Fast Luck Bags from Guatemala and something called Four Thieves Vinegar.

"So," Paris says, "you have no idea what any of this stuff is used for?"

"A little. Most of Santeria is harmless as far as I know. People casting spells for a new job, a new car, a new house. Mostly for a new lover."

"Of course."

"Hey, didn't you ever pray for some girl to like you when you were a teenager?"

Teenager? How about last *week*, Paris thinks. "I guess I did," he says. "Okay. All the time."

Mercedes laughs and attacks the last bite of her egg sandwich as Paris's pager goes off. He excuses himself from the booth. Two minutes later he is back.

"There's been another murder," Paris says, grabbing his coat from the booth, slipping it on. "A woman."

Mercedes covers her mouth for a moment, then checks her watch, makes an entry in her notebook. "Are we going there?"

"Yes. One of the other detectives is the primary on this, but there appears to be evidence that might link this murder to a case I'm working on."

"You think it may be the same person who did this other killing?" Mercedes asks as she slides out of the booth. "The one involving Santeria?"

"Way too early to tell," Paris says. "But this one's a little different already."

"Different how?"

Paris decides to see what she's made of. A little severe, perhaps, but necessary. "Well, for one thing, she's missing the top of her head."

"Oh my God," Mercedes says, the color vacating her face. For a moment, it looks as if she just realized what the Homicide Unit actually does.

"And so far," adds Paris, dropping a tip on the table, "no one's been able to locate her brain."

The Reginald Building, at the corner of East Fortieth Street and Central Avenue, is a shabby, six-room structure that still holds on to ruins of its long list of tenants. One side of the building boasts faded Jheri Curl and Posner's ads; the other side, a hand-painted takeout menu for Weeza's Corner Café.

When Paris had been a patrolman he had spent many a dinner break parked across the street, partaking of Weeza's short-rib dinners, washing it all down with RC Cola, the only soft drink Louisa Mae McDaniels would stock. He knew that the owner of the building—one Reginald G. Moncrief, also known in those days as Sugar Bear—had had big plans for the building and its adjacent lot at one time, having even rented out a pair of rooms in the back for a short period, until the housing authority shut him down. Everything, of course, changed the night someone in the men's room at the Mad Hatter disco parted Reggie Moncrief's Afro about four inches too low with a slug from a .44 Magnum.

The yellow crime-scene tape is wrapped around the entire building and, in spite of the snow, in spite of the cold, a crowd is beginning to gather in front of the vacant lot across East Fortieth Street.

The front doorway to the Reginald Building is busy with SIU activity. Paris and Mercedes are routed to the side door, facing Central Avenue. Paris leaves Mercedes Cruz in the care of a uniformed officer for the time being and steps into the building and is immediately solicited by the smell of death, by the damp perfume of neglect. A quick scan of the room: crack vials, spent condoms, broken glass, fast-food trash. The temporary lighting that had been brought in is throwing more light than the interior of this building has seen for years. Cobwebs hang in thick cascades from every corner; the floor is dotted with dead insects, animal feces, tiny bones. Paris notices a pair of small black mice scurrying along one wall, probably wondering why their home has been so loudly and brightly invaded.

Paris locates Greg Ebersole in this scene. He is standing near the SIU team, talking on his cellular phone.

Sergeant Gregory Ebersole is forty-one, spare, and red-haired: a mongoose in a Chess King suit. Paris had seen him get physical with suspects a few times and remembers being surprised and impressed at Greg's speed and agility. What was scary about guys like Greg Ebersole, Paris had always thought, was not the cards they showed you, but the ones they didn't. Behind the cool, jade eyes, beneath the freckles and affable exterior, lurks a man capable of all manner of explosive behavior.

But as Paris approaches Greg he sees the sallowness of the man's skin, the weariness in his eyes. Greg's six-year-old son Max had recently undergone heart surgery, a fairly routine procedure, it was said, but one that thoroughly exhausted the Ebersoles' insurance, and then some. Greg had once confided that he would owe tens of thousands of dollars before it was all over. Paris knew of two part-time jobs Greg worked. He suspected there were more. This very evening there is a benefit for Max Ebersole at the Caprice Lounge. Looking at Greg now, Paris wonders if the man is going to make it.

Greg sees Paris, nods in greeting, points toward the body.

Paris acknowledges him and finds the victim in the back room, near the rusted ovens that once prepared bread pudding and the like for customers of Weeza's Corner Café. The body is covered with a plastic sheet, and next to it stands a very nervous, bespectacled black officer. Paris approaches, mindful of the small areas of chalk-circled evidence on the floor.

"How ya doin'?" Paris says, stepping into the room.

"Just fine, sir," the officer lies. He is heavyset, clean-shaven, no more than twenty-two years old. Paris locates the man's name tag: M.C. Johnson.

"What's your first name, Patrolman Johnson?"

"Marcus, sir."

"How long have you been on the job, Marcus?" Paris asks, putting on a pair of rubber gloves, recalling that, when he was a young officer, he always appreciated ordinary conversation at moments like these.

Patrolman Marcus Calvin Johnson looks at his watch. "About six hours, sir."

Six hours, Paris thinks. He remembers his own nerve-racking first day in blue. He was absolutely certain that he and his mentor—a highly decorated street cop named Vincent Stella, a lifer well into his forties at that time—would stumble upon a bank robbery in progress and that Patrolman John Salvatore Paris would shoot his own partner. "Tough assignment right out of the box, eh?"

"*Oh* yeah," Patrolman Johnson answers at the entrance to a deep breath, one that swells his cheeks for a moment, the kind of breath that generally precedes a roll of the eyes and a quick trip to the linoleum.

"Hang in there, Marcus," Paris says. "It's not always this bad."

"I'll try, sir."

Paris tucks his tie into his shirt pocket, nods to the officer, then hunkers down next to the body. Patrolman Johnson pulls back the sheet. Immediately, Paris wants to amend his pearl of wisdom for the rookie cop.

It's *never* this bad.

Because there is something so very wrong about what Paris is looking at. It is the body of a partially clothed young white woman, lying prone, her face turned to the left. She has very pretty legs, is wearing a short white skirt, white high heels. She is wearing no blouse or bra, and Paris can now see that the same symbol he had seen on Willis Walker's tongue is carved between her shoulder blades. The primitive-looking bow and arrow. But even the horror of that symbol, at this moment, cannot not compare to the hideousness that is to be found just a few inches away.

The victim—a formerly alive, vibrant woman, a woman

who surely had friends and family and coworkers and lovers, a woman who quite possibly had children of her own—simply stops at her forehead. Above it, above her ears, there is nothing.

Air.

Paris forces himself to look at the top of the woman's head. It is lying next to her right shoulder, a clotted, empty bone-bowl, framed by tendrils of blood-blackened hair that seem to reach for him like Medusa's snakes.

Like deadheading a flower . . .

"Okay," Paris says to the grateful Patrolman Johnson, who has been staring at the ceiling and hyperventilating. "You can cover her."

"Thank you, sir."

Paris walks over to Greg Ebersole, who is standing near the front door; he can see that Greg is pumped and primed for this one: arms crossed, nostrils flaring, fingers beating out a rhythm on his biceps, detective's eyes redrawing the crime scene over and over in his mind. Floor, ceiling, wall, door, window. Silent witnesses, all.

And while it is true that homicide detectives have absolutely no power to prevent murders from occurring, whenever something like this happens—an arrogant, vicious killing after which the perpetrator does not even have the decency to turn himself in or kill himself—it is tantamount to saying to the detectives that I, a murderer, am much smarter than you are. And, to some cops, that is almost worse than the murder itself.

Jack Paris is just such a cop.

Greg Ebersole, too.

"Who found her?" Paris asks.

"Fifteen-year-old kid and his girlfriend," Greg says. He flips a page in his notebook. "Shawn Curry and Dionna Whitmore."

"Any reason to hold them?"

"Nah. We've got their statements." He gestures to the mattress in the corner. "This was just their love shack."

"How'd they get in?"

"Back door," Greg replies. He turns another page, holds up his notebook, showing Paris the now familiar bow-and-arrow emblem, a replica Greg had drawn in pencil. "That your symbol?" he asks, staring straight ahead.

"It sure looks like it," Paris says, then lowers his voice. "Did I hear this right? No one's found her brain?"

"Nope," Greg says. "We've cleared the building. Nothing."

"You think this fucker took it *with* him?"

Greg turns, fixes Paris with an adrenaline-charged stare, a look that Paris had seen a thousand times before, the one that says: *We have eleven-year-old hit men in this country, Jack. People who fuck and strangle their own children. We have guys who dress up in clown suits and bury thirty boys under their houses; drug gangs that harvest unborn babies right from the womb. We've both seen these things. Shall we now be shocked that someone is making doggie bags of human brains?*

"I guess I have my answer," Paris says.

"I guess you do," Greg replies, nearly salivating at the prospect of this new chase, this fresh opportunity to catch a murderer and put him on the other side of the bars. Or, preferably, in this case, the other side of the sod. "I guess you *do*."

❖ 11 ❖

MURDERER.

The word caroms in her mind, around and around and around, a white-hot billiard ball that won't find a pocket. *Mur-der-er.* Three syllables, three cushions. Constant. It used to be a word that she applied to *real* criminals, gangsters, the people you see in prison documentaries, their fingers wrapped tightly around the bars, their eyes boring through you with hatred and violence. But now the word applied to her. She would *be* one of those people soon.

"Murderer" is at the top of her résumé now.

How long had it been? One day? Two? She hadn't slept a minute, of course. The first two pints of Jack Daniel's had passed through her like perspiration, a thin brown mist that paused neither to calm her nerves nor to salve her Christian soul. Her commandment-shattering, burn-in-hell-forever soul.

Remember Mary? Isabella's mother?

Oh yeah. The killer, right?

That's her. Hear what happened?

No, what?

Died in a lesbian prison riot.

No.

Yep. She killed that black guy and they sent her to the Ohio Reformatory for Women. Died in a small pool of bloody vomit and urine.

The thought makes her crack the seal on the third pint. There is one more bottle after this one. After that . . .

She is sitting on the floor in her kitchen, lights off, save for the steady glow of her cigarettes, each one lit from the last. She is waiting for the knock on the door, the hard rap of a police-issue flashlight that will signal post time at the gates of hell.

Options?

Let's see. If she leaves town she will never see Isabella again. That's a lock. If she stays and somehow beats the rap, they will *still* never give her daughter back to her.

One option left. Take the money. Take her daughter.

And run.

Willis Walker had the right to be mad. No question about it. Given. Nolo contendere, your honor. He even had the right to call the police and have her arrested. After all, she had drugged him and robbed him, right?

Right.

Hell, he probably had the right to punch her in the mouth. The recollection returns her mind, momentarily, to the ache that had settled into the left side of her face.

But Willis Walker did *not* have the right to kill her. And that's precisely what she felt he was going to do. He fired actual *bullets* at her. She had no choice. Put a thousand women in that situation and 998 of them would do exactly the same thing. Bash his fuckin' brains in.

She takes another deep swallow, this one reaching her nerves, beginning to calm them. She feels one rung better. Then, the facts come into focus.

The woman at Vernelle's was blond.

She *wasn't* blond.

No one saw her at the Dream-A-Dream Motel.

No one saw her when she picked up her car at Vernelle's. Besides, she was wearing a knit cap and a dark raincoat.

She was all but positive she had wiped down everything in the motel room.

She was fine. She will take her fifty grand—only three

thousand or so to go now, she thinks with some twisted measure of accomplishment, thanks to Willis Walker—and leave this horrible life behind her.

She rises, puts the bottle on top of the refrigerator. Enough with the booze, she thinks. Enough with the worry, the guilt. She doesn't need to apologize to anyone.

What she needs to do is work *out*.

The night is clear and cold, perfect for jogging, but the four or five packs of cigarettes that she has smoked in the last twenty-four hours had prevented her from achieving any real aerobic benefits from her lackadaisical run around the block.

She slows to a walk as she turns the corner onto Lee Road and sees that there is a man standing in front of her apartment building. The area is well lighted so she isn't too worried about getting mugged. Besides, she has her pepper spray in her right hand.

But maybe it's not a mugger, she thinks.

Maybe it's worse.

Maybe it's a *cop*.

She stops for a moment, gathers her wind, and decides there is no real reason to be concerned. The man in front of her building is probably a tenant, just a guy getting ready for a run himself—stretching, doing a few deep knee-bends. Had she seen him around the building before? She wasn't sure. But she was absolutely *certain* that she wouldn't mind seeing him again. Tall, wavy hair, big shoulders. He is wearing an olive and black Nike jogging suit, the kind with reflective white stripes on the elbows. He also wears black wool gloves and a black waist pack.

He is standing in front of the door, so there will be no avoiding him, no sidestepping a conversation if he chooses to start one. She approaches, unafraid, but still keeping her finger on the pepper spray's trigger.

"Hi," the man says.

"Hi."

"Just starting your run or just ending it?" he asks. Another knee-bend.

"Just finished," she says, glancing past him, cringing at her reflection in the glass door. She looks like a wet collie. Of course. "Enough for me tonight."

"What a pity. What's your name?"

Her mind whirls. It is a little forward of him, a little too fast for her taste, but that's not what throws her. What throws her is that she had not anticipated being *anyone* tonight. "Rachel," she answers, as if the name were simply the next name up on a never-ending roster of deception. "Rachel Anne O'Malley."

"You're Irish."

"Yes," she says, telling the lie by rote. "Well, half. I'm Irish on my father's side. My mother's Italian."

"Pretty volatile combination," the man says, flashing a smile. "Italian and Irish."

"Constant battle," she jokes, surprised at her acumen at this after so long, shocked at her growing ease with the events of the last twenty-four hours. "Eat, drink, eat, drink, eat, drink . . ."

The booze, it appears, had finally kicked in, in spite of her halfhearted run around the block. Rachel Anne O'Malley is a little loaded after all.

He puts his foot on the decorative concrete bench and begins to stretch his leg muscles.

She has an insane thought: Maybe she'd take stud-boy upstairs and give him a freebie. Why the hell not? Maybe sleeping with a complete stranger will make the specter of Willis Walker go away.

Then, just as suddenly, she comes to her senses. She decides to run a little more, but alone. The last thing she needs is some cock she can't get rid of, some pretty-boy lover to hang around just long enough to fuck up everything she's worked for in the past two years.

But it seems that stud-boy, and his cock, are not quite finished with her.

"So, could I interest you in a late supper, maybe?" he asks. "A run and a shower won't take me more than forty-five minutes."

"I don't think so."

"Anywhere you'd like," he continues. "Just paid off Visa. I'm golden again."

"No thanks," she says, the phrase *late supper* crazily making her mind return to the late-night breast-feedings in the darkness of her living room, the pleasure and pain of Isabella at her nipple. The sorrow ignites within her. "Some other time. For sure."

"Okay," he says, agreeably, adding to his charm. Not the pushy type. "I'll leave it up to you. I jog around here all the time. Look for me one of these nights. Maybe we can run together."

"Sure," she replies. She pulls open the door to her apartment building. She'll walk through the lobby, down the service hallway and exit on the parking lot side of the building. Maybe have a real run through Cain Park, hope she doesn't embarrass herself by running into him. "Nice meeting you."

"The pleasure was all mine, Rachel," he says, and with that he takes off down the street in long, powerful strides.

She watches him disappear into the night and feels a strange nervousness building inside her. Not necessarily about what just happened. She had handled the advances of a thousand men in her time. But, rather, about what *almost* just happened.

She'd nearly let someone in.

And she hadn't even asked his name.

❖ 12 ❖

I AM CARVED of moonlight.

I follow the jogging figure at a distance of no more than one hundred feet, sliding from shadow to shadow, heading south on Lee Road, waiting for the long stretch of gloom we will both soon enter, the colonnade of darkness leading into Cain Park.

The jogger makes a left, past the squat stone columns, past the huge dedication rock, into the all-but-deserted park. I follow on the access path that winds down the hill.

To the casual observer we might look entirely unconnected, two hardy citizens of Cleveland Heights, Ohio, out for a late-night winter workout, one maintaining a slow jogger's pace; the other—the one carrying the odd-looking device—an even slower, but still quite graceful, power walk.

And yet we are connected in a way that most casual observers—indeed, most people on the planet—could never imagine nor understand.

The noise flourishes the moment I move within range of the jogger. This time: fat punches of thunder on the inside of my skull, a desperate pummeling of bloodied hands in a sealed coffin.

The jogger stops at the shuttered kiosk near the Alma, the smaller of the park's two theaters. I approach from the west. In my right hand is a small-caliber pistol, loaded with hollow-point rounds. In my left I carry a four-quart pail, bottomed with a three-inch layer of hard rubber and wire mesh, a handle on its side.

I step to within five feet of the jogger.

The jogger, a handsome young man clad in an expensive-looking olive and black Nike jogging suit and black wool gloves, doesn't see me. The reflective stripes on the elbows of his jacket made it embarrassingly easy to follow him.

"Hey," I say.

The man freezes in place. A veteran of the streets, it seems. He doesn't turn around. "My wallet is in my waist pack," he says. He spins the nylon belt around his waist, slowly, until the pack faces me.

I step closer, take the wallet, say: "I have a message for you."

The man swallows hard but remains very still. "What . . . what are you *talking* about?"

I place the barrel of the gun near his left temple. "She's mine." I lift the pail by the handle—as if wielding a giant coffee mug—and position it on the other side of the man's head. *"Mío!"*

I pull the trigger.

The puff of smoke is insignificant in the darkness, as is the popping noise, no louder than the sound of a child flicking his thumb out of an empty soda bottle. What *is* significant is that the pail catches not only the bullet—a feat accomplished without putting a hole in the bottom—but also a good portion of the man's brain. The police will not find a slug nor a shell casing, nor more than a drop or two of vaporized membrane on the shrubbery.

I look at the figure on the ground, then into the pail, at the pink tissue, the off-white bone, warm and gaseous in the December night air.

For my cauldron, I think. My *nganga*.

For the spell.

❖ 13 ❖

HIS MOTHER SLEEPS on the couch by the space heater, a Jetson-age-looking Norelco model designed and built in the seventies. The heater, as always, is on full blast and leaning perilously close to the orange and brown afghan—Cleveland Browns colors—the coverlet that had seen its best days when Brian Sipe had quarterbacked the team and Mayor Perk's hair had been the hottest attraction in town.

The small second-floor apartment on Baltic Road has a clock radio in every room, including an old Magnavox on the back of the toilet, just beneath the macramé ballerina toilet-paper cozy. Today, from the kitchen, comes an Italian-language news program.

He kneels next to his mother, brushes a soft strand of white hair from her forehead. She had been Gabriella Russo when his father swept her off her feet nearly fifty years ago, a raven-haired siren of a lounge singer who strung Frank Paris along for five years before giving in to his repeated proposals of marriage.

An only child, Paris had been sixteen when his father died. His mother had worked two jobs to help put him through college, sometimes three. She is an undereducated woman, having finished only high school, but she is, and will always *be,* the smartest woman he has ever known.

She is content now, he thinks, nearly seventy-four years of

age, still on her own, still a force at gin rummy. Still a force at gin *gimlets*, too. Two of them at lunch every day with her bingo cronies Millie and Claire. Followed by her nap.

He moves the space heater a safe distance from the couch and sits at the rolltop desk. The bills, as always, are neatly pigeonholed on the right side. He pays them. It is a monthly ritual for the two of them, one that has proceeded like clockwork for the past few years or so. At first, his mother would drift off to the bedroom when he paid her bills, ashamed that she could no longer work even part time. Sometimes, she would busy herself in the kitchen, and somehow, in the space of twenty minutes, produce a dish of baked ziti or linguine with calamari.

Now she just sleeps through it.

When he finishes, he closes the desk, then crosses the living room to the small pullman kitchen. He takes the sandwich that is always on the top shelf of the fridge, wrapped in Saran Wrap, a pickle on the side.

Should he wake her? No, he decides. Let her sleep. She will know that he has been here.

She always does.

He puts on his coat, stands at the door, surveys the apartment: the old waterfall furniture; the shabby armchair that he had once, as a six-year-old, accidentally wet during *Ben Hur* on TV; the oval braided area rug she'd had for so many years that it was no longer possible to replace; his academy graduation photos on the mantel.

Jack Paris opens the door, steps through, closes it behind him, checks the lock.

Merry Christmas, Mom, he thinks as he wraps his scarf around his neck, a *Casa di Gabriella* hand-knitted special.

Merry Christmas.

The houses on this small section of Denison Avenue, near Brookside Park, are a collage of Eisenhower bungalows, paint-blistered pastels of powder blue, sea foam green, buttercup yellow, all washed gray by the impending dusk, the winter drizzle. Paris is parked at the curb, heater chugging, oldies station on low.

After leaving his mother's apartment, he had spent the remainder of the afternoon canvassing a three-block circle around the Dream-A-Dream Motel. No one at any of the half-dozen bars had seen anyone running from the motel with a dripping butcher knife in the middle of the night, it seems. In the end Paris had interviewed three dozen bleary-eyed men and collected the expected: shrugs, urban apathy, temporary amnesia. Hear no evil, see even less.

He now sits in his car on Denison Avenue, the front seat covered in police reports, all from Michael Ryan's murder book. He had signed them out, not really certain what he is looking for. An earlier connection between Sarah Weiss and Mike Ryan? A disgruntled cop on the inside who lost his cut of the ten grand?

A little yellow car?

Paris had taken Sarah Weiss's acquittal much harder than usual. He had put so much of himself on the line during the investigation. No cop likes letting a killer off. But when it's a cop-killer, there is a piece of every police officer that never forgets.

There was alcohol in Michael's system that night, but it was nowhere near the limit. There was also trace evidence of an extremely powerful hallucinogen. Traces of the hallucinogen were also found in a flask that was inside the killer's bag. The record shows that Michael was officially off-duty when he was murdered.

According to the defense, Michael was an alcoholic, drugged-up detective who sold confidential police files for ten thousand dollars to fuel his vile habits. According to the defense, Mike Ryan was a very bad cop who got precisely what he had coming.

To this day, Paris refuses to believe it.

Before leaving the Justice Center for the day, Paris had called Dolores Ryan and asked if she still had Michael's papers: financial records, notebooks, and the like. She said everything was in storage. Dolores also said that Paris was welcome to all of it, without, mercifully, asking him why. Mercifully, because he couldn't give her an answer if he tried.

Paris turns off the engine, but before he can exit the car, his cell phone rings. "Paris."

Loud music. Ice cubes in glasses. The drone of roadhouse chatter. "Hi, it's Mercedes, can you hear me okay?"

"Just fine."

"Am I catching you at a bad time?"

"Not at all," Paris says. "Where are you, Atlantic City?"

"I'm at Deadlines."

Paris knows the place. A venerated old Cleveland tavern favored by journalists. "So what's up?"

"Well, at the moment, there is a fabulously handsome, ethnically diverse male sitting right next to me, trying to ply me with fruity cocktails."

Paris smiles. "How's he doing?"

"Lemme look." Mercedes is silent for a moment. "Still have my shoes on. Not that well, I guess."

"It's still early."

"Es verdad."

"So what can I do for you?"

"What do you mean?"

"As in, the reason you called?"

"Oh *yeah*. Right. Sorry. Listen. I'm going to need a photograph or two of you for the article, but the paper is too friggin' cheap to hire a second photographer. At least for my stuff, anyway. I left a message for my brother Julian, who is a really *good* photographer, if he would just get off his ass and do something about it, but that's another story, okay? Sorry. Anyway, it's a million to one shot that he'll show up, which means that me and my Instamatic might have to do, but if you see a cute guy with a camera hanging around, don't get scared, okay?"

"Thanks for the heads-up."

"No problem."

Paris asks Mercedes if she needs a designated driver. She declines. Paris signs off, crosses Denison Avenue, considers walking up the long wheelchair ramp, the sturdy-looking U-shaped structure made out of two-by-sixes and rusting bolts.

Too icy, he thinks. For a man of my advanced years.

So, holding firmly onto the wrought-iron railing, Jack Paris climbs the narrow stone steps to Dolores Ryan's house.

She looks thin and blanched, a brittle outline of the brunette bombshell to whom Michael Ryan had introduced him one night at the Caprice Lounge; a night now entombed almost twenty years in his memory. That night, Dusty Alessio had the attention of every man in the place, including a woefully young John Salvatore Paris.

Now her hazel eyes are cloudy, veined, tired. Her hair, shocked with silver. She wears old denim jeans, threadbare espadrilles, a faded maroon Ohio State University sweatshirt.

They are sitting in the small tidy living room, across from each other, coffee between. In the corner, next to the muted TV, squats a large, artificial Christmas tree, its heirloom ornaments placed haphazardly, hurriedly.

Dolores points at his coffee, asks: "You want something else?"

"No. No thanks."

"You want something in it?"

"I'm good, Dusty."

The old nickname makes her smile, blush deeply, run a hand through her hair. "No one calls me that anymore."

"That's the first name I heard and I'm stickin' with it," Paris says.

"You know where that nickname came from?"

"No."

"I got it from Michael, the day I met him. Michael was going to Padua High School. I was going to Nazareth. I was sixteen. Six*teen*, can you imagine?"

Paris sees the color start to rise in Dolores's cheeks, the flush of a woman recalling the day she met the love of her life. "I can," he says.

"I used to see Michael and his friends at the baseball diamond at State Road Park. I'd see him all the time there, but never had the guts to talk to him. Remember how we used to just die of embarrassment at that age?"

"*Oh* yeah," Paris says, thinking he hadn't really progressed all that much in that department.

"So one day my friend Barb and I are tooling around in her old Ford Fairlane convertible, top down. We hit the Manners, the Dairy Queen, the McDonald's, the Red Barn, then the baseball field on State Road. And suddenly I see him.

" '*There's Michael!*' I yell. Barbara, of course, panics, swings into the parking lot, knocking her Dairy Queen cup on the floor, completely covering the brake pedal in chocolate milkshake. The car jumps the curb and heads right for the baseball game. Barbara is stamping and stomping and trying to hit the brake pedal, but it's too slippery. We're going, like, thirty miles an hour now, smacking into garbage cans, benches, lawn chairs. Finally, after making everyone scatter, she hits the brake pedal squarely and we fishtail around the middle of the diamond, coming to a stop right on the pitcher's mound. And, because the top is down, there is now an inch of dust on everything—the car, the seats, the books, the burgers, me. Worse than that, ten boys our age are watching us in complete awe, knowing they had just seen what will probably be the story of the year at school.

"Well, it turns out that my history notebook had flown out of the backseat, landing God knows where. So, out of the cloud of dust, notebook in hand, comes Michael Patrick Ryan—black T-shirt, blue eyes, long eyelashes, sweaty muscles. He says: 'Hey, *Dusty*, this yours?' " Dolores looks at Paris with a half-smile that is somewhere adrift between inconceivable heartache and the joy of indelible memory. "Everybody laughed, but I didn't really hear them, you know? All I saw were those blue eyes. I was a goner."

Paris watches as Dolores absently fingers the ribbed cuff of the sweatshirt, wandering through her reverie, and realizes it is Michael's. She is still wearing his clothes.

Dolores returns to the moment. She checks the grandfather clock in the hallway, pours more coffee, allows the levity of her story to come to a full rest. After a minute of silence, she says, "He was scared, you know."

"Michael?"

"Yeah."

"Scared of what?"

Dolores looks out the bay window, at the rain turning to snow, at the ice crystals starring the tips of the hedges in front of the house. "Everything." She waves the back of her hand at the long-ago widened doorway leading to the first-floor bathroom; the gesture, a full explanation of life with a family member in a wheelchair. "He was scared all the time after we came back."

A decade or so earlier, Michael Ryan had pulled up stakes, moved west, taken a job with the San Diego PD. But after his daughter was injured by a hit-and-run driver, a driver never caught, as Paris understood it, he moved the family back to Cleveland to be near Dolores's mother, a police widow herself.

"He was a great cop, Dusty. An even better man."

Dolores considers Paris for a moment, then leans forward, as if to share a secret. With one carefully measured exhale, she concedes the real reason for Paris's visit in the first place, saying: "I knew."

These are words that Paris does not want to hear. Michael Ryan is dead. As is his killer. Paris would just as soon hang on to the notion that Michael was on the job when he was murdered, was following up a lead, got ambushed. But, against his will, his mouth opens and forms the words. "What do you mean?"

Dolores reaches for a tissue, dabs at her eyes. "That's why I don't look in the storage, in the boxes. I just can't."

"You don't have to tell me this."

"Michael and I had . . . had a *deal*, you see. We made it the day of Carrie's accident. Michael told me that she would never, *ever*, want for anything, as long as he was alive."

Paris considers just standing, hugging her, leaving, letting all this go. Instead, he asks:

"What was your end?"

"My end?" She looks up at him, her eyes leaden with pain. "My end was never to ask where the money came from."

The tiny lock opens with a satisfying click. Paris is proud of himself. He hadn't picked a desk lock in years but, for some reason, the touch seemed to be back. Maybe he'd start carrying his pick-set again. He is in bay number 202 at the My-Self Storage on Triskett Road. Dolores had given him the key, but asked if he would drop it back off as soon as possible. Dolores and Carrie Ryan are moving to Tampa, Florida, soon.

The bay is large, perhaps ten by fifteen feet, and stacked ceiling to floor with the detritus a man acquires in forty-some years of life: a rusting band saw, mismatched golf clubs, a delaminated poker table. Along the back wall are Dolores's things. Hatboxes, white-handled shopping bags stuffed with clothes, along with a few big boxes from Petrie's, a ladies' retailer whose name Paris hadn't heard in years.

The space smells of mildew, mice; the damp ennui of shelved memory.

Within ten minutes or so, by the light of the single forty-watt bulb in the ceiling, Paris had sifted through all the musty books and folders and papers on the desk. Nothing pertinent to any investigation Michael had been working on. Nothing that leapt out at him. He had tried, unsuccessfully, to pull open the small floor safe serving as a stand for Michael's old Remington manual typewriter. The safe did not open, but, after a few long-unpracticed turns of a bent paper clip, the bottom right-hand drawer on the desk did.

In the drawer is a solitary item: a nine-by-twelve envelope.

Paris removes the envelope, opens it. Inside is a black-and-white photograph of a corpse, the mutilated, naked body of a man lying in a gravel parking lot. There is a white brick wall to the right, the wheels of a big Dumpster behind the man's right shoulder. The man is horribly disfigured, slicked with blood nearly head to toe. With disgust, Paris can see that pieces—large pieces—of the man's midsection are missing; chunks that appear to have been torn away, eaten, as if animals had been at the body.

But it is the appearance of the man's head that runs a cold finger up Paris's spine.

The man's head is completely wrapped in barbed wire.

The photograph looks like a standard police crime-scene photo but is not marked in any official way. The yellowing edges and slightly sienna whites tell him the picture is old. Fifteen, twenty years maybe. In the upper-right-hand corner is an address, handwritten in faded blue ink. An address on East Twenty-third Street.

Paris flips the picture over and what he sees on the back tricks his eyes for a moment, then comes swimming back into focus.

It is a sentence. A simple, handwritten, five-word sentence that should not be written on the back of a picture in a dead man's desk, a man who had not drawn breath in two years.

Scrawled in red, from the coldness of his grave, Michael Ryan says:

Evil is a breed, Fingers.

PART TWO

❖ ❖

SPELL

❖ 14 ❖

Belmont Corners, Ohio
Thirty years earlier . . .

THE WOMAN WAITS in the emergency room at Our Lady of Mercy Hospital on Greenville Road, her face a purplish mass of swollen tissue, her womb a capacious medicine ball beneath her dress. It is New Year's Eve and the woman's ex-husband had stopped by the trailer at around five-thirty that evening, supposedly to drop off a late Christmas present for his daughter, but what he really wanted was what he *always* wanted. Drug money. The scene had escalated so quickly that the woman had not even had time to lock her daughter in the bedroom for her own protection, although the man had never once laid a finger on the little girl.

The little girl's mother was far too satisfying a target.

Lydia del Blanco is twenty-seven years old, an unlicensed hairdresser of moderate skill, a folk singer of unexplored talent, a slender young woman with clear amber eyes. But today her eyes are a muddied rust; her skin, a rough topography of distended, yellowing welts. Anthony del Blanco had taken a belt to her, one of his favorite weapons of intimidation.

To Lydia's left sits her four-year-old daughter Fina, a slight, dark-haired bundle of worry who seems, for the moment at least, to have abandoned her circuitous route around the waiting room, her sobbing and her flopping-around in oversized blue rubber galoshes. Since she had been a toddler, Lydia had not been able to fool her daughter about the beatings, although they had come in decreasing frequency since Anthony had left the trailer and moved in with one of his never-ending parade of whores.

But Fina knows who her father is, and what he sometimes does to her mother. Still, she is far too young to hate him. She just wants the yelling to stop and her mom to be happy.

And so she cries . . .

In the corner of the emergency room sits a black-and-white portable television, its picture fading in and out with the snowstorm rolling over the Ohio Valley. From time to time, Lydia looks at the screen. Guy Lombardo and his Royal Canadians. Bobby Vinton. The King Family.

When her name is called, Lydia rises slowly to her feet and approaches the frosted glass window. Amid the usual details, the usual lies, she tells the woman that her ex-husband is dead; which, in Lydia's mind and heart, he is. But it is Anthony del Blanco's violent act of rape eight months earlier that gave seed to this formerly restless child in her womb, this child Lydia del Blanco had alternately hated and loved, this child who had not kicked her for more than three hours.

As Lydia is helped to a wheelchair, her daughter begins to cry again, her tears now thin, meandering streams down her cheeks. She dutifully walks alongside her mother's chair until they reach Examining Room One. Then, without tantrum, her utter exhaustion preventing such a display, she stops as they lift her mother onto a gurney and wheel her away.

A pleasant young candy striper named Constance Aguillar takes Fina's hand and leads her over to the vending machines, where she buys her an O Henry! bar and a Coke.

But before the little girl can take a single bite, she crawls onto one of the padded chairs and, within moments, falls fast asleep.

* * *

At the stroke of midnight, the moment when just about everyone living in the eastern standard time zone of the United States is popping champagne corks in celebration; the moment when Anthony del Blanco is taking carnal pleasure with a prostitute named Vickie Pomeroy in Room 511 of the TraveLodge on Cannon Road; the moment when four-year-old Fina is asleep and dreaming of a place where her father doesn't raise his voice or his hand, Lydia screams in agony, just once, a long, solitary call of admonition to all those who would harm her or her family in the future.

And Lydia del Blanco has a baby boy. A healthy, seven-pound-five-ounce boy born of a brand new day, a brand new year.

A boy, Anthony del Blanco would one day discover, born of violence.

❖ 15 ❖

THE DEAD WOMAN'S name was Fayette Martin.

At the time of her murder she was thirty years old, never married, no children. A graduate of Mayfield High School on Cleveland's far east side, a real computer buff when she wasn't raising prize-winning orchids in her spare time; this according to a phone interview Paris had conducted with her brother, Edgar, a resident of Milwaukee, her only living relative.

She had been identified through the Department of Motor Vehicles. Her late-model red Chevy had been parked a few blocks from the Reginald Building, where her body was found. Prints taken at the scene matched prints found in the car, and the ID was made. She had worked at a florist shop in suburban Chesterland for the past twelve years.

The official cause of her demise would be recorded as "blood loss due to severe head trauma," but that would tell only part of the story. What really happened to Fayette Martin was that someone took a very large, very sharp knife— a machete, perhaps, or a hefty steel saber—and sliced off the top of her head. One clean blow. The coroner found no serration on the woman's skull, no evidence of sawing. And there is a good chance that the woman was engaged in intercourse at some point either before or during the bloody event, but not after. Reuben says during, but has decided to keep that opinion unofficial for the time being.

Paris finds small solace in the fact that, on top of all this, they are not chasing a necrophiliac.

Generally, when there is evidence connecting the methodology, if not the motive, of two murders, there is some similarity in the victims: college girls, prostitutes, insurance salesmen. But this time, the two deceased could not be more disparate:

A dead black man found in a room at the Dream-A-Dream, robbed and castrated.

A dead white woman found in the Reginald Building on East Fortieth Street, the top of her head lopped off, her brain removed from the scene.

What makes them kin, in death, is that both victims had a strange symbol of a bow and arrow carved somewhere on their bodies. A symbol as yet unidentified.

As of two days before Christmas, the official position of the Cleveland Police department is that these killings are not related.

Three photographs are taped to the chalkboard in the common room on the sixth floor of the Justice Center. Around the trash and file-strewn conference table sit three police officers: Detective Jack Paris, Detective Greg Ebersole, and Sergeant Carla Davis of the Sex Crimes Unit.

Carla Davis is black, thirty-five, a stunning six-one, with broad shoulders and kelly green eyes flecked with gold. Even if she wasn't married, most of the guys in the department would be far too intimidated by Carla to have the guts to make a move on her. She looks like a big sexy forward in the WNBA, a woman who took no shit when she worked vice—where she was the undisputed queen of the prostitution sting—and takes even less now as second in command of the Sex Crimes Unit.

The past twenty-four hours have yielded a forming of this task force, as well as a shifting of assignments.

All police officers believe that there is something special about being the very first investigator to physically step into a crime scene. The smells, the sounds, the very *feel* of the air, the position of the body, the possibility that, in many cases, the last person to have stepped out of the room is the killer.

And while it is true that, if another detective takes over the investigation, and ninety-nine percent of the evidence is conveyed through witness reports and affidavits and photographs and videotaped interviews, there is still that one percent held dear by detectives everywhere, and having a case yanked is never pleasant.

Although, this time, Paris is clearly getting the better deal, if there is a better deal to be had here. He wasn't anxious to poke around in Willis Walker's life, any more than he was anxious to poke around the man's pants.

The trade is not lost on Greg Ebersole. Or his demeanor. Greg's vast array of drug connections were working against him. He'd take over the Walker investigation for the time being. Paris got Fayette Martin. Carla Davis will liaison with Sex Crimes.

At eight-fifty, Captain Elliott enters the room and the task force meeting begins.

Paris at the chalkboard, notebook in hand. "We have a dead male black, one Willis James Walker, forty-eight, a resident of East Boulevard. Mr. Walker's body was found in Room 116 of the Dream-A-Dream Motel on East Seventy-ninth Street and St. Clair Avenue. The coroner's office says Mr. Walker was struck on the back of the head by a heavy, flat object, but that is not what killed him. Nor did the large quantity of Rohypnol and alcohol in his system. The cause of death has been ruled to be loss of blood resulting from the removal of Mr. Walker's penis and testicles, none of which were recovered at the scene.

"What *was* found was an unlicensed twenty-five-caliber semiauto, discharged twice. Both slugs were recovered. There is no evidence that anything human was struck.

"We also have one female white DOA, a woman named

Fayette Martin, thirty, formerly residing in the Marsol Towers in Mayfield Heights. Ms. Martin's body was discovered in an abandoned building at the corner of East Fortieth and Central. The coroner believes Ms. Martin was partially beheaded by a large knife or machete-type weapon. Her brain has not yet been recovered. In both cases a body part or parts was missing. In both cases a symbol, a carving, was left behind."

Paris points to the first two pictures. One is of the symbol carved into Willis Walker's tongue. The second one is of the symbol carved into Fayette Martin's back.

"Reuben says that the mark may have something to do with the religion of Santeria, or one of its darker offshoots. I'm following up on that now. He believes that the mark on Mr. Walker's tongue was made postmortem. The mark on Fayette Martin's back was made before she died. But *minutes* before she died."

"Who found Willis Walker?" Carla asks.

"Cleaning woman," Paris says.

"And the two kids who found the woman?"

"Neighborhood kid and his girlfriend. The girl is the one who called it in. Greg got their statements."

"What do you have on Martin's family, friends?" Elliott asks.

"Both parents deceased," Paris says. "She had a brother in Milwaukee.

He's flying in to claim the body. She worked at a place called The Flower Shoppe in Chesterland ever since high school. According to her brother there was no boyfriend. As far as I can tell, Fayette Martin and Willis Walker did not know each other."

Paris meets the eyes of everyone in the room, sees no further questions. He sits down.

"Greg?" Elliott says.

Greg Ebersole remains seated. To Paris, he looks like a man on the verge of physical collapse. "Willis Walker was married and had—are you ready for this?—*eleven* children. Five different women. Two of them had the brief privilege of being called Mrs. Willis Walker. Three of Willis's progeny are doing hard time, one of them in the Ohio pen. Willis was co-owner of Kinsman Products, a print shop specializing in calendars, letterheads, business cards. He also fronted a record label called Black Alley Records. But mostly Willis Walker was in the business of getting away with petty crime. Twelve arrests, two convictions, both misdemeanors. Never spent more than forty-eight hours behind bars. No connection yet to anyone into voodoo or anything like that. Willis wheeled and dealed, so the possibility that he owed, or *was* owed, a large sum of money is extremely likely."

Greg flips his notebook shut.

Elliott says: "Obviously, the last thing we want here is the FBI, people. Let's try and clear these. Also, let's look into the gangs, especially the Latino gangs, see if we can match this to some kind of initiation rites. Let's check the index of gang tattoos, see if this mark means anything. Carla?"

Carla Davis sits up straight, crosses her legs. Today she is wearing a red wool skirt, cut just above the knee and a white silk blouse. All three men do their very best to look her straight in the eye. "Sex Crimes will look into the tattoo freaks, as well as the guys who like it in public. If Fayette Martin was having sex in that doorway, right before she was murdered, maybe this guy has done this before, and this time it got out of hand. Also, anybody who's shown a propensity for recreational carving."

"That happen a lot?" Paris asks.

"You'd be surprised," Carla says.

"Doubt it."

"Had a guy, few years ago," Carla continues. "Creepy crawler. He used to prowl Tremont in summer, looking in windows, watching girls undress. His thing was sneaking in after the girls had gone to sleep, chloroforming them, then carving a series of numbers on their foreheads with a hat pin."

Paris and Ebersole exchange a glance. "And that's how he got off?" Greg asks.

"Well, he used to masturbate while he carved. Never raped any of them. Did it five times."

"Please tell me he's in Mansfield now," Paris says.

"*Oh* yeah," Carla says, standing, collecting her papers. "And are you ready for what the numbers meant?"

"What?"

"It was his locker combination," Carla says. "His damn high school *locker* combination."

"Jesus," Greg says.

"The worst part is that he'll be out in eighteen months and there are five women walking around Cleveland with this asshole's locker combination written across their foreheads in scar tissue."

No one in the room feels it would be appropriate to laugh, considering the serious nature of the crime. They are professionals and they take the violation of a citizen under their watch very seriously. Laughing would be unprofessional.

So, instead, they grab their papers and coffee and cigarettes and head for the door as fast as they can.

"Are you Detective Paris by any chance?"

They are in the Justice Center lobby. It is noontime, crowded. Paris turns to see a young man of his height, nice looking. A Nikon hangs around his neck.

"By *every* chance. You are?"

"Julian."

Paris arches an eyebrow, waits for more.

The man continues. "I'm sorry. Mercedes Cruz is my sister."

"Ah, yes, okay," Paris says, extending his hand. "Jack Paris."

"Julian Cruz," he says, shaking hands.

Julian is clean-cut—khakis, suede hikers, leather flight jacket, tortoiseshell sunglasses, trimmed mustache—and perhaps a few years older than Mercedes.

"Nice to meet you," Paris says.

"Same here. I called upstairs but they told me I just missed you."

"Yeah. They have to let me out sometimes. Union thing." Paris buttons his coat, smooths his hair, anticipating having his picture taken with little notice. "How'd you know it was me, by the way?"

"Believe me, my sister described you to the last detail. She's awfully good at detail." He unsnaps the leather case around the Nikon and holds it up. "I'll make this as quick and painless as I can."

"Where do you want me?"

Julian gestures to the huge windows overlooking Ontario Street. "Light looks good there."

They walk across the lobby. Julian positions Paris, steps away, focuses, says: "You know, I probably shouldn't be telling you this, but Mercedes is awfully taken with you."

"Is that right?"

He snaps a picture. "Well, maybe *taken* is the wrong word. It's just that this is the biggest assignment she's ever had. She just is glad to be working with such a professional."

"Well, it's my pleasure."

Snap. "I love her very much and I hope she sets the world afire. That's all."

"I have no doubt she will. I hope I can help," Paris says.

"Don't tell her I said anything, okay? I don't know if you've gotten a taste of that temper yet. She'd kill me."

"I understand."

"A few more?"

"Sure."

Julian snaps a third, fourth, and fifth picture, then caps the lens. "Thanks. All done. I'll make sure you get copies."

Paris lies: "I look forward to seeing them." They are near the door to the parking garage. Paris points to the garage. "Can I give you a lift anywhere? I'm heading east."

Julian holds up an RTA pass. "West. Thanks anyway. Nice meeting you."

"My pleasure." Paris pushes open the door, wondering— about twenty seconds too late—if his cowlick had been sticking up on the top of his head, a tonsorial battle against gravity he has waged with his hair, on a daily basis, since he was eight years old.

The Flower Shoppe is a tan, rough-cedar-and-glass building on Caves Road in semirural Chesterland, conveniently located across the street from the LaPuma-Gennaro Funeral Home.

The sky has brightened but the day is still cold enough to make the snow crunch beneath Paris's feet as he approaches the garland-and-ribbon-bedecked building. His breath describes small cirrus clouds of vapor before him. He opens the door and is immediately enveloped by the humid fragrances of pine and spruce and balsam.

The interior of the store is packed with seasonal flora, every surface covered with snow-flocked wreaths or huge red and yellow poinsettias. Behind the counter stands a man wearing a green apron, starched white shirt, and raspberry red bow tie, just wrapping up a sale of two large wreaths to an even larger woman. When she leaves, he turns to Paris.

"Can I help you, sir?" the man asks.

Paris badges the man. Then he notices a name tag that identifies him as Gaston Burke.

"I'd like to ask you a few questions, Mr. Burke."

"This is about Faye, isn't it?"

"Yes."

"I haven't slept since I heard," Gaston says. He is fifty, pear shaped and well tended. His hair is a dyed copper, slicked back like that of a barber from the 1930s.

Paris takes out his notebook. "How long did you work with her?"

"Twelve years or so, on and off. She came to work here right out of high school, I think. This was my parents' store then. I worked here part-time, off and on, until five years ago, when I took over the shop."

"Was she a good employee?"

"The best," Gaston says, his voice breaking a little. "In early, out late, always willing to come in on her day off when we were busy or if we had some kind of emergency. Three weeks after my parents died in a car accident, I had an appendectomy. Faye slept in the back room for five days in order to run the shop. Faye wasn't just an employee, detective."

"What else can you tell me about her, Mr. Burke?"

"I can tell you that she was a true artist. Had a real talent for floral design. Had a natural ability with orchids. These are Faye's," he says, gesturing to a tall, narrow glass case behind the counter. Inside are a dozen extraordinarily delicate flowers of rose, lilac, and yellow, long-petaled flowers of a beauty Paris had never seen. "I can't believe her Ladies Tresses are still alive and she is not."

"What can you tell me about her personal life?"

Gaston thinks for a moment. He smiles ruefully. "Only that she didn't have one. Faye was the kind of sad woman you see all the time now. Pretty woman beaten by life. Guess she got burned once, then it was *check please* as far as romance goes."

"What do you mean?"

"Well, she never really talked about it, but I always got the sense that she had had a pretty serious relationship once, and had been rather unceremoniously dumped. I guess she never got over it. Holidays would come around and I would see her usually pleasant demeanor start to slump and it would break my heart. Every year I invited her to spend Thanksgiving or Christmas with my family. Every year she begged off."

Paris asks: "So no one ever came to pick her up after work some Friday or Saturday night?"

"No. Never."

"She never came in on a Monday morning and talked about a date she might have had over the weekend?"

"Maybe once, years and years ago. But nothing in recent

memory. She was a lonely young woman, detective. I am going to miss her terribly. I loved her very much."

"You loved her."

"Yes."

"Was there ever a time that you two . . ."

"Dated?"

"Yes."

"I'm gay, detective."

"I see," Paris says, choosing not to jot that bit of information in his notebook. "I hope you didn't expect me to just *know* that."

"No," Gaston says. "I suppose not. But I trust it answers your question."

"It does. But only one of them."

"Touché."

"Did Fayette work on the twentieth of this month?"

Gaston checks the calendar blotter on his desk. "No. She was off that day."

"Can I ask where you were on the twentieth?"

"I was here. I closed the shop at six-thirty, stopped at the CVS and bought every cold medication they had. I then went home, took said drugs, and curled up with *The English Patient.*"

Paris is going to assume he is talking about the book or the movie. "And you didn't go out?"

"Ever take NyQuil, detective? No. I didn't go out. I was comatose."

Paris flips shut his notebook. "Anything else you can add, Mr. Burke?"

"Only that Faye was also very good with computers. She set up everything here. The accounting software, the database for our mailing lists." Suddenly, Gaston brings his hand to his mouth. "I just realized something."

"What's that?"

Gaston Burke says: "I am absolutely *dead* without her."

❖ 16 ❖

THE DEAD LIVE HERE.

The cauldron, the *nganga*, sits in the center of the room, a room decorated with black shag carpeting, black walls, black ceiling. Twelve feet by twelve feet. The sparse light from the half-dozen votive candles deployed in a loose six-foot circle seems to soak into the darkness like moon-silkened blood into virgin snow.

Outside, in the hallway, there are red and green lights strung along the crown molding; a pine-scented wreath between the elevators, just above the call buttons. In the lobby, there is a huge silver tree, ringed with multicolored lights and laden with dazzling ornaments.

In here, there are no lights. In here, it is always midnight. In here, it is a place called Matamoros, a place called El Mozote. In here it is My Lai. Srebenica. Amritsar. Phnom Penh. In here, in this undying darkness, the silence is interrupted only by the screams of the dead, cold and un-avenged, their pleadings a brutal red sea at the bottom of my cauldron.

But the black room doesn't hear them. The black room stores their pain, nurtures it.

I made the *nganga*, my first, from an old Charmglow gas grill I found on a tree lawn on Neff Road. I waited until the middle of the night to bring it up in the service elevator. If anyone had seen me, they most certainly would have wondered what I was going to do with a huge, dilapidated gas grill in an apartment building with no balconies.

No pets, no kids, no barbecues, the building super had told me when I scoped the Cain Towers apartments on Lee Road for the first time. Of the twenty or so apartments, it was hard to believe there wasn't a cat, a kid, or a hibachi lurking in one of them, but these were the rules.

I sanded and painted the round, deep bowl, then emblazoned *Ochosi* onto its side. It now contains flesh. Flesh of this earth. Flesh that is rotting. It will only be a matter of time until the smells reach the hallway, the elevator.

I must act.

I squat next to the cauldron, sip the Metusalem rum laced with the very last of the *Amanita muscaria*, the rarest of magic mushroom. I will need more. I light the cigar and exhale smoke in a casual orbit around me. Smoke draws the gods. Smoke masks the overwhelming odors of human meat gone bad.

I inhale deeply, drawing strength from the ill-starred spirits in the *nganga*, filling my lungs, my being, with the power of such tormented flesh. The brain of a whore. The brain and hands of a seducer . . .

I close my eyes.

I am *nkisi*.

I begin to dream of Mexico as the amanita takes hold. I dream myself fourteen, standing nude, drenched in my own sweat, the sweat of others. I am in the room over Cedrica Malo's bodega, waiting for the dry creak of the first step, the first of eighteen dry, wooden steps that will bring a watcher, a toucher, a torturer. The fan overhead turns slowly, barely molesting the air so thick with sour smells. There are soiled black silk sheets on the bed; gold-veined mirrors above.

Suddenly, the step cries out again, its aching back wondering how many more.

Yet I know that, outside, the hot Tijuana sun still sears the sidewalks, the streets, the very *minds* of the reprobates who come here. It is just afternoon. Hours to go.

So they come. Eighteen steps, turn to the left, one or two more steps. Push. There is no lock on the door to the room above Malo's. One is not needed. The door opens and the noise intrudes quickly after, crashing inside me like a black gale; followed, always, by the hideous touching, by the fantasy of skulls caving in, razors carving flesh, throats, gurgling with contrition.

All the men who climb the stairs are big-fisted, like my dad.

All the women, rich and violent.

Because I am the grail. Fourteen years old, unlined, shoulders and hands like a man. I am the prize that Cedrica Malo offers in her lottery, the one it costs five hundred dollars to play, the one that will make us both rich.

Sometimes the lottery winners ask me to trade in pain. Sometimes, in sacrifice. But always I am bound to deal in pleasure, and to collect its many debts.

The black room swoons.

El brujo esta aquí.

The witch is here.

And I will look you in the eye and tell you I am an itinerant farmworker from Culiacán, and you will believe me. I will tell you I operate a hot air balloon over Napa Valley, and you will believe me. I will tell you I am a baker from New Orleans, and you will believe me.

I will fuck you in your marriage bed, my workman's fatigues around my ankles, while your husband fetches the mail.

The blood will flow, sweet and plenteous.

I will tell you that I love you.

The world will fall silent.

And you will believe me.

❖ 17 ❖

SHE SCANS THE newspaper for details, but this day, there is no mention of the Willis Walker murder in the *Plain Dealer*. It had made the second section for one day, a small item that said a man named Willis James Walker, forty-eight, had been found dead in a room at the Dream-A-Dream Motel, and that cause of death had not been determined. Nor were there any suspects in custody.

She is sitting at a window table at Shooters on the west bank of the Flats, watching the icy river flow, sunglasses down, an untouched plate of *al pomodoro* with angel hair pasta growing old in front of her.

She had managed to sleep through the night, which frightened her a little. Somehow, the image of Willis Walker on the floor of that filthy bathroom had not invaded her dreams. She had thought she would be haunted by the image for years to come—probably as she sat in a jail cell at the ORW—but, so far, it isn't happening. And that is a little unnerving.

Perhaps it's because she knows that she has a job to do. To get this money into a trust. To raise her daughter. Willis Walker was a big, violent man standing between her and that goal. Fuck him, she thinks. He took his chances and lost.

He hit on the *wrong* damn girl.

She pays the check, bundles up, and steps outside. She walks down Main Avenue for a few blocks, to Center Street, where her car is illegally parked. She turns onto the nearly deserted street and is happy not to see a bright orange ticket on her windshield, her mind already a deadfall of numbers, apprehension, sorrow, promise, fear.

And that's when she notices the man breaking into her car.

"Hey!" she screams, before she can stop herself. She looks up and down the street. No one to hear her. Or help.

The man looks up, around, but not at her. He is fortyish, white, dressed shabbily in a hooded green sweatshirt and stained chinos. He has something that looks like a crowbar in his right hand. He looks a little too old to be doing what he was doing, but there he was, trying to jimmy the passenger door of her not-even-close-to-being-paid-off lemon-yellow Honda.

Her fear folds into anger. "*Hey*! Are you *deaf*? Get the fuck away from my *car*!"

At this, the man staggers back a few feet, finds her in the twisted landscape of his vision. He is clearly drunk. The f-word seemed to register something with him. As did her volume. "Wuss your prollem, bitch?" he says.

Bitch? She is incredulous. "That's my car, *bitch*. *You're* my problem." What the hell had come over her? What was she doing? She should be keeping as low a profile as possible, and here she was threatening a car thief. On the other hand, she isn't all that anxious to call a cop. She shoves her right hand into her coat pocket and takes a nervous step forward. "Now take a friggin' hike. We'll pretend this never happened."

The man glares at her, obviously weighing the possibility that she might be some kind of militant career woman feminist type with a Mauser .380 in her pocket, just waiting for some fuckup to cross her path.

The ploy works. Without a word, the man slowly drops his hands to his sides and begins to back his way up the sidewalk, not taking his eyes from her. When he nears the corner, he shakes the crowbar at her in a final, pathetic attempt at caveman bravado, before disappearing down an alley.

That is *it*, she thinks. One hundred percent friggin' *it*. Doesn't matter what it takes, how it happens. Even if she does it with less than fifty thousand dollars. Even if she has to disobey a court order and live with Isabella on the run for the rest of their lives. She was *outta* here.

Fuck this place.

She walks over to the passenger door. No damage. Well, no damage that wasn't already there. All she can think about now is sinking into a hot bubble bath, a glass of herbal tea at her side, Andre Previn on the stereo, something in the oven on slow. Nearly heaven. Only Isabella frolicking amid the bubbles, her laughter echoing off the old fixtures, would make it so.

She brushes the snow off the door key, inserts it into the lock, turns it, and—

The first thing she smells, as the man's hand closes around her mouth, is DL Hand Cleaner. Her father had been a tinkerer when she was very small, fixing the family cars himself, rebuilding lawn mower engines, and when he would hoist her upon his lap before dinner she would smell the rich, petroleum-based cleaner mixed in with his cigar smoke.

But this time, the smell does not make her feel warm and protected.

This time it is making her sick.

"Who the fuck you think you're *talking* to, bitch?"

It is her car thief, back to assert himself for real.

She tries to scream but the sound is muffled by his grimy half-glove. She struggles, and, for her trouble, she is clubbed to the ground with a heavy forearm. The earth reaches up to her—icy and hard and unforgiving. She lands on her left shoulder, rolls to her right; dazed and disbelieving, thoroughly demeaned.

Then, she hears shouting.

Hey, someone yells.

HEY!

Footsteps approaching. She sees a pair of brown hiking boots, the cuffs of denim jeans. She hears more shouting, but the words are unintelligible, considering the steam shovel that had just begun work inside her brain.

Then, footsteps crunching the snow, staggering away.

Then, silence. *God* her head hurt. Am I alone? she wonders.

No.

Strong hands grab her by the arms; strong arms lift her to her feet.

A moment of vertigo, then everything comes swimming back. Center Street, in front of her. Her car, roughly where she'd left it before her quick trip to the ground. A total stranger beside her, holding her up.

"Are you okay?" the owner of the strong hands asks.

The words echo in her head for a few moments before registering. She takes a deep breath, and looks. It is a man. A nice-looking young man.

A *very* nice-looking young man.

And, it appears, he has just saved her life.

❖ 18 ❖

Lakewood, Ohio
Twenty-six years earlier . . .

LYDIA DEL BLANCO sits on a thirdhand rattan love seat, by the front window of her small apartment on Lake Avenue, a glass of warming lemonade in her hand. It is just after noon on the Fourth of July and the sheers are blowing in the windows on gentle waves of sweet alyssum, followed by a lush duet of just-mowed grass and smoldering briquettes.

Fina is on the living room floor, teaching her little brother how to fold paper napkins for the picnic they will have later. A car cruises slowly up Lake Avenue and Lydia can hear the strains of a Young Rascals song float up from the car's stereo. She begins to cry, softly, a strange habit of hers of late.

She cries because she has survived a brutal marriage.

She cries because her two children are healthy and bright and curious and beautiful.

She cries because they are safe here. It has been three years since she has seen her ex-husband. Two years since she's had to hang up on him in the middle of the night and park herself by the front door, dozing off with a baseball bat in her lap.

She cries because, at long last, she and her children have a real life. Sure, the clothes are from Value City, not Higbee's, and, true, she herded her little brood into McDonald's more often than she liked, but they were making ends meet.

Plus, for the first time in her life, she has four hundred dollars saved. *Four hundred.* A miracle. It is stashed in the living room inside her favorite book of all time: *The Secret Garden* by Frances Hodgson Burnett.

The dream house with a yard? Now *that* is a still a few years away, she thinks.

She senses a presence, looks around to see that Fina is standing in front of her. A very *concerned* Fina.

"Mom?"

"Yeah, honey?"

"You okay, Mom?"

Am I okay? Lydia thinks. What does she mean? Lydia looks behind her daughter. Her son is standing there, grave apprehension narrowing his small face. Then it hits her. The tears. They think she is crying because she *hurts*.

"Come here."

The children crowd around. She wraps her arms around them, holds them close. Her daughter, the tall, slender tomboy. Her son, the solid little man.

"Hey," she says, breaking the huddle, wiping her tears with the back of her hand. "Who wants ice cream?"

The boy and the girl both raise their hands. She finds her purse in the dining room, hands them two dollars.

"Come right back," Lydia says. "We're leaving in an hour."

"Okay, Mom," her daughter says.

As the back door closes, Lydia walks to the front window. She looks out, watching her children walk down the steps, hand in hand, then down the sidewalk toward Dinardo's Superette, two blocks away. In an hour, the three of them will head to Edgewater Park to stake their place on the beach in order to watch the big fireworks display later.

Lydia busies herself, retrieving the basket from the hall closet, counting out napkins, plastic forks, paper cups. They will have hot dogs, potato salad, and root beer, her children's favorites. Hers too, if she had to confess. Of all her talents, the culinary arts were screamingly absent. Maybe one day.

Let's see, she thinks, is that everything? No. They'd need mosquito spray, of course. On the windowsill over the sink.

She closes the wicker picnic basket, lugs it to the kitchen. "*It's a beau-ti-ful morn-in,*" she begins to sing, echoing the Young Rascals tune.

But what she finds in her kitchen has nothing to do with beauty.

In fact, what she finds there has nothing to do with *sanity*.

Anthony del Blanco is standing just inside the back door. He is older, heavier, clean-shaven, and well dressed, but the demon is still in his eyes. Cocaine is still his bottom bitch, as he used to be fond of saying. She could smell the Early Times bourbon from ten feet away.

"Hi, babe," Anthony says, closing the door behind him.

"Please," Lydia says, her voice sounding small and weak and nothing like it had sounded in her dreams for the past three years, that booming, powerful voice of vengeance she had used as she pummeled her ex-husband to a bloody pulp.

"I need a couple of bucks, Liddie. Can you help me out?" He begins to cross the kitchen.

"Anthony . . . please. The kids will be back any second."

"The *kids*. How are they?"

"Anthony."

"Kinda hard to find you guys, you know?"

"It's over between us," Lydia says, taking one step backward for every step forward her ex-husband takes. "Over."

"I understand that, sweetheart. And I'm willing to work with you on it. I really, truly am. Today, though, I need a couple of bucks. Okay? Today it's about finances. So, why don't you, for the first time in your *stupid* fucking life, do the smart thing?"

"I don't have any money, Anthony. Look around. Does it look like I have money? We're eating hot dogs for God's sake."

"You save, Lydia. You always did. Don't know how you

did it, but you always managed to put a couple of bucks away."

"Please. Can't you just be a man and walk away?"

The fire spreads in her ex-husband's eyes.

She'd said the wrong thing.

Anthony pins her to the wall, holding her by the neck with his powerful left hand, a hand that easily wraps all the way around her throat. "I'm the *only* fuckin' man you've ever *known*, Lydia. The *only* man." His right hand goes to his belt buckle. "Want me to fuck you right now on the goddamn kitchen floor? Want me to show you what a man I am?"

Before Lydia can stop it, the revulsion rises within her, then boils over. She spits in his face.

Anthony rears back, sets himself, and explodes her nose with a pile-driver right hand.

Lydia sags, her vision clouded by a thick, crimson fog. Anthony holds her up with his left hand, threatens her again with his right, the timbre of his voice rising with his rage, his breath a warm breeze over a landfill.

"You gonna tell me where it is? Because there's plenty more. You know that, right? *Plenty* more. I got *all* fuckin' day."

Lydia, at the very brim of consciousness, cannot speak. But she can raise her eyes. And her eyes speak volumes to a man with whom she lived for four years.

Anthony steps to the side and smashes her in the kidney with his right fist. Once. Twice. Three times. Hard, leveraged punches, expertly thrown. Anthony del Blanco was once a promising amateur middleweight boxer. "I'm sorry, what did you say, Liddie? 'Cause I coulda swore I just saw the cunt look and I don't remember asking you no questions like *Are you a cunt? Please show me*." He tightens the grip on the bloodied bodice of her dress. "Now *where's . . .* the *fucking . . . money*?"

Lydia tries to lift her head, fails. Instead, she succumbs to the nausea. A foamy river of pinkish bile leaks out of her mouth, onto her ex-husband's pantleg and shoes.

Anthony del Blanco now becomes the full animal, and the beating begins in earnest.

Primal.

Methodical.

Complete.

At the moment when Anthony begins to wonder if he has finally gone too far, he remembers. He walks into the living room, finds *The Secret Garden* on the bookshelf, removes it. He laughs, wipes his bloody, damaged hand across his mouth. "Shoulda known," he says, extricating the stack of bills from the book. "Nothin' ever changes around here."

He stuffs the four hundred dollars in his pocket, already tasting that first line of coke rocketing up his right nostril. A sensation he will surely reward with a second line, this one up the left. Toot, toot, he thinks, and tosses the book onto the kitchen floor.

"*The Secret Garden*," Anthony del Blanco says to no one in particular, stepping out into a dazzlingly bright July day in Lakewood, Ohio, dropping his mirrored aviator sunglasses in place. "Yeah. Right. *Big* fuckin' secret, Liddie."

Lydia del Blanco is prone on her kitchen floor. Her jaw is broken in three places, her right cheekbone is shattered. The first punch had demolished her nose; the cartilage now hangs from her face in a corrupt red mass. Three ribs on her right side are broken, two on the left. The ulna of her right arm is fractured and there is a laceration that runs from the middle of her forehead to the left side of her mouth—the result of being thrown through the glass door of the dining room china cabinet—a deep cut that will require nine hours of surgery in order to repair the muscles, and more than two hundred stitches to close.

She is unconscious and bleeding heavily.

Her son and daughter stand in the doorway, holding each other, trembling in the suffocating summer air that is suddenly brassy with blood, their all-but-destroyed mother lying before them, a trio of melting Eskimo Pies at their feet.

But no tears.

The girl lets go of her brother for a moment, steps forward, kneels on the floor. She makes the sign of the cross, then places her right index finger into the pool of warm blood near her mother's left ear. She returns to the doorway, considers her brother's face, the way he stands, now, with his hands clamped tightly over his ears, as if to blot out the silence of this horror.

Without a word, she places her finger gently to her brother's mouth, leaving a small slash of bright scarlet blood on his lips. It is how she would think of him for years—his dark, frightened eyes; his sweat-matted shock of russet hair; red lips giving him the appearance of a sad little girl. She glances down at her mother one last time, then kisses her brother delicately on the lips, their mother's blood all that they would ever say of this day.

Nine years later, when Lydia del Blanco dies, a jaundiced stick figure in the charity ward at St. Vincent's, it will finally free her two children of this moment, free them from all the responsibility of the coming horrors in their lives, free them from the life of an addict mother who will live with a half-dozen men, sleep with ten dozen more, eventually running from heroin fix to cocaine fix to alcohol fix, her face a twisted, scarred mess, never again to resemble the slender young flower in the one photograph her son would keep forever.

A moment, the boy and girl would come to agree, that would free them from fear.

❖ 19 ❖

MARY SAYS: "I have to meet someone."

She *thinks*: What's happening here? Two beauties in a row. First the jogger in front of my building. Now this guy. My knight in shining armor. I'm going to have to jump onto one of these boxcars soon. One of these days the train ain't gonna *run* this way.

He is in his late twenties, early thirties maybe. When he had helped her to her feet she had supported herself against his right thigh and found it was rock hard.

The pain on the left side of her head, where the man had struck her, was minor compared to the wounding of her pride, the swelling of her embarrassment. To be lying face-down in the snow on a city street, humiliated and violated by a common thug, was far worse.

But the man standing in front of her didn't seem to care.

"Well, at least let me take you to the hospital," the man says. "I saw him hit you. You might have a concussion. We'll stop at the police station. You can fill out a report."

"No thanks," she says. "I'm okay, really."

He waits until her eyes meet his before he responds. His eyes are dark, expressive, the color of semisweet chocolate. "Are you sure?"

"Positive."

The man lets go, and she finds that she is still a little wobbly.

"My name is Jean Luc Christiane," he says.

"Tina Falcone," she answers, before she can bottleneck the words in her throat.

"Nice to meet you, Tina."

"You're French?"

"No," he says, smiling. "Born in the *vieux carré* in New Orleans. My family is in baking. I'm as American as beignets."

"Well," she says, rubbing the side of her face, thinking about how she had managed to go through most of her life without getting hit, only to be punched twice in one week. "All I can say is thanks. Who knows what that guy would have done."

"It was both a duty and a pleasure," he says. "Although I wouldn't recommend this method of meeting to the rest of my unmarried friends."

The word, *unmarried*, ripples between them for a moment. He is telling her he is unattached. If she is to play the mating game, this is where she lets him in on *her* marital status in some witty and urbane manner. Instead, she says: "No. I wouldn't either."

"So . . ." he begins, ". . . how do you want to pay me? The standard 'I can call you in the middle of a snowstorm for a ride to the airport because I saved your life' contract? Or do you have something else in mind? Because, clearly I cannot let you leave without settling this matter."

He holds her gaze until she submits. She's willing to bet that that stare has been awfully effective for him throughout his life.

"Well, what do *you* have in mind?" she asks.

"Seeing as I do this quite often—pulling pretty young women out of snowbanks—I do have a standard fee. If I'd had to run the perpetrator down, or produce some type of firearm, or even call the city crews to have you dug out of the snow, the remuneration would increase geometrically."

"How fortunate I am."

"Indeed," he says, flicking the last snowflake from her shoulder.

"So . . . your standard fee is . . ."

"Dinner. Eight o'clock. Cognac at eleven. Home by twelve. Guaranteed."

She considers his offer for a coquette's moment. What the hell, she thinks. Maybe she'd get a hug or two out of it. She really needed a hug. Maybe even, God forbid, a long, dreamy kiss. It had been *ages*. "Yes. Okay. I'm game. Sure," she says. "Why not?"

Jean Luc smiles. "Is that five dates, or just the one?" he asks. "I'll have to check my calendar."

Mary laughs.

It hurts her head.

But, for the first time in a long time, it's a good hurt.

❖ 20 ❖

PARIS IS SITTING in Fayette Martin's kitchen. He is alone. Greg Ebersole is running down leads on Willis Walker's girlfriends, interviewing the regulars at Vernelle's Party Center, a few of whom were already in the unit's Rolodex.

Evil is a breed, Fingers.

He had not been able to shake those words. What breed? Evil how? If Mike Ryan wrote those words, it couldn't possibly have anything to do with something current, so what was the point? Besides, there was no case number on the photo, so it would be impossible to follow up, just a faded street address on the front.

But what if that dead body has something to do with Mike Ryan's murder?

Could he possibly have been wrong about Sarah Weiss?

Is Mike Ryan reaching out to him from the grave?

Ancient history.

Focus, detective.

Unless he is mistaken, Fayette Martin's apartment—a one-bedroom in Marsol Towers, furnished in Kronheim's sale items—is exactly how Fayette left it the night she was murdered. She had, most likely, showered and dressed and hurried out the door, but surely not before making certain that all the cigarettes were out, that the coffeemaker was unplugged, that the deadbolt was turned, never for a moment realizing that none of these things would matter in the end. The shorted cord, the flaming ashtray, the midnight intruder: specters of a different realm, now.

And then there are the plants. Every flat surface, every tabletop in Fayette Martin's apartment is devoted to some kind of healthy, exotic houseplant. In the small pantry there are three dozen boxes of fertilizer and other plant-care products. Fir bark. Hydrolite. Epsom's salts. Coltsfoot. Nettle.

It appears that Fayette had made a Swanson's turkey dinner the night she was murdered. Paris immediately recognized the box, the familiar logo, peeking out of the Hefty bag plopped by the kitchen door. There are several of the same empty boxes in Paris's kitchen wastebasket, too. Crazily, he wonders if Fayette liked the stuffing. To him it always tastes like wet stucco.

But there were probably many nights when, like him, she didn't even notice.

Her computer is on the round Formica kitchen table in front of him; the monitor is black and cold, but the computer itself was on when the super had let him in. It is clear that Fayette Martin took many of her meals here, perhaps cruising the Internet as she ate. On the kitchen table there is also a mouse, manuals, a pair of floppy disks.

Paris has found nothing to indicate the presence of a lover in Fayette's life: no letters, no Hallmark cards, no photographs at Cedar Point or Kings Island held to the refrigerator with a magnet.

Paris thinks: I know the feeling, Fayette. Got a blank fridge myself.

Then, the dead woman speaks to him.

Out loud.

"Hello."

Paris jumps nearly a foot. It sounds like it might be a recording of a phone conversation, but there is no tape recorder or answering machine in the kitchen. No radio, no TV either. So where was the—

It is then that Paris realizes that his hand is on the mouse.

The voice must have something to do with a computer program he started by moving the mouse. The sound is coming from the computer speakers.

Fayette Martin? Paris wonders. Is that her voice? Is that the voice that belonged to the woman he had seen so torn apart in that building on East Fortieth Street?

"Hello," a man answers.

"Are you the police officer?" she continues.

Police officer? A shiver runs through Paris. Please, he thinks. No cops.

"Yes," the man says.

"Just home from a tough day at work?"

"Just walked through the door," he says. *"Just kicked off my shoes."*

"Shoot anyone today?"

"Not today."

"Arrest anyone?"

"Yes."

"Who?"

"Just a girl. A very wicked girl."

The woman laughs.

Paris thinks: It's a sex tape. This is a recording of some sort of 900 call. Cops and maidens. Fayette Martin worked for a *sex line*?

The conversation continues.

"The woman you saw on the top floor. Did you like her?"

"Yes," the man answers. *"Very much."*

"Did it turn you on to watch her?"

"Yes."

As the conversation proceeds, Paris presses the power button on the front of the computer monitor, hoping there is some sort of video accompaniment to this. Although he doesn't know much about computers, he knows enough to realize that a light should come on if the monitor is working. It appears to be broken. No light, no heat. He checks the cord in the back. It is frayed, unplugged. He decides not to take the chance.

"That was me, you know. I was the whore," the woman says.

"I see," the man says.

"Do you like to watch me do that to other men?"

"Yes. I love it."

"Spread your legs."

As Paris listens to this exchange, he has a hard time reconciling the supposedly shy young woman who worked at The Flower Shoppe with this sexual animal. The more he learned, it seemed, the less he knew about people.

Great trait for a detective.

"Like this?" the man suggests.

Maybe the world was full of Fayette Martins, Paris thinks. Maybe it is just naive, over-the-hill cops who—

"Meet me," she says.

Paris sits upright in the chair. Yes. *Talk* to me. Talk about getting *together.*

"No."

"Meet me tonight."

The woman's voice sounds pleading.

"No," the man repeats.

"Meet me and fuck me."

A few seconds of silence. Paris holds his breath, hoping The Lead is about to fall into his lap. He doubted that such synthesized versions of these voices would ever stand up in court as proof of anything, but you never knew.

Just say the words.

Say them.

"If I say yes, what will you do for me?" the man asks.

"I . . . I'll pay you," the woman says. *"I have cash."*

Paris thinks: Fayette Martin didn't work for a sex line.

Fayette Martin is the *caller.*

"I don't want your money," the man says.

"Then what do you want?"

Pause. *"Obedience."*

"Obedience?"

"If we meet, you will do as I say?"

"Yes."

"You will do exactly as I say?"

"I . . . yes . . . please."

"Are you alone now?"

"Yes."

"Then listen to me carefully, because I will tell you this once. There is an abandoned building on the southeast corner of East Fortieth and Central . . ."

Paris's heart leaps, spins, settles. His stomach follows suit. Fayette Martin is talking to her killer. Fayette Martin is talking to the man who cut her in two.

"There is a doorway on the East Fortieth side," the man continues. *"I want you to stand there, facing the door. Understand?"*

"Yes."

"Do you truly have the courage to go there? To do this?"

The slightest hesitation, then: *"Yes."*

Paris realizes, amid his revulsion, that it was indeed courageous for Fayette Martin to go there that night, to be so committed to her fantasy that she would risk it all. And all is exactly what she lost.

"Do you understand that I am going to fuck you in that doorway? Do you understand that I am going to walk up behind you and fuck you in that filthy doorway?"

Paris closes his eyes. The scene begins to draw itself in his mind. Watercolors, this time. Blue and purple and gray. Weeza's Corner Café. Neon in the distance. A woman in the doorway. Petite. Pretty.

"I . . . God. Yes."

"You will wear a short white skirt."

Paris sees the dead woman's accordion-pleated skirt against the filth of the frigid concrete floor; the brown gouache of her blood.

"Yes."

"You will wear nothing underneath it."

"Nothing."

Now, the curve of her buttocks. Pink, dimpled with the cold.

"You will wear nothing on top either, just a short jacket of some sort. Leather. Do you have one?"

They had found no leather jacket. Paris dresses her in one.
"Yes."

"And your highest heels."

"I'm wearing them now."

He sees the bottom of her shoes. Blood-flecked, stiletto-heeled; the Payless price tag barely worn. Special-occasion shoes.

"You will not turn around. You will not look at me. Do you understand?"

"Yes."

"Say it."

"I will not look at you."

"You will not speak."

"I will not."

"You will submit to me totally."

"Yes."

"Can you be there in one hour?"

"Yes."

"If you are one minute late, I will leave."

"I won't be late."

"Then go."

The conversation ends, the speakers fall silent, the hard drive of the computer turns twice, then stops. Paris finds himself staring at the speakers, waiting for more. An address, a name, a nickname, a background sound.

Nothing. He moves the mouse again. Still nothing.

Just the electric-clock silence of a dead woman's kitchen.

Paris stands, looks into the living room. His gaze finds Fayette's high-school picture propped on an end table. It is a soft-focus shot, head slightly back, eyes looking heavenward. Her lips are parted slightly, her sweater is burgundy, perhaps angora, and the color deepens the blush in her cheeks. Around her neck is a thin gold chain bearing a heart-shaped locket.

Paris wonders: What was the path that took her from that

moment—sitting in an Olan Mills Studio, eighteen years old, her whole life an uncluttered horizon before her—to that doorway on East Fortieth Street? Through which of life's portals did she need to pass to make that journey make sense?

And yet Paris believes that whoever she was in life, whatever she did, she had the right to be alive, and that a killer had butchered this woman and left her lying at his feet.

In *his city*.

And thus, as she lay cold and blood-shorn and disassembled on a stainless-steel table at the morgue, he begins to feel that strange and special relationship with Fayette Marie Martin, as he had, at least to some degree, with every victim since his first homicide call.

Paris closes his eyes, conjures Fayette's devastated body in the crime-scene photo, and asks of her murderer: *Which way did you like her better, you son of a bitch? Dead or alive?*

Which way did you prefer *her?*

He glances one last time at her portrait, her eyes.

"You will not look at me," Paris says, aloud, the sound of his voice a dagger through the stillness. Fayette Martin's stillness.

He looks at her lips.

You will not speak.

❖ 21 ❖

PARIS'S PHONE RINGS at Carnegie and East Ninety-third Street.

"Paris."

"Jack, it's Reuben."

"What's up, amigo?"

"I just got the full report on Fayette Martin," Reuben says. "There's something I think you should see."

Paris is glad they are not meeting in the autopsy theater. The labs, although possessed of a full range of their own macabre sights and grotesque smells, at least had the occasional spider plant, the half-eaten peanut butter cup, the air of the living.

Reuben looks wiped out. He leans against a marble-topped table bearing a bank of three microscopes, listlessly drawing on a straw stuck into a beaker of flat Pepsi. On the table, to the left of the microscopes, are a pair of covered lab dishes.

"Hey, Reuben. You look like shit."

"Just pulled a thirty-six," Reuben says. "And, with all due respect, detective, you ain't no *centavo nuevo* either."

Paris has no idea what Reuben said, but figures he has it coming. "What do we have?"

Reuben considers Paris for a moment, blank-eyed, taking his time finishing his drink. He then puts the beaker of cola down, flips on the task light over the table, and says:

"We found something strange inside one of Fayette Martin's shoes."

"It was under the inside label in her left shoe," Reuben says. "There was no reason to look under there so no one did. We almost missed it. Looked like an ordinary brand label you find in half the women's shoes sold."

"Who found it?"

"The lab was finishing up taking blood samples from the heel of the shoe and someone noticed the corner of the label turned up slightly. They peeled it up a little more and saw the edge of this sticking out. Then they called SIU." Reuben takes a pair of evidence photos of Fayette Martin's left shoe out of an envelope.

"Could it have gotten there at the factory by accident?"

"No," Reuben says. "The label on the inside of that shoe was peeled back and reglued very recently."

Paris looks at the evidence bag on the table, at the small item found in the murder victim's shoe: a strip of purple cardboard, about two inches long by a quarter inch wide. On it are what appear to be the bottoms of red letters, as if someone had cut off the bottom quarter inch of some kind of packaging label. It looks like two, or possibly three, words. It looks like the first letter might be a *T*. Or an *I*. Or a *P*. Paris counts two letters that look like an *S*. Beyond that, to Paris, it might as well be Sanskrit. "Any fluids?" he asks.

"Just Fayette's. We also found Fayette's blood mixed in with the glue that secured the shoe company's label, which means the glue was soluble at the time of her murder. This was done at the scene, Jack. And we were *definitely* supposed to find it."

Paris thinks for a moment, asks: "Do you think we have enough of the label to get a lead on what it says? Is there software that can do that?"

"Not sure. But I know the man to call."

"Fed?"

"Who else?"

Shit, Paris thinks. Should he clear this with Elliott? It is up to the unit commander to reach out to another agency, especially at the federal level. If this leads somewhere, Paris is going to have to explain why he broke procedure. On the other hand, if Reuben's contact is willing to forget the paperwork, maybe the CPD can nail this psychopath without the almighty Justice Department taking all the credit, as it usually does. The Cleveland Police Department could use the shot in the arm.

Paris asks: "How well do you know this guy?"

Reuben smiles. "Hang on."

Reuben crosses the lab, enters his office. Ten minutes later, he returns. "I sent it over to the Federal Building via secure courier. He called to confirm receipt and said it isn't much, but he also said he sleeps an average of two hours a day. The rest of the time he sits in front of his computer. He said the strip of cardboard is definitely cut from a commercial consumer product of some sort. He thinks he has the font and point size already. He also has the poundage of the cardboard."

"What about the original?"

"It's on the way back already."

"And you trust this guy?"

"Absolutely. Believe me, if anybody is going to tell us what we have it's Clay Patterson. He said he'll call when and if."

"What about the paperwork?" Paris asks.

"He says the invoice will read DigiData, Inc.," Reuben replies. "And that they take cash."

❖ 22 ❖

"WHAT DO YOU think, Bella?"

She pulls her Anna Sui from the closet, holds it up in front of her, glances at the cheval mirror. As always, Isabella's picture, sitting atop the armoire, remains silent.

"Yeah, I think so, too. The little black dress. There's simply no defense against it." She laughs at her joke, then feels guilty, the way she always feels guilty having fun without her daughter.

As she steps into the shower she runs down her itinerary. She will meet Celeste on the way into town and get the money from the sale of Elton's jewelry. Although she so desperately wants to tell Celeste about what happened at Dream-A-Dream Motel—as crazy as it sounded, Celeste is indeed the only person in the world she can trust—she has decided to wait.

She will tell her in due time.

And only if she needs to.

Jean Luc wears a Zegna wool suit, navy blue, and a subtly patterned dove gray tie. They dine at the Sans Souci restaurant at the Renaissance Hotel, the fare consisting of fusilli with roasted peppers and eggplant, sautéed scallops with fresh fennel and saffron broth, and a glorious, shared ice cream sundae topped with boysenberries and Grand Marnier.

The leisurely stroll around Public Square—window-shopping, watching the skaters twirl amid the Christmas lights—is even more glorious.

Jean Luc tells her about his job as the creative director for a major downtown ad agency.

Jean Luc tells her that he finds her extremely attractive, in a very young Natalie Wood kind of way.

Jean Luc tells her that *Movieline* is his favorite magazine.

Incredibly, it is her favorite magazine, too. It is the only one to which she subscribes. The new issue is, at that moment, sitting in the lobby of her building.

They stop in front of the window display at Dillard's, ponder each other in the warm lights from the Christmas display in the windows. Overhead, the speakers offer a tinny "Silver Bells."

Jean Luc asks her if she would like to have coffee, or if she would like to be taken home.

It was somewhere around the scallops that she had arrived at the answer to *that* one. She takes his hand in both of hers, squeezes gently, and says:

"Both."

They are sitting on her couch, a single lamp lit behind them, the television on. They watch a few scenes from *Anatomy of a Murder* with Lee Remick on the AMC channel. They talk about dating, about travel, about movies, carefully skirting politics for this, their first date. By one o'clock, the coffee is gone. The film ends at one-fifteen.

Then comes the awkward silence. The first of the evening.

She decides to break it. "Well, in case I've forgotten to say it for the three-thousandth time, thanks for a wonderful evening," she says, snapping on the table lamp next to the couch. She tries for levity. "I'm glad we, um, ran into each other today."

"Uh oh," Jean Luc replies. "Sounds like I'm leaving."

"I have to get up, I'm afraid. Working gal."

"Just one more cup?"

"Coffee's gone."

"Then so am I," he says with a smile, rising, slipping on his charcoal gray coat. "But you've only begun to chip away at your debt to me. You do realize that, don't you?"

"Of course," she says, standing, trying to stretch her cramped legs without being obvious. "I intend to work it off at Sfuzzi, The Watermark, Piccolo Mondo, whatever it takes. I pay my debts, no matter what the personal hardships."

Jean Luc laughs. "Such nobility in the face of so many calories."

"And anytime you want to go back to Sans Souci . . ."

"Isn't it fantastic? It's my personal favorite."

"The food was incredible. Thanks again."

"Well . . . it was my pleasure," he says, pulling on his leather gloves. "Beats the fare at Vernelle's Party Center, I'll bet."

Suddenly, everything in the world is at a forty-five-degree angle to everything else. She is looking around her apartment, but nothing in it makes sense. Sure, it is her couch, her coffee table, her books on the shelf. But now the room is huge, ventless. The walls seem miles away.

She asks: "I'm sorry? Where?"

"Vernelle's Party Center. On St. Clair Avenue. They serve chitterlings and ribs and collard greens there, if I'm not mistaken. Somehow, you don't strike me as the soul food type."

She can hear him speaking, but the words seem to rush by her ears, as if she is in motion. "I've never been there," she says. "And you're right. I'm not the soul food type. Way too fatty."

"Oh, but I bet you were Willis Walker's type," he says. "I'd almost bet everything on that one."

"Get out."

"Please. Just listen to me."

"Get out."

"You'll understand completely once I tell you the whole story."

"Get *out*!"

"I'm afraid you have no choice *but* to listen," he says, reaching slowly into the inside pocket of his coat.

"I have plenty of choices," she answers. She squares herself in front of him, puts her hands on her hips. Her eyes remain riveted on the hand entering his coat, while her peripheral vision estimates that the knife on the kitchen counter is less than eight feet away. "I have every fucking choice there is." It is an old defense. Whenever she got scared, she got vulgar.

He removes his hand from the inside pocket of his coat and drops something on the coffee table in front of her. It is a five-by-seven black-and-white photograph. At first, it looks like an abstract of some sort, the kind of optically challenging picture you might see in gaming magazines— *Identify This!* But when she looks at it more closely, she knows it is no game.

It is a picture of her running from Room 116 of the Dream-A-Dream Motel.

Her head swims. Tears begin to limn her eyes, in spite of efforts to stop them.

How could she have been so stupid?

She tries to gather her thoughts, her breath. "What . . . what do you want?"

"I just need your help. No violence," he says. "I'm just settling an old debt. And you can help me."

"And this is how you *ask* me? By fucking *blackmailing* me?" She begins to pace around the apartment. Then, it hits her. "*Wait* a minute . . . you hired that guy to attack me, didn't you?"

"He wasn't supposed to lay a finger on you," he says. "On the other hand, he wasn't supposed to run away like a ten-year-old girl at the first sign of danger, either. Him coming back? That was all his idea. I guess you wounded his homeless-man pride. But, you have to admit, it made my rescue a lot more swashbuckling, don't you agree?"

Everything that made this man attractive over dinner has

now dissolved into a pool of disgust at the base of her roiling stomach.

But, she had to confess, it's not like she didn't deserve having some con run on her. It's not like she didn't have it coming. She is, by anyone's standards, at any time in the history of the world, a thief. And a murderer. Even if it was self-defense.

It's just that she feels so *violated.*

"What do you want me to do?" she asks, sitting back down on the couch, her tears turning to sniffles, her mind turning to business.

"I want you to do what you do best," he says, his face brightening, flashing the smile that got her into this mess. He sits down next to her. "Be yourself. Your charming, beautiful self."

She draws a cigarette from the pack on the table, her hands no longer shaking.

He lights her cigarette, rests his hand on her knee, continues.

"Let me tell you a short story," he says, offering her a starched white handkerchief. "Then I'll go. I promise."

For some reason, his soft, elegant voice is beginning to calm her. She is beginning to believe that he means her no physical harm, at least not at this moment. She takes the handkerchief and dabs her mascara-streaked eyes. "A story?"

"Yes. It takes place a few years ago. I was barely a teenager. If I remember correctly, the Indians beat the Minnesota Twins that day . . ."

❖ 23 ❖

Cleveland, Ohio,
Seventeen years earlier . . .

TONY B'S EMPORIUM carries a little bit of everything—
soda, chips, candy, cigarettes, condoms—but mostly it carries lottery tickets and fifteen different brands of fortified
wine. Seventy percent of Tony B's daily receipts are from
one or the other. Twenty percent are from cigarettes. The
other ten percent are from the idiots either too dumb or too
lazy to walk the extra five blocks to buy their milk and eggs
from the Kroger's on East 105th Street.

It is late September, a steamy Indian summer day. The
heat shrieks off the pavement in waves, punishing the water-
starved trees in front of Tony B's. From the apartment above
the store comes the sounds of the Cleveland Indians playing
the Minnesota Twins.

Tony B's Emporium is empty, save for its proprietor, who
is sitting high behind the counter, reading his paper, trying
to keep absolutely still, trying to let the ancient, asthmatic
air conditioner above the front door do its job.

Suddenly, something is wrong.

He can *feel* it.

It is the same premonition he used to get in 'Nam, seconds before the first sniper round would crack out of the
hills and send everyone at the base camp scrambling. The

store is small, well lighted, and unless someone decides to lie on the floor and roll under a display, Tony B, with the aid of his three convex mirrors, can see every square inch. He knows when people are in the store. The bell on the door tells him when they come in. The bell on the door tells him when they leave. So why does he have the feeling that—

There. A shadow to his left. Next to the chip stand.

There are two people standing there. A boy and a girl.

How had they gotten in? Tony B wonders, his heart racing a little. Why hadn't he heard them? Had they come in the *back*?

They are young—the girl is in her late teens, the boy even younger, maybe sixteen—and they are staring at him. The girl is one hot-looking little bitch, that's for sure. Trim. Brunette. She isn't dressed sloppy like a lot of the other girls who come in the store and tease him; the black girls with their baggy jeans unbuttoned and their tube tops wrapped tightly around their budding breasts. This one is white, slender, seductive, wearing a short denim skirt and flowered blouse, the kind of girl who always went for a man like Tony B. Sure he was into his forties now, but he was a *young* forties. Still had most of his hair, all of his front teeth. And he still had all the charm in the world when he needed it.

"We know each other?" he asks, bending the top of his *Racing Form* to make eye contact with the girl. He reaches over and drags a Pall Mall from his pack, lights it. "We been introduced?"

"No," the girl says. "You just look like someone we know."

The girl's voice is deep, like a woman's. Her blouse is sheer and Tony B can just about make out the shape of her right breast. "Oh yeah?" he answers, trying to float a smile. "Burt Reynolds, maybe?"

"No," the boy says. "Like an uncle or something."

The boy's age is less determinable after he speaks. The kid is on the tall side, dark hair, dark eyes. He now seems younger than sixteen. Like a big thirteen-year-old with a man's hands. His voice hadn't fully broken yet. Smart-ass punk, for sure.

"Well, I ain't your uncle," Tony B says, realizing he isn't going to make any time with the girl if this little shit is hanging around. "So now that we've established that piece of business, you buyin' something?"

"We're just looking," the girl says. "We're allowed to look, aren't we?"

Cocky little cunt, Tony B thinks. Reminds him of the first ex, the one he did the stretch for. Looks a little like her, too. He'd gone up for an eight-to-ten ride on an attempted murder charge for beating the shit out of Lydia that day, but less than a year into his sentence they found a mistake somewhere and had to spring him. "Who said this is America, girly-girl? This ain't America in here. This is Tony B's. Capeesh? Now, either you buy something, or you take it on the arches. Those are the rules."

She turns to the side and Tony B can see her nipples poking up against the inside of her blouse. God*damn* she's a sexy little thing. Tony doesn't know whether to yell or get hard. She grabs a pack of Gillette single-edge razor blades off the rack.

"We'll take these," she says, gliding over, placing them on the counter.

As she walks, Tony B is mesmerized by the shift of her breasts beneath her blouse. Up close he can see that her eyes are almost black.

He rings up the razor blades, an item he keeps stocked for the cokeheads. Cokeheads prefer the single-edge blades to cut up their lines. It used to be *his* ax of choice, back in the day. "That's three-sixty-two, miss," Tony says, not taking his eyes from hers. "Including tax."

The girl reaches into her pocket, produces a five-dollar bill. As she hands it to him, Tony B would swear that she intentionally lets her hand linger on his for a moment. When he hands her the change, he repays the flirtation in kind.

"Need a bag?" he asks.

"No," she replies.

"Now, you be careful with those razor blades, miss," he adds, shutting the cash drawer, sounding far more paternal than he wants to. "Wouldn't want you to cut that pretty skin of yours."

The girl turns to face him fully. She smiles a smile that sends shock waves through Tony B's libido. But the sensation cannot compare with what he feels as she unbuttons her blouse and reveals most of her left breast to him. There, right above her pink nipple, is a small tattoo of a flower. "I can take the pain," she says. "Can *you*?"

"I . . ." is all that Tony B can muster as she buttons her blouse, turns on her sandals, and sashays to the door, where the boy awaits her. Somehow, Tony B manages to tear his eyes from the girl. He looks at the boy, and immediately wishes he hadn't.

The boy is smiling at him.

And he suddenly looks a lot more like a man.

Tony B is drunk. It is two in the morning, and he is leaning against the wall outside his store, in the alley, a cigarette dangling from his lower lip, searching the same pants pocket for the tenth time, hoping that a full pack of matches might have spontaneously generated there since his last visit. Nothing.

Fuck it, he thinks. I'll wait until I get inside.

He slowly continues up the alley, toward the back parking lot.

He'd had an unbelievable night at Big Ray Amato's poker game. Walked in with two hundred, walked out with six. Drank Ray's booze all night, ate his food. It's a good thing Ray's house was only two blocks away, within walking distance of the store, which is precisely where Tony B has decided to sleep it off. No *way* is he going to drive all the way up to Fortieth Street. He steps into the small pitted gravel parking lot behind his store. There are two cars, including his own, along with a beat-up van. The lot is dark, empty, still; the day's wet heat seems to radiate from the ground like a colossal steam iron buried in the earth, just inches beneath his feet.

Tony B begins the ritual of searching for his keys.

And, for the second time that day, finds that someone is standing right in front of him. Someone who does not make noise. Tony B looks up, takes a wobbly step backward, and sees that it is a woman. A beautiful young woman with pale skin and shiny hair.

Where had he seen her before?

Man, the short-term memory is shot, he thinks, laughing to himself. Guess thirty-some years of drug and alcohol abuse will do that to you. It's the brunette bitch from the *store,* of course. The cocky one. The little girl with the tattooed tit. But now she is made up like a woman. Tight leather pants, spike heels, hair piled high on her head.

"Hey, baby," Tony B says.

"Hey yourself," she answers.

Tony B thinks: She dumped her little turd friend and she came back for Tony Fuckin' B. Before he can take a step in her direction, he hears a sniffle from nearby and sees the boy sitting on a packing crate next to the Dumpster in a dark corner of the lot. The pungent smell in the air tells Tony B that the kid is smoking a joint. Right out in the open.

Right behind *his store.*

Ah, who gives a shit? Tony thinks. He is loaded, there's a foxy little bitch nearby, and he hadn't smoked a joint in five years. "You're gonna get in trouble smoking that shit," Tony B says, smiling, staggering over to the Dumpster. "Got a hit for your Uncle Tony?"

The boy looks at the girl. She nods. The boy hands the giant joint to Tony B.

"Man," Tony B says, drunkenly examining the double-long spliff. "Where the fuck you from, Jamaica?"

The boy and the girl both break into stoned laughter. Tony B takes a huge, lung-rattling drag on the joint. He holds it for a few moments, his cheeks puffed out like Dizzy Gillespie's.

More laughter. It causes Tony B to lose the hit. "Hey . . . quit makin' me laugh," he says, already feeling some of the effects of the pot. "Damn," he adds. "This is good shit."

"Only the best," the boy says. "Take another hit. Help yourself."

What the fuck, Tony B thinks, and complies. This time, after holding it only a few seconds, the pot begins to excavate the top of his brain. Street sounds from Euclid Avenue, a half-mile away, are suddenly crystal clear. Somehow, he can smell the trash from behind China Garden, all the way up on East 105th! His mind is unclouded but, suddenly, his limbs weigh a *ton*. "I don't . . ." Tony B says. "How come I—"

The kid laughs. "You've been dusted, man."

"What?"

"You've been dusted. Angel dust."

Before he can react, Tony B remembers the girl. He wants to get a good look at her with this new, scary buzz on. He turns on his heels and can suddenly smell her perfume—rich and flowery and sexy. His erection begins to form even before she steps out of the shadows and opens her blouse to reveal two of the most perfectly shaped breasts Tony B has ever seen. Ever. "God almighty," he exclaims. "God. All. *Mighty*."

The girl covers up, giggles.

"How much?" Tony B asks.

"How *much*?" the girl answers.

"Don't play with me. How much? You say it, it's yours."

"How much do you have?"

Tony B rummages his pockets. He has cash everywhere. "Six hundred," he says.

"Six hundred will get you everything you want," she says, stepping very close. She begins to unbutton his shirt.

"What about *him*?" Tony B answers, nodding at the boy, who is now back next to the Dumpster, in the shadows, his eyes staring out like lucent black stones.

The girl removes Tony B's shirt, letting it fall to the

ground. "He doesn't care," she replies, unzipping his pants, backing him over to the pile of flattened cardboard boxes against the building. "He likes to watch."

Tony B knows this is a huge mistake, just as he knows that he isn't going to stop. Within a minute or so he is completely naked—save for his short black socks and soiled Reeboks—and half-sitting, half-leaning against the waist-high stack of boxes, the sultry night air pouring over his body, the angel dust and the alcohol in full control of his reflexes.

The girl backs up a few paces. She removes her white blouse and begins to dance, topless, in front of him, gently swaying her hips to one side, then the other.

Jesus jumped up Christ on an Easter palomino, Tony B thinks. I've died and gone to fuckin' heaven. He glances over at the Dumpster.

The boy is gone.

Then, for Tony B, everything begins to happen at once; all of it shrouded in a pasty gray light, all of it lurching to a maddeningly unsyncopated beat.

Movement to his left. The crunch of gravel. A young man's rhythm.

A shadow from Da Nang? Tony B wonders.

Am I back *in country*?

The beautiful girl in front of him begins to exaggerate her slow, liquid movements. A pale arm lashes out in the moonlight; the curve of a young breast flashes before him.

Now—hot breath on his neck. Sounds from behind him. *Sliding* sounds.

Now—the girl's leg rises toward him. *Fast*. A cobra strike from the darkness.

The kick to his exposed testicles is so swift, so *precise*, that at first Tony B thinks it is part of her dance routine. He knows he should feel it, but, for the moment he does not. For the moment, he cannot feel *anything*.

Then, a loop of wire is cast over his head. "Razor wire," the boy whispers in his ear. "Concertina." The boy is behind him now, kneeling on the boxes. "You move an inch you puncture your jugular vein. Don't fucking move." Wearing thick leather gloves, the boy continues to wrap Tony B's head in the razor wire, slicing tiny cuts and nicks in the man's head, neck, shoulders.

Tony B's mind is a morass of confusion, indecision, anger. *You've been dusted.*

"She's dead," the girl says.

Dead? *Who's* dead? Tony B wonders. *And why can't I move my hands, my feet? Why does everything weigh . . . a fucking . . . ton?*

"She's finally dead," the girl repeats. "You've finally killed her."

And, in an instant, Tony B knows.

Jesus Christ.

Lydia.

He begins to cry as his daughter takes his now-flaccid penis in her right hand.

The sobs become a deep, soughing wail as his son produces a single-edge razor blade and examines it in the heat-shimmered moonlight.

Tony B tries to scream, but the pain now generated by his crushed right testicle, the fear generated by the razor wire at his throat, prevents him from making any coherent human sounds.

Instead, Anthony del Blanco opens his mouth, and all that pours forth is a series of small, wet whimpers, sounds of fear and defeat and failure and humiliation, sounds that return to his ears with full dynamic range and echo like a young woman's footsteps across a long, dark gallery of remembrance.

For five minutes, they do not stop. The baseball bats they had fitted with the single-edge blades first demolish the man's head, pounding the razor wire deep into his flesh, caving in his forehead, occipitals, cheekbones, jaw, clubbing his upper torso into a crimson mess, snapping his collarbone into dozens of pieces.

In spite of the girl's wishes, in spite of her decade of prayers, her father is dead by the time the two begin work on his ribs, stomach, hips, legs.

When they are finished, heavily lathered after such a workout in such heat, the boy reaches into the Dumpster and retrieves the gallon plastic bottle he had placed there earlier in the day. He completes his task by pouring the contents— the full measure of two thirty-ounce cans of beef broth— over the length of his father's corpse.

The boy and girl agree that they have done the world a favor. Of course, the law enforcement agencies will not see it that way. And thus they must split up. She will return to her foster home, where she is, at that very minute, on the third floor, asleep. He will take the Greyhound to San Diego. From there, a cousin will bring him into Mexico, a place where he will be safe.

They hold each other in a long, silent embrace, just as they had held each other in that doorway nearly a decade earlier. Then, for her own safety, the girl gets in her car, a car belonging to her foster mother, a late-model Toyota for which the girl had made a duplicate key months earlier. She meets her brother's eyes one last time as he readies the key at the back of the van. He had stolen the van earlier in the day and will leave it a dozen or so blocks from the Greyhound bus station at East Thirteenth Street and Chester Avenue.

They had collected the dogs for the past two weeks, alternately starving them, then throwing them the slightest morsels of rancid beef. The dogs are ravenous, insane with hunger, and long bereft of any notion of their place as domesticated animals in a civilized world. There are four of them in the back of the van. Two Rottweilers, two Dobermans.

The boy opens the door and carefully, one by one, removes their muzzles. Within seconds, the four big dogs are out, their huge paws chewing up the gravel to get to this fallen cousin so freshly and mortally wounded in the primordial mist of their need.

As the boy and girl look on, the dogs descend upon the body with a viciousness that has lived in their beings, untapped, for centuries. The boy and girl understand completely, for they too have carried a dark violence within them for years, a visceral craving for this moment.

And so they watch, still and silent and rapt, two children of the same mother.

But, at this moment, their thoughts are one.

Rest now, Lydia.

Rest.

The girl pulls out of the lot first, leaving the boy in the driver's seat of the van, idling, lights off, watching the last of the carnage unfold.

Mexico, he thinks. He does not know it yet, but Mexico is a place where he will learn the way of the road, the way of the night, the way by which all things must pass at least once as the devil smiles upon them. The way beside which all other ways pale.

In Mexico, he will learn the way of the saints.

❖ 24 ❖

SHE IS HORRIFIED. Disgusted. More than a little afraid. And completely bewildered.

Here's what she knows. Or *thinks* she knows.

Jean Luc and his sister beat their father to death because their father was an animal and abused their mother. Then they let dogs eat him.

But how does she know the *story* is true? How does she know that Jean Luc is really the boy in the story? And what can it *possibly* have to do with her? Did he tell her that story just to frighten her? On top of the blackmail?

She looks up to see him cross the room, pick up Isabella's photo.

Fighting her growing nausea, she sprints across the room, takes the photograph from him, as forcefully as she dares, and places it in the end table drawer. "What do you want from me? Just tell me what the *fuck* you want from me."

"Tonight? Nothing." He takes her chin in his right hand, angles her face toward his. "But tomorrow. Tomorrow is Christmas Eve."

"Yeah? What about it?"

"It is a magical night and I want you to have the best time possible."

She remains absolutely still, silent.

"Tomorrow night you are going to a party," he continues.

"A party filled with laughter and goodwill and all the other joys of the season."

She looks at his handsome face, thinks about him as a thirteen-year-old boy, a bloodied baseball bat in his hands. She considers the will that must have propelled that fury. She feels it seething from him as he moves ever closer. She retreats, little by little, until her back is to the wall. Is *any* of this true? She has no idea. But she is a realist, if nothing else, and knows the box score. As long as Jean Luc has those pictures of her at the Dream-A-Dream Motel, it doesn't really matter if the story is true or not.

Jean Luc says: "All I want you to think about, between now and tomorrow night, are three little words."

He touches her cheek.

For a moment she feels, what, *charmed*?

In the middle of all *this*?

"What three words?" she asks.

He tells her, counting each word off with his fingers.

"Merry Christmas, Jack."

❖ 25 ❖

JACK PARIS STANDS in the checkout line at the Rite Aid drugstore at East 113th Street and Euclid Avenue, a ridiculous parody of a Christmas tree in his hands. Actually, he is holding a box no bigger than a boot box, a box that allegedly contains a "full 36-inch-tall Christmas tree, great for small spaces!"

He has decided that he will not let this Christmas pass without some sort of cheer in his otherwise cheerless apartment.

The line is moving slowly, but that is not the worst of it. The worst of it is the incessant, mind-scrambling ring of the Salvation Army bell, courtesy of the Santa-clad volunteer standing just outside the door. Paris, like everyone else in the store, would like to take Santa out with a spinning back kick and stomp that bell flatter than a tuna can on the freeway.

Instead, after paying for his tree in a box, he nods at Santa as he passes him and, as per routine, walks another ten feet or so, spins on his heels, saunters back, and dumps a buck in the bucket.

"Thank you," Santa says. "And Happy Holidays."

"Yeah, whatever," Paris answers, his grumpiness a receipt for his small generosity.

Paris reaches his car and opens the trunk. At least one-third of his life stares back at him. After some clever maneuvering, he is able to slip the Christmas tree box into the left side, next to the gym bag containing workout sweats that have already survived two full years in the trunk without ever having seen the inside of a gym.

Then, from behind him, a sunny voice says: "What a *softie*."

Paris turns around to see Mercedes Cruz. They had planned to meet here and she is right on time. "Hi," he says.

"Saw you give in to the Christmas spirit there, detective."

"Don't let it get out, okay?" Paris says, slamming the trunk, hoping, for some reason, that Mercedes hadn't seen his pathetic tree-thing. "Cops have four million charities and I'd never have a minute's peace. In fact, tonight is the annual Cleveland League Christmas party. Bunch of conscience-plagued cops and inner-city kids. I go every year. It's my penance."

"You *are* a softie. I admire that in a . . . married man?"

"Divorced," Paris says.

"I admire it even more," she says, then instantly covers her mouth with a magenta-mittened hand. "Oh my goodness, was that sexual harassment?"

"Let's see. Who has the power here?"

"I'd say it's equal. I've got a pen. You've got a gun."

"Then it was a compliment."

"Whew," Mercedes says.

"But let's keep it to a minimum," Paris says. "First it's compliments, then the next thing you know people will think the press and the police are getting along."

"I won't let it happen again."

"By the way, I met your brother. He took a few photos of this crooked face and busted nose."

"You've *got* to be shittin' me," Mercedes says.

"What?

"My brother actually did something I *asked* him to? Un-believable."

"Nice kid," Paris continues. "Good-looking, too."

"Yeah," Mercedes says, rummaging in her bag. "He's a real thief of hearts, let me tell you. Girls have been knocking on our front door ever since Julian turned twelve. I'm just stunned he stopped by."

"It was painless," Paris says.

"Good. Maybe getting these pictures published will get him off his ass." She gestures toward the city. "So, where to first, detective?"

"West side," Paris says. "I think it's time to visit the botanica."

"Want me to drive?" Mercedes asks, holding up her key chain, pointing to a sparkling, midnight blue Saturn.

Paris looks at his listing, rusted Olds, caked with road salt, and makes his first mistake of the day when he says: "Sure."

They are on Detroit Avenue, going thirty-five miles per hour, sliding on ice, and about to slam into the rear end of a primer-prepped old Plymouth; a Plymouth whose driver decided to pause, at a green light, to empty his ashtray into the middle of the street.

In the middle of a snowstorm.

On the way, Paris and Mercedes had stopped at Ronnie's Famous for a few minutes and Paris had switched thermoses. He had also turned Mercedes Cruz on to Ronnie Boudreaux's vaunted beignets. She had agreed instantly. World's best, no contest.

Now, though, as they hit a patch of ice on Detroit Avenue, Paris can feel the coffee and the beignets in his stomach begin to head north. They do a three-sixty. Then another. Then, the Saturn comes to a full stop, somehow pointed in the right direction, somehow just inches to the right of the Plymouth. No damage.

Yet.

Mercedes gathers herself, waits a few beats, lowers her window, smiles, gestures to the other driver to do the same. He reaches over, a confused look on his face, and rolls down the passenger window.

"Hi," Mercedes says, all charm and innocence.

"Hi," the driver says.

"Chinga!" Mercedes yells out the window. *"Chinga tu MADRE, tu PADRE, tu 'BUELA!"*

Although Paris is monolingual, having plenty of trouble with English alone, you don't have to be Roberto Duran to know what Mercedes just said about the other driver's sainted mother, father, and grandmother. The driver, a fair-sized young Latino kid, promptly flips Mercedes the bird, then floors it, fishtailing his way down to West Thirty-eighth Street, where he makes a hurried left turn and disappears into the squall of falling snowflakes.

Winter silence ensues for a few moments. Mercedes looks at Paris. Paris speaks first, realizing he had just witnessed the temper Mercedes's brother Julian had mentioned. "You okay?"

"Fine. Sorry about that."

"No harm done."

"I said a bad word."

Paris laughs. "A bunch of them, actually. Nice talk for a Catholic gal."

"You understood that?" she asks as she carefully scans her side mirror and gingerly pulls back out into traffic.

"Well, if you work the inner city, you learn the f-word in many languages. I had an Arab flip me off in Farsi once. I'm sure of it."

"I'm *so* embarrassed."

"Don't be. I offer the same sentiment to my fellow Cleveland motorists quite often. Usually in Italian, though."

"You're Italian?"

"My grandfather on my father's side was named Parisi. The *i* got chopped off at Ellis Island somehow. My mother's father was Italian, too. What about you?"

"Puerto Rican on my father's side. My mother's family is English/Irish."

"Which heritage do you feel more strongly?"

"I guess I consider myself Hispanic. My brother and I are both pretty close to my *'buela,* my grandmother. She is a wonderful woman. My role model. I look a lot like her when she was younger. I think we're the same type."

"Type?"

"You know. Independent. Mysterious. *Darkly* exotic."

"I see."

"Kind of a cross between Ava Gardner and Eva Peron, the way I see it." Mercedes looks at Paris, affecting a glamour pose. "What do you think?"

Paris, completely cornered, ever the diplomat, says: "Actually, I never saw *Evita*, so I'm going to have to give it some thought, you know?"

Mercedes laughs, snaps on the radio, grabs her third beignet out of the oily white bag between the seats, and says, "I've got all day, detective."

❖ 26 ❖

LA BOTANICA MACUMBA occupies one corner of Fulton Road and Newark Avenue, on Cleveland's near-west side, next to a used-shoe mart run by lay personnel at St. Rocco's called The Deserving Sole. Beneath the botanica's large red-lettered sign is a legend that reads: *Hierbas Para Banos/Todas Clases.*

Paris finds no small irony—now that he has a little background on Santeria and knows how it came into being—that the reflection in the window of La Botanica Macumba is of St. Rocco's across the street. The botanica's window is a patchwork quilt of brightly colored banners, decrying the shop's exotica: Spanish Cards! Sugar Candy! Pompeia Perfume! Blue Balls! High John Root! Maja Products!

Yet there, in the center of the window, is a diaphanous cruciform, a cross reflected from the facade of St. Rocco's. Next to the likeness, a neon sign that claims that La Botanica Macumba is a "grocery store for the body and soul."

As Paris enters he is immediately beguiled by a seductively sweet aroma. He sees the smoldering cone on a nearby brass plate. A tented, hand-lettered card reads: *nag champa.*

There is one other customer in the shop, a Hispanic man in his seventies.

Paris and Mercedes look around the small store a while, waiting for the proprietor to wrap up his business with the other customer. On one wall there is a huge rack of oils, incense, and soaps, many promising a variety of benefits: from keeping away spirits to drawing money or love to keeping one's spouse at home. "Stay With Me" one of the oils is called, Paris notes with an inner smile, thinking: Coulda used some of that. On another wall is a magazine and book rack, along with a dozen cardboard display bins of candles, herbs, voodoo supplies, gris-gris, dolls, artwork, CDs, T-shirts, tarot decks.

After a few moments, the customer leaves. Paris and Mercedes approach the counter.

"My name is Edward Moriceau," the man behind the counter says. He is sixty, thin and wiry, dark-skinned, of indefinable heritage. North African, perhaps. There is a ring on each of his fingers, including his thumbs. "*Mojuba!*"

"I'm sorry?" Paris says.

"It is a Lucumí term of greeting. It means 'I salute you.' "

"Oh," Paris says. "Thanks."

"How can I help you?"

Paris shows the man his shield. "My name is Detective Paris. I'm with the Homicide Unit of the Cleveland Police Department. This is Ms. Cruz. She's a reporter with *Mondo Latino*."

Moriceau nods at Mercedes, says, "Yes. I am familiar with your paper, of course." He gestures to a wire newspaper bin near the door, where a small stack of *Mondo Latino* newspapers reside.

"I'd like to ask you a few questions," Paris says.

"Certainly."

"Do you recognize this?" Paris holds up a pencil sketch of the symbol found on both Willis Walker and Fayette Martin.

"Yes. It is the symbol for Ochosi."

"Could you spell that for me, please?"

Moriceau does.

"What does it mean?" Paris asks.

"Ochosi is a hunter god. The bow and arrow are his tools."

"What is it for?"

"For?"

"Why would someone pray to this god?"

"For many things, detective," Moriceau says as he turns to the display case behind him, removing a small iron replica of the bow-and-arrow symbol. "It depends upon what is in the heart of he who prays. If you are a decent man, a law-abiding citizen, you might pray to Ochosi for bounty. If you are a thief, with the proper sacrifice, the hunter god Ochosi can ward off arrest, police, jail."

Paris and Mercedes exchange a glance. "Sacrifice?" Paris asks.

Moriceau offers a sad, lopsided smile. "I'm afraid there are more misconceptions than truths about the Afro-Caribbean religions. The notion of human sacrifice is one of the most insidious."

"I didn't say anything about human sacrifice," Paris says.

"You are a homicide detective," Moriceau says. "I trust you are not here because of some disemboweled rooster."

Paris doesn't particularly care for the man's attitude, but lets the snide remark slide for the moment. "I didn't say there was a disemboweled *anything*. I'm here to ask some basic questions about Santeria. Mind if I continue?"

"Not at all."

"Are there many followers of Santeria in Cleveland?"

"Yes. But Santeria is not a centralized religion. It is impossible to count the number of worshipers in this or any city."

"Do you have any regular customers who've mentioned this Ochosi lately?"

"None that come to mind. There are many subtle variations in the Afro-Caribbean religions. Many different names for things."

"So, there's no way to pin down which sect might use this god for, say, darker purposes?"

"Not really. It is as if someone says that they are a practicing Christian. Are they Methodist? Baptist? Mormon? Adventist? Roman Catholic? If a *brujo* were to purchase items for an altar, there are many different combinations of symbols, candles, cards, incantations he might use. Brazilian Macumba, Haitian voodoo, Mexican Santeria. Santeria and its offshoots like Palo Mayombe are very complex, very secretive religions that differ from country to country."

For some reason, Paris is feeling a bit defensive about Catholicism, even though he knows he hardly has the right. "And what exactly is a *brujo*?"

"A *brujo* is sort of a wizard, a seer. A male witch, to some. But these words have completely different meanings than they do in English."

"Are there any of these *brujos* in Cleveland?"

"A few. Although, if I may anticipate your next question, I do not keep a list. We generally do not ask to what use our customers put our goods."

Paris jots a few more notes in his book, liking Moriceau's attitude less and less. "What sorts of items might a customer ask for if he were doing evil things?"

"Well, followers of Palo Mayombe sometimes ask for *palo azul*—blue stick. It is an item many botanicas do not stock. This one included. But there are many exotic things used for good and evil. One botanica in New York City regularly stocks dried cobra. Some stock something called *una de gato*—cat's claw."

"Have you had any unusual requests lately?"

"No," Moriceau says. "Nothing like that."

Paris closes his notebook. He looks at Mercedes, who shakes her head slightly, indicating she had no questions, nor anything to add.

Moriceau says: "Now, may I ask *you* a question, detective?"

"You can ask," Paris answers, buttoning his coat.

"Obviously, there has been some sort of tragedy. A murder, most likely. My hope is that the police department is not going to conduct some sort of a witch hunt against the Hispanic and Caribbean people of this city. Most of the people who follow Santeria are peaceful, tax-paying citizens. They believe in the magic and the magic works for them. They just want to win the lottery. Or have a healthy child. Or hang on to their wife or husband for a few more years. These are not criminal acts."

Paris leans over the counter. He brings his face to within inches of Moriceau's. "If I'm not mistaken, witch hunts are where the authorities round up people with no evidence. Only suspicion. I'm here for a *reason*, Mr. Moriceau."

The two men look at each other for a few hard moments, exchanging will. Paris wins.

"I did not mean to imply—" Moriceau begins.

Paris leans back, holds out his right hand, shows it empty, both sides, then produces a business card with a quick flourish. It is an easy sleight-of-hand, a holdover from his amateur magician days as a teenager.

"Very good, detective," Moriceau says.

"But not magic, Mr. Moriceau. Merely a parlor trick. Which, upon closer examination, I have always found the supernatural to be."

Moriceau takes the card and glances at Mercedes. He finds no quarter there.

Paris continues: "If you remember anything else, or if you have any customers who request paraphernalia relating specifically to this Ochosi, please give me a call."

Moriceau examines the card, remains silent.

"One last question," Paris says. "Is there a Santerian term for 'white chalk'?"

"Ofún," Moriceau says. "It is a chalk made from eggshells."

Mr. Church, the weirdo who had phoned about the missing woman, had said: *"You will take her place in ofún."*

The chalk outline.

This prick had *called* him.

"Thanks for your time," Paris says, and turns for the exit, the *nag champa* filling his senses.

As Paris opens the door for Mercedes, and an icy wind

greets them, he shudders for a moment. Not from the cold, but rather from the irony of Edward Moriceau's words.

Brujo, Paris thinks.

It might be a witch he is hunting after all.

❖ 27 ❖

THE BACK ROOM of La Botanica Macumba is a shambles, littered with wooden packing crates bearing seashell candles, Indian incense, and cheap T-shirts from Korea bearing African incantations. Amid the mess sits a slight brown man with graying hair, a rainbow skullcap on his head, his fingers and thumbs adorned with gaudy paste jewelry.

His name is Moriceau.

He trembles before me.

Edward Moriceau is a man who, perhaps, once wielded some power in this life, once seduced young women with a flex of his back muscles or a wink at closing time. A man now reduced to a shuddering clerk amid a minefield of cheap trinkets and brightly colored trash.

"It is not something so easily obtained," Moriceau says.

"I understand this," I say. "But I have faith."

"And you want it within three days?"

"No. I will *have* it within three days."

I can see the resistance flare for a moment in Moriceau's eyes. "And what is to stop me from calling the police?" he says. "They were just here, you know."

"I know."

"Then why me? Why here? Go talk to Babalwe Oro."

"The Mystic Realm? They are bigger charlatans than even you. The truth is, I am *here* and I am talking to *you*. I am asking you to perform a service for me, to obtain an item within your grasp, just like all the other items you have obtained for me over the past year. I am not asking for this thing for free. I intend to pay full price for it, as well as some reasonable surcharge for the rush service. Each day you stand there and you sell love potions to lonely *tías* who think they will win the heart of some elderly gentleman of means. Do you care that you sell them false hopes? No. You just pocket their money like a common thief."

"Yes, but they *want* to believe it works. Are you saying there is no magic here?"

"I am not saying that," I answer, knowing enough to fear even my own practice of the dark arts. "But your drugstore magic has no *true* power. This is Potions-R-Us. Don't insult me again."

"But what if I cannot get you what you want? What if it is completely out of my hands?"

I cross the room, towering over Moriceau. "Then I will visit you. Perhaps in a month. Perhaps a year. One day, I will be in the closet when you open it. One day, I will be in the kitchen when you descend the stairs in the middle of the night for a drink of water. One day, I really *will* be the man sitting behind you at the movies."

I genuflect, kneel, stare into the man's small, sable eyes.

"Listen to me, Edward Moriceau. If you do not bring me what I demand, I will be more than the sum of your earthly concerns." I take my small knife from its ankle scabbard, touch its razor-sharp tip to my right index finger. Blood responds. I touch this shiny dot of scarlet to my mouth, lean forward, kiss Moriceau on the lips. "I will be the shadow within the shadow you fear the most."

❖ 28 ❖

THE BUILDING ON East Twenty-third Street is a Veterans Administration–assisted nursing home, six stories of grimy brown brick, just west of a boarded-up factory that once produced ball bearings, just east of a failing discount tire mart. Behind it, the constant moan of the I-90 interchange. The address, almost faded to oblivion on the front of the crime scene photo Paris had found in Mike Ryan's desk, hadn't promised much in the first place, and, as Paris traverses the run-down lobby, he expects even less.

Mercedes Cruz is off to interview the other detectives at the unit. Before driving to East Twenty-third Street, Paris had checked in with Reuben. Still no word from his contact in the document division of the FBI on the strip of purple cardboard.

Paris badges the attendant at the front desk. The deskman—tattooed, late sixties easy—is watching a soap opera on a rabbit-eared twelve-inch. His name is Hank Szabo.

"These guys are mostly WWII vets," Hank says, after giving Paris the basics, his GI-bill dentures slipping on every sibilant. "A couple of guys from the *police* action," he adds with a glare, a look that tells Paris that Korea was Hank Szabo's war. Paris glances at the man's left forearm tattoo. USS *Helena*. "But most of *us* ain't quite old enough for the heap yet, I guess."

"This is the heap?" asks Paris.

"This is the heap."

"How many men live here?"

"Twenty-two, current count," Hank says.

"Were any of these guys ever cops that you know of?"

"Yeah. Demetrius used to be a cop."

"Demetrius?"

"Demetrius Salters. I think he was a sergeant in the Fourth District for a lot of years. Gone now."

"I'm sorry. He *doesn't* live here?"

"Oh, he lives here. Room 410. He's just *gone* gone. In the head." Hank points to his temple, rotates his finger. "Old-timers, y'know?"

"I see," Paris says. "Does he still have contact with anybody at the department that you know of?"

"Not that I know of."

"Does he have friends or family?"

"I don't think so. Never seen anyone visit him."

Paris scribbles a few notes. "And how long have you worked here?"

Hank Szabo smiles, gives his uppers a northward shove. "Let me put it this way, Detective Paris. I started the day they stopped shooting at me."

Paris walks down the fourth-floor hallway, a grim, cracked-linoleum corridor decked with faded holiday decorations. From somewhere below, a scratchy-voiced Patsy Cline sings about life's railway to heaven.

He finds 410 with the door open, knocks on the jamb, looks around the corner into the room, then steps inside.

The smell is almost a living thing, instantly bullying him back a step. Camphor and pea soup and feet. A half-century of filterless cigarette smoke. Paris adjusts somewhat, breathing through his mouth, then steps inside to see a gaunt black man in his seventies sitting in a wheelchair, a moth-eaten afghan covering his legs. A bed, a small bookshelf, and a nightstand are the only other objects in the room. Sadly,

Demetrius Salters is sitting by the window, equally inanimate. Another furnishing.

And, it is easily ninety degrees in the room. Paris begins to sweat for a wide variety of reasons. "Sergeant?" he asks, thinking that he is probably speaking louder than he needs.

Nothing.

Paris knocks on the jamb again.

"Sir?"

Demetrius Salters doesn't move or acknowledge him in any way. "Sergeant, my name is Detective Paris. Jack." He steps around to the front and holds up his shield. For a brief moment, the daylight plays off the badge onto Demetrius Salters's face and, for that moment, Paris senses that the old man recognizes something. Then, a collapse of his features says no. Paris picks up the old man's hand, shakes it gently, returns it to his crumb-littered lap. "It's a real pleasure to meet you, sir."

Paris glances around the room, searching for a touchstone that might create a link to the here and now. On the bookshelf is a vintage framed photograph of a smiling Demetrius Salters standing on the bow of a destroyer. Another shows Demetrius in a different uniform, this one CPD dress blues. Demetrius is standing near a girder in right field at Cleveland Municipal Stadium, his arm around the slender waist of a pretty, toffee-colored woman.

"Back in the day, eh?" Paris says wistfully, pointing to the photographs, trying to fill the room with noise, any noise, more for himself than anything. "Yeah, boy. I used to *love* seeing the Browns at the stadium. Especially when it was cold as hell. Remember those days? Jim Brown, Dick Schafrath, Jim Ninowski, Galen Fiss. The way the wind would cut off the lake? *Man.* My father took me to at least one game every year, right up until . . . yes, sir. Back in the *day.* The hawk was *out.*"

Paris glances at Demetrius.

Stillness.

He waits a few moments. He tries a new angle. "So . . .

how long were you on the job, Sergeant?" he asks, shoving his hands into his pockets, rocking on his heels. "I'll bet it was a completely different town then, huh?"

More silence. The man's deeply creased, implacable face reveals nothing. Paris crosses the room and sits on the edge of the bed. He looks into Demetrius Salters's eyes, searching for the young man who must certainly still dwell there, the swaggering beat cop who once trolled Hough and Glenville and Tremont instilling respect and fear, the handsome young sailor on watch.

They are gone.

And thus Paris realizes that his pleasantries, however heartfelt, are not really going to be noticed. Might as well get down to business. "Sergeant, I'm working a case that I think you can help me with."

Then, even though Paris knows it is wrong, even though he feels in his heart it is probably *cruel*, he does it anyway. He stands, looks up and down the hallway, then clicks open his briefcase. He takes out the crime scene photo of the mutilated corpse lying in the parking lot. He holds it up in front of the old man's face.

At first, it appears as if Demetrius can't focus his eyes at the distance at which Paris is holding the photo. But, soon, recognition ascends, like a violent sunrise.

And Demetrius Salters begins to scream.

❖ 29 ❖

CARLA DAVIS SITS at a desk in a small room on the ninth floor of the Justice Center, a pair of computer terminals before her, as Paris knocks on the door.

Paris, having felt like a pimp for showing the crime-scene photo to that harmless old man, made his apologies to the stern-faced nurse and made a quick exit. Michael Ryan's case, although not officially closed, was dormant. If there is a fact to be had, if there is something lurking that will shake up the inactive investigation, it would have to come to *him*.

Fact: There is a fucking lunatic loose in his city. Now. Today. And it is his job to catch him. And that job does not include shocking old men to death.

Paris stands behind Carla, looking over her shoulder, trying his best to focus.

"I ran the file with the woman and man talking," Carla says. In front of her sits two computers. One belongs to the department. One is Fayette Martin's. "But there is no video portion. No em-pegs, nothing."

Paris frowns. "You'd better give me the 101, first."

"Okay," Carla says, hitting a few keys. "The format is loosely called videoconferencing. I got the ins and outs at a seminar the Sex Crimes Unit had last year on cybersex predators." She hits Enter and launches a program.

Videoconferencing, Paris thinks. Where had he just heard

that? When the program starts, and he sees the window open, he remembers.

Beth.

"Now, recording the audio is one thing. There's a lot of fax and voice software out now that can be used like an answering machine. Recording audio still takes up a lot of hard drive space, but not nearly as much as recording the audio *and* video from a session. Recording full-motion video is still an expensive and disk-consuming process. First and foremost you need a video-capture card, which was not installed on Fayette Martin's computer."

"So, I was listening to what might have been the audio portion of an audio/video session?"

"Absolutely. I've listened to it twice myself. Now, the woman could have been watching the video stream and not recording it. Most people do it that way. But there's no question that the woman could see the man she is talking to. Unless these are *extremely* creative people."

"How do you think they hooked up?"

"Most of the commercial, noncorporate usage of video-conferencing is devoted to sex, of course. Lots of pay sites. You can watch women strip, men strip, men and women having sex, men and men having sex, women and women having sex—"

"I get it," Paris says.

"I was just getting started," Carla says. "You didn't even let me get to the barnyard."

"Spare me the muskrat love, okay?"

Carla hits a button and, in one of the six frames on the screen, the two of them appear. Carla looks stunning, even in the shitty light. Paris looks like he needs a shave, a haircut, and two months' sleep.

"Most pay sites let you watch, without having a camera of your own," says Carla. "But most individuals who cruise the Net insist that you have your own camera."

"So, what you're saying is that Fayette Martin perhaps dialed into one of these pay-per-view sex lines?"

"Perhaps."

"And that our actor perhaps worked for that sex line?"

"Perhaps."

"How would we find out which one she may have called? Are these sessions set up over the phone like phone sex?"

"Know a lot about phone sex, do ya, Jack?"

"Not a thing," Paris lies, knowing full well that he had once rung up a ninety-six-dollar call one Friday night when the Windsor Canadian had a choke hold on his libido. "I read a lot."

"Well, Internet sex is a little different than phone sex. Most of it is set up online. You click onto a site, give them your Visa or MasterCard number, and they let you in for x amount of minutes, hours, whatever."

"But there won't be a phone record?"

"Afraid not. The only phone call is the call to the local Internet service provider. On the other hand, every time you log on you are given something called an IP address, which is unique to your computer until you log off. So the Internet service provider might have a record of where Fayette Martin went the night she was killed. I'll look into it. Most of the pay-per-view male solo performance stuff is gay. But if there's an adult site that offers solo male performances geared to the heterosexual female, I'll find it."

"When do you think that might be?" Paris asks, then immediately regrets it. Carla gives him the look that probably makes her husband Charles—all five-six and one hundred forty pounds of him—roll over, cut the grass, fix the sink, and take out the garbage. Before breakfast.

"When it *is*, detective."

Luckily, for Paris, at that moment Matt Sullivan sticks his head in the room. Tall and fair-haired, Matt is the youngest detective in the Homicide Unit at twenty-nine. "You guys hear what happened in Cleveland Heights?"

"What happened?" Paris asks.

"They found a body in Cain Park. Male white. Shot in the head. Hands are gone. Some kids were sledding, saw a foot sticking out of the snow."

Paris and Carla exchange a glance, the sage look of two veteran cops who know that when hands are missing, someone is serious about delaying identification. However, the challenge of solving this *particular* murder would never engage them officially. This body belongs to the Cleveland Heights PD.

"Teeth intact?" Carla asks.

"No idea."

"How long was the body there?" Paris asks.

"A couple days, I guess. Snowstorm covered it completely."

"No ID at all, eh?"

"None," Matt says. "John Doe, so far. Body's on the table now."

"Shit," Paris says. "And here I was thinking of moving to Cleveland Heights."

"The whole world's a zone, Jack," Matt replies. "See ya."

Matt Sullivan moves down the hall as Paris absorbs the information for a moment, then looks back at the monitor screen. Mercifully, his hangdog video image is gone. "Is it possible to go to one of these sex sites now?"

Carla laughs. "I can do better than that," she says, reaching under the desk and producing a rectangular, soft nylon shoulder bag. She puts the bag on her lap and unzips it. Inside is a laptop computer. Carla flips it open. "I loaded all the software you need to cruise the Web and the Internet Relay Chat channels. Sign it out and take it home, get familiar with it."

"I have no idea how to use any of this, Carla."

Carla reaches into another of the bag's many pockets and produces a thin manual called *Internet for Idiots*. She hands it to him, along with a look that dares him to say he is incapable of learning from any book with the word *idiot* in the title.

The two of them stare at the Christmas tree.

"There's no *way* that's three feet," Paris says. "Is it, Manny?"

Manny, at just under twelve inches tall, is an expert in only the first few feet of tree trunks. He cocks his head, glances back, as if to say that a scrawny tree like this isn't even worthy of him lifting his leg.

Paris rummages in a kitchen drawer, finds his tape measure. He squats next to the tree and measures. Thirty-four inches. He *knew* it. Then he notices the snap-on plastic base in the box. He attaches it to the bottom of the tree and re-measures. Thirty-six on the button.

"Man oh man. Can't even give you an extra freakin' inch, can they? Some spirit of giving."

Manny barks once, clearly in agreement.

The two of them set about the task of decorating the tree, with Manny shuttling individual ornaments from the box in the dining room, dropping them gently at his master's feet, and Paris trying to find a spot for them. Small tree, big bulbs. In the end, Paris manages to fit only ten or twelve ornaments on the tree and, although the scale makes it look a little ridiculous, and the green of the branches is a shade not to be found *anywhere* in nature, when he plugs in the lights, it makes the corner of the apartment suddenly come aglow with a toasty radiance.

Not bad, Paris thinks. Not bad at *all*.

He puts the small star on the tree.

Manny wags his stub of a tail.

And it is officially Christmas Eve.

❖ 30 ❖

IT IS CHRISTMAS EVE and I am in the white room. I have one session left, something set up weeks ago. A woman who, were I not so embroiled in my current activities, I would pursue mightily. She is divorced, in her mid-thirties. Or at least that is the role she is playing. We have had two sessions; both with her watching me.

Tonight, though, she has promised to appear on camera, to show herself to me.

I am in the white room early, nearly beside myself in anticipation. When the video stream opens at eight o'clock I see her for the first time. She is sitting in a desk chair, wearing a dark scoop-neck dress. Behind her, a bedroom.

She leans forward, tilts the camera slightly upward so that I may see her pretty face. In doing so, I am privy to a maddening few inches of cleavage. It appears as if she is wearing a black lace push-up bra.

"Hi," she says.

"Hello."

She sits back, crosses her legs. I can now see the hem of her dress, a hint of her slip. "Merry Christmas."

"And the same to you," I say. Her hair is a light color, strawberry blond perhaps.

"Do you like what you see?" she asks.

"Very much."

"Do you feel it was worth waiting for?"

"Yes."

"If I can get away, I will be at Jayson's Pewter Mug on Chagrin Boulevard in one hour," she says. "Do you know it?"

"Yes."

"I will save the seat next to me until ten."

"I understand."

She stands, unzips her dress, slips out of it. She is wearing a black bra, matching slip. She turns to the side, places one of her spike-heeled shoes on the computer chair and adjusts what I can now see is a thigh-high nylon.

Then, incredibly, she turns off her camera and closes the session.

Is *she* baiting *me*?

I look at my image reflected in the now-black monitor. The reflection tells me the truth.

It is a mistake.

This is my chorus as I shower, shave, dress, and head for the Pewter Mug on Chagrin Boulevard.

She is nowhere to be seen. The Christmas Eve crowd is thin, just a handful of couples scattered around the room, invisible in their sameness; just a pair of Asian businessmen at the far end. I sit at the bar, near the door, sip my Ron Rico, wonder. Perhaps she had car trouble. Perhaps she was in an accident. Perhaps her husband had intervened.

Perhaps I have no business doing this when I am so close to my goal.

I wait another ten minutes, drain my drink. I decide to pay the bill and leave. It was a mistake to come. I have appointments.

A few minutes later, waiting for my change—my mind adrift on the scent of a doorway on East Fortieth Street and Central Avenue, on bleached white skin, blued by moonlight—I hear, from just behind me, a man's voice:

"Could you stand up please?"

The noise erupts. This time, a loud, discordant blood rush in my ears. The blaring brass of imminent violence.

Again: "Sir?"

My hand moves slowly toward the knife sheathed on my left hip. Heart slips into high. Exits mapped—front door to my right, back door through kitchen. I calm myself enough to speak. "I'm sorry?"

I turn around to see a graying, Asian businessman of sixty, pointing to my stool. His jacket is hanging from the back.

It is nothing.

I get up, blow past him, rage out of the bar.

The cacophony in my head begins to recede slightly as I walk to the parking lot, disgusted with myself for coming in the first place. I start the car, pull into westbound traffic, drive toward the auditorium, my fury, for the moment, turned inward, my heart beating in my ears like some ancient metronome counting down a coda of inescapable madness.

❖ 31 ❖

MADNESS: TWO HUNDRED children between the ages of one and twelve, all fully charged on cheap frosted cake, Tootsie Pops, and Faygo root beer. The cavernous Masonic Temple on Euclid Avenue and East Thirty-sixth Street is awash in brightly colored snowsuits, rubber galoshes, and neon-hued knit caps.

Billy Coughlin, a lifer from the Second District, is Santa again this year, his decades of holding down the first stool at the Caprice Lounge and a back booth at Elby's Big Boy Restaurant providing a bulbous red nose and a billowing gut that negated the need for makeup or pillows. Billy sits on his makeshift throne, once again bracing for the onslaught, once again looking as if he's about to hit the door at a crack house.

Earlier in the day Mercedes insisted that she had no plans for the evening and would be delighted to show up and help out. Paris tried to talk her out of it, never having been one to foist his charity efforts on anyone, but she was adamant. At the moment, Mercedes F. Cruz—aproned and adorned with a red satin bow in her hair—is behind a huge coffee urn, dispensing coffee with what Paris is beginning to believe is a perpetual good mood. Except, of course, for those few minutes that she wanted to kill that kid in the Plymouth.

Paris is sitting at the back of the auditorium, near a heat duct, trying to get the warmth into his hands. After a few moments, he looks up to see a very small person studying him.

Happy Holidays! My name is Kamal Dawkins! the young boy's name tag declares. He is black, braided, no more than four years old.

"Hi," Kamal says. "Are you a policeman?"

"I am."

"Ever shoot anybody?"

"No sir," Paris says. "Never have."

Kamal thinks for a minute, apparently trying to reconcile all that gunplay he's seen on TV. "Ever take someone t'jail?"

"Oh yes. Now *that* I've done. All the time. Every day if I can."

"Were they bad guys?"

"*Very* bad guys," Paris replies, lifting Kamal onto his knee. "Very, very bad guys. And now they're all locked up."

Kamal takes a deep lick on his cherry Tootsie Pop. "My daddy's in jail."

Ah *shit*, Paris thinks. *Now* what the hell do I say? "Well, see, sometimes really good guys do a bad thing. Just once. And sometimes they get caught and have to go to jail for a while. But that doesn't necessarily mean they're bad guys. They just did a bad *thing*."

Kamal ponders the concept for a moment. "I do bad things."

"You do? What kinds of bad things?"

Kamal looks at his boots, confesses. "I push my sister."

Paris sees an opening. "Does your mom punish you for pushing your sister?"

"Yeah. I have to sit on the time-out step."

Perfect. The old time-out-step-as-juvenile-metaphor-for-jail argument. "Well, see, the time-out step is kind of like jail. Sometimes adults do bad things and they have to go sit on the time-out step."

This seems to register with Kamal. As does the overwhelming question: "Then why can't my daddy sit on the time-out step at *my* house?"

With this admittedly savvy question, Kamal throws his hands into the air to emphasize his point. As he does, the Tootsie Pop goes flying straight up in the air, twisting, end over end, like the bone that turns into a space station in *2001*.

For a moment, Paris and Kamal watch it rise, hover, then begin its descent.

Paris reaches out to grab the plummeting sucker before it hits the floor, but instead of wrapping his hand around something warm and sticky, he wraps his hand around something warm and *soft*.

Someone else's hand.

He looks up to see who he is holding hands with. It is a very pretty young woman—lustrous brown hair pulled back into a ponytail, dark caramel eyes, twenties. She is holding a two-year-old blond girl dressed in a red velvet jumper.

"Ya gotta be quicker than that, officer," she says with a smile, but makes no move to extract her hand from his. Paris lets go, a little embarrassed.

The woman is slender, shapely, wearing a black turtleneck sweater, tight denim jeans. Paris is accordingly tongue-tied. "I . . . uh . . . I guess we both—"

"Former shortstop," she says, interrupting him. "We always put the worst kid in left field. Nothing ever got by me."

"Yeah, well, I was always the kid in left," Paris says.

Kamal looks back and forth, between the two adults, apparently wondering when the part about him getting his Tootsie Pop back was going to be brought up.

"I'll get you a new one, sweetie," the woman says. She puts the little girl down, who immediately toddles off toward Santa.

"Rebecca," the woman says, holding out her hand to Paris. "Rebecca D'Angelo."

"Jack Paris."

They shake hands and immediately become glued together. Rebecca laughs, covers her mouth with her other hand, realizing what she'd done. She'd shaken hands with her Tootsie Pop hand. "I'm so *sorry*," she says, unsticking herself, slowly, from Paris. "Let me go get some water and some napkins."

"That's okay."

"I insist."

"Really," Paris says. "It's—"

But the young woman is already on her way to the coffee stand. Paris watches her walk across the room, then sits back down, next to Kamal. His little inquisitor. "See that lady?" Paris asks, pointing toward Rebecca.

Kamal nods.

"Follow her, okay?"

"Okay."

"She'll get you a new Tootsie Roll."

"Tootsie *Pop*," Kamal says.

"Tootsie *Pop*," Paris corrects.

With that, Kamal gives Paris a hug and runs off after the woman. And Paris has to laugh. *Kamal Dawkins, Esquire.* He could see the shingle now.

After a few moments, Mercedes sidles up next to Paris. "Pretty gal," she says.

"Yes, she is."

"Thinking of adopting?"

Paris notices a little jealousy in her voice. Or does he? "Smart-ass," he says. "I just met her. She's probably somebody's daughter."

"I'm an investigative reporter, detective. I'd be willing to go to print with the fact that she's *somebody's* daughter."

"You know what I mean. The daughter of some cop I know. Guy about my age."

"Hmmm. A guy your age. What age would that be?"

"Somewhere between Huggies and Depends," Paris says. "Right about halfway."

"I see," she says, lifting her pen and notebook. "And can I—"

"Miss Cruz?"

Paris and Mercedes look over to see two young girls,

around eleven or twelve years of age. Melissa's age. Paris notices how similar they are to his daughter; trying to shed their girlish ways, bodies poised to become women, yet still a bit coltish and sharply angled, a bit clumsy. One of them whispers something into Mercedes's ear. It seems that Mercedes Cruz has become an instant role model.

"I'll be right back," Mercedes says, and lets herself be led off. "Don't leave the area."

❖ 32 ❖

HIS CAR SMELLS of old onions. I hadn't expected show-room cleanliness from the man, yet I *had* expected a certain order, considering his profession. You would think as much.

And yet it is *good* news. A car in such a state is never scrutinized.

I clip the inexpensive crystal transmitter—one that allows me no more than a three-hundred-foot range, but operates well above the FM band—under the passenger seat, draw a deep breath, savoring his essence, and step back into the frozen night.

❖ 33 ❖

AT NINE-THIRTY the party begins to wind down, the dolls and race cars and action figures having been duly named, adopted, and secreted away. Rebecca had returned not with a handful of napkins and a paper cup of ice water as Paris expected, but rather a warm washcloth with which she gently washed his palm. They chatted as she did, and for Paris, so long out of a woman's arms—any woman's arms—the experience was highly erotic and ended way too soon.

Then, the requisite old-fart feelings return and he begins to feel silly.

"You're sure you don't mind?" Rebecca asks. "I can take a cab."

"I won't hear of it."

"It's not out of your way?"

"Not at all," Paris says, wondering how he was going to clean the inside of his car in the next ten minutes.

"You're sweet. Let me get my coat and say good-bye to some of the kids."

"No problem," Paris says. "I'll meet you by the back door."

Paris watches her walk away again, wondering, again, how he got to this age, this volatile state of his heart. When he cruised the nightclubs in his twenties, he would look at the guys in their forties—hanging around the bar, drinking their Scotch-and-somethings, surveying the human landscape like hairsprayed jackals—and laugh at their feeble attempts at picking up young women. Now he *is* that guy. When the hell did *that* happen?

The hall is just about emptied when Mercedes returns, her coat on, her shiny black boots in hand. "Where's your little friend?"

"Don't know," Paris says. "Lost track of him when he went for his new Tootsie Pop."

"I meant the one in the tight jeans."

Paris laughs. "Off to say good-bye to the kids, I guess."

"Ah . . ."

"She just needs a ride home, that's all. Said her car broke down."

"I guess they don't make Big Wheels like they used to."

"C'mon. She's not *that* young. Is she?"

"No," Mercedes says. "Just giving you a hard time."

They stroll to the door. "So, what do you have planned for the rest of the evening?" Paris asks.

"Not much. Home. Bubble bath. Snuggle up with Declan and watch *It's a Wonderful Life* for the thousandth time. Cry like always."

"Uh . . . Declan?"

"Yeah. Dec's my twenty-year-old houseboy from Dublin. Soccer legs, eyes like Gabriel Byrne's."

Paris isn't going to fall for it. "I see."

"Declan is my dog. He's a Jack Russell terrier. Jack Russells are a smaller version of the English Fox terrier that a guy named Reverend John Russell . . ."

Mercedes keeps walking and talking, but Paris is frozen in his tracks.

Mercedes stops, turns. "What?"

"You have a *JR*?"

His car smells like Taco Bell. He had done a quick cleaning job, shoving everything into the backseat and covering it all with that quilted moving blanket he carries around just in case he sees a spinet piano on a tree lawn someday, all the while reprimanding himself for offering a ride to a pretty woman before thinking about this. He is now parked by the back door of the auditorium, both doors flung open, heater on.

Paris looks around the emptying lot. There are only a handful of cars left. Then, on the other side of the lot, next to the parking kiosk, he sees Mercedes's brother, Julian, standing with some teenaged boys. Nearby, a fifty-gallon drum burns. Paris waves, but Julian doesn't see him.

Catholics, Paris thinks with a smile. Mercedes must have told him about the party and he had volunteered, too. He looks for Mercedes but doesn't see her. A few minutes later he notices Rebecca approaching from the auditorium wearing a long dark coat and matching beret, compounding Paris's schoolboy dread. He has always been a sucker for women in berets.

"Sorry to keep you waiting," she says.

"No problem," Paris says. "You all set?"

"Yep."

They both get in the car, buckle up. Paris pulls out of the parking lot, heads east, absolutely dispossessed of clever conversation. Rebecca breaks the silence first.

"So, how long have you been doing the Cleveland League party?"

"Let's see," Paris says. "This was my fourth."

"Wow. You're a real vet."

"I've got the broken eardrums to prove it, too. How about you?"

"Just my first. There was a little article in last Sunday's *Plain Dealer*. Some of the kids were quoted in there about what they wanted for Christmas. Some said they wanted a family. Some said they just wanted a friend. It broke my heart and here I am."

"They appreciate it," Paris says. "They really do. And they won't forget you."

"I hope not. But you. Four *years*. You must really love kids."

Paris thinks about it for a moment. It was true. "I do. The part that hurts, though, is that some of those kids are going into the system one day. Some of them soon. Guaranteed. And there isn't anything we can do about it."

"I know," she says. "It's sad."

Rebecca turns her back to her door, crosses her legs, smooths her coat. Paris can feel her eyes on him, but does not have the courage to look over. The silence lasts for four or five stoplights. Paris fills it by turning on the radio, finding a station with Christmas music. Finally, at University Circle, Rebecca asks, her tongue firmly in cheek: "By the way, can I chip in for gas?"

"Sure," Paris says, deadly serious. "I was just going to bring that up, in fact. I think it comes to twenty-six cents. But don't sweat the penny. A quarter's cool."

Rebecca laughs. "Okay, then. But at least let me buy you a cup of coffee."

Paris almost blurts out: "Sure. That would be great."

The Starbucks at Cedar-Center is busy with Christmas Eve revelers, mostly kids in their late teens and twenties. Paris takes a corner table. Rebecca soon joins him bearing espresso. She places the cups on the table and removes her coat, reminding Paris what a great body she has.

"Gosh I'm getting old," she says, sitting across from Paris. "It used to be that everyone behind the counter here was my age or older. Now I feel like somebody's mother."

Right, Paris thinks. What a hag. "I wouldn't worry too much about that for a while," Paris says. "Take it from someone who knows."

Rebecca smiles. "So *you're* Father Time then, huh?"

"Sometimes I feel a thousand years old. And those are my ginkgoba days."

"Well, as a semiyoung single woman, all I can say is you look pretty good for a thousand." She sips her espresso. "Besides, like Groucho said: You're only as old as the woman you feel. Or something like that."

Wow, Paris thinks. She even quotes the Marx Brothers. *I'm in love.*

Over the next ten minutes or so they discuss their lives, their respective romantic pasts. Paris, divorced, one daughter. Rebecca, divorced, no kids. The conversation flows freely and comfortably.

"So, can I ask an unbelievably personal question, considering the time we've known each other?" Paris asks.

Rebecca examines every square inch of his face before answering. "Okay."

"What happened? In your marriage, I mean. That is, if you don't mind telling me."

"I don't mind telling you. What happened was I was married to a man who thought he was going to hit me and screw me in the same twenty-four-hour period. Took me a whole year to figure it out. I was young. That's my only defense. One day I woke up, looked at the newest bruises, grabbed a few dresses, and walked. Never looked back."

"Good for you," Paris says. "What happened to your husband?"

"Long gone. Texas, I hear. Although I do expect him to turn up someday. Most likely in a post-office photo." Rebecca sips her espresso. "What about you?"

Paris thinks for a moment. He hadn't had to encapsulate his marriage and divorce in a long time. He finds that the pain hasn't receded a bit. "The day I joined the Homicide Unit is the day my marriage began to crack, I think. The hours, the things I see every day. The fact that I couldn't seem to leave the job at the office like I had before. Add to that too much booze, an average of four hours' sleep every night, along with the attitude of a macho shithead cop trying to be protector to the world while ignoring his family, and you have the story. Old story at that. One day I awoke in a stupor, asked for a second chance, sobered up, and realized she'd already given me ten."

Rebecca offers a compassionate smile and touches the back of his hand. "Do you have a picture of your daughter?"

"What do *you* think?" Paris retrieves his wallet, takes out an old snapshot of Beth and Missy. Beth's hair is long; Missy is in a two-piece bathing suit, wearing orange sunglasses and a floppy yellow sunbonnet, brim up. "It's a few years ago."

"She's *such* a little doll."

"All that heaven will allow," Paris says. "She's my light." Rebecca hands back the photo. "How old is she now?"

"She's going to be twelve this coming February."

"Yeow. Twelve. *Look* out."

"Thanks. Can't wait for the wholesale hormones." Paris returns the picture to his wallet, spins his cup idly for a few moments. "So, do you mind if I ask you another really personal question?"

"Oh, why stop now?"

"What the hell do women want?"

Rebecca laughs. "That's *easy*. I can't believe you don't know this one by now."

"It's on a very long list."

"Women want three things in a man, Jack. One, strong hands."

"Okay."

"Two, soft heart."

"I see," Paris replies. "And third?"

"Fast horse."

It is Paris's turn to laugh. "Well, I have two covered."

"Oh yeah? Which two?"

"The two that don't involve gravity or inertia."

For Paris, the next twenty minutes are a warm, pleasant blur. The conversation is all over the map. Rebecca shares his interest in film, especially cop movies, especially Al *Pacino* cop movies. They agree that the grocery store scene in *Sea of Love* is about as sexy as it gets. Rebecca seems to share some of his core political beliefs. Rebecca has dimples.

They leave Starbucks and drive the short distance to Rebecca's apartment building. Paris doesn't remember any of it. They sit at the curb, headlights off, heater on low.

"Thanks for the ride," she says.

"You are more than welcome."

"I'm glad we met. I feel like I have a new friend."

"Me too."

"It kind of made my Christmas Eve."

She really has no idea, Paris thinks. "Mine, too," he says. "And thanks for the espresso."

"Sure."

They contemplate each other for a few moments, afield in that place where men and women sometimes find themselves after a little harmless flirting, after a brief encounter dusted with the casual flattery, the occasional touch, the silent sexual nearness.

Mercifully, Rebecca moves first. She leans over, kisses Paris on the cheek, and says:

"Merry Christmas, Jack."

❖ 34 ❖

CHRISTMAS MORNING BREAKS silently over Lake Erie; milk-glass sunlight struggles first through thick lavender clouds, then splays like a wash of yellow tempera along the ragged shoreline that stretches from Ashtabula to Toledo.

At ten-thirty, as per their arrangement, Paris is sitting in Beth's kitchen, watching her make breakfast. Melissa is in her room, trying on her new Christmas clothes. And blasting some God-awful music.

"So," he begins, trying, and failing, to sound conversational. "You guys got plans for New Year's Eve?" He used the word *guys*, hoping Beth and Melissa were going to do something together, thereby indicating that Beth did not have a date.

"Missy is going over to Jessica Manno's house. I guess Jessica's mother is putting on a pretty big spread for the kids. I heard she was even hiring a rock band."

"Wow," Paris says, stoking a tiny ember of hope in his heart. "That sounds like fun."

"You can actually *say* that after watching that group the other night?"

Paris laughs as Beth places a plate of eggs, home fries, and toast in front of him. He takes a bite of toast, remains silent for the moment. But the next question is in his eyes. There is no need to say it out loud. Beth puts down the butter knife. "I have a date, Jack."

187

The words ping around his heart for a moment or two, leaving welts. "Oh, okay. Anyone I know?" He tries to float it as a small joke, but it sinks.

"Why?"

"Why what?"

"Why do you torture yourself?"

"It's not torture. It's . . . conversation, that's all."

"*O*kay," Beth says.

Paris furrows onward, heart first. "Somebody from work?"

"Nope. I met him on the Internet, actually."

"*What?*" Paris drops his fork.

"You asked, right?"

"You're *kidding*."

"Jack, you want to know where I met him? I met him in a Christian singles chat room, okay? Is that safe enough?"

Paris throws his hands skyward. "Safe? Are you *nuts*?"

"What are you talking about?"

"I've got two words for you, okay? David. Koresh."

"Jack . . ."

"Do you want to know how many people I've locked up who've gone to church every Sunday of their lives?"

"How many?" Beth asks with a smile, one that Paris knows she uses when she is trying to break the tension in what will certainly become an argument. An argument they are no longer authorized to have. It works.

"A *lot*," Paris says. "It's just that—"

"It's just that you love your daughter very much and you want the very best for her."

Paris would add Beth to that list, but doesn't. "Well, yeah. *That*. But I—"

"And that is why Melissa adores her father," Beth says. "She knows."

Knockout punch. Paris doesn't even bother getting off the emotional canvas. "Okay. Just be careful, all right?"

Beth salutes him, then gives him a brief hug. "Missy

loved her present from you, by the way. She thought it was cool."

He had returned the perfume and gotten her a gift certificate to The Gap. He was glad that The Gap was still in the realm of hip for girls his daughter's age.

Beth leaves the room for a moment, then returns, a gift-wrapped shirt box in hand. Missy's gift to him. He takes the box, opens it. There, inside, is a white Calvin Klein dress shirt, spread collar. A very nice tie as well, clearly his weakest suit when picking out dress clothes.

But, also in the box, is a smaller box, something that looks like a jewelry case. Paris glances at Beth, knowing that she broke the rules. The shirt may be from Missy, but whatever is in the leatherette jewelry box is from Beth.

"No fair," Paris says. "I thought we had an agreement."

"Just open it, Jack. You'll understand."

"But we *agreed*," Paris says, feeling like an idiot for not having the brains to have brought a contingency present for Beth in case this happened.

"I know," Beth says. "But if you'd just open it, you'd understand."

Paris opens the small, square jewelry box to find a pair of beautiful silver cuff links.

Beth says: "It's a French cuff shirt. Completely useless without cuff links, right?"

After an early dinner at his mother's—the usual belt-loosening holiday spread that includes a *primi piatti* of homemade gnocchi, followed by a main course of roast capon, followed by warm hazelnut biscotti—Paris spends the remainder of the day in his apartment, stumbling around the Internet.

He had first skimmed the *Internet for Idiots* book Carla had given him, addressing it in a manner in which he addresses most technical material, that being with one perfectly glazed eye. He discovers that Internet Relay Chat, or IRC, is where one finds the chat channels: real-time "rooms" where people meet to discuss any of thousands of different interests.

From four until nearly six o'clock, Paris is absolutely fascinated by this new form of communication. Not only is IRC completely anonymous, due to the fact that people are known only by a nickname—Paris is *TSMcPhee* for the time being, after his favorite blues guitarist of all time—but it is also a place where role-playing seems to have been elevated to a fine art.

Granted, many of the IRC channels are devoted to cybersex and its myriad permutations. And granted, channels like #preteensexpics make Paris want to jump into the channel, bitch-slap a few sick twists, and cuff them to a moving bus. But there also seem to be a lot of helpful channels devoted to everything from alcohol recovery to cancer support groups to help rooms for the IRC newbies, of whom Paris had to be the newest and most blatantly ignorant.

Like a jerk, from six to seven, Paris sits in #christian-singles, a twofold purpose in mind. One, just to see what kind of people were in there. Two, to put his detective skills to work in the hope of determining if any of the half-dozen or so feminine-sounding nicknames on the channel might be Beth.

After jogging Manny over to Ronnie's Famous and back, Paris spends the rest of the evening reading about videoconferencing. At eleven, with *Internet for Idiots* tented over his eyes, Paris falls asleep on the living room couch.

Usually, whenever he pays a visit to his ex-wife's apartment, he has the standard dream about Beth, one where she spends a pleasant day with him, laughing and touching and hugging, only to say good-bye forever at the end, breaking his heart anew every morning. But this time he doesn't dream about his ex-wife and their long-cooled love affair.

This night, lost on the guile of *nag champa*, he dreams about a beautiful young woman with burnished bronze hair.

❖ 35 ❖

THE DAY AFTER Christmas in most major cities brings a brief respite in violent crimes. If people are going to kill each other around the holidays they seem to get their licks in on Christmas Eve or Christmas Day. Or they wait until New Year's Eve.

At noon, on December 26, the halls of the sixth floor at the Justice Center are quiet.

Paris and Carla Davis are meeting with Greg Ebersole in Greg's office. Greg looks like a beaten man. The benefit for Max Ebersole had gone well, but not as well as Greg had hoped, Paris had learned. It is the holidays, they all said, a reassuring hand on Greg's shoulder. A lot of people are out of town. A lot of people are simply tapped out. Paris considers the possibility that Greg had not been to sleep for more than an hour or two at a time since leaving the Caprice that night.

Greg says: "I've got a sketch coming this afternoon. Composite of a woman that Willis Walker was seen with at the bar at Vernelle's on the night he was killed. White woman."

Paris and Carla exchange a glance. "White woman? Anybody recognize her from before?" Carla asks.

"No," Greg says. "And they all say that they would remember. The men anyway. They said she was all that *and* a bag of chips, you know?"

Carla laughs. "You say that pretty good for such a dough-boy, Greg."

"I took Homeboy 101 at Cleveland State."

"Get us copies the minute you see them," Paris says.

"You got it."

Greg stands, puts on his coat.

"Where are you off to?" Carla asks.

"Gonna reinterview the night clerk at the Dream-A-Dream. He was three sheets to the wind the first time I talked to him. He's on days now. Maybe he hasn't started drinking yet and I'll get a straight answer from him. If you see me back here in an hour dragging a screaming and kicking redneck by the hair, you'll know it didn't go well."

"How's Max?" Carla asks.

"Max is good, Carla. Max is tough."

"If I don't see you later, tell him I said hi."

"I sure will. See you guys."

"Careful," Carla says.

"Always," Greg replies and takes his leave.

Paris and Carla exchange a different kind of look now, one laden with concern for a fellow officer who might be on the very edge of the very edge, a precipice that can lead to many places, all bad. Paris asks: "What did you get this morning?"

Carla says: "I visited Fayette Martin's Internet service provider. OhioNet Services on Buckeye. Got a fix on where she went online the day she was killed."

"Where'd she go?"

"She logged on three times, went three different places on the Web," Carla says. "But I think we need to be concerned with only one of them."

"Which one?"

"The site is called CyberGents. I've traced the ownership to an address in University Heights. The website is run by a company called NeTrix, Inc."

"What is CyberGents exactly?"

"Like I said, if there was a live, pay-per-view videoconferencing site devoted to straight females, I'd find it. This is one. And it's local. As soon as the street address came up, I knew I'd been right about these people."

"What do you mean? What people?"

"I've been working this pleasant group of folks for six months. I knew there was *something* beyond the usual swapping. I think I can get us an invite."

"An invite?"

"It's a group of east-side swingers."

"So, you're saying that Fayette Martin may have called in online to this CyberGents in University Heights?"

"I *know* she did."

"And that they have men there who do things online?"

"Yep."

"In *University Heights*?"

"Well, they may not be right there at the house in University Heights. The men could be anywhere. But someone has to clear the credit-card transactions. Someone has to set up the session with the performers, either by phone or by e-mail. Unless they're routing the calls elsewhere, I'd bet that they do it there."

"So how do we get in?"

"Well, I know for a fact that they meet three times a month for parties. They're having one tonight."

"What kind of parties?"

"Hard to say exactly what goes on there," Carla replies. "But I think I can get us in."

"How are you going to do that?" Paris asks.

Carla lowers her head, then raises her eyes. "Are you serious?"

At two-thirty, Paris walks to the Cleveland Public Library at Superior Avenue and East Fourth Street. He had reserved another book about Santeria in the United States, as well as one about ritual murder in the inner city.

As he rounds the corner of the BP Building he stops. Rebecca D'Angelo is standing right in front of him, looking into the window at a holiday display. She has her back to him, but she looks just as he remembers. She is wearing a navy blue wool coat, knee-high boots. Paris is just about to tap her on the shoulder when it appears as if she sees him reflected in the window. She turns abruptly around.

It is not Rebecca.

"Sorry," Paris says. "I thought you were a friend of mine."

The woman glares at him, then makes a rather quick retreat down Superior Avenue, toward Public Square, turning twice more to look at him.

Paris shakes his head. He jaywalks to the library entrance. *Why can't I stop thinking about her?*

He is halfway across the underground lot at the Justice Center when he hears a man call his name from the shadows. It is Hank Szabo, the front-desk attendant from the VA nursing home on East Twenty-third Street.

"Mr. Szabo," Paris says. "What brings you down to the Justice Center?"

"Not sure, really." Hank steps forward into the fluorescent light. He is wearing a beat-up old pea coat, a nubby watch cap. "I was just coming up to see you."

"What about?"

Hank lowers his voice. "I'm not sure if this means anything at all. But Demetrius did something."

"Did something?"

"Yeah. Well, something kind of out of the ordinary for him."

"And what was that, Mr. Szabo?"

"He did this right after you left. And call me Hank, okay?"

Hank shows Paris a copy of *Cableviews* magazine.

"And what is *this* exactly?"

"Magazine, of course. It's what Demetrius did *inside* I'm talking about. Something he did all on his own." Hank opens the magazine to page 15 and points to the bottom. "See there? See how that's circled?" The number 15, in the lower right, is circled in a shaky red ink.

"Yeah," Paris says. "*Okay.*"

"And look here." Hank now flips to page 28. Same thing. Then he flips to page 35, where the page number is once again circled very carefully in red. A quick scan of the magazine shows that these are the only pages with circled page numbers.

"Mr. Salters did this, you say?"

"Absolutely. I watched him do it."

"And it was right after I left?"

"Well, it was right after he was sedated," Hank says. "Don't know what you did, but you scared the fuckin' shit out of him. Literally."

"Sorry about that."

"No big deal. We usually have one or two of the boys go nuclear by lunchtime every day."

"And what do you think it means?"

"No idea. I looked at the pages, at the articles, but they didn't seem to be about anything, so as I can figure. As you can see, two of them are full-page ads for aluminum siding. One is a story about Helen Hunt. She was that lady on—"

"*Mad About You.* Right, Hank. I'm just not sure why you think this has something to do with me."

"Can't say for sure," Hank says. "But Demetrius doesn't hardly ever do *any*thing. Ever. So, for him to pick up a pen is pretty weird. This took him almost an hour, you know."

"Did he say anything?"

"Yeah. Well, kind of. Up until the drugs kicked in, he kept mumbling something under his breath. I got close, but not too close, if you know what I mean." Hank taps the side of his nose. "But I could hear him saying something over and over again. Like a prayer, almost."

"What was he saying?"

"Well, I'm not *totally* sure about this. But it sounded like—you're gonna think this is crazy."

Paris almost smiles. "Trust me on this one, Hank. Crazy is what I do for a living. What did Mr. Salters say?"

"Once again, I wouldn't swear to this," Hank says, looking around the underground lot, as if the very act of entering the Justice Center parking garage had automatically put him under oath. "It sounded like he was saying '*secret garden.*' "

❖ 36 ❖

RANDI BURSTEIN HAD never seen the man at the counter before, but she seemed to recall hearing the name somewhere. On the younger side of thirty-five, she thinks. Too well dressed to be a cop. Too handsome to be a civil servant.

Lawyer.

Definitely.

Who else ever comes in here?

"I can get that file for you right away," Randi says. "Going to need some ID of course. Social security number at the very least."

"Of course," he says, handing her a social security card. "May I ask you something . . ."

"Randi."

"Randi," he repeats. "May I ask you something, Randi?"

"Sure," she says, hopes awakening. In the fifteen years she had worked in the records office of the Veteran's Administration, she had yet to meet a man she had seen, socially, more than twice. Now that she was over forty, and a few pounds south of svelte, the opportunites seem to be diminishing every day. But, still, hope springs and all. "What would you like to know?"

"Have there been other folks requesting these files lately?"

"Now, now," she says, a little disappointed, but still happy to engage in banter with someone so handsome, someone so

197

much younger than the usual fossils with whom she deals. "You *know* I am not permitted to tell you that."

"Well, I believe that rule exists because no one ever asks as nicely as I just have."

"That may be true," she says, crossing the room, pulling out the file drawer marked *Saar-Salz*. She finds the file, then closes the drawer with a slightly exaggerated bump of her ample hip. She makes a quick photocopy of the requested file. "I am *still* not allowed to break it." She lays the form on the counter, slashes an X with her pen. "Sign for me there, please."

The man scribbles a signature with his own pen.

"Any special plans for New Year's Eve?" she asks, retrieving an envelope from beneath the counter, hoping to keep the conversation going.

"*Oh* yes," the man answers. "I'm going to have a party."

"Well, that sounds like fun," Randi says as she slips the photocopy into a manila envelope, seals it. "Big or small?"

"Huge," he says. "In fact, I'm thinking of inviting the whole world."

"That would include me, of course," she replies, amazed at her boldness. Maybe it's just the holidays, she thinks. Or maybe the two eggnogs at lunch. She lays her left hand atop the counter with great deliberateness. The hand that sports no wedding or engagement ring whatsoever. "What should I wear?"

The man pauses for a moment, dramatically lost in thought. "A black leather jacket," he says with a smile. "I think you would look very sexy in a black leather jacket and a little white skirt."

Two full minutes later, long after the man with the dark eyes and the darker lashes had left without a further word, Randi Burstein finds herself still standing at the counter, a little flushed, a lot intrigued, her mind giddily rummaging through her closets.

❖ 37 ❖

DETECTIVE JOHN SALVATORE PARIS—whose brain had already formed an exasperating Möbius strip of the numbers *152835*, all wrapped around the words *secret garden*—meets Sergeant Carla Davis at the Kaufmann's in University Heights.

Greg Ebersole and a team of six officers from the University Heights PD stand by in two locations, less than a block from the Westwood address.

The swingers party is a long shot, there had been unanimous task force consent on that point, but, for the moment, it is all they have. The neighborhoods around the two murder scenes had been canvassed and recanvassed. Forensics had uncovered nothing useful so far.

Carla drives the rest of the way to the house on Westwood Road, where she finds a spot on the street that is ten houses east of their destination. The number of cars on the street indicate that this is a rather large gathering.

As they approach the house at the crest of the hill—a stately gray colonial—there is only a dim light on in the curtained picture window; there is no loud music. Nor is there a light on over the side door, where Carla was instructed to go.

From his vantage, at the foot of the drive, Paris stops for a moment, conducts a quick inventory of the house, the neighborhood. Sleepy, bucolic, suburban; mostly brick houses with occasional lavish Christmas displays, surgically plowed driveways. A place where dogs don't bark after ten and nobody needs a new muffler.

Yet, Paris thinks as he makes his way up the drive, it is also a place that might be plugged directly into a pair of unspeakable crimes.

Carla rings the doorbell, steps between Paris and the door. She had said on the way over that getting in was still a fifty-fifty proposition, even though they had been invited to the party on a probationary basis. But Carla Davis knows what she has and figures, rightly, that if she is the first thing that whoever opens the door sees, they'll get in. She is wearing a bulky wool coat; her long hair is down around her shoulders and her perfume is driving Paris around the bend. In contrast, Paris is wearing a black blazer, black T-shirt, black slacks, no overcoat. He looks like a gay Johnny Cash.

After a few moments, the door is answered by a short, heavyset white man in his early fifties. His hair, jet black and thinning, is swept into a dramatic comb-over, the individual strands making the top of his pasty head look like a UPC bar code label. He is wearing a green alpaca cardigan, with bell sleeves, the kind that were popular when Paris was in junior high school.

"*Hi*," he says, very enthusiastically. "You must be Cleopatra." He opens the storm door.

"Yes." Carla extends her hand. The man takes it, kisses her on the fingers.

"Charmed, I'm sure," he says.

They're not even in the door and Paris is ready to puke.

"My name is Herb," he says, finally releasing her hand. "But you can call me Dante, my dear. Please come in." He steps to the side, letting Carla into the small vestibule, deliberately making her pass by him in the narrow doorway so he could achieve maximum friction.

"And let me guess," he says, looking at Paris. "Marc

Antony, right?" Herb laughs at this, as if it were the most extraordinarily clever thing ever thought of.

"You can call me John," Paris says.

Paris extends his hand, but Herb looks away at the last second, into the kitchen, pretending he doesn't see it. Clearly an attempt at belittling the new male arrival in front of the new female arrival. "Come on *in*," he finally says to Paris, as if scolding him. "You're letting all the heat out."

"Whatever you say, *Dante*," Paris replies, wanting to introduce Herb to the back of his hand before asking him about the heating bills here at the Inferno, but opting against it.

For the time being.

Perfectly ordinary kitchen, very tidy. White toaster, white can opener, something that looks like a bread machine, a small dinette table with a frosted glass top. The overhead lights are off, but there are a dozen candles distributed around the kitchen. Paris can hear some seventies disco coming from somewhere, but it is extremely faint.

Carla and Paris bunch together in the small kitchen and wait for Herb. He shuts the door, steps inside, climbs the three stairs to the kitchen, rubbing his hands together. "So, who was it that nominated you for memberships again?"

"Teddy and Sue," Carla says.

"Oh that's right," he says. "Teddy and Sue. Have you swung with them before, Cleopatra?"

"No," Carla says. "Only some cyber. They like to show, you know."

"Do they ever," Herb says. "And Sue is *such* a sub."

"Really? Every time I cybered with them Teddy was the submissive. Not Sue. Sue was always the dom."

Paris's head is spinning with the terms, the Cleavers-in-bondage atmosphere of this kitchen. For a moment, he thinks they've been made.

"Is that a fact?" Herb says, staring intently at Carla, his neck craning upward at what looks like a painful angle.

Then his resolve breaks. "Sorry. Just testing you a little. We've got to be careful, you know."

"I understand."

"Sue really *is* the beastmaster around here. There's a half-dozen guys scared to death of her."

"I'll bet," Carla says.

"But they like it that way," Herb adds. "Here, let me take your coat." He steps behind Carla, purposely in front of Paris. Paris can smell the scotch, the breath freshener. Herb also reeks of moth flakes and old Jade East.

When Herb slips Carla's coat from her shoulders, he gasps slightly, an involuntary heterosexual male reaction that Paris himself has to stifle. Carla is wearing a skintight white dress, cut nearly down to her waist in the back, the hem about halfway up her thigh. Her toned back muscles and narrow waist accentuate her hips, her long, sinewy legs; her coal black skin looks smooth and radiant in the candle-light.

She turns to face the two men, taking her coat from Herb. "I'll carry it, thanks," she says.

If Herb has an objection, seeing Carla Davis from the front makes it jailbreak his brain. It is just chilly enough in the kitchen to clearly define the contours of Carla's breasts, the outline of her nipples through her dress. She wears a dazzling silver cross on a delicate chain. Herb is nearly cata-tonic with lust. Paris isn't too far behind him. He'd never seen Carla Davis in anything but business suits or blues.

"Oh *my*," Herb says. "You are . . . you are . . . you are . . ."

"I am what, honey?" Carla says, flashing a smile, touch-ing Herb's cheek lightly.

"You are . . . . going to be *very* popular."

"You're a doll," Carla says. "Now, do you have a little girls' room where I can freshen up a bit?"

"Of course," Herb says. "Right this way."

Paris is left by himself in the kitchen for a minute. The de-sire to start opening cupboards and drawers and cabinets is almost overwhelming, the need to know what kind of cranberry sauce people who do this sort of thing prefer.

Herb returns, flushed from his interaction with such a new and delicious and by God black and gorgeous amazon female. He motions to Paris to sit at the dining room table, a thoroughly unused walnut French provincial set. Paris sits, knowing that Carla needs a few minutes to activate the small camera and recorder she's carrying in her clutch purse.

"So how long have you two been in the lifestyle, John?"

Paris hesitates for a moment before answering. "A year, maybe."

"First party?"

"No," Paris says, and leaves it at that, hoping Herb might get the point that he is the strong, silent type. Herb does not.

"Cleopatra is stunningly beautiful."

"Yes," Paris says.

"Are you two married?"

"Yes."

Herb pauses for a moment. "How long?"

"Writing a *book*, Herb?"

"No . . . I . . ." Herb begins, starting to color. "We just like to know a little about the people we let into our homes, that's all. Surely you can understand that in this day and age."

Paris actually does understand. He sure as hell wouldn't want Herb at *his* house. "Five years."

Herb nods, silently absorbing the notion of five years with a woman like Cleopatra. "You are a very lucky man, John. A *very* lucky man."

Paris leans forward and smiles at Herb in a man-to-man, swingin'-cat-to-swingin'-cat kind of way. He says, softly: "Luck has nothing to do with it, Herbie. Nothing at *all*."

Herb, thoroughly outcocked, laughs, but it is a dry, mirthless sound, a sound born of intense envy and plain macho rivalry.

"Either of you boys wanna escort a lady to a party?" Carla says, inches behind Herb.

Herb nearly knocks his chair over as he stands up. "I know *this* boy would."

Paris rises, buttons his blazer. He looks at Carla's purse. Although he knows it is there, he cannot see the tiny lens of the hidden camera.

Perfect.

"Allow me," Herb says, once again ignoring Paris, offering his arm to Carla. She takes it, but not before glancing at Paris with a look all police officers recognize.

The look that precedes the door.

Except, this time, the door is deceptively benign. It is a door that Paris had originally thought might lead to a closet or a pantry. A door behind which one might ordinarily find an ironing board, or a broom closet, or any other of a thousand kitchen adjuncts in this waxed and pine-scented version of Battle Creek suburbia.

Instead, Herb opens the door and Paris can see that it leads to a rather undistinguished stairwell. A stairwell leading downward. Paneled walls, soft lighting, a narrow wooden handrail. Paris can hear polite conversation, subdued rock music.

"Shall we?" Herb says.

Carla looks at Herb and offers a slight angling of her head, a very seductive half-smile. It is another look Paris has seen before, perhaps on the Discovery Channel, or maybe in an old episode of *Wild Kingdom*: the mien of the young jaguar in that airless instant before its legs uncoil.

Herb takes his arm from Carla's, clasps his hands together, smiles at his two new recruits, then gestures for them to enter his *carnivale*—a grinning, false-toothed doorman to another kind of suburbia altogether.

❖ 38 ❖

FORTY-EIGHT THOUSAND three hundred and fifteen dollars is not an easy thing to hide. Not if it is in small bills. And the biggest bill she has is a twenty. Plus, she has at *least* twelve thousand dollars in singles. Every time you think you have found a perfect place to hide it in your house or apartment—a place you are certain no burglar in the world would think of—you realize that it is the absolute *first* place any burglar with five functioning brains cells *would* think of.

So you move it.

Again. And again. And again.

She takes the cash from the Winkelman's hatbox, stuffs it into a WVIZ tote bag, and covers it with a bath towel. She has decided to break down and finally rent a safe-deposit box somewhere with one of her myriad sets of ID. Tonight she will sleep with the bag's canvas handle wrapped around her wrist; a butcher knife on the nightstand.

She knows she has to end this. And that the best defense is a good offense. And that there are two things she must do if she has any chance of surviving.

One. She has to get the photographs and negatives of her running from the Dream-A-Dream Motel.

Two. She has to find a way to get Isabella back before the police kick her door in.

A pair of seemingly impossible tasks she knows she cannot accomplish alone. A pair of dangerous endeavors that will probably require the mind of a master thief, the hands of a magician. She knows of only one person with that reputation.

She stashes the tote bag back in the hatbox, puts the hatbox in her closet for the time being. She then picks up the phone and dials Jesse Ray Carpenter's pager number.

It is time to meet in person.

❖ 39 ❖

PARIS TAKES IN the room. Twenty or so people, mostly white, a mix of men and women in their forties and fifties. They descend the steps into the recreation room. Herb elbows them to the center of the room, introducing them to the other guests. Peg and Chazz. Lisette and Wolfie. Barb and Tug, a lesbian couple.

You are a very beautiful young man, Fayette Martin had said to her killer. No one here, as yet, seems to fit that bill. Nor does anyone resemble the sketch of the woman from Vernelle's.

Except for Rebecca D'Angelo, Paris thinks crazily. Then instantly boots the thought from his mind.

They reach the far end of the room, where there is a green leather pit couch. Sitting on the couch are three couples in their forties, chatting softly, drinks in hand. They glance up as Carla and Paris approach them.

"Everyone," Herb says. "I'd like you to meet Cleopatra and John."

Paris surveys the men. No one even promising.

"This is Maggie and Mort," Herb says, gesturing to the couple on the left. They are a handsome couple—she is platinum blond, busty; he is tall, indoor tanned.

"This is Jake and Alicia."

Jake is older than Paris thought initially. He looks closer to sixty at this range, wearing a very expensive rug and a tailored suit. Alicia, on the other hand, is a bombshell. Petite and part-Asian, forties, heavy on the Suzie Wong. She is wearing a tight fuchsia cocktail dress and the most painful-looking stiletto heels Paris has ever seen.

"And last but not least, Ed and Gilda."

There clearly *was* a reason to leave Ed and Gilda to the end. Straight out of the late seventies, Ed wears a navy blue leisure suit; Gilda, a red-sequined tank top and hot pants. Paris isn't sure if they are in costume, or simply stuck in time.

"What can I get you to drink?" Herb asks Carla, rubbing his hands together like a Borgian alchemist.

"I'll have a Perrier," she says.

Herb appears crestfallen, as if just now realizing—and rightfully so—that the only way he would stand a snowball in a microwave's chance of getting anywhere *near* Cleopatra is for her to be so shitface drunk she couldn't see what he looked like. He asks: "Is Cotton Club soda water okay? We, uh, ran out of Perrier."

"That's fine, Dante," she says.

The saying of his *nom de boudoir* reenergizes Herb, who scoots off to the bar.

The next twenty minutes of conversation is a bizarre mix of politics, suburban woes, and thinly veiled sexual innuendo. Paris takes every opportunity to covertly examine rings and pendants and earrings and bracelets—anything that might bear a symbol remotely resembling the Ochosi sign. Or even anything looking vaguely Mexican in motif.

But he finds nothing.

The next hour and a half yields even less. Everyone seems to behave like people would behave at a regular cocktail party. No more sex talk than usual.

At ten o'clock, having gathered what Paris believes to have been zero evidence, they find themselves in the kitchen with Herb again.

"We want you to come back for our New Year's Eve party," Herb says.

"Both of us, right?" Carla asks, slipping on her coat, arching her back in such way as to bring her breasts to within inches of Herb's face.

Herb zones for a moment, then, clearly meaning precisely the opposite, says: "Of *course*. I asked around. You were both a big hit tonight."

"You noticed the door, too?" Carla asks. They are sitting at a red light on Silsby Road, having just gotten off the radio with the University Heights PD, standing down the operation.

"Yeah. I leaned against it for a minute while Gilda was telling me about her love for maraschino cherries and highballs mixed with Vernor's, not regular ginger ale. It was locked."

"But you heard the music, right?"

"Oh yeah. It was faint, but it was definitely coming from another room."

At the Kaufmann's parking lot, Paris's pager goes off. He holds it up to the streetlight. "It's Reuben," he says. "And he's tagged it urgent."

Paris looks at Carla; she at him.

He doesn't have to ask.

Carla edges out into the intersection, looks both ways, throws a blue light onto the roof of her car, and heads west on Cedar Road at a high rate of speed, toward the morgue on Adelbert Road.

The old man is laid out on a table, naked, his genitals covered by a powder blue towel, his bony, hairless skull so flowered with liver spots that at first Paris thinks he is looking at mummified remains of some sort.

"Hey, *Jacquito*," Reuben says. Reuben is wearing a bloodied apron, no mask. "And hel*lo* Sergeant *Davis*. How ya doin'? You look *great*."

Reuben Ocasio is middle-aged, overweight, and, by any community standard, has the face of a bulldog with mumps, yet he is still willing to tread where younger, fitter, better-looking men fear to go. Over a dead body, in the morgue, he is trying to sweet-talk Carla Davis.

"I'm well, Dr. Ocasio," Carla replies, all business, wisely leaving her coat on. The white dress would all but incapacitate Reuben. "What do we have?"

"Call me Reuben. Please."

"Reuben," Carla says, getting it over with.

Reuben smiles at her, as if he had scored some kind of point, then looks at his clipboard. "We have Isaac Levertov, seventy-nine years of age. My preliminary findings are that Mr. Levertov died by strangulation." Reuben points to the deep purple welt at the base of the old man's neck. "His wife reported him missing a few days ago. Found him on the roof of his building. She said he ran a kosher hot dog cart in the neighborhood. Right up until the day he turned up missing."

"Why are we here, Reuben?" Paris asks. "Who's the primary detective on this case?"

"Ivan Kral is the primary. But I found something I know you'll be interested in."

Reuben picks up a nine-by-twelve envelope, opens the clasp.

And Paris knows. "You found more of the purple cardboard."

"Yep."

"*Damn* it," Paris shouts. He walks across the room, back, hands on hips. He calms. "How much?"

"Not much." Reuben places five or six eight-by-ten black-and-white photos in front of Paris and Carla. The top photo is of the first strip of cardboard they had found in Fayette Martin's shoe. The second photo is of an almost identical strip, this time containing other parts of the letters.

"Where was it?" Paris asks.

"Underneath the old man's upper plate. Not enough surface area for prints. Saliva belongs to only the deceased. SIU is going through all of Willis Walker's effects now. If our boy is planting one puzzle piece per corpse, there might be something there."

Paris looks at the final few photographs. Composites of the pieces of cardboard put together in a variety of ways.

"I still don't see anything," Paris says.

"The middle word is *is*, definitely," Carla says. "And it looks like it ends in *g*."

"Yeah," Reuben says. "That's about as far as I got."

"Did you send it out?" Paris asks.

"Yeah. I brought it over myself about a half hour ago. Clay Patterson says it just might be enough to extrapolate the rest of the letters. Waiting for the fax right now."

"Who is the guy on the table?" Carla asks. "Where did he live?"

Reuben looks at the chart again. "Let's see . . . he lived at 3204-A Fulton Road."

The address trips a switch in Paris. He removes his notebook from his pocket, flips back a number of pages. "Say that address again."

Reuben does.

"Holy *shit*," Paris says.

"What?"

"La Botanica Macumba is at 3204 Fulton," he says. "This guy lived upstairs. What the hell is going on here, Reuben?"

"I don't know, amigo. I just sort through blood and guts."

"Have you found anything on him like the Ochosi symbol?"

"Nothing like that," Reuben says. "But I haven't *been* everywhere on him. I'm by myself here tonight. As soon as I get the fax I'll—"

No sooner does Reuben say the words than the fax machine in his cubicle at the other side of the autopsy theater hums to life. The three of them cross the room, crowd around the fax machine.

First comes a cover page with a hand-scrawled note on a DigiData letterhead.

Reuben. These cardboard strips were cut from the top end of a videocassette box. The ASIN is 6304326289. Unfortunately, it is a commercial release available just about everywhere—Best Buy, Wal-Mart, amazon.com. Maybe that's why it took all of ten minutes to nail it down. The full graphic follows.

The fax machine pauses an excruciating twenty seconds or so, its red lights blinking like a railroad crossing. Finally it begins churning out the second page, a five hundred percent blowup of the videocassette box end label, the cryptic letters to all three words now filled in.

It is a movie title, a 1990 release that runs for seventy-eight minutes and answers a question posed by an earlier film. A movie title made up of three words on a dark background.

Three words that pass through the room like an electrical storm.

Paris Is Burning.

❖ **40** ❖

SHE HAD NOT known what to expect when Jean Luc opened the door to his apartment. She had been in so many houses and homes and apartments and penthouses over the past two years that she had become quite the expert at predicting things like motif, wallpaper, furniture. One of her marks was a sixtyish Italian American, a concert promoter who'd sported a two-carat diamond pinkie ring in a setting of gold when she'd met him at the lounge at Morton's. It didn't take a genius to know he'd have a paneled recreation room with a black Naugahyde nail-head bar.

Yet every one of those times she had been in complete control of the situation. If not the man. This time, it is different. This time, *she's* the mark.

The real shock, the part that unnerved her as much as anything that had happened so far, is the fact that Jean Luc lives in the building next door to hers. The Cain Towers apartments. It explained how he knew so much about her, but it made her feel stupid. Dumber than the dumbest of her marks.

Earlier in the night she had paged Celeste four times and, for the first time since she had begun doing business with Celeste, she had not gotten a call back within a half hour.

Something is wrong.

Jean Luc had said for her to come over at ten-thirty and he would explain everything she was supposed to do. He had

213

said that this would be the second to last of their meetings, and that she would soon be done with him.

Jean Luc greets her at the door to his apartment dressed in a black cashmere sweater, gray flannel slacks, loafers. His hair is swept straight back today, à la Michael Corleone.

She follows him to the kitchen, a kitchen full of modern, almond-toned appliances. But there is something beneath the fragrance of Glade aerosol and scented candles. Something that has gone off. Something dead.

She looks down the hallway where she figures the bedrooms and bathroom are located. Four doors, all closed, a single sconce at the end. To the left, a small living room, unfurnished. To the right, the tidy little kitchen. Not particularly lived in. Not septic either.

But where might he have the photographs and negatives?

Jean Luc takes her coat without a word and hangs it in the hall closet. He closes the door, leans against it, studies her. After an excruciating silence, a silence during which she could actually hear her pulse in her ears, he says, "I don't want you to hate me."

"I don't hate you."

"I'm glad."

"I'd have to *know* you to hate you. I don't know you at all."

"We can change that."

"No. We cannot."

"Why?"

"We have a business deal, Mr. Christiane," she says, realizing that it is the first time she has referred to him as *anything*, much less something as formal as Mr. Christiane. "It is ugly, it is something I never asked for. But it is now on my plate and I can't get it off. Or can I? Can I just turn around and walk out of here right now?"

"No."

"See? Now, let's just tolerate each other for the next day or two and then go on our separate ways."

"If you only knew my pain, for a single second, you would understand why I am doing what I am doing."

"Believe it or not, I really don't care why you're doing it. What I care about is why *I'm* doing it."

Jean Luc's face is unreadable. Had she pushed him too far?

He crosses his arms, considers her for a few more long moments. Then, as if a key was turned somewhere within him, his face softens and he says: "Can I get you something? Coffee? A soft drink?"

"Nothing, thanks."

"Sure?"

"Positive," she says, relieved that she hadn't overstepped any boundary. She has to keep reminding herself that this is a man who beat his father to death with a baseball bat, poured beef broth on the body, and let four big dogs eat what was left.

Jean Luc offers his hand, like an old lover on a beach.

For some reason, she takes it.

He says, "Let me show you a very special room."

❖ 41 ❖

PARIS PRESSES THE button at 3204-A Fulton Road for the fifth time. He steps back onto the sidewalk, glances up. There are no lights on in the apartment. He looks into La Botanica Macumba. It is dark also, save for a small spotlight over the cash register, which sits with its empty drawer open.

Paris tries the door to the stairwell that leads to 3204-A. Locked. He had circled the building twice when he arrived, but the back and sides of the two-story structure offered no lighted windows, no open doors, no fire escape. He takes out his phone, dials the Levertov number. There is no answer, nor is there an answering machine.

Five cars are parked along the curb within a block of the doorway. Paris jots down the license plate numbers. He calls them in, and at the same time requests an address.

Fifteen minutes later, Edward Moriceau is in custody.

Moriceau sits in Interview One at the Justice Center. It is nearly eleven and this is Paris's third run at the story.

"And you never saw anyone argue with him, threaten him?" Paris asks.

"No. Never."

"And you've never had any business dealings or personal dealings with Mr. Levertov?"

"No."

Moriceau is lying. Time to ratchet things up a bit. Paris drops a photograph in front of the man, a medium close-up of Willis Walker's tongue. The Ochosi symbol is very clear. Moriceau brings his hand to his mouth.

"Look familiar to you?"

"Yes," Moriceau replies, his voice a little thin. "As I said . . ."

"Oh yeah . . . that's right," Paris says, knowing it is time to toss out the first bomb, the last vestige of cordiality. "You said something about a disemboweled rooster, didn't you? This look like a rooster?"

With this, Paris places a full body shot of Willis Walker onto the table. The impasto of thick maroon blood is spread on the white tiles, giving the dead man's body a bloated, mothlike shape. A rose-colored sprout of viscera extends from where Willis Walker's genitalia once grew.

Moriceau dry heaves, turns away. Then vomits on his feet.

Paris grimaces, looks at the two-way mirror, and can almost hear the buck being passed down the food chain among the police officers on the other side. Low man gets to fetch the bucket and mop.

Paris circles to Moriceau's side of the table, carefully skirting the foul debris on the floor. In a moment, Greg Ebersole enters, mop in hand. He hands Moriceau a ten-inch stack of napkins, runs the mop over the vomit, and makes a lithe and rapid exit from the room.

"Mr. Moriceau," Paris begins, "somebody is doing terrible things to the people of this city. Right now, nobody here thinks that person is necessarily you. Do you understand?"

Weakly, Moriceau nods, dabs his chin.

"Good. The problem is, as time goes on, and there are more and more connections to Santeria, or the address on Fulton Road, the more likely it is that our attitudes will begin to change. Do you understand this also?"

Again, Moriceau nods.

"I want you to think about something for a moment.

Somebody killed the old man who lived over your store. There is a good chance that that person is into Santeria or Macumba or Candomblé, or maybe he's just a wanna-be asshole who gets his rocks off pretending to be some kind of witch. Either way, the link to your store, the link to the products you sell, is *awfully* compelling."

Moriceau looks up, and Paris is nearly frightened by what he sees. The terror in the man's eyes has no bottom. "They will know. . . ."

"They?" Paris asks. "What are you talking about? Who is *they*?"

Moriceau gazes back at the floor. Paris is almost certain he is about to puke again, but instead Moriceau says, in his increasingly disjoined voice: "The seven powers."

Paris had come across the term *seven powers* in his readings on Santeria. But it was all beginning to blend together in his mind. He imagines it would be like someone trying to learn all about Catholicism or Judaism in seventy-two hours or so. "I'm sorry?"

"Eleggua, Orula, Ogun . . ."

Paris could barely hear him now. "What are you talking about?"

"Obatala, Yemaya, Oshun, Shango . . ."

"Mr. Moriceau?"

Moriceau looks up, holds his gaze, his red eyes searching, his hands now trembling like those of a man in violent, freezing waters. "I . . . I . . ."

Paris remains silent for a few moments, waiting for the answer this man will almost certainly not supply. He is right. "You *what*, Mr. Moriceau?"

"I . . . want . . . a lawyer."

Paris studies the shivering figure in front of him. This is no stone killer. Whatever legal horrors Moriceau might be facing, whatever apparitions of prison life eddy in his mind, they seem to be nothing compared to the flames of his personal hell.

The stench reaches Paris at that moment—sour and pervasive and cloying. He looks into the mirror, at himself, at the cops on the other side. They all know that there is no way they will be able to hold Edward Moriceau, just as they know that surveillance on La Botanica Macumba will begin within the hour.

The building has taken back its silence, reclaimed its mysteries. Paris is alone. He directs the beam of the flashlight along the cobwebbed wall, the skewed shelving, opaque with dust. Some of the hand-painted menus for Weeza's cuisine are still visible beneath the layers of time.

Paris Is Burning.

He is unsure why he had come back. Boredom and loneliness certainly had something to do with it. The building had probably given up what it knew about the last moments of Fayette Marie Martin's life, had most likely disclosed all its veiled wisdom.

But what the Reginald Building had not told him is why would someone like Fayette Martin come here in the first place. Why did she agree to meet with someone who, by all appearances, had been a total stranger, a man she had met online? Why didn't she drive up to the building, take one look, then drive back home and lock her doors and ask herself what the hell she was doing?

How lonely had it *gotten*?

He stands in the doorway leading to what was once Weeza's kitchen, listens to the night sounds, the constant bray of the wind. He wonders if Fayette *knew*. Did she scream when she saw the big knife? Did it come as a complete surprise? Did she have a second to reflect, or did the end of her life come as a brutal blindside, like a drunk driver running a red light at eighty miles an hour? Hadn't she known it *might* happen?

Or was that the kick?

Paris decides to go home, to rest, to take the whole story apart and reassemble it from the bolts up. He plays the flashlight beam across the floor at his feet and heads for the door just as the wind picks up again, a doleful gust that rattles the glass panes of the building's few remaining windows, loose in their mullions like rows of diseased teeth.

❖ 42 ❖

THEY HAD ENTERED through the second door on the left. The room is *searingly* white. The one splash of brilliance is the velvet wing chair in the center of the room, a deep purple in color. Across from it, against the far wall, is a white table holding a computer and a monitor. Against the wall to the right is a white ultramodern desk, very slender, no chair.

That's it. No other furniture, no paintings nor posters on the walls, no books nor magazines nor ashtrays nor table lamps. Just . . . *white*. And a hell of a lot of track lights hanging from the ceiling. There had to be twenty of them. And every one of them is blazing.

"Do you have anywhere to be tomorrow, early evening?" he asks.

She sits on the velvet wing chair. Whatever she had smelled in the kitchen is stronger here. Spoiled beef, maybe. But this room is almost sterile, and she finds it hard to imagine that Jean Luc would have another room in such disarray as to have rotting food strewn around. Perhaps it is coming from the next apartment.

"No," she answers. One of her part-time jobs is secretarial work for a small company that writes grants for charities and foundations. They had closed the offices for the week. Besides, if she had said yes, she had the distinct feeling it wouldn't really matter that much.

"Good," Jean Luc says. He crosses the room, opens the

closet door. Inside hangs a solitary item, a black leather jacket. He removes it from the hanger and walks over to the velvet wing chair. Without a word, she stands and he slips the jacket on her. It feels warm. She does not question what he is doing. There is no longer any point to that.

There are other ways to win.

Jean Luc reaches into his pocket, then holds up a small card. On it is the address of an Italian specialty market on East Sixty-sixth Street. "He'll be there at six-thirty P.M. tomorrow. He goes there like clockwork, every week."

"What do you want me to do?" she asks, standing closer, looking deeply into his eyes. She unzips the jacket halfway.

"I want you to take him on a little voyage." He walks over to the desk, opens a drawer, removes a soft cloth. She looks into the drawer. No photos. Jean Luc returns, gently buffs everywhere on the jacket he has touched. "A little *cruise*, if you will."

"A cruise?" she asks. "What kind of cruise?"

Jean Luc smiles. "A cruise I'm certain he will enjoy. A cruise on the *Mare di Amore*."

❖ 43 ❖

THE ICE ON the back of his head melts during his fourth cup of coffee, but the hangover does not. He had stayed up until almost dawn, finishing the final three inches of four different kinds of booze he had found lurking in his cupboards. Scotch, rye, schnapps, Cuervo. He had also found a pair of Lynchburg Lemonades loitering in the back of his fridge.

What had he been *thinking*?

He had been thinking about not thinking, that's what he had been thinking.

Paris Is Burning is what he had been thinking.

He had watched old movies, he had smoked old cigarettes, he had poured his booze carefully, adding ice until every drop was gone, shooting for blotto.

He arrived.

He has most of the day off and has at least ten errands to run before his tour starts. He pours himself another cup of coffee, promising movement soon, and scans the *Plain Dealer,* pleased by not seeing a huge headline, above the fold, with the words *voodoo* and *killer* in it.

Paris inserts the VHS tape. It is a low-angle shot of himself standing in front of the Justice Center. He is younger in the shot, wearing a dark suit, burgundy tie. He looks heavier than he remembers being, which is one of the reasons he had not watched the tape for more than a year. The reason for the tape to begin with? Pure vanity. He had worn his best suit that day, in the hope he would be interviewed, in the hope that Beth would see it and it would impress the hell out of her. Only the interview part happened. He had caught it on the eleven o'clock news that night.

"This was a cold-blooded killing of a police officer in the line of duty. . . . I think the evidence will show that the defendant, Sarah Weiss, pulled the trigger."

This statement is followed by a barrage of questions shouted from the dozen or so reporters in front of him. Although he doesn't remember hearing it, one of the questions must have been about Mike Ryan's own investigation, the Internal Affairs inquisition as to whether or not Mike had extorted protection money from a man who owned a chain of adult bookstores.

"Mike Ryan was a good cop . . . Mike Ryan was a family man . . . a man who woke up every day and chose—chose— to strap on a gun and jump into the fray. . . . Mike Ryan died in the line of duty protecting the people of this city. . . ."

Here is the part Paris hates. He shouldn't have said any of it, and took plenty of heat from the brass for opening his mouth. He had been to dinner, had had a few drinks, and should not even have been back at the Justice Center. But that's where he went, and that's where the cameras surrounded him. Even though he had come within a hairbreadth of a reprimand, he doesn't regret a word.

"So the next time you find yourself picking through a pile of garbage, or hiding in the bushes like some pervert, or running down the street with a forty-pound video camera just so you can invade the privacy of a heartbroken ten-year- old girl in a wheelchair, I want you to stop, take a deep breath, and ask yourself what the hell it is you do for a living. . . . Mike Ryan took a bullet for the people of this city. . . . Mike Ryan was a hero. . . ."

Another shouted question.

Then, his answer. The part he *does* regret saying.

"*Sometimes, the monster is real, people,*" his video voice says. "*Sometimes, the monster has a pretty face and a perfectly ordinary name. This time, the monster is called Sarah Weiss.*"

With that, the younger, heavier video Jack lifts his hand, waving off further questions, trying to salvage a little cop macho from the encounter. The tape then cuts back to Stefani Smith, the infoblond anchor on Channel 3 at that time, and, within a few seconds, the image fades to the movie that was on the tape originally.

The movie, Paris notes with a strained smile, is *Network.*

Two o'clock. Paris shakes out four or five Tylenols, wiggles them down with cold coffee. He grabs his coat and keys, deadbolts the door, descends the steps, stops.

Someone is standing on the platform at the bottom of the stairs.

It is Mercedes Cruz. He had forgotten to call her. They were supposed to meet the previous afternoon and he had forgotten to call her.

Shit.

"Hi," Paris says, his tone landing about three miles short of innocence. "I was just going to call you."

Mercedes's ever-sunny demeanor is now clouded with gray. Even her barrette is gray. "The *Plain Dealer* is working on a story about a ritual killer in Cleveland," she says. "A ritual killer who carves up his victims with a Santerian symbol."

Fucking leaks, Paris thinks. The department had not officially released the information that Willis Walker and Fayette Martin were mutilated. Nor anything about the Santerian angle. "Yeah. There've been a few calls from the paper."

"So, let me get this straight. I ride around with the lead detective on this case and I have to overhear the details in a booth at Deadlines?"

"I'm sorry," Paris says. And means it. Mercedes Cruz has

been a trouper. "Things have been moving kind of quickly on this case."

"I have a car. Two good legs. I move quickly, too."

"I know. But that's not it."

"Then what is it?"

"It's just that I've never done this before. Had someone watching me think, okay? In case you haven't noticed, the department is always nervous as hell that some fact will leak out about a homicide and the suspect goes to ground for good."

"Look, I didn't tell you about this before, because I didn't want to involve her, but my grandmother used to practice Santeria. Okay? I can help, detective. Let me do this. Let me write the biggest story of my life."

Paris thinks about it. "Come on. Walk me out." They descend the stairs.

Mercedes F. Cruz continues to plead her case. "You think I want to write for a friggin' west-side Latino newspaper the rest of my life? You think this is some kind of dream job? I'm as good as any writer in this town. I can *do* this, detective."

Paris caves in. "Okay," he says. "Tell you what. There is a task force meeting coming up. I'll let you sit in on it. But you have to swear to me that nothing you hear in there will see print until this is all over. I don't want to read *sources close to the investigation say* and have to wonder if it's you. Okay?"

"Okay."

For some reason, Paris can never find the deceit in Mercedes Cruz's eyes. "I'm not kidding about this. Not a word in print."

They are now standing in the parking lot behind Paris's apartment building. Mercedes smiles and holds up her hand in a Girl Scout salute. "Promise."

"Man," Paris says. "Girl Scouts, too?"

"Are you kidding? I've got three cases of cookies in the trunk."

"Not Caramel deLites," Paris says, glancing at the blue Saturn. "Please don't tell me you have Caramel deLites in the trunk of your car right now."

"And only three bucks a box. I'm helping my niece."

"Caramel deLites are my personal demon, you know. Had to enter a twelve-step once."

Mercedes Cruz takes her car keys from her pocket, and jangles them. "Welcome to the nightmare."

At three o'clock Paris's head begins to clear, though his hangover still feels like a cast-iron walnut at the base of his skull. He scans the now-dwindled number of yellow Post-it notes that are stuck onto his refrigerator. One of them leaps out. He had promised Beth that he would get her mother's ring from the safety-deposit box.

It was pointless to put it off further.

He grabs his coat and his keys and begins the process of chiseling off the last piece of his marriage.

After retrieving the entire contents of his safety-deposit box at Republic Bank, and closing out the account, Paris looks at the pile on his dining room table, items no longer worth safekeeping.

Among them, he sees the yellowed old police report, and his shame returns. He had all but forgotten about it. The incident report, which had been in his safekeeping for more than seventeen years, brings him back to that night so long ago, the night he and Vince Stella had come upon a middle-aged man fondling a sixteen-year-old runaway in an alley behind the Hanna Theatre on East Fourteenth Street. It was the much older of the two police officers who took charge that evening, recognizing the assistant county prosecutor immediately. God only knew how often Vince Stella had traded on that night in his years on the beat.

Paris decides he will get rid of it. The man is now a municipal judge and the incident, albeit sleazy, is ancient history.

*   *   *

On the way to meet Beth at Shaker Square at five o'clock, to give her back her mother's ring, Paris makes every light on Belvoir Boulevard, every light on South Woodland. He arrives at the square ten minutes early. He trots across the parking lot and is just about to head through the stone breezeway leading to the square when he spots Beth standing next to the ATM machine at the National City Bank. Paris is just about to raise his hand to draw her attention when he sees she is not alone. She is talking to a tall man in a tailored overcoat. Although the man has his back to Paris, Paris can see that he has dark, wavy hair. Certainly on the younger side of forty. Broad shoulders, gloved hands.

Paris is frozen for a few moments, watching his ex-wife talk to someone, as yet undetected. Should he stay? Go? Watch? Leave? Step in and make a fool of himself? He is enough of a voyeur to want to find a better vantage point from which to spy, to see how Beth acts when she's not around him. But he is also enough of a sissy to not want to see Beth give this guy some kind of big sloppy soul kiss.

The sissy wins.

Paris walks to Yours Truly, grabs a booth, orders coffee. Five minutes later, Beth arrives, lipstick intact.

Jack Paris decides to take it as a positive sign.

❖ 44 ❖

HIS NAME IS Axel Westropp. Nice suit, shitty tie. Shitty loafers, too.

"I hope you realize it's nothing personal," Axel says.

"Of course. Business is business. No offense taken."

Axel leans in, as if sharing a secret, even though we are alone in the coolly lit conference room at Cable99, the local access channel whose offices are located on Shaker Square. "It's the fucking politicians that screwed it up for everyone. But what's new, eh?"

Axel is certainly referring to the fact that political types have a nasty habit of ordering air time, using it, losing the election, then refusing to pay. Nothing of the sort is going to happen here, I assure him. Especially at these prices.

"Cash okay?" I ask.

"Cash is fine," Axel answers.

"And you say the modem hookup won't present any problems?"

"None at all," he replies. "Of course, you realize that the video quality won't be the greatest. We did a simulcast with Pere Ubu recently and it was cybercast worldwide on the Net. Our only problem was the video lagging slightly behind the audio. Other than that, everything went smoothly."

"And I'll be able to feed from two locations?"

"Absolutely. As long as the software is right on your end, whatever comes through will go right on the air."

"Outstanding," I say, rising to my feet. "Where do we take care of this nasty money business?"

"Money is never nasty around here," Axel says with a huge grin.

Ten minutes later I pay for thirty minutes of airtime on Cable99, buying the eleven-thirty-to-midnight slot on New Year's Eve, paying a substantial premium for the short notice. The audience won't be that large, of course, but neither are the demands regarding standards and practices. I can safely assume that what I have planned would never be suitable for broadcast on the network affiliates.

Not until it becomes news, that is.

❖ 45 ❖

AT FIRST, he figures it is just a hallucination, just another by-product of middle-aged myopia mixed with extreme sexual deprivation. He had thought about her so much over the past few days that he had begun to berate himself each time she danced across his memory, which seemed to be every forty-five seconds or so. He had even said her name aloud on a few occasions.

Why couldn't he get her off his mind?

He had no idea. But of all the places he might have expected to run into her, inside Pallucci's had to be down there near the bottom of the list. Right around monster-truck show.

Had he told her of his nearly twenty-year habit of stopping at Pallucci's on East Sixty-sixth Street every week at this time so he could get the fresh mozzarella with basil? He couldn't remember. The conversation at Starbucks is a smudge. He may have.

Regardless, this time it is no hallucination. She is standing at the end of the aisle, posing, her right leg cocked, her dark hair swept back from her face, her lips a damp, glistening scarlet. She begins to walk slowly toward him, her eyes fixed on his. She is wearing a tight black skirt and a black leather jacket, the kind with a million zippers, a cream T-shirt beneath. She looks tough. And cocky. And *very* sexy.

As she approaches, a tiny smile graces her lips, and Paris

suddenly realizes that she is not going to speak to him. He also notices it is not a cream T-shirt at all, but rather creamy *skin*. The jacket is unzipped halfway. She is wearing nothing beneath.

She walks past him, to the end of the aisle, turns, glances back.

Sea of Love, Paris thinks. The grocery-store scene in *Sea of Love*.

This can't be happening.

And, being the cynic that nearly twenty years on the force will make anybody, he begins to wonder what is wrong with this picture.

Yet, when he walks down the aisle, turns the corner, and sees Rebecca D'Angelo standing by the small produce rack, when he sees the way the fluorescent light plays off her alabaster skin, something other than logic propels him. He sidles up next to her, giddy with her perfume. She unzips her jacket another inch, leans in front of him, taking a handful of fennel, sniffing it. She runs her other hand slowly up his thigh, back down. Paris can now see inside her jacket, her white breasts against the black leather. She holds the pose for a moment, then puts the fennel back, strolls toward the small bakery counter—the sound of her heels clicking on the hard tile, along with Jimmy Roselli's "Mala Femmena" playing on the store's speakers, making the perfect surreal backdrop to the moment.

Slowly, Paris follows. When Rebecca reaches the counter, she turns, leans against the glass. When Paris stops in front of her, she grabs the lapels of his coat, pulls him between her legs.

The kiss is long and slow and deep. Paris slides his hands between her short skirt and the warm glass of the bakery display case. She kisses him again, and this time Paris wraps his arms around her, the leather, warm and sensual in his hands; the aroma of freshly baked *scallette* filling his head. Rebecca runs her tongue gently along the tip of his earlobe, whispers:

"Happy New Year, Jack."

Paris is speechless.

They kiss one last time, a kiss that delicately, yet unquestionably, conveys the promise that the next time they meet they will make love.

Rebecca slides from his arms, then turns and walks toward the register. She leans over, pecks Carmine Pallucci on his stubbly gray cheek, opens the door and is gone. One moment she is deep in Paris's arms, and the next moment he is greeted by a cold blast of air and the sloppy sounds of traffic sloshing down East Sixty-sixth Street.

Paris looks at Carmine, dumbstruck.

Carmine, who had seen the whole thing from behind the register—who had in fact seen quite a bit from that perch in his seventy-one years—looks at Paris, the shape of Rebecca D'Angelo's lips a neon sign on his right cheek. Then, with a big grin, and a whopper of a story to tell his grandsons in the morning, Carmine reaches under the counter and pulls out two small glasses and a bottle of his special-occasion *grappa de Vin Santo*.

Three hours later Paris sits in the backseat of his car, across from La Botanica Macumba, his legs outstretched in front of him, his mind trying to rein in his thoughts about his erotic grocery encounter. He can still smell Rebecca on his hands, his collar.

What was she doing?

What was *he* doing?

It was very clever, very sexy, very *mature* for someone her age. Maybe she *is* thirty or so, he rationalizes. Which would give him a little hope. Which is probably what scares him so much. He knows that there is a big sign called Hurt at the end of this. Guaranteed. Perhaps that is why he is starting to feel like Emil Jannings in *The Blue Angel*, the middle-aged schoolteacher who literally makes a clown, as well as a complete asshole, out of himself for Marlene Dietrich.

Paris looks up at the bay window above La Botanica

Macumba, the front window of the Levertov apartment. Shades still down, no lights.

Ivan Kral, the detective in charge of investigating the Isaac Levertov murder, had said that he had not been able to interview Levertov's wife in person since the old man's body had been found. He said that he had spoken to her at some length on the phone, and that she had come down to the morgue to make an official ID of the body, but that he has not been able to make contact with her since. It will take a search warrant to enter the premises and there wasn't nearly enough credible evidence to support probable cause.

Yet.

So they wait.

Paris repositions himself, brings his knees to his chin. He had learned how to wait the summer his father had died. Every morning that summer the sixteen-year-old Jack Paris would sit in the blue Naugahyde recliner at the foot of his father's bed, cocooned in that thick, closed-window air of infirmity, his lap covered with his many books on magic: *Blackstone's Modern Card Tricks, Keith Clark's Encyclopedia of Cigarette Tricks, The New Modern Coin Magic.*

His father had been a six-footer at a time when the heavyweight champion of the world was five-eleven; a maker of things new in his basement workshop, a fixer of things broken in the garage. Frank Paris was a machinist all his working life, a self-sufficient man who checked the locks every night, changed the furnace filters every fall, shoveled the driveway with his huge coal shovel every winter.

But, in that darkest of summers, leukemia made Frank Paris small.

On those rare and precious days when his father sat up, took real food, smiled at him, Jack Paris had performed his magic tricks on an aluminum TV table at the foot of the bed. Cups and Balls. The Traveling Deuce. The Vanishing Glass and Handkerchief. Good sometimes, more often not. His father had nonetheless applauded each and every time, his thin, osseous hands meeting in an almost soundless smear.

Jack Paris sat in the blue chair for three months, standing guard over his father's health, a bewildered, downhearted sentry. At the end of August the ambulance came in the night while Jack slept soundly. Three days later, the call from the hospital came at six o'clock in the morning.

He's dead, isn't he? his mother had said in the kitchen that fog-laden late-summer morning, her pink waitress uniform suddenly a widow's mantle. Jack waited for her gentle tread on the stairs, for the news.

All that spring and summer, from the balmy April day his father had come home, grim-faced, from Dr. Jacob's office, to the rainy funeral at Knollwood cemetery on Labor Day, Jack Paris had rolled a silver dollar through his fingers— palming, transferring, producing, vanishing, concealing.

His father's unhurried death may have taught him patience, but it was magic, he would reaffirm every *good* day he spent as a police officer, that taught him how to look at the other hand, how to see through the shadows.

It was magic that taught him illusion.

Paris rubs his eyes. He glances up at the Levertov front window, wondering how long he'd been gone, realizing that an entire performance of *Guys and Dolls* could have taken place in that window and he would have missed it.

You're on the job, Fingers.

Paris straightens his legs, does a quick scan of the immediate area with his binoculars. Deserted, except for a lone hot dog vendor on the corner of Newark and Fulton. Paris gets out of his car, stretches his legs, does a few kneebends, allowing the frigid air to revive him, his stomach now rumbling at the sight of the vendor. He'd managed to miss dinner again. Before he can head over, his two-way blares: "Jack?"

"Yeah?"

"I'm on my way," Carla Davis says, sounding agitated. "Five blocks out."

"You're *way* early. What's up?"

"Big fight with Charlie *Davis* is what's up."

"Oh yeah?"

"Gonna bust a cap up his skinny black *ass* is what's gonna *be* up."

Paris knows enough to leave it alone. Especially on an open channel. "Got it."

"Where are you parked?"

Paris tells her.

"I'll park closer to Trent, so we're not in the same spot," she says.

"Okay," Paris says, eyeing the vendor and his cart, two blocks away, famished now that he's seen it. "Listen, there's a vendor on Newark and Fulton. Grab me something, okay?"

"No problem. What do you want?"

"I don't know. Dog with the works, I guess. Coke."

"You got it."

"And listen, I know it's Ivan's case, but why don't you pump this guy a little about the old man. Isaac Levertov peddled his cart around here. Maybe he saw something."

"You got it."

Carla pulls very close with her car. She hands Paris the hot dog—wrapped in Christmas themed wax paper—and the freezing can of Coke.

Paris asks: "Did he know the old man?"

"No," Carla says. She holds her notebook up to the streetlight. "Mr. William Graham of Memphis Avenue in Old Brooklyn has been at this job exactly two weeks. Said he heard about the old man getting killed, but that's about it." She closes her notebook.

"What do I owe you?"

"Nothing," Carla says, yawning already. "Just bring coffee in the morning. And every damn McMuffin there is. Now get *outta* here. Go have a life."

*   *   *

The snow falls; hushed, relentless, orderly. The sparse traffic crawls up the center of Lorain Avenue, wisely making two lanes out of four.

It just didn't add up.

Willis Walker. Fayette Martin. Isaac Levertov.

What the hell ties these three people together?

Paris opens the Coke, sips, places the can between his legs. He grabs the hot dog, unwraps one end, lifts it to his lips, a third of his mind on Rebecca, a third of his mind on the road, the final third adrift on a stagnant sea of meaningless clues.

It is the smell that brings him back to shore.

The smell of death.

Paris slams on his brakes and begins to slide, sideways, up Lorain Avenue. Luckily there is no oncoming traffic. After a few terrifying moments he rights the car, brings it to a halt, straddling the center of the road. He opens the driver's door and all but dives onto the icy street.

"God *damn*, man . . . *shit!*"

Jack Paris begins to pace around in the middle of Lorain Avenue, fighting the nausea, holding his shield up to the car behind him, directing it around his car. He stops, rests his hands on his knees for a moment. He spits on the ground—once, twice.

Fat snowflakes catch on Paris's eyelashes. He brushes them aside, then dares to reach back into his car. He retrieves the blue light, puts it on the roof, and as he does he glances at the festive, brightly decorated wax paper, the beige-colored bun resting on the passenger seat.

"You are going *down*, motherfucker," Paris says as he takes out his flip phone, dials the Second District precinct house, his fury now a living thing within him. He spits into the gutter again. "You don't *see* a fucking courtroom. I swear to Christ."

Paris listens to the phone ring, absolutely certain that the hot dog vendor is going to be nowhere in sight when the squad cars get to the corner of Newark Avenue and Fulton Road; absolutely livid that he had been taunted with that name, Will Graham, the tormented FBI agent in Thomas Harris's *Red Dragon;* absolutely revolted by the knowledge that he had just come to within an inch or two of biting into Willis Walker's penis.

❖ 46 ❖

I CAN HEAR the police sirens in the distance and know that they are coming for me; a sober, urgent aria, rising and falling.

The old woman sits on the plastic-slipcovered dining room chair, her eyes a dead pool of defiance. I know that she has been through worse than whatever I can offer her now. Much worse. She has survived the horrors of Buchenwald, has witnessed an encyclopedia of inhuman behavior.

Initially, she had refused to tell me where the keys to the garage could be found. I needed them to get at her husband's hot dog cart. She had lost the tip of the little finger on her right hand to this stubbornness, yet still refused. When I brought the steam iron to within an inch of her face she pointed to a drawer in an old desk, her frail shoulders sagging under the weight of her shame.

She is very tough, clearly from another time, another era. Not soft and complacent like so many of my generation. She really has nothing to do with my plan, and my instincts are to just leave her apartment, take my chances. These are my instincts. And yet I know I cannot do this. I have no hatred for her, but I need until New Year's Eve at the very least and she has seen my real face.

My *father's* face.

I look out the window as two police cars converge on the corner of Trent Avenue and Fulton Road, their blue lights a sparkling, prismatic display on the ice-crystalled facade of St. Rocco's church.

The old woman struggles against the ropes. It appears that life, complete with all its horrors and barbarism and cruelty, is still precious to her. She tries to plead with me, but the tape over her mouth catches her fear, mutes it.

When we met, I had told her and her husband Isaac that my name was Judah Cohen. I kneel in front of her and say, in very apologetic Hebrew, acquired just for this occasion:

"Ani ve ata neshane et haolam."

You and I will change the world.

Edith Levertov's eyes open wide, wider.

She screams.

She has met the devil once before.

❖ 47 ❖

PARIS MOUNTS THE steps to the Levertov apartment, his sidearm drawn. He is followed by Carla Davis and two uniformed officers from the Second District. Paris has not pulled his weapon in the line of duty for more than eight months, and although he had requalified at the range since, it suddenly feels foreign in his hand, heavy.

Three scenarios are possible at the top of these stairs, Paris thinks, ten treads from the door. One. Nobody home. Isaac Levertov's widow is staying with relatives, too grief-stricken to return to the apartment. Two. A dazed and confused and heavily medicated Mrs. Edith Levertov will come to the door, having never heard the doorbell or the ringing phone.

Three?

Well, three has too many variables, even for someone of Jack Paris's experience.

The top of the stairs brings a collective breath from the four police officers. Paris tries the knob and the old door opens, just a few inches, creaking in protest. Paris makes eye contact with Carla, who is standing directly behind him. Paris will open the door wide, go in high. Carla will go in low.

After a silent count of three, Paris pushes open the door fully. The squeal of the hinge is louder this time, a shriek of rusty disapproval in the silence of the hallway.

No movement. No voices inside. No TV nor radio.

Paris waits a few heartbeats, peeks around the jamb. Small kitchen ahead, enameled yellow walls, a wrought-iron dinette table, plastic plants. He smells old frying oil, Lysol, cat litter. Whereas there had been no lights on when Paris had staked the apartment out earlier, now, it seems, every light in the small apartment is blazing.

Paris rolls in high. Carla follows. Spotless kitchen floor, except for the two slightly sullied size-eleven footprints made of melted snow. Paris silently apprises Carla, who skirts them.

To the left, an archway into the living and dining rooms. Paris sidles against the refrigerator, holds his position. Carla moves low, to the far side, glancing through the archway as she does. She stands on the opposite side of the arch, nods at Paris. Paris steps into the dining room, his 9 mm pistol at a forty-five degree angle to his body.

The shadow appears first, then the outline, then the form. Someone is sitting at the dining room table.

Paris raises his weapon, draws down on the shape in front of him, his heart flying. *Shoot don't shoot.* It never changes. Shoot.

Don't shoot.

Paris lowers his weapon slightly, the sweat now gathering at the nape of his neck, running down his back in a lattice-work of icy threads.

There is no threat from the person at the table.

Carla rolls the corner, weapon high, sees what Paris sees, hesitates—the macabre scene distracting her for a moment—then silently moves forward.

Ahead, a small cluttered living room: an old twenty-five-inch rock maple TV, a tall étagère full of glassine objects, overstuffed chairs. Empty, silent, ominous. Carla nods toward the hallway that certainly leads to the bedrooms, bathroom. Paris moves to the hallway opening, Carla spins into the hall. The two other uniformed officers position themselves in the living room. Paris nods to one of them, who then skirts Paris, and moves down the hallway. Paris repeats the action with the second officer. He follows. They search the rest of the apartment.

Bathroom. Empty.

Bedroom One and closet. Empty.

Bedroom Two and closet. Empty.

Paris walks back to the dining room and looks at the figure seated at the table. He returns his weapon to his shoulder holster.

"Clear!" Carla Davis yells from a bedroom.

Carla emerges from the hallway, her pistol at her side. The two other police officers—rookie patrolmen from the looks of them, pumped and full of adrenaline from the search—follow her out. It is usually a moment, a very *special* moment for police officers, to decelerate, to slap each other on the back, to take that deep, nervous breath that says *we went where the danger was and we didn't flinch.*

But it is not a time for camaraderie.

Not this time.

"My God, Jack," Carla says softly.

The two other police officers in the dining room holster their weapons, avert their eyes. They are both young enough to have living grandmothers and they are appalled at the sight in front of them. One of them leaves the room, ostensibly to cover the front door to the apartment. The other studies his shoes.

The old woman, Edith Levertov, is sitting at her dining room table, as she most likely had for many years—partaking of her kreplach, playing mah-jongg, diapering the parade of Levertov babies and grandbabies, dispensing her years of wisdom.

Except, this time, there is a difference.

This time, her head is turned completely around, facing the flower-print wall of cabbage roses and olive green vines. This time, her exanimate eyes are wide open and she appears to be staring at a symbol, roughly slashed into the plaster on the dining room wall. An ancient emblem made of six lines, two of them curved into a gentle arc.

Paris, suddenly the scholar in Santerian symbology, doesn't bother to look.

❖ 48 ❖

THE CAPRICE LOUNGE is all but deserted and Carla Davis is about as looped as he had ever seen her. The fact that Carla had had their actor right in front of her both infuriated and, if the fact that she is on her third Cutty Sark is any indication, frightened her more than a little.

Right around last call, after a long silence, Carla asks: "I've been wanting to ask you something."

"Okay."

"Nothin' to do with the case."

"Good."

"You ever think about getting married again?"

"Never," Paris lies.

"Really? How come?"

"A million reasons, none of them good enough on their own. But *collectively* . . ."

"I understand."

"Let me put it this way," Paris says. "At this stage of my life, I like my women like I like my first pot of coffee of the day."

Carla plays along. "You mean, hot, black, and sweet?"

"Nope," Paris replies. "I mean gone by seven-thirty."

Carla laughs. "Okay, okay. I hear ya."

"Now I've got a question for *you*. It's got everything to do with the case." Paris reaches inside his suit coat pocket and retrieves an old newspaper photograph of Jeremiah Cross. "You know this guy?"

Carla squints at the photo in the dim lights of the bar. "Not sure. Who is he?"

"Defense attorney. He defended the woman who killed Mike Ryan."

Carla takes her glasses from her coat pocket, puts them on, holds the photo up for better light. "No," she says. "But, on the other hand, pretty-boy lawyers all kind of blend together for me, you know what I mean?" She reads the caption. "Jer-e-mi-ah Cross. Nope. Doesn't ring a bell. Why?"

"This is gonna sound insane."

"It's almost two-thirty, Jack," she says, draining her drink, calling for the tab. "Believe me, it won't."

"Is there any chance that he might have been our unsub?"

Carla looks at Paris. Deep, cop-trance look. He has her attention now. "*This* guy? Our unknown *subject*?" She grabs the photo back. "Shit, I don't know. Maybe yes, maybe no. My guy had a big beard, tinted shades, ball cap. Probably a wig. I think I saw his lips and his nose. How tall *is* this Jeremiah Cross?"

"Six feet or so."

"That's about right," Carla says.

"What about an accent? Did he sound southern at all?"

"No. Sounded like a guy from Rocky River, actually." Carla scrutinizes the photo again. "Why on earth would you like *this* guy as our actor?"

Paris gives her a brief rundown.

"That ain't much," Carla says.

"I know."

"Just because you'd like to go upside on this guy doesn't exactly make him our voodoo mass murderer."

"You're right," Paris says. "Forget I said anything."

They drop the money on the bar, sign off for what they know will only be a few hours. Paris walks Carla to her car. They assess each other's ability to drive and give themselves a pass.

Thirty minutes later, as Paris flops into his bed, chilled to the marrow, fully clothed, deprived of any direction in this brutal abattoir he calls a career, he falls instantly into a deep, troubled sleep.

Evil is a breed, Fingers.

An hour later, Paris does not hear the car pull into the parking lot across the street, nor does he see the glow of the cigar ember inside, phosphorescent in the blackness, strobing through the night like a rosary made of fire.

PART THREE

❖ ❖

BRUJO

❖ 49 ❖

**New Year's Eve
Cleveland, Ohio**

THE BOY IS a man. Thirty years of age this day. In his
time, he has broken every law of God, almost every law
of man. In his time he has taken the lives of eleven people, including a *cholo* who once approached him in a
Sinaloa café, a foul-breathed wretch with a pedophile's
eyes over slick yellow teeth. He had been so revolted by
this man's repeated advances that he had paid for the
man's drinks well into the night, left with him, then lured
him to a dark place and gutted him like a *pescado*. He
had been fifteen. He had fed the man's insides to some
strays.

Another life became his around the time his mother had
been walking the streets near East Fifty-fifth Street in Cleveland. One night she had brought home a man who looked
and smelled like a hobo, like someone who rode the rails. In
the morning the boy had seen the man searching the kitchen,
looking for cash. The man found the cookie jar that held
sixty-one dollars. The boy had dressed, followed the man to
a vacant building on Prospect. He watched while the man
made an elaborate job of hiding the money in a coffee can.
He watched while the man curled up on a stinking mattress.

When the boy was certain the man was sound asleep, he

sneaked up on him and, with one powerful blow, pounded a rusty wood chisel into the man's left ear, deep into his brain, killing him instantly. The boy had been twelve at the time. He and his sister had then dug a hole in the lot behind the building and buried the man. Two weeks later, they stood across the street as the building was torn down, filled in, leveled. A month later it was paved over.

The sixty-one dollars was replaced in the cookie jar before their mother even knew it was gone, as was an additional four dollars and ten cents the boy had found in the dead man's pockets.

As the clock winds down to a new day, a new year, the man knows his future is uncertain, as unpredictable as death itself. And yet, as he showers and shaves and readies himself for the day, he knows one thing with certainty.

He knows that Detective John Salvatore Paris will die, by his own hand, before this day is out.

❖ 50 ❖

MERCEDES CRUZ HAS taken on the waxy pallor of the newly deceased. All the ghastly visual details of the murders of Fayette Martin, Willis Walker, Isaac Levertov, and Edith Levertov are displayed in front of her in brilliant, living color. Forty-eight photographs in all.

Paris feels for Mercedes. He knows her well enough to know she has a good heart and this is something she had not anticipated.

The task force meeting begins promptly at eight o'clock with every available detective in the Homicide Unit sitting in the room. Four of the eight unit commanders are also in attendance, as are the coroner and deputy coroner.

In addition to the crime-scene photographs of the victims, there are two photographs of the cardboard strips found on Isaac Levertov and Fayette Martin, as well as two photographs of the shoeprints found in the Levertov apartment. Also, a pair of computer-generated composites are tacked on the board. One is of a young blond woman, the woman last seen with Willis Walker. The other is really two composites side by side. The bearded, bespectacled young man at the hot dog cart on the left; and a clean shaven, glassless version of the suspect on the right.

During the past twenty-four hours, the net had widened to include law-enforcement agencies at the county and state levels. Images of the hot dog vendor had been distributed to police and sheriff's departments all over northeastern Ohio, some already to Pennsylvania, Indiana, Kentucky, and West Virginia. The image had also been uploaded to a dozen law-enforcement Websites.

The task force had also rerun the tape taken from Carla's hidden camera at the party. Poor quality, terrible lighting, absolutely unusable.

In the past few days, the buzz that had flowed through the department regarding the *Paris Is Burning* evidence had taken on a far more serious tone than if the rumor that a police officer might be targeted by a killer had not been prematurely floated. There are about eighteen hundred men and women on the force and more than once, over the past days, a few more vests than usual had been quietly removed from lockers and strapped into place.

The investigation had also confirmed what they already knew; that video-rental businesses, including the big ones like Blockbuster, do not rent the original cardboard packaging with the movie. In the past forty-eight hours, the factory packaging of all thirty-one rental copies of *Paris Is Burning* in the greater Cleveland area had been examined and cleared. Not one of them had a missing label.

Greg Ebersole begins. "There were no usable prints from the motel room. Most of the surfaces were wiped down rather thoroughly, but there *were* traces of Willis Walker's blood found on the nightstand and the inside doorknob, indicating that the killer wiped the bludgeoning weapon first, which was most likely the toilet tank cover, then proceeded to wipe down the room with the same cloth. A towel with what looks like blood on it was found in a culvert along I-90 last night. Lab's got it now.

"SIU has also lifted no fewer than fifty prints and par-tials at the Fayette Martin crime scene. Of the twenty on file, eleven were incarcerated at the time of the murder, three no longer live in the area and have provided work al-ibis. Two are over seventy, being a pair of pensioners who routinely visit the building looking for aluminum cans. That brings us to one Jaybert Louis Williams, thirty-four, whose sheet begins and ends with a pair of shoplifting charges in North Randall, and one Antoinette Viera, thirteen years of age."

"Thir*teen?*" Paris asks. "Why the hell are her prints on file?"

Greg scans his notebook. "She stole some supplies from her junior high school."

"And she went through the system for that?"

"Computer supplies, Jack. As in four brand-new laptops."

Everyone in the room absorbs the information, then discards it. There is nothing there.

"Any reason to like the shoplifter?"

Greg holds up the man's Polaroid photograph. Jaybert L. Williams is black, no less than three hundred pounds. He is certainly not the hot dog vendor. But it doesn't rule him out as an accomplice or accessory.

Carla asks, "And what's his excuse for being on someone else's property?"

"Actually, he copped right to it. Said he was in there getting a blow job. Said it was so good he had to hang onto the counter."

A collective sigh skirts the room, buttressed by some boisterous laughter.

Paris asks, "Did he say *when* this blow job of a lifetime occurred?"

"Last summer," Greg says. "The lab supports that. It's an old print."

Dead end. Elliott turns to Carla.

Carla begins. "The shoeprints found in the Levertov kitchen are from a man's hiking boot, size eleven and a half. Unfortunately, it is an extremely popular model, available everywhere: Dillard's, Kaufmann's, Saks. The material on the floor was mostly water, with particulate matter consisting of mud, soot, road salt. Another shoeprint matching these was found in a small snowbank near the entrance to the stairwell. Everything on the stairs themselves is too smudged."

As he had the first time he had seen it, Paris looks once again at the sketch of the young blond woman, as described by the regulars at Vernelle's Party Center, and sees Rebecca.

Why?

Granted, the cheekbones and eyes are familiar, as is the hint of a dimple, but that's about it. Beyond that, it doesn't look like her at all.

Does it?

Or is it just this spell he's under?

Job, Jack.

Everyone concurs that their suspect had to have listened in on Paris's and Carla's radio traffic and known that Carla would be buying the hot dog for Paris, which is one of the reasons why Paris had phoned the Second District to move in and not radioed Carla. There had been no time to establish a scrambled command frequency. They had, of course, found the hot dog cart abandoned and currently had it in the lab.

It still didn't nail down the *Paris Is Burning* connection, but there was no longer any doubt that Paris is the subject of this psychopath's attentions. He's not just baiting the department, the system, the city.

This is personal.

Paris holds up the composite of the hot dog vendor, sans spectacles and beard, says: "No one at the party looked anything like our actor. As far as we know, he wasn't even *at* that party. Now, if he *is* some kind of rent-a-cyberstud for this NeTrix, Inc., he might show up at the big New Year's Eve bash. In fact, he may not have any idea that we made the house in University Heights yet, or established any kind of connection. Just because he has some kind of thing for me doesn't mean he knows anything about the last party."

Elliott asks: "How do you know that someone at the party didn't tell him about you and Carla?"

"Believe me, nobody looked at me. Carla's the only reason we got in the door in the first place. They know us as Cleopatra and John. I don't think he has any idea we would come at him from this side. I vote for hitting that party tonight."

Elliott looks at Carla Davis. "You agree?"

"Absolutely," Carla says. "If we bring in Herb now, or whoever actually lives in that house, and sweat him, we tip our boy for sure. We lose the possibility that he shows up at the party. He's in the wind. I say we raid the party at midnight."

"What time does this thing start?" Elliott asks.

"Ten o'clock," Carla says. "Herb sent me an e-mail this morning."

❖ 51 ❖

THE STAIRWAY TO the basement is narrow, unlit, paneled haphazardly with three different types of Masonite, all overlapping each other by a few inches or so, all banged into place with bent and tortured sixteen-penny nails. At the bottom of the stairs is a rack of garden tools—rakes, picks, shovels, hoes, mattocks—hung on a Peg-Board. Paris and Mercedes reach the bottom, turn to the right: low ceiling, crosshatched with exposed wire, heat ducts, copper pipe. A single bare bulb hangs, casting brusque shadows.

They turn the corner, skirting the furnace, and see a slight brown woman of seventy, her chalky hair pulled back into a bun and infused with an elaborate network of colorful shells and beads. She wears a multicolored caftan and Dr. Scholl's sandals. Behind her oversized, cat's-eye framed glasses, Paris can see that she has a lazy left eye.

"This is my *'buela*," Mercedes says after hugging the old woman. "My grandmother. Evangelina Cruz."

"Mrs. Cruz," Paris says. "Pleasure to meet you."

Evangelina Cruz holds out her small calloused hand. Paris shakes it, noticing that Mercedes is right to say they favor each other. For a moment, when Evangelina Cruz smiles at him, he can see the young woman rise to the surface.

"Bienvenido," she says.

"Thank you," Paris replies.

Evangelina Cruz looks to her granddaughter for a sign,

258

then turns and parts the curtain of garnet-colored glass beads in the doorway behind her, steps through. Paris and Mercedes follow.

It is a small, square room, perhaps ten by ten feet, damp concrete floor, painted masonry walls. Against the far wall is an altar, a four-foot-tall, three-foot-wide structure that appears to be a series of five steps, leading upward, covered in a bright white cloth. Each of the treads bears a number of items—candles, bowls, loose shells and shell necklaces, statues, cards, small pieces of pottery. But mostly candles. There are candles everywhere, all of them scented. The mélange of sweet and bitter and earthen aromas is overpowering.

Then there are the animal smells.

The smells of cages.

Evangelina Cruz steps to the right of the altar, reaches beneath the white cloth, presses a button. Within seconds, music begins to play, a vibrant African beat, mostly drums. She looks heavenward, then reaches into the pocket of her caftan and produces a cigar. She lights it slowly, methodically. When it is fully lighted she draws the smoke into her mouth, then exhales it over the altar. She then blows smoke at Paris and places the cigar onto a brass incense plate.

"Donde está tu fotografía?" Evangelina asks.

"She needs the photographs now," Mercedes whispers.

Paris reaches into his pocket and produces photocopies of the photographs of the four victims. Fayette Martin, Willis Walker, Edith Levertov, and Isaac Levertov. He hands the paper to Evangelina Cruz. Without looking at the photographs, she drops them into a large terra-cotta bowl on the bottom step of the altar. She then leans over and picks up an earthen cruet and pours what appears to be water into the bowl, half-filling it. She places the pitcher back onto the altar, then dips her fingers into the liquid and flicks them over the altar.

Before Paris can react, she turns and flicks the last few drops over him.

"Maferefún ashelú!" she says.

Then, without a word, she leaves the room, the glass beads clapping behind her. Paris hears a door open and close. Then again, fainter. After a few moments, Evangelina returns, carrying a chicken. A *live* chicken. She turns up the music.

Paris looks at Mercedes and lets his right eyebrow do the talking.

Mercedes leans close. "Don't worry. She eats them after."

Up goes the remaining eyebrow. "She's going to *kill it*?"

Mercedes smirks. "And I suppose you send condolence cards to KFC when you're done with a bucket?"

She has a point, Paris thinks. He just wasn't prepared for some kind of barnyard slaughter in the basement of a house on Babbitt Road. He directs his attention back to the altar.

Evangelina Cruz puts the body of the chicken under her left arm, and with her right hand she reaches into the pocket of her caftan. This time she produces a pearl-handle switchblade, clicks it open, and cuts the chicken's neck, deeply, taking the head nearly off. It flutters wildly under her arm, but Evangelina Cruz doesn't even flinch. She holds the chicken's exposed throat over the bowl containing the four photographs, and Paris watches as a series of bright scarlet spurts cloud the water, blurring the photographs completely.

In the background, the tribal music plays.

Evangelina chants. *"Maferefún ashelú!"*

The chicken's blood squirts into the bowl.

"Maferefún ashelú!"

Paris looks at Mercedes. "Do you know what that means?" he whispers.

"Yes," she says. "She is offering praise to the police."

Paris is shocked. "There's a *saying* for that?"

Mercedes smiles as the ceremony continues.

Within three minutes, Evangelina has the chicken plucked and the white feathers scattered about the altar.

Mercedes emerges from the house, walks over to the driver's door of her car, gets in. Paris sits in the passenger seat, a little rattled by what he has just seen.

As soon as the ceremony was over, Paris had thanked Evangelina Cruz and quickly made his way out the side door, the smell of sour smoke and chicken blood filling his sinuses. The cold air had done wonders. He had agreed to meet with the old woman at Mercedes's request, hoping to further his knowledge of Santeria. And although he could honestly say that he knows more about it now than he did yesterday, he isn't entirely certain how this newly acquired wisdom is going to help.

Paris asks, "So . . . what did she say?"

Mercedes buckles her seat belt, starts the car. "She said you seem like a very nice young man."

"Young?" Paris says. "I think your *'buela* may need a new 'scrip for those glasses."

"She also said that the man you are looking for is not a real *brujo*. He is an impostor."

"*What?* What the hell does that mean?"

"It means he was not ordained into *brujería* or Palo Mayombe or even Santeria itself. He is just using these things to frighten people. He is like . . . like a *pimp* she says. A cardboard bully."

"Those dead bodies are not cardboard, Mercedes."

"I know. I told her that. She says that the man you are looking for will crumble when you close your hands around him. Like paper. It's kind of tough to translate, okay?"

"Okay."

"But . . . she says that if you want to know him, if you want to catch him, you have to know what breaks his heart."

Paris's mind races around the evidence, trying to plug all this into a reality socket. "She really thinks the Santeria angle is just window dressing?"

"Yes."

"How can she be sure?"

Mercedes looks out the side window for a moment, then back at Paris. "This is going to sound a lot worse than it is."

"It already does. Just spit it out."

Mercedes fumbles with the settings for the car's heater,

stalling. "She says that if he were the real thing, he would have sacrificed a child by now."

Paris goes cold for a moment, remembering Melissa in the hands of a psychopath. "Please. No. Don't tell me that—"

"No," Mercedes says as she looks both ways, then backs out onto Babbitt Road. "She really doubts that he will do that. She thinks this guy is a player. A hustler. No more a *brujo* than you. She says he has an angle, a reason for doing this that is of this earth. Nothing more mystical than that."

Paris is silent for a few moments. "And what did she say about that spell she cast?"

Mercedes smiles broadly as she puts the Saturn in gear and heads toward the Shoreway. "She said you will have your killer within twenty-four hours."

❖ 52 ❖

THE LITTLE GIRL tries to lift the ball of tightly packed snow; her short arms are wrapped only halfway around the circumference. It is the snowman's head she hoists, the third and final level of the rather portly, misshapen fellow that is already taller than she is.

She tightens her grip. Up, up, up, up . . . *no*. Not this time.

The snowman's head falls to the ground and rolls a few inches.

The little girl circles the ball of snow, her face a twist of concentration. And it is such a beautiful face. Big eyes, raven hair, loose curls beneath her tam-o'-shanter—dark, springy ringlets that frame a face of such angelic power and purity and innocence.

She will try again. But not before consulting her almost life-size playmate, the huge bundled-up doll that is sitting on a nearby snowbank, blankly observing. The little girl whispers into the big doll's ear, sharing little-girl strategy, little-girl tactics. She then walks back over to the snow-man's head, bends over, wraps her arms as far around as she can.

One, two, three.

Boom.

She falls facedown in the snow.

I count the seconds until the first tear appears but am amazed that they don't come. She gets up, brushes the snow from the front of her navy blue wool coat. She stamps her right foot in disgust and walks away for a few moments.

But sheds no tears.

I would love to jump in and help her, but that, of course, would make all hell break loose.

An old woman sits on the porch, a cup of steaming coffee or tea in her hands. Quiet street, old ethnics. Nothing could possibly go wrong in bright daylight.

I am fascinated by the false sense of security people have over their domain, with their deadbolts and lamp timers and Rottweilers and phony security company signs.

I am more fascinated by the feeling I get when I watch the little girl romp in the snow—trying to dominate all within her little-girl horizon—and how very much like her mother she looks.

GLOBAL SECURITY SYSTEMS the sign on the side of the van proclaims in sleek euro-style letters. The two men working on the locks to the front doors of the Cain Manor apartments hardly look like global systems analysts, but, nonetheless, I have to figure them capable at the very least.

New locks. A problem. My key to Cain Manor came from a duplicate I had cut from a wax pressing, a pressing I made while helping an elderly lady with her groceries a year or so ago.

But why new locks today?

Might it have something to do with a body being discovered in Cain Park?

Regardless, I do not have time to press a new key. I pull the Yellow Pages from the backseat. Cleveland Retail Supply on Chester Avenue. Problem solved.

I will pay them a visit today on my way to Jack Paris's apartment.

Earlier this morning, before Paris had met up with the reporter and driven out to Babbitt Road, while I was well within range of his car and my crystal transmitter, he had been on the phone with his commanding officer and was kind enough to give me his precise itinerary for the day.

It seems we both have much to do.

I swing the car onto Euclid Heights Boulevard and head for the city. Later, after making my purchase at the retail supply house, I believe I'll make a brief stop at Ronnie's Famous Louisiana Fry Cakes on Hough Avenue.

I hear the beignets are very good.

❖ 53 ❖

IN HIS CAREER on the street, Arthur Galt was known as a man without fear. A cop who would push other cops out of the way to get to the door, a First District legend who never took a dime and, in spite of a dozen incidents in his twenty-odd years with the CPD, never had a bad shoot.

But now, over the phone at least, he sounds like a man who has settled quite comfortably into the baronial life of country constable. Arthur Galt is the very popular, very connected chief of police in Russell Township.

The two men get their pleasantries out of the way and get to business.

"This is ongoing, Jack," Galt says, a chief's cautionary tone lying right on the surface.

"I understand," Paris says.

"We've got a couple of witnesses who now say they saw Sarah Weiss at the Gamekeeper's Taverne earlier that evening."

"Alone?"

"No. These two guys who work at the treatment plant in Chagrin Falls say that they both did their duty by hitting on Sarah Weiss early in the evening, but were shined on. They said later in the night, she gave some time to a yuppie type in a dark business suit, who left after a half hour or so. But even *later* in the evening, they said, she spent at least a couple hours talking to a woman. A real looker they said. Redhead, although, according to these guys, it looked like a wig. She says the two women left together."

"Who reported the yellow car on the hill?"

"A woman named Marilyn Prescott. Her house is about a hundred feet from a clearing that looks right onto the hill. She said it was a full moon that night and she could clearly see the two cars parked there around eleven-thirty. She said she then went to bed, woke up an hour later when she heard the gas tank explode. I've already checked to see if the moon really was full that night."

"And?"

"It was."

Paris processes the information. "Do you have a sketch of the business type or the redheaded woman?"

"Nothing yet. We're still canvassing on this, Jack. It's still officially a suicide."

"They left the bar together. . . ."

"Yeah," Galt says. "These two guys wrote them off as gay, of course. They work at a fuckin' sewage treatment plant and neither of 'em could figure out any other reason as to why they were shut down."

St. John the Evangelist, the imposing cathedral on East Ninth Street and Superior Avenue, is nearly empty at this hour, with just a handful of widely spaced penitents in the afternoon gloom. Paris walks through the vestibule, steps inside. The echo of his footsteps in the enormous church recalls the other times of his life, the times that being a Catholic had been important to him, the times that seemed to elate and frighten and entrance him all at once, the times during which he had leaned on his faith for strength.

But that all changed on his third night as a police officer. All of that changed the night he saw three young children—ages four, five, and six—blasted apart with a shotgun in a stifling third-floor apartment on Sonora Avenue. Besides the torn flesh and the sea of gore, Paris's lingering memory—the remembrance that has led him to deny a benevolent God for so many years—was the Etch-A-Sketch he had seen, still clutched in the hands of the four-year-old; the Etch-A-Sketch sheened with blood that had borne the half-drawn *Happy Birthday Daddy!*

It was the little girl's father, insane with seventy-two hours of methamphetamine and fortified wine, who had placed the barrel against her head and pulled the trigger.

No. No God of John Salvatore Paris would allow this to happen, he had thought at the time, and it has been that conviction that has shielded his heart and mind and memory from the abundance of horrors he had witnessed since.

Until today. For some reason, the need has returned.

He selects an empty pew.

Mercedes Cruz, nearing her deadline, had gone home to write the first draft of her story, having argued with Paris for nearly an hour about the possibility of accompanying the task force on the raid later that night. It is, of course, entirely out of the question. But still she pressured him. In the end, Paris had said that he would call her later that night, regardless of the time, and give her an exclusive. It wasn't what she was lobbying for, but it was the best he could do.

And then there is the image of Evangelina Cruz, covered in blood and feathers.

Paris thinks about the ceremony in Evangelina Cruz's basement, how foreign and violent and pagan it seemed. But Catholicism certainly has its rituals, he concedes, looking around him. Odd-seeming ceremonies that people of other faiths might find bizarre.

Willis Walker. Fayette Martin. Isaac and Edith Levertov.

Mike Ryan.

Sarah Weiss.

What am I doing in St. John's after all this time?

He leans forward, kneels. Automatically, his hands find each other, a loose tenting of fingers, a long unutilized mainstay of his Catholic upbringing.

Am I praying?

Yes, he thinks. I am. After all these years I am praying

again. I am praying for every Fayette Martin out there. I am praying for Melissa. I am praying for all the little girls who will one day grow up, dress like a woman, and say yes to a man with sorcery in his smile.

Dolores Ryan's outgoing phone message had stated that she and Carrie would be out of town for the New Year's holiday, and to please call them at a Tampa, Florida, number. Not the smartest move, Paris had thought, considering the world as it is these days, but it was common knowledge that the patrols on this stretch of Denison Avenue were a little more frequent in the past few years. Widows of cops killed on the job rarely had to worry about break-ins.

On the other hand, there is no need to advertise. After Paris had called in his location, then made his way around back, through calf-high drifts of snow, he noticed the note pinned to the doorjamb, a note from Dolores to her newspaper carrier, instructing the carrier to put the newspapers into the covered wooden box near the back door: a bright beacon of invitation to any burglar who happens to come by. Paris takes Dolores's note down, shoves it in his pocket, makes a mental note to call the *Plain Dealer* circulation department and tell *them* to tell the carrier.

Then, not without a sliver of guilt, Paris acts like a burglar himself.

He looks three-sixty.

And knocks out a pane of glass.

The storage bay is an icebox. He had waited for the glass repair company to arrive and replace the pane, paying the man in cash, then had retrieved the key from the corkboard in Dolores's kitchen. He is once again standing in front of Michael Ryan's desk in bay number 202, not really certain as to why, not really comfortable with the desperation that had settled over him of late.

He finds a suitable rag and cleans off the dust-covered dial on the small floor safe.

Then, in the dim light of the single overhead bulb, he looks at Demetrius Salters's scrawlings on the *Cableviews* magazine, even though the page numbers had stalked the edge of his conscious thought for so long he knows them by heart.

15, 28, 35.

It had occurred to him somewhere in the middle of a daydream. Carla's creepy crawler. The one who used to carve numbers into the foreheads of his victims.

Combinations are six numbers.

Before he can talk himself out of it, he hunkers down, spins the dial.

Fifteen, right.

Once around. Twenty-eight left.

Thirty-five right.

Paris takes a deep breath, grabs the cold iron handle on the door to the safe, absolutely certain the door will not open, thoroughly convinced that a sequence of numbers circled in a cable TV guide by a retired cop with Alzheimer's could not *possibly* be the combination to a safe that has been sitting in—

The door swings open.

Paris's stomach flutters wildly as he looks inside and sees two dog-eared manila folders. He removes them. The first one contains an old charcoal police-artist sketch of a teenaged boy. High cheekbones, long dark hair, wraparound sunglasses. Paris flips it over. On the back is glued a one-paragraph newspaper article from the *San Diego Union-Tribune*: HILLSDALE GIRL, 4, VICTIM OF HIT-AND-RUN DRIVER. The article is about Carrie Ryan's accident.

Paris looks at the sketch again.

The hit-and-run suspect?

He opens the other folder. This one contains an old police file. On top is an aggravated assault complaint by a woman named Lydia del Blanco sworn out against her former spouse, Anthony C. del Blanco. Paris notices that it is a photocopy, not the original.

But that's not what makes his mind spin. *That* dizzying feeling is courtesy of the fact that Anthony del Blanco lived at 4008 Central Avenue. Anthony del Blanco lived in one of the rooms in the Reginald Building, not more than fifteen feet from where Fayette Martin's body was found.

The arresting officer that day was Michael P. Ryan, then a rookie patrolman. And Paris sees the mistake right away. The wrong address is on the search warrant. Michael had typed in 4006 Central Avenue. The room *next* to Anthony del Blanco's room. And it was in 4008 that the investigating officers found Anthony's clothes, covered with his ex-wife's blood, the evidence needed to prosecute him.

Also in the safe is a news clipping, a small *Cleveland Press* article about how Anthony del Blanco was released from prison after spending only ten months in jail on a ten-year stretch, having been sprung on a technicality.

The body in the parking lot, Paris thinks.

The mutilated man with the barbwire crown.

Paris looks again at the bottom of the arrest report. He is not surprised to find that Mike Ryan's partner that day was Demetrius Salters.

He flips a page, reads on. Lydia del Blanco had two children: a boy and a girl. There are two photos. One, taken of the crime scene where Lydia del Blanco was beaten, tells one story. The woman is not in the photo, just the huge Rorschach of her blood. There is also a book lying on the kitchen floor, near the refrigerator.

The Secret Garden.

The old man's mantra.

The other photo is one from happier times, a color-faded photo of the woman and her two children at Euclid Beach. Pretty woman, white-rimmed sunglasses, white dress. Her daughter, sitting on her lap, is maybe six or so; the little boy a toddler.

Is this little girl Sarah Weiss? Paris thinks.

And what about the little boy?

Evil is a breed, Fingers.

Paris is no linguist, but he knows enough German and Spanish to know that Weiss equals White. And that White equals *Blanco*.

Mike Ryan's murder had nothing to do with a deal gone bad, Paris thinks, his hands trembling slightly with the knowledge. Nothing at all.

Mike Ryan was executed.

❖ 54 ❖

SHE STANDS IN the lobby of the Wyndham Hotel, the box under her left arm. She is wearing a short platinum wig, tinted glasses, a Givenchy suit. She looks at her watch for the hundredth time in the past ten minutes, cocks her right foot out of her shoe for a moment, giving her toes a break. Her gray pumps are a half-size too small.

At three-ten, the young man in the Ace Courier jacket enters the lobby, looks left and right. He sees her—his eyes giving her body a quick twice-over, once he realizes that the silver hair is attached to a shapely young woman—then approaches, smiling, clipboard in hand.

"Hi," he says.

"Hello," she replies.

"Are you Miss O'Malley?"

"Yes, I am," she says. "I'd like to have a package delivered."

❖ 55 ❖

FIVE O'CLOCK. Paris checks the Cleveland White Pages. Zero. He runs a computer check on *del Blanco*. Nothing. He runs an Internet white pages search for Ohio and gets nothing. Not a single del Blanco in Ohio.

Shit.

At five-ten, Paris learns that two agents from the Cleveland field office of the FBI are meeting with all unit commanders. Paris had expected it, although it means he will soon be a back-bencher on this case. There is evidence of serial murder here, plus a lot of forensic material with which the lab at the Justice Center is ill equipped to deal.

And what to do with what he found in Mike Ryan's safe? Was Mike Ryan killed for messing up a search warrant? Is this enough to activate the investigation into Mike's murder? And wouldn't producing a stolen police report that was in Mike Ryan's possession just smear his name further?

On the other hand, how could the fact that Anthony del Blanco once lived in the Reginald Building be coincidence?

Five-thirty. The photographs of the victims, along with all the other players, and potential players, are in a loose square on the floor in Paris's office. As are all of the sketches. Furniture has been pushed to the walls. Paris circles the pictures, stalking the clue hidden there.

A grim spectacle stares up at him.

Faces of the dead.

Sarah Weiss. *Burned to death in a car.*

Michael Ryan. *Shot in the head.*

Willis Walker. *Bludgeoned and castrated.*

Isaac Levertov. *Strangled.*

Edith Levertov. *Broken neck.*

Fayette Martin. Paris pauses, as he has every time he has looked at her picture, and considers those innocent eyes. Someone had looked deeply into those eyes, seen the life there, and then slaughtered her.

And then there is Jeremiah Cross.

If the little girl in that photo is Sarah Weiss, then she is central to this. And if Sarah Weiss ever had an advocate, literally and spiritually, it is Jeremiah Cross.

Paris asks himself: What do we know about Jeremiah Cross?

We know that Jeremiah Cross just *happened* to appear like magic on the Cleveland high-profile defense scene when Mike Ryan was killed. We know that Jeremiah Cross blames the department for his client's suicide. We know that Jeremiah Cross has a hard-on for Paris every time they see each other. We know that Jeremiah Cross could easily fit the general description of the hot dog vendor. We know that Jeremiah Cross shares a last initial with the man, "Mr. Church," who had called before Christmas and warned Paris of the *ofún.*

Church.

Cross.

Religious terms.

But, if Sarah Weiss changed her name from Blanco, why Cross? Why would he pick that name? What is Cross in German?

No idea.

And what about Spanish? What is Cross in Spanish?

Cruz.

No, Paris thinks. Don't *even* go there.

He looks once again at the photograph of Lydia del Blanco and her two children. Knowing it's a long shot, and deciding to keep it to himself for the time being, he picks up the phone, punches Tonya Grimes's number. Tonya is one of the two investigators on duty.

"Grimes."

"Tonya, Jack Paris."

"Hi, handsome. What can I do for ya?"

"Two things. One, I need a full workup on a Jeremiah Cross, local attorney." He spells it. "All I have is a PO box in Cleveland Heights."

"That's it?"

"Sorry." Paris gives her the box number.

"No sweat. Don't need more than that when Tonya is on ya."

"That's why we call."

"And you need it . . . when?"

"Any time this year," Paris says, treading lightly.

Tonya laughs. "*Boy* are you lucky that law enforcement is my first and only love."

"We love you on six, Tonya. You know that."

"Doesn't *that* sizzle my slippers on New Year's Eve. What else?"

"I need you to cross reference a homicide by the victim's name."

"Who's the vic?"

"Anthony C. del Blanco."

"Got it."

"Thanks, Tonya. Call me."

"On the case, detective."

Paris hangs up, glances back at the mess on the floor.

All right. Where is the *straight* line from Mike Ryan to Fayette Martin to Willis Walker to the Levertovs?

Before the line can begin to be drawn in his mind, Paris hears Greg Ebersole's heels clicking down the hall. Fast. Greg grabs onto the doorjamb, pokes his head into Paris's office.

"We've got physical," Greg says, out of breath.

"Lay it on me."

"Just walked in the front door."

"What are you talking about?"

"Just got a package via courier. Inside was a leather jacket. The delivery kid said he picked it up from a woman in the lobby at the Wyndham. He's with a sketch artist now."

"You think it's the jacket Fayette and the killer talked about online?"

"I'm betting on it."

"Why?" Paris asks.

Greg finds his wind, says: "It's covered in blood."

Paris stares at the jacket on the lab table, trying to think of a single reason why it doesn't look *exactly* like the jacket Rebecca wore when he had seen her at Pallucci's, the jacket that had felt so sexy in his hands. This jacket is a motorcycle type, studded and multizippered. So was Rebecca's.

But there are millions of them, right?

When Greg had said "covered in blood" he meant, as many cops do, that there was trace evidence, not that it was blood-*soaked*. There certainly is not a great deal visible to the naked eye, but as Paris watches the lab techs work, he sees that they are retrieving samples from all over the jacket, inside and out.

At seven-forty P.M., December 31, the break comes. Buddy Quadrino, head of the CPD's latent print unit, is standing in the doorway to Elliott's office. Paris and Carla Davis hold down the chairs.

"Have good news, BQ," Carla says wearily. "*Please* have good news."

Buddy holds up a sheaf of paper, grinning broadly. "We've got patterns," he says. "If he's anywhere in anybody's database we'll have him in four or five hours."

Paris and Carla high-five, then bolt for the door.

Captain Randall Elliott picks up his phone, slams a button, and barks a command he'd held inside for the past six days: "Get me the prosecutor's office."

❖ 56 ❖

THE SOUTH EUCLID library, the splendid, multilevel stone building that was once the William E. Telling estate on Cleveland's far-east side, has an archive of back issues of the *Plain Dealer,* as well as the long-defunct *Cleveland Press.*

Mary sits down at one of the microfilm readers, loads the film, her heart accelerating with the whirring of the reels. Days, weeks, months fly by in a blur of light gray. So many stories. She zeroes in on the date. It hadn't taken her long to find it. What had Jean Luc said that night?

It takes place a few years ago. I was barely a teenager. If I remember correctly, the Indians beat the Minnesota Twins that day. . . .

After a little digging, and a little math based on Jean Luc's age, she finds only three likely dates. The first two produce nothing. She forwards to the day after the third date and feels her skin begin to crawl when she finds the small article in the Metro section.

CLEVELAND MAN FOUND BEATEN, MUTILATED.

The dead man's name was Anthony C. del Blanco.

She follows the story for the next five weeks, checking every page on which a follow-up story might be run. Nothing. It seems the investigation just evaporated. No arrest, no suspects, no justice for the dead man. Even if the dead man was a pig.

279

Jean Luc and his sister had simply gotten away with murder.

On page B-8 of the current *Plain Dealer*, she finds another story of interest, one that tugs at her heart. It is accompanied by a photo of Jack Paris standing next to a tall, fair-skinned guy. She reads the caption. The event was a benefit for Max Ebersole, six. A Fraternal Order of Police benefit that raised more than twenty-nine hundred dollars.

She looks into Paris's eyes, at his smile, the way his presence just fits so perfectly in this setting, a benefit for someone else. She looks at his big hands, recalling them on her body and how protected she had felt, how good.

And knows, without question, that it is over.

❖ 57 ❖

THE CAULDRON IS FULL. I can watch the tape again. I put my coat on, cross the living room, power-up the VCR, hit Play.

"This was a cold-blooded killing of a police officer in the line of duty," the man in the old video begins. *"I think the evidence will show that the defendant, Sarah Weiss, pulled the trigger. . . . Mike Ryan was a good cop. . . . Mike Ryan was a family man . . . a man who woke up every day and chose—chose—to strap on a gun and jump into the fray. . . . Mike Ryan died in the line of duty protecting the people of this city. . . . So the next time you find yourself picking through a pile of garbage, or hiding in the bushes like some pervert, or running down the street with a forty-pound video camera just so you can invade the privacy of a heartbroken ten-year-old girl in a wheelchair, I want you to stop, take a deep breath, and ask yourself what the hell it is you do for a living . . . Mike Ryan took a bullet for the people of this city. . . . Mike Ryan was a hero."*

This is where the woman reporter asks a question I cannot hear.

But I hear the man's response. Loud and clear and full of arrogance. I have heard it every ten minutes, like maddening clockwork, for a very long time. As I listen, my silence momentarily gives way to the sound of a beast, stirring in its nap.

"Sometimes, the monster is real, people," the man says. *"Sometimes, the monster has a pretty face and a perfectly ordinary name. This time, the monster is called Sarah Weiss."*

❖ 58 ❖

RONNIE'S FAMOUS IS fully lighted, empty. Paris had called Ronnie earlier in the day and asked him to put together two dozen doughnuts and coffee for the stakeout team. And damned if there aren't a pair of bulging white bags on the counter, right next to the register, right next to a tray of large white foam cups and one of Paris's thermoses. Even on New Year's Eve. Paris had said he would be by at nine-thirty, and he is right on time.

Paris makes a U-turn, parks in front of the shop, grabs his empty thermos, steps inside, his mind afloat on the increasingly bizarre facts of a case that is starting to look like it began twenty-six years ago when a woman named Lydia del Blanco got beaten nearly to death by her ex-husband, a man who once lived at Fortieth and Central.

Is this why Fayette Martin was lured to the Reginald Building?

Is this why Michael Ryan was murdered?

If God is doling out luck this New Year's Eve, he will begin to get some of these answers in the next few hours. One way or another.

Paris looks around Ronnie's. No customers at the short counter. No one behind the glass. Paris can hear the whine of a vacuum cleaner in the back, the sound of a television.

"Ronnie?" Paris yells.

Nothing.

"Ronnie?"

Just the mewl of a motor and some kind of sitcom. Paris grabs everything on the counter, drops a twenty, then turns to leave before Ronnie Boudreaux can come out of the back room and object.

"Happy New Year, Ronnie!" Paris yells, but he is certain the drone of the vacuum has drowned him out.

As Paris approaches his apartment building he sees two men standing by the front door. Two familiar shapes. Bobby Dietricht and Greg Ebersole. At *his apartment*.

A first.

Something must be going down. Why hadn't they called?

Paris parks on East Eighty-fifth Street, grabs his thermos. "Hey, guys," he says, climbing the steps, letting the surprise register on his face. "What's up? We have a name?"

"Hey," Bobby Dietricht says, reading the surprise, ignoring the question.

The three men step inside the lobby of Paris's building as an icy gust wraps around the building. "What's goin' on?" Paris asks, checking his watch. He is due at the Westwood stakeout in thirty-five minutes. "We starting a doo-wop group?"

Greg laughs a little too hard. Although he is on the task force, he is not part of the raid team. Early that evening, amid Greg's violent protests, Captain Elliott had taken one look at him and ordered him off duty.

Bobby Dietricht reaches into his overcoat and pulls out a manila envelope. "Full lab reports are in."

"What?" Paris says. "Why the hell didn't someone call me?"

"This is it, Jack," Bobby says. "This is the call. I just got the report ten minutes ago."

"What's Elliott's take?" Paris asks.

"He hasn't seen them yet."

Wrong answer, Paris thinks. Wrong, *wrong* answer. *Why not?* "Talk to me, Bobby."

"We've got matches. All over the fuckin' map. Blood, prints."

"No shit."

"None. Most of the blood is Fayette Martin's. But there was also trace evidence of Willis Walker's blood, too."

"What about the prints?"

A look passes between Greg and Bobby. "Yeah. We've got a match. And we've got it a half-dozen times."

"Do we *like* someone? Please tell me we *like* someone."

"Yes and no," Bobby says. "Mostly no."

"What the hell are you saying? We have a hit on the prints or not?"

Bobby nods.

"Great," Paris says, his stomach starting to centrifuge with tiny needles that soon work their way down to his groin, where the real fear lives. And he knows why. "We've got the connection."

"Not so great," Greg says, a look of distilled heartbreak on his face.

"The prints," Bobby says, cop-stare locked in place, cold and unnerving. Paris had never been on this side of it.

"What about them?" Paris asks.

Bobby: "They're yours."

❖ 59 ❖

THE FIFTH TIME she dials Jesse Ray's pager number she stops, halfway, then quietly hangs up the phone, defeated, her tears no longer an enemy. No one is going to save her. No one is going to wave a magic wand and keep her out of prison. This had gotten so bad, so fast, that everything she had worked for in the past two years seemed to be slipping away. If she had just been able to get the money into a trust for Bella, to show her father that the little girl's future was secured, she might have had a life.

Jean Luc had told her to call no one, to stay inside her apartment until he came for her.

But she knows that if she can just get to her car, she will find the courage to drive down to the Justice Center, walk inside and start talking before she can stop herself.

She puts on her navy wool parka. In her right pocket she slips her Buck knife. In her left pocket is her pepper spray.

Keeping the lights off, she crosses the apartment, tiptoes through the small foyer, sidles up to the door. She checks that the security chain is on, the deadbolt turned. She looks through the peephole: just the fish-eye view of the hall, exactly the way it looks every time she gets paranoid and peers through it. Quiet, empty, monastic. She puts her ear to the door, listens. Nothing. Not even the hum of the elevators. She looks through the peephole again, then takes a step back, turns her deadbolt to the left and silently rotates the knob, opening the door an inch.

She is alone.

She steps through the door, locks it, eases her way to the stairwell, cringing at the sound of the squeaky hinge. A few moments later she steps into the small, deserted Cain Manor apartment lobby. Earlier, she had come home to find a pair of men working on the front doors. They told her that, due to the recent murder in Cain Park, they were putting in new, high security locks. The thought had made her feel a little better, but only a *very* little.

Now it no longer matters.

She glances around the empty lobby, then floats silently down the corridor and out into the rear parking lot.

The first thing she notices is the deep lavender moonlight on the snow. As she approaches her parking space, the light on her car returns a greenish cast to her eye, a color that makes her pause for a moment, disoriented, thinking it may not *be* her car. A glance at the license plate. It *is* her yellow Honda. Right where it is supposed to be. Then why is—

She stops in the middle of the thought, her mind tripping over an image that her heart doesn't seem to want to process. She cannot understand why someone is sitting in the passenger seat of her car. She cannot understand why this person looks so familiar.

She cannot understand why *Isabella is sitting in the passenger seat of her car.*

It is Bella's tam-o'-shanter, her round face, her dark curly hair. Yet, although most of her daughter's face is obscured by shadow, one thing is clear to Mary, and that is this:

Her daughter is not moving.

"Bella!"

Mary sprints to the car, slipping on the ice, fumbling with the keys, a spike of raw terror in her heart. It seems like a full minute before she can get the key in the frozen lock, the frosted window now clouding with her breath, concealing her daughter's tiny form.

She whips open the door and grabs her child from the front seat. Too hard, too light, not a child not a child not Isabella *not Isabella*—

The world stops. Relief washes over her in a huge hot wave, taking her legs out from under her. She falls to her knees.

It is not her daughter.

It is Astrid, her daughter's big doll, the one she herself had sent by UPS for Isabella's last birthday. *Astrid wearing Isabella's old clothes*.

Release, first.

Then confusion.

Then, a reprise of her fear.

Because there, in the plum-colored moonlight, pinned to the doll's coat, is a directive that Mary has no trouble at *all* understanding, a square of white paper bearing a simple message:

Go back.

❖ 60 ❖

THE BLUE SATURN turns the corner for the third time. It has the look of a car well maintained, the imperious sheen of a vehicle that is the very first automobile ever purchased off a showroom floor after a series of beaters. And, although things like road salt, cinders, slush, and goopy carbon by-products abound on such a winter night, as the blue Saturn passes I can see the occasional streetlamp reflected off its smooth, muscular lines in starry patterns.

The woman at the wheel looks left and right, left and right, searching for a parking space, a block or so south of Carnegie on East Eighty-fifth Street. She finds one, squeezes the Saturn in expertly, then exits the car, moves to the trunk, opens it. As I approach I see her reach inside and remove a camera case. She is wearing a long double-breasted coat, a knitted red scarf.

She has courage. I will give her that. By the way she is skulking around, I can tell she isn't supposed to be here. I guarantee that Jack Paris has told her not to come to his apartment.

I have no hatred for her, but she will certainly get in my way.

At the last second, the crunch of snow beneath my feet alerts her to my presence. She spins around, looks into my eyes. And remembers.

Just like a reporter.

"Hola, chica!" I say. "Buy you a fruity cocktail?"

❖ 61 ❖

AS SOON AS Bobby said the word *midnight,* Paris knew
that it was not going to be enough time. He also knew that
it was a favor he would probably never be able to repay,
one for which he had not even presumed to ask. Bobby Dietricht and Greg Ebersole are both in possession of conclu-
sive forensic evidence in a capital murder case and are
willfully delaying the submission of these facts to their superior officer. This is obstruction of justice at the very
least, not to mention the violation of a truckload of other
laws.

Serious jail time.

At midnight, Bobby Dietrich will have no choice but to
place the file on Randall Elliott's desk. And at that time,
Captain Elliott will have no choice but to issue a warrant for
the arrest of John Salvatore Paris.

"You all right with this?" Paris asks.

"Wouldn't be here if I wasn't," Bobby Dietrich says.
Greg just nods.

Paris had told them everything. Rebecca. Mike Ryan. Jeremiah Cross. Demetrius Salters. It had come out in a flat-
ulent roar, the tension with it. He could deal with someone
setting him up.

But, by *midnight*?

The problem is that they could not get a search warrant
for Rebecca's apartment without cause, and cause could

not be established until the lab reports were submitted. Besides, there is nothing physical tying her to the jacket. To search Rebecca's apartment, legally, would be to implicate Paris.

Bobby Dietricht and Greg Ebersole will work Rebecca D'Angelo's apartment on their own time. Starting right now.

Bobby adds: "Besides, I'm married, Jack. I ain't fuckin' dead. I saw her at the Cleveland League party. You don't have to explain a damn thing."

"You don't think I—"

Bobby holds up his gloved hand, stopping him. "I don't know a cop in this city who would."

Paris immediately regrets every negative thought he'd ever had about Detective Robert Dietricht. "I don't know how to thank you two."

"Three," Greg says.

"Three?"

"Yeah," Greg says with a wink. "I guaran*tee* you Mike Ryan's working this detail."

Paris heads upstairs, opens his apartment door, sees a FedEx envelope on the floor. "Do Not Bend: Photos" a label says on the outside. The photographs Mercedes's brother took. Paris is not exactly in the mood to look at himself. He tosses the envelope on the table, pours himself coffee, gulps a cup. Twenty minutes until he has to be at the Westwood Road house. Bobby and Greg are off to the Heights.

How could he have been so fucking stupid? How could he have thought, even for a minute, that a woman like Rebecca—or whatever the hell her name is—would be the slightest bit interested in him?

She is good though, he thinks. Jesus *Christ,* she is good.

But why is she doing this?

Could he have been *that* wrong when he looked into her eyes?

Or does the killer have something on her?

Regardless, he does not relish the idea of her on a witness

stand. He grabs his keys, his Kevlar vest from the dining room table. Manny perks for a moment, but soon senses he isn't involved. He rolls over on the couch.

Paris is almost out the door when the phone rings.

"Paris."

"Jack, Tonya Grimes."

"What do you have?"

"I have half. I have a listing of a homicide victim named Anthony C. del Blanco. The funny thing is, that's *all* I have."

"What do you mean?"

"I mean, all I have is a *stat*. There's no paper."

Paris's heart sinks.

Mikey.

No.

"Nothing at all?" Paris asks.

"Not a shred. No interviews, no photos, no autopsy reports. Zip. I looked under other spellings, just in case it was misfiled, but nothing turned up. Just a computer entry listing him as a vic. Weird, huh?"

"Yeah," Paris says, absently. "Thanks, Tonya."

"Listen, I'm getting a fax right now. It may be about this Jeremiah Cross. Let me call you right back."

"Okay." Paris hangs up the phone, his mind beginning to connect the dots between Mike Ryan and Sarah Weiss. It is then that he notices the blinking message light on his answering machine. He pours a half-cup of coffee from his thermos, glances at his watch. He has time. He hits Playback.

"Hi . . . it's Mercedes . . . 'bout nine-thirty . . . I was wondering . . . what's the penalty for killing a little brother in Ohio? . . . can't be much . . . probably like a fine or something, right? . . . anyway . . . I know you're not there . . . you're off to the big raid I'm not allowed to attend and all . . . kidding . . . anyway . . . I just talked to my brother Julian and, after enduring much threat, he confessed that he never showed up to take your picture, so whoever you met that day was definitely not my brother . . . anyway, seeing as

*he's only fifteen and can't exactly drive over there tonight,
especially with my foot up his ass, I'm going to get in my car
right now and drive over myself and wait for you . . . sorry
again . . . you can't trust Puerto Rican/Irish people . . . what
can I tell you . . . good luck . . . okay . . . bye . . . happy new
year . . . bye."*

Fifteen, Paris thinks. What the hell is she talking about?
Her brother Julian is only fifteen? Who the fuck was it at
the Justice Center that day, then? And who the fuck was it
in the parking lot at the Cleveland League party?

It hits him.

What was it that Mercedes had said the day she called him
from Deadlines, the day she had told him that her brother
might show up to take pictures?

*"Well, at the moment, there is a fabulously handsome,
ethnically diverse male sitting right next to me, trying to ply
me with fruity cocktails. . . ."*

Paris dives for the dining room table and the FedEx envelope that contains the photographs. He tears it open to find
an eight by ten of himself standing by the window in the Justice Center lobby, a bright red hole drawn in the center of his
forehead.

He has seen his *face*.

Before he can pick up the phone to call in the description
of the devil himself, he notices something hanging from the
inside of his apartment door. He tries to move toward it, cannot.

As the *Amanita muscaria* begins to rocket through his
veins, he understands.

He understands why no one came out of the back room at
Ronnie's. He understands that every single move he has
made in the past week or so has been watched, observed,
noted. He understands that the psychopath the entire department is looking for had known he was heading to Ronnie's
for coffee and had made sure that Jack Paris had gotten a
special brew, a brew of whatever was in Mike Ryan's blood-
stream the day he died, a brew intended for the entire stake-

out team, and Jack Paris suddenly knows that, if the feeling beginning to surge through him now is any indication of where he is going, it will surely end in a dread that is deeper, and colder, than any he has ever known.

❖ 62 ❖

THE BOYS ARE ten and eleven. They are supposed to be watching television in their grandmother's basement, but, instead, they are standing at the corner of Fulton Road and Newark Avenue, across from the St. Rocco's rectory, passing a Winston Light back and forth, cupping it in hand as they had seen the older kids do.

At a few minutes after ten they see a cop car trolling Fulton, so they work their way down the alley that runs behind the strip of stores that begins with Aldonsa's Tailors and ends with that heebie-jeebie voodoo place on the corner.

The younger boy looks around the Dumpster for a piece of foil in which to wrap the sacred remains of their last smoke. There is foil all *over* the place, courtesy of the take-out, but it all seems to be covered in barbecue sauce or spilled Pepsi.

Too short to see inside the Dumpster, the younger boy reaches over the rim, feels around the debris, and feels something wet. Something thick and viscous and sticky.

More barbecue sauce?

"Shit," the boy says, pulling back his hand. And realizes immediately that it doesn't smell like barbecue sauce at all. In fact, it smells like *shit*. Actual *shit*.

The two boys hoist themselves up to the rim of the Dumpster.

The corpse inside was, at one time, a man. This much is

obvious, due to the fact that the man is naked. But there is also a huge hole where the man's middle used to be. The area from his throat to his groin is cut into a long, flayed crescent, the fat and skin and muscle pulled to the sides in a surprised rictus of a smile, the contents glistening beneath the overhead vapor lights like maroon slabs of liver at the West Side Market.

The boy had reached directly into the man's lower intestine, into fully digested *arroz con pollo*.

Although the dead man has rings on every one of his fingers—huge shiny stones that shimmer like multicolored prisms—the boys do not take them. Instead, they run as fast as they can, wind-whipped and mind-shattered, and do not stop until they reach West Forty-first Street and the arms of Jesus in the close, blessed safety of their grandmother's basement.

Light snow, bitter cold. Ten-fifteen P.M.

The Ochosi task force, eight officers strong, is deployed in two locations, neither more than a block from the Westwood Road house. One team of four SWAT officers is in an unmarked tech van at the corner of Edgerton and Fenwick Roads. The other is in an SUV down the street from the Westwood Road address, at the bottom of the hill, a distance of less than half a mile. Within ninety seconds, both teams could arrive at the scene.

Sergeant Carla Davis sits in an unmarked car a half-mile away, in the Kaufmann's parking lot, dressed in civilian clothes. The raid is scheduled for midnight, now less than two hours away. The task force has established a scrambled command frequency, so even if someone in the house is monitoring the channels, they will not pick up the task force traffic.

The bad news, on Westwood Road, is that it appears as if every house on the street is having a party. Every few seconds another car passes the tech van's position, brake lights aglow, looking for a parking space, a space that is becoming harder and harder to find. People seem to be coming and going from every house on the block.

A half-mile north, Carla Davis tries to reach Jack Paris.

Greg Ebersole's cell phone rings at ten-twenty-one. He is on Cedar Road, heading to the Cain Manor apartments. Bobby Dietricht is in the car behind him.

"Greg Ebersole."

"Detective, this is Tonya Grimes."

"Yeah, what's up, Tonya?"

"I can't reach Jack Paris. I talked to him ten minutes ago and now I can't find him. Is he with you?"

Greg shoots a protective glance at the rearview mirror. Bobby is good. *What's going on here?* "No. I just left him, though. What do you have?"

"Got one Jeremiah David Cross, attorney at law."

"I'm listening."

"Mr. Cross is a Caucasian male, twenty-nine years old, six feet, one-eighty-five, brown over brown. Got his law degree from American University in Mexico City. No wife, no kids, no—"

"Address, Tonya. *Address.*"

"Mr. Cross lives at 3050 Powell."

"Where is that exactly?"

"Cleveland Heights. Right near the Cain Towers apartments."

Five minutes later, Greg Ebersole, Carla Davis, and Robert Dietricht meet at the Lee Road entrance to Cain Park.

All three police officers have something to do before midnight.

❖ 63 ❖

THE FIRST SENSATION is one of near-weightlessness. Floating an inch or so off the floor. Light head, light arms, light legs. He feels as if his body is suddenly manufactured of smoke, as if he possesses no footsteps, as if a slight breeze might urge him around his apartment, cornice-high, allowing him to cavort along the ceiling for a while, leaving no trace of his presence, no residue of his passing. Light and ethereal and vaporous and . . .

Invisible.

That's the feeling. The dream of every adolescent and postadolescent boy. To have the ability to become invisible and tread where laws and rules and adults and signs do not allow.

As he looks around the mysterious landscape of his own apartment, the sensation becomes amphetamine-like. He had popped a few white crosses in his first year on night duty, a few orange-triangled Benzedrines to ward off those sleep demons, but had never indulged in LSD or mescaline or psilocybin or any other of the hallucinogens along his crazy path through the seventies. As a cop, of course, he had seen way too much collateral carnage to the hard drugs like cocaine and heroin to consider them anything but a scourge on urban life.

But this . . .

He can *use* this. He suddenly understands everything

about everything. He suddenly knows exactly what he needs to know about everything he needs to know about.

This is *cop fuel*.

Behind him, a door slams. He turns, slowly, and sees a note pinned to the inside of his apartment door.

A note to *him*?

On the inside?

He floats toward it. No, not a note. A note*book*. A spiral notebook covered with red and blue hearts. It is nailed to the door with a huge spike.

Soon, the blue hearts begin to caper and swirl and, before Paris can place the image, he hears a noise, a soft footfall on the carpeting behind him. He turns to see a slender woman approaching—black hair, pale skin, almond shaped eyes. She wears a short white skirt, a black leather jacket. She seems to be gliding toward him.

Across *his living room*.

Paris is unable to respond to her presence in any way. Who is she? Where had he seen her before? She is surely from a dark place in his past, a room currently unavailable to his memory.

She continues toward him. Graceful, confident, like a runway model. She has full lips. The blackest eyes.

She stops in front of him.

And that's when Paris feels the tap on his shoulder. He turns, dream-slow, to see the familiar face of the man standing behind him, to hear the *whoosh* of an arm breaking the stillness, to feel his head suddenly detonate into a glittery flourish of Technicolor, a painless implosion of red and orange and yellow sprites. He slumps against the wall, reveling in the ascension of the magic mushroom, reeling with remembrance.

And, before he falls unconscious, knows.

The woman is Sarah Weiss.

❖ 64 ❖

IT WAS THE hardest phone call she had ever made. She had not spoken to her father in more than ten months and was terrified he might answer the phone. But she had no choice. Luckily, her cousin Anita was visiting for the holidays and had answered and told her, with a rather subdued voice, that Isabella was fine, was trying her best to stay awake until midnight.

She also said that someone had recently stolen Astrid, Isabella's big doll, from the back porch. Anita said Bella's tantrum—eased somewhat by back-to-back viewings of *The Little Mermaid* and *The Lion King,* and a small bag of Famous Amos—wasn't fully over yet.

Mary had hung up the phone and found that her difficulty breathing had begun to ebb.

Slightly.

She knew the police couldn't help her this night, not if Jean Luc could so easily get to her. How could she take the chance?

If she could just speak to Celeste. To Jesse Ray. If she could just have someone to *talk* to.

She had paged Jesse Ray a dozen times in the past twenty minutes.

At ten-thirty the phone rings. She whips the phone from the cradle.

"Celeste?"

A lot of static. Through it, she hears: "No. This is Jesse Ray."

It is the first time she has ever spoken to him. His voice seems deep, a baritone. But it is too scratchy to tell anything else. A cellular call from the fringe of its range.

She begins to talk. She tells him everything, the words tumbling out—how she helped set up Paris, how Jean Luc had threatened her this night, how Jean Luc had threatened Isabella. When she finishes her tale, Jesse is silent for a few moments. If not for the static, she might think he had hung up.

Then, as casually as someone might agree to help you move furniture, Jesse Ray saves her life. "I'll take care of this for you," he says. "We'll be there in five minutes."

Her heart soars.

Maybe there *is* a way out of all this.

She wears black jeans, hikers, a thick sweatshirt. Her parka is on the couch, as is her shoulder bag. For the hundredth time in the past ten minutes, beginning the moment she'd hung up the phone, she steps over to the front window, looks out.

And, suddenly, in the carbon blue light of the Dairy Barn sign, he is there. Jesse Ray's dark sedan is parked across the street, its exhaust pipe spewing big, gray reassuring fumes, his left arm sticking out of the window, gold watch gleaming, his hand holding the ever-present cigarette, just like always.

Then, the passenger door opens and Celeste, wearing a broad-brimmed hat and huge fur coat, exits the car, crosses the street, toward the apartment building.

The phone rings.

"Hello?"

Static. Interference from the neon across the street. "Celeste is in the lobby. Buzz her in."

She vaults across the room, hits the button, hoping the new locks work with her old buzzer. "Okay?"

"Yeah. She's in," Jesse Ray says. "Listen, she's got a gun with her. Let her in, lock the door behind her, and wait for me."

She moves back over to the window. "All right."

"And keep the damn lights down. I can see you up there."

"Okay. I'll turn them off."

"Do you know how to use an automatic?" Jesse Ray asks.

"No."

"Have you ever fired a gun before?"

"No."

Pause. "Well, Celeste has."

Before she can respond there comes a knock at the door.

Mary puts down the phone, runs across the living room, her heart hammering in her chest, hardly believing that Celeste will be on the other side, hardly believing that her friends, her *only* friends, have come to help her, hardly believing that this nightmare is about to come to an end.

She opens the door.

It is not Celeste.

It is Jean Luc. In his right hand is Celeste's hat, along with a bloody silver earring, shaped like an icicle.

In his left hand, a gun.

Jean Luc points the gun at Mary's forehead, eases back the hammer, and says: "You shouldn't have called them."

❖ 65 ❖

CARLA DAVIS RUSHES across the icy parking lot at the Cleveland Heights city hall. Bobby Dietricht has gone to Jeremiah Cross's address on Powell Road. Greg is on his way to the Cain Manor apartments. It is Carla's job to reach out to the Cleveland Heights PD before they begin banging on doors. Even though time is incredibly tight, it is absolutely necessary.

In the lobby of the Cleveland Heights city hall Carla sees two grim-faced men chatting by the elevators; one weasely and rail thin; the other portly, pockmarked. Carla recognizes the older, heavier of the men as Denny Sanchez, a Cleveland Heights detective.

She takes out her badge, and all three cops exhibit the usual camaraderie, tempered by the usual rivalry.

"What can we do for the city?" Sanchez asks.

Carla explains, in minimal detail, the need for Cleveland Heights assistance.

Sanchez buys half the loaf, says: "I think the chief will want a little bit more."

Carla glances at her watch. A *little bit more* puts Paris in the middle. "That's classified for the time being."

"Then so are the Cain Manor apartments," Sanchez says. "Just give me a name. I won't take it."

Carla hesitates for a moment. "Cross."

The skinny cop barks a laugh.

"Something funny?" Carla says, leaning in, towering over him.

"No," he says. "No ma'am."

Sanchez asks: "Is there somewhere we can call you?"

Carla holds the skinny cop's stare until he looks away, then says, "I can wait right here if you've got to talk to someone, Denny."

"Well, we have to clear this from *high* on high. You understand. It's New Year's Eve, for God's sake. Let me talk to Chief Blake. I'll call you right back."

"Like tonight?"

"Like in ten minutes," Sanchez says.

Carla flips him a card, holds up her phone. "Brand-new batteries, gents."

❖ 66 ❖

AN UNKNOWN ROOM. *Beyond* dark. Black walls, ceiling, floor. A large round object in front of him, like a kettle or an old gas grill. He is surrounded by candles, but the light is instantly devoured by the gloom, immediately digested into the air, thick with death. Thumping music comes from somewhere.

He had traveled, definitely. He had been in a car. He looks at the object on his lap.

It is a gun. *His* gun.

The smell is coming from the huge bowl in front of him. He leans forward and, as he does, in the scant light, he sees the putrefacted flesh, the blackened organs, the shimmer of a thousand maggots, fat with marrow. He bolts to the corner of the room and, like the inevitability of vomit itself, gives in to the nausea and retches on the floor, near the corner. His vision vibrates with colors around the edges.

He wipes his mouth, tries to steady himself, a deep paranoia rummaging inside him. He hallucinates wildly, thoughts and sounds and emotions whirling. He finds the chair, pulls it back to the wall, sits heavily.

One minute of black silence passes, then:

"Son?"

Paris raises his head. He sees a chair on the other side of the big kettle. A figure is sitting on it. Sitting? No. More like floating just an inch or so off the surface, a weightless, matterless being.

It is Frank Paris.

"Dad?"

The figure on the chair shimmers, disappears, returns, like a pixilated image coming and going from clear focus. His father is robust and healthy again. His hands look huge and nicked and dad-grimy.

For some reason, the sight of his father, dead these many years, does not scare him. What scares him is his father's *scrutiny*. After all this time his father can now assess him as a full-grown man, instantly, as he might a too-young doctor holding onto a clipboard that would chronicle the end of his life.

Jack Paris wonders: Am I tall enough? Am I smart enough? Am I man enough?

Am I *father* enough?

Frank Paris will say no to that one. *No, son, you are not father enough. You couldn't make your marriage work, and you will never be father enough to my granddaughter.*

Shimmer.

His father is suddenly thinner, young-old again, his face is drawn downward in a sallow avalanche of skin. In his hands, a battered Etch-A-Sketch.

Happy Birthday, Daddy!

"Do a trick for me, Jackie," his father says.

"What, Dad?"

Silence.

You've got to know what breaks his heart.

"Dad?"

Again, silence. The definition of empty.

His father is gone.

Then, suddenly, all the lights of hell explode in Jack Paris's eyes.

❖ 67 ❖

AT FIRST, to the 617 people tuned to Cable99 on New Year's Eve, it looks to be a scaled-down version of *Hollywood Squares*. Or *The Brady Bunch*. Four windows dividing the TV screen into four equal sections.

Closer examination, to those in the know, would yield the understanding that these are four separate computer-cam feeds, the sort of cybercast videos that jump and lurch and produce, overall, a rather vertiginous effect in the viewer.

Still, anything can happen on Cable99, and often did.

In the upper-left-hand frame is a disheveled man, early forties, maybe. He is sitting in a chair, staring blankly at the camera. But not moving. The room he is in looks to have very dark walls, and the bright lights cast harsh shadows across his face.

In the upper-right-hand corner is a still photo of a very exotic-looking young woman, a fashion model head shot, a real dark-eyed beauty. The lower two squares are blank.

In the control booth at Cable99, Furnell Braxton, the unlucky low man on the totem pole who drew New Year's Eve tech duty, casts a disinterested eye toward the monitor as he eats his Tony Roma's.

At eleven-thirty-one, a videotape begins to play in the lower-right-hand frame. It looks like a video of a man standing in front of the Justice Center, a place Furnell Braxton tries to avoid at all costs. The video is pretty jerky, as always, but Furnell is not a big believer in computer video anyway and truly hopes all concerned here understand.

Still, the audio seems to be running smoothly.

"This was a cold-blooded killing of a police officer in the line of duty," the smeary video image of the guy in front of the Justice Center says. *"I think the evidence will show that the defendant, Sarah Weiss, pulled the trigger."*

Performance artists, Furnell thinks. What a bunch. Still, anything's better than the woman who dresses her dogs up for tea once a month, then tapes the whole damn thing.

The tape continues: *"Mike Ryan was a good cop. . . . Mike Ryan was a family man . . . a man who woke up every day and chose—chose—to strap on a gun and jump into the fray. . . . Mike Ryan died in the line of duty protecting the people of this city."*

Furnell pops open his diet Dr Pepper, adjusts the skew, checks his light levels.

"So the next time you find yourself picking through a pile of garbage, or hiding in the bushes like some pervert, or running down the street with a forty-pound video camera just so you can invade the privacy of a heartbroken ten-year-old girl in a wheelchair, I want you to stop, take a deep breath, and ask yourself what the hell it is you do for a living. . . ."

"Damn straight," Furnell says as he unwraps his dessert.

"Sometimes, the monster is real, people," the man says. *"Sometimes, the monster has a pretty face and a perfectly ordinary name. This time, the monster is called Sarah Weiss."*

There is a break in the video, then, a new video image.

A young man, wearing Ray-Bans, sitting in a wing chair, in a brightly lit room.

Furnell nearly chokes on his soft drink when the man in the sunglasses says the words.

Within sixty seconds he is talking to his cousin Wallace. Wallace Braxton works the night shift at WKYC, the Cleveland affiliate station of NBC.

"Are you *sure*?" Wallace asks for the second time, already punching in his boss's speed-dial number.

"Absolutely," Furnell says. "Abso*lutely* sure. He said, 'Here, tonight, *live*, a police officer is going to commit suicide.'"

❖ 68 ❖

THE HOUSE IS DARK.

Bobby Dietricht had rung the bell, knocked on the front door, knocked on the back door, listened for a dog, listened for footsteps, peered in the windows. He had even tossed a few pebbles at the upstairs windows before hiding behind the huge maple tree on the front lawn.

Nothing.

Then he had repeated everything, just to be sure.

The house is unoccupied, he had concluded.

Or else someone inside sleeps the sleep of the dead.

Carla rolls up in front of Jeremiah Cross's house, headlights off. She meets Bobby around back and apprises him of her meeting with Denny Sanchez. Together they climb the small back porch, position themselves on either side of the door. Bobby pulls open the storm door and knocks one last time. He presses the doorbell and, in the stillness of the night, they can both hear the bell, loud and clear.

No answer, no lights flipping on upstairs, no response at all.

They draw their weapons.

Bobby holds open the storm door, tries the handle of the inner door, turns it. It is unlocked. He nods at Carla.

Weapons out front, the two police officers step inside, knowing that establishing probable cause to enter these premises, at this moment, is going to be uphill all the way if Jeremiah Cross has anything to do with these homicides.

But Jack Paris is in trouble, and thus there is no hesitation.

Silently, they agree to take their chances in court.

Five minutes later, at eleven-forty, the house has been searched, but not scoured. The first floor and basement contain nothing out of the ordinary, nothing any other upwardly mobile lawyer wouldn't have in his house. They had found no bodies, no blood, no sacrificial altars, no body parts in the freezer. If Jeremiah Cross is a serial murderer, he is one of the tidiest ever.

As Bobby Dietricht and Carla Davis begin to mount the stairs to give the second floor a more thorough search—drawers, nightstands, some boxes they had seen in closets—Carla's phone rings. "Hang on," she says, but Bobby continues up the stairs.

Carla steps into the kitchen. The raid is coming down in twenty minutes and this is probably the call. Thankfully, she is still within five minutes or so of the Westwood Road address. She steps into the kitchen, pulls her phone from her pocket. "Davis."

"Sergeant Davis, this is Dennis Sanchez."

"Yes, Denny, thanks for calling me right back. I appreciate it."

"Have you got a minute right now?"

"Absolutely."

"I think we've got something," Bobby yells from upstairs. *"There's a door at the back of the bedroom closet. . . ."*

"Wait for me, Bobby," Carla says, then puts her finger in her other ear. "Go ahead. I'm sorry."

Sanchez continues: "I talked to Chief Blake and he asked me to call you. Earlier, you made an inquiry about a man named Cross, yes?"

"That's right."

Bobby yells: *"It looks like . . . like some kind of altar. I think we've got this prick."*

Sanchez asks: "As in *Jeremiah* Cross of Powell Road, Cleveland Heights?"

"Yes," Carla replies, trying to pay attention to two things at once. "Why?"

"Can I ask what your interest is in Mr. Cross?"

"We like him in a homicide," Carla says. "That's really all I can say at this point."

Bobby says: *"Holy shit."*

Sanchez takes a deep breath and exhales slowly. "Bad news, then, I'm afraid. We just got the dental lab records an hour ago. Jeremiah Cross was shot to death in Cain Park a week ago. Had his hands cut off, too."

Jesus, Carla thinks. *Cross is not our actor.*

Cross was the DOA in Cain Park!

And that means—

Sanchez adds: "As of an hour ago, my John Doe became a *good* lawyer. I've got a team on the way to his house right now."

—setup.

Bobby.

From upstairs: *"There's some kind of . . . hel-lo . . . what the fuck is this?"*

"Bobby, *no!*"

In the instant before the explosion, as Carla rounds the corner and mounts the steps, she feels the air being sucked out of her lungs, even before she feels the searing heat of the blast.

On the third step, something punches through the drywall, just over her head, showering her in blackened gypsum. Then, a streak of flames chases down the stairs to her left, followed by a dark shape.

Carla Davis falls to her knees, lungs full of smoke, eyes burning, and realizes that the smoldering shape is Bobby Dietricht.

❖ 69 ❖

THE GUN IS in his coat pocket. For the moment. He had stepped inside her apartment and shut off most of the lights. She looks at the bloody silver earring on the coffee table. Celeste's earring. She chances another look out the window. Jesse Ray is still waiting in his car.

Her one thought is: *Can I throw something that far?*

"I . . . I don't care anymore," she says, trying to stall. On the mantel is a heavy bronze bust of Beethoven, about the size of her fist. If she could just get the window open, or broken, she would have one shot at pitching as far as she could, hopefully hitting somewhere, anywhere, on Jesse Ray's car. "I'm done. I'm not going to hurt anybody. My daughter will be cared for. Do what you gotta do."

"Do you know how much could happen to you by the time your friend makes it up here? A *lot*. All of it bad."

"Take your best shot."

"I want you to pick up the phone, call him, tell him everything is all right."

"No."

Jean Luc steps over to the window. Mary takes a step back, away from him. They look at the parking lot together, where the dark sedan idles next to the pay phone, at the cigarette smoke curling up into the night sky.

Jean Luc laughs. "That's your savior?"

Mary is just about to pick up the bronze bust when a white

313

van pulls into the Dairy Barn lot across the street, screeching to a halt. On its side is the NBC peacock logo. On the roof, a satellite rack.

What the hell's going on here? she thinks. *Why is a news crew setting up across the street from my apartment building?*

When Jean Luc removes his coat and begins to roll up his shirtsleeves, she knows. But it is a wisdom she does not want, a keen palisade of memory that tells her that the horror of this night had been ordained a very long time ago.

Because, there, on Jean Luc's forearm, is the tattoo of a bright orange rattlesnake.

This is the man who was fighting with Celeste in the hotel lobby two years ago, she thinks. *My life has been on a collision course with this moment for two . . . years.*

Her knees trick painfully, her mind reels out of control, her stomach revolts. She grabs onto the windowsill to steady herself and looks down to see the driver of the NBC van angling his vehicle toward Jesse Ray's sedan. It looks like the driver wants to get to the phone, but Jesse Ray isn't taking the hint.

The man puts the van in park, exits, crosses over to Jesse Ray's car, stops. He turns to glance at his partner, a quizzical look on his face, then reaches for Jesse Ray's arm and removes it from the car window. It is a mannequin arm clad in a black coat sleeve and a bright white cuff, the hand holding an all-but-burned-down cigarette.

The man from NBC scratches his head and smiles.

The cigarette falls to the ground.

Four floors above, Christian del Blanco—known over the years as a hundred different men, including a bon vivant named Jean Luc Christiane and a shadowy grifter named Jesse Ray Carpenter—laughs as he closes the shutters and draws the blinds, sparing the night this tableau for the moment, denying those madmen, who can surely hear such things, the song of Mary's scream.

❖ 70 ❖

PARIS CHECKS THE DOOR, the stench from the cauldron a thick, fetid fog that invades every cubic inch of air in the room. The door has an ordinary interior door lock, reversed. The door itself is solid core. The lock would go first. He feels along the ink black wall, finds the heavy plywood over the window, the black-painted heads of the lag bolts. Solid, too.

He surveys the small room, made smaller by the blackness. The cauldron, dead center. A sturdy wing chair. And, across from the chair, a small table with a computer and keyboard.

Not his father.

The computer is on, but the screen is deep blue, blank. Paris sits in the chair, tries to clear his head. He checks the magazine in his weapon. One bullet. The son of a bitch had left him with one bullet. He returns the magazine, jacks the round, clicks on the safety.

He checks his pockets. Right pocket. Twenty or thirty dollars in a paper clip. A packet of relish or ketchup from Subway. Left pocket. Empty.

One bullet, with condiments and hallucinations to go, Paris thinks.

Great.

❖ 71 ❖

THE MAN IS tall and thin, red-haired. He wears a cheap overcoat, sturdy black lace-up shoes. In the stale light thrown from the caged bulb on the wall in the underground service tunnel linking the Cain Manor and Cain Towers apartments, he looks tired and wan and deeply etched with worry. A man running on coffee, sugar, animal fat, liquor.

A cop.

"Evening," I say, the barrel of the twenty-two up against Mary's back. We stop walking. We are now about ten feet from the man.

"Evening," the red-haired man replies.

I feel Mary tense, about to bolt. "What's the weather like out there?"

"Getting pretty bad," the man says, turning his body slightly away from me, the sort of move a left-hander would make if he were going to unsnap the holster of a gun on his left hip, a weapon hiding beneath his coat. His voice echoes slightly in the concrete tunnel. Above us, a water pipe clangs.

"Looks like *we're* in for the evening," I say. "Wife's a little under the weather. Had to leave the party next door. Thank God for this walk-through, eh?"

"*Oh* yeah." The cop takes a step forward. "Are you all right, ma'am?"

"Like I said, she's a little nauseous. Bad shrimp or something, you know? Can't trust those bargain basement caterers."

"If you don't mind sir, I'd like to hear it from her. Now, ma'am, are you—"

Suddenly, the crackle of two-way radio traffic bursts from inside the red-haired man's coat.

Our eyes meet again.

And we are linked forever.

Before he can make his move I step behind Mary, lock an arm around her throat, put the barrel of the gun to her temple. The redheaded cop freezes.

I say: "Put your hands behind your head and interlace your fingers. Officer."

Slowly, reluctantly, he does. But he does not take his eyes from mine. His eyes are a deep green, unreadable, stoic in their calm. I know that this man can do me great harm.

"You have your handcuffs with you?" I ask.

The cop just stares.

I say: "Cuff yourself to the drainpipe."

"No."

I cock my weapon. Mary goes rigid beneath my hand. "Beg your pardon?"

"I'm not going to do it."

"And why is that?"

The cop looks at me with a weariness I have never before seen in a man his age. A resignation of *soul*. "Because I'm a beat-up cop, pal. You hear me? A used-up old flatfoot. Letting you handcuff me is a nightmare far worse than anything you could do with that gun. Believe this."

"Do you think I won't kill her?"

"Oh, don't get me wrong," the cop says. "I think you're *going* to kill her. I think you're going to kill me, too. You're just not going to do it to me while I'm cuffed to a drainpipe. I'm leaving my son more than that. Sorry."

I do not want to hear anymore of this.

I shoot him three times.

He stumbles backward and goes down, hard, flat on his back.

Mary shrieks. I cover her mouth. I put the gun to her head until the reality of her own death becomes apparent in her eyes. I lead her to the service elevator, then hit the button with my elbow. The car soon arrives.

I hear fire engines in the distance.

As we step inside I can also hear the traffic on the cop's radio. The elevator doors close just as a woman's voice says:

"Greg . . . Greg . . . you'd better get out . . . all hell is starting to break loose out here . . . Bobby's down . . . repeat . . . Bobby's down . . ."

❖ 72 ❖

HE LOOKS SO ORDINARY, Paris thinks. Better than average looks, he had thought when the man had played the part of Julian Cruz. Charming and easygoing.

He had shaken hands with a monster and not known it.

But now, seeing him sitting in a chair on the computer screen, in the upper-right-hand frame of four, he looks ordinary. In the upper-left-hand frame, Paris sees himself, sitting on the chair, live, courtesy of the small digital camera clipped to the monitor and the track lights overhead. In the lower right is the old video of himself on the steps of the Justice Center.

"Mr. del Blanco," Paris says.

"Christian, please, detective," the man says.

"Call this off."

"Did you enjoy your hot dog? Tasty?"

"Call this off."

"Too late for that."

"Let me ask you something," Paris says, trying to sound a lot more in control than he really is. The magic mushroom is still making his mind take wing in a thousand directions. "I understand why you're after me. I even understand why you went after Mike Ryan. But why the Levertovs?"

Christian reaches off camera. He brings back a trio of photographs. To Paris, they look like pictures of Christian coming and going from La Botanica Macumba. "Can you

319

believe these? Clandestine pictures of *me*." He laughs, holds them closer to the camera. "Turns out old Ike wasn't just selling kosher hot dogs on that corner, detective. He was one of these block-watch assholes. I had seen him around the corner a few times, passed the time of day with him, even met his wife. But about the fifth time I visited the botanica, he started to become suspicious, it seems, began taking *pictures*. Guess I wasn't the right breed. Believe me, the minute a voodoo murder and a sketch of the suspect showed up in the press he would have been on the phone. I needed time. Old Ike just meddled in the wrong man's business. Edith made the mistake of loving him." Christian puts the photos aside, leans forward, adds: "The important question is, how did *you* feel?"

"What do you mean?"

"To be a suspect. Even for a minute. How did it feel when people, people you've known for years, looked you straight in the eye and thought you were a monster? Did the shame of it all make you want to kill yourself? Make you want to get drunk and set yourself afire? *Hmm?* Show the world that Paris is, indeed, burning?"

In his mind's eye Paris sees Bobby's face, and how only ninety-nine percent of it believed him. "I know who my friends are. They know the truth."

"Truth," Christian says wistfully. He reaches out of frame, returns with a sterling flask, sips from it. "*Amanita muscaria*. Very potent. Have you ever tried it?"

Paris remains silent.

"Where did it take you on its brief, exhilarating voyage?"

Dad, Paris thinks. "You wouldn't begin to understand."

"Oh, I bet I would. The Hinchi Indians say it invokes ancient memories. What are *your* ancient memories, detective?" Christian leans forward, taps a few keys. Instantly, in the lower-right-hand frame, a picture appears. A picture of Frank Paris. A picture that was in the *Sun* newspaper next to his father's obituary. The anger rises in Paris's chest. His training pushes it back. Barely. He now knows what triggered his hallucination.

Christian says, "The first thing you should know is that I am in the very next room." On-screen, Paris sees Christian walk out of frame. Then, faintly: "Hear this?"

Paris hears a muffled pounding from behind him. "Yes."

Christian walks back into frame. "As I'm sure you know by now, you have only one bullet. In your life, right now, that bullet is currency. How will you spend it? The lock on the door? You could shoot it off, but then your gun would be empty and I would kill you."

Before Paris can stop himself, he looks back at the picture of his father, thinks about the photograph in this butcher's hands. He says: "Fuck *you.*"

Christian stares into the camera. Silent. Motionless. *Hurt.* As if a videotape had been put on freeze frame. Then, in a smear, he bolts out of frame, and, for twenty seconds the screen is a gray, out-of-focus blur. Then, the point of view changes to a longer shot, and Paris can now see that, in the bright white room next door there is an altar not unlike the chantry in Evangelina Cruz's basement. But this one is larger, covered in a huge, brilliant white cloth. There seem to be candles everywhere, staring up the lens of the digital camera. On the steps of the altar Paris sees dried animal claws outlined against the cloud white sheet. He sees earthen cruets bearing ancient symbols. He sees a half-dozen brass plates bearing cones of incense, stacks of copper coins.

But it is what Jack Paris sees behind the altar that terrifies him.

There, against the white wall, behind the shimmering candles and mysterious pottery and vaporous urns, is a huge white crucifix. And on it hangs a figure.

A familiar figure.

The figure of Rebecca D'Angelo.

❖ 73 ❖

I REMOVE MY shirt, pants, underwear, shoes, and socks. I slip the long white caftan over my head, my skin now electric with the feel of the rayon. I have never felt more the *brujo*, so full of power.

I undress my *madrina* on the crucifix. Her skin looks soft, sepulchral, white. I take out my big claw hammer. "Have you ever witnessed a real sacrifice, detective?"

"Listen to me," Paris says. "If she's dead, there isn't a rock big enough to hide under. Hear me?"

"She's not dead."

"Kill yourself. *Now.*"

"She is tied there," I say. "But, if you don't do exactly what I say, it can get worse." I hold up the silver spikes, sharpened to a razor point. "Much worse."

❖ 74 ❖

HE HAS TO keep the man talking. "How do we end this, Christian? Stop what you're doing and let's talk."

"I want you to draw your weapon."

Paris obeys. "Now what?"

"Put your bullet in the chamber."

"It's already loaded."

"Of course," Christian says. "Safety off?"

"Safety's off."

On-screen, in one of the four frames, is now a local news break-in. Paris can see a pair of Cleveland Heights zone cars in a Dairy Barn lot and thinks:

We are in the Cain Towers apartments.

Christian says: "You will now place the barrel of the weapon against your forehead and pull the trigger."

"What?"

"If you do this within . . . let's see . . . four minutes . . . I'll let her go. If not, I am going to drive nails into her hands and feet and then I'm going to cut off her head. Which do you think our viewers would prefer?"

Viewers? Paris thinks. This is being *broadcast*? "What are you talking about?"

"You're the main attraction on Cable99 right now. Dare I say, soon, worldwide."

"You're out of your mind."

"Perhaps. But seeing as you're really not that much of a

detective, I doubt seriously that you are qualified to make such a damning diagnosis. No *offense*."

"This isn't going to happen."

The lower-right-hand frame flickers with still pictures now. Christian, in front of a rusty old Bonneville. Christian and his sister at Cedar Point.

You've got to know what breaks his heart.

"She didn't kill herself," Paris says, knowing now that the real Sarah Weiss is dead. The woman in his apartment had been an impostor. "It wasn't suicide."

Christian freezes, his face contorting with rage. "Shut up."

"It's true. They're reopening the case. They're treating it as a homicide."

"Shut up!"

"I know you blame me for prosecuting her, but I was doing my job. The evidence was there. But now—*now*—there is evidence that she was not driven to suicide. It is much worse."

"I don't want to hear this."

"Don't you want to see whoever did this to your sister pay for it? Isn't that what all this has been about?"

Christian steps away from the crucifix.

Yes, Paris thinks.

Stall him.

"So, I can walk away from this?" Christian asks. "You and me'll hit the trail and round up the bad guys, sheriff? Please."

"Of course not. But you . . . you can get *help*. And I can see that justice is done for you."

"Shut up," Christian says. "Not a word." He holds up a pair of spikes. In the other hand, he holds a crown of razor wire. "If you say—"

"No!"

"What did I just tell you?" Christian screams. "You *killed* her, you asshole."

"*Wait!*"

Christian does not wait. He crosses the room, walking right up to the camera. In an instant, Paris's computer screen goes blue again.

But Paris can still hear. Christian has left the microphone on. Christian screams: "Pull the trigger, detective! Pull the trigger *now!* You can still save this woman! You have ninety seconds! *The whole world is watching you!*"

Paris hears Christian's footsteps storming around the room. He hears the music, which had been a faint, scratchy noise in the background, suddenly jump in volume.

"Christian!"

"Save her life!" Christian says. "Pull the trigger *now!*"

"Stop!"

But he does not stop. Paris hears the ugly, hateful sound. The icy clank of hammer on steel.

Then come the screams.

FURNELL BRAXTON IS bathed in sweat. For a single, crazy instant, he sees himself on stage in a huge ballroom at the Marriott picking up a local Emmy. He checks his levels. The audio level is dead center; the video, although lagging slightly, is clear. There are now four separate feeds. The lunatic in the white room with the girl. The looping video of all the old pictures. The cop in the black room with the gun. And the NBC live-news cam.

Furnell had taken the live network feed and inserted it into his cablecast like Harry Blackstone dovetailing two halves of a bridge deck. He hadn't the slightest idea if he had any right whatsoever to grab the feed, but on the other hand, at the moment, he simply didn't care.

This is Emmy time.

On-screen, in the upper-right-hand frame, the lunatic is poised, ready to slam home a nail he had begun to pound into the nude woman's left hand. The nude woman is tied to a cross. The lunatic is watching his monitor, his hand over the woman's mouth.

In the lower-left frame, now, a medium shot of the Cain Towers apartment shot from across the street. Cop cars everywhere. You can hear a helicopter, too.

The lower-right-hand frame is a video feed showing an old crime scene photo, a kitchen floor covered in blood.

But it is the frame in the upper left that has Furnell, and

everyone else, watching, spellbound. In that frame sits the police officer, on the verge of suicide. He has a 9 mm pistol reversed in his hands, the barrel against the center of his forehead, his thumb is on the trigger, his face is corded with fear. At exactly midnight he says:

"I know you will see this one day, Missy. I hope you won't, but I know you will." His voice breaks. "I love you and your mother with all my heart."

He pulls the trigger.

The sound is more of a muffled clap than a bang, but the body bucks and shakes, then Furnell sees the hole, dead center on the man's forehead. The cop slumps into the chair, still and silent.

In the upper-right-hand frame the man in the white caftan steps away from the woman on the cross. He walks up to the camera, stares. He is looking at his monitor in disbelief. Then, he begins to laugh, high and loud and long, spinning in a circle, shouting in tongues.

Death, Furnell Braxton thinks as he turns and deposits his Tony Roma's dinner all over the control panel, his acceptance speech on hold for the moment.

He had broadcast death.

Live.

❖ 76 ❖

THE *AMANITA MUSCARIA* is in full, adolescent blossom in my brain, my muscles, my blood. I feel primally fit, cunning.

Jack Paris is dead.

The world might think he sacrificed himself to save the woman, that he is some kind of noble savage, but we know the real reason:

Guilt.

My very first spell.

My *madrina* screams but I can barely hear her over the mad rumbling, the swelling chorus of the music. I select the machete, comforted by its heft, its balance.

I will behead her with one stroke of steel.

I look directly into the camera lens as the floor beneath me begins to quake and shudder, to shake the very foundation of the building.

To this world I say: "This is for Sarafina. *Mi hermana.*"

"And this is for Fayette Martin."

The voice comes from right behind me. *Inches away.* I spin.

It is Paris. He has big hands, like my dad's.

For the first time in my life, everything goes quiet.

I spring.

Dad fires.

VOODOO KILLER PLEADS GUILTY
BY THE ASSOCIATED PRESS
Filed at 12:31 PM

CLEVELAND (AP)—The man who killed his victims, then mutilated their bodies with Santerian symbols, pleaded guilty today to seven counts of aggravated murder, admitting that he had killed one victim by chopping off the top of her head; another, by castration.

The plea bargain promises Christian del Blanco, 30, a life sentence without the possibility of parole. He would have faced the death penalty if he had been convicted of first-degree murder on any of the counts.

After his arrest early New Year's Day, Mr. del Blanco confessed to murdering Fayette M. Martin, 30, last December after luring her to an abandoned inner-city building, as well as Willis James Walker, 48. It is unclear as to how Mr. del Blanco knew Mr. Walker, or what drew the two men to the Dream-A-Dream Motel, a motel on Cleveland's east side.

The other victims, Isaac C. Levertov, 79, and his wife Edith R., 81, were apparently victims of a sacrificial killing.

Another victim, Edward Moriceau, 60, was the proprietor of an herb shop that specializes in Santerian artifacts.

As he entered his plea, Mr. del Blanco shocked the prosecutors and his court-appointed defense attorney by mentioning two other victims. One, a female accomplice named Celeste L. Conroy, 26. Police found Ms. Conroy's body in the basement of a building on East Eighty-fifth Street and Carnegie Avenue where they say she was strangled. The other, a shooting victim found in Cain Park in Cleveland Heights, a victim only recently identified as Jeremiah D. Cross, 29, a Cleveland Heights attorney who once represented the defendant's sister on a murder charge of her own.

Due to injuries sustained during his arrest, Mr. del Blanco appeared in court in a wheelchair. Before being returned to his cell, he apologized to the victims' families in fluent Spanish.

Sentencing is set for January 15.

❖ 78 ❖

THE FALLOUT FROM any case the size and weight of the Ochosi murders is always far-reaching. There are two books in progress. A four-part series is under way in the *Plain Dealer*.

Bobby Dietricht had suffered first-degree burns on his right arm and leg that night, as well as a fractured ulna in his left arm. Greg had taken three .22 caliber bullets to the left side of his vest, breaking two ribs. Both are scheduled to be back on the job within a few weeks.

After murdering Jeremiah Cross, Christian knew that eventually the Sarah Weiss connection would be made. It was then that Christian must have taken a few of his extra trinkets and set up a makeshift altar on the second floor of Jeremiah Cross's house, rigging some plastique to a mercury switch.

Just in case.

Records at the Veterans Administration showed that a man named Jeremiah Cross had requested a file on Demetrius Salters around a week after Jeremiah Cross had been murdered. It explains where Jeremiah Cross's ID had gone after he was killed, as well as the fact that Christian del Blanco was moving in on the old cop.

Ronnie Boudreaux had called Paris on New Year's Day. After having been sapped in the back of the head by Chris-

331

tian del Blanco the night before, Ronnie proclaimed that, although he was grateful unto the Lord that Christian del Blanco had spared his life, he and Paris are finally *égal*—that all debts have officially been paid.

As far as Paris could piece together, courtesy of the thick packet of letters they had found in Christian's apartment, Christian and Sarafina del Blanco—who signed all of her letters "Fina" —had split up after the murder of their father. Christian went first to San Diego, then into Mexico where he spent the next dozen or so years of his life. Sarafina had worked as an escort and a model, mostly trade shows, traveling the country under a variety of names. Delia White, Bianca del Gato, Sarah Weiss. Her past had turned up very little when she had stood trial. The letters from Sarafina to her brother also kept tabs on Michael Ryan, the man they blamed for letting their father get away with what they felt was murder.

When Michael Ryan moved to San Diego, it became an unexpected opportunity for Christian to sneak across from Tijuana and take a shot at him. But Michael Ryan was not that easy a target in San Diego. He had been a patrolman in a heavily armed zone car.

Carrie Ryan was a different story. A beat-up old Bonneville was seen tearing around a corner, leaving the girl's small, ruined body behind. Descriptions of the driver were given, but the teenager was never caught.

By the time Michael had moved back to Ohio, Sarafina and Christian had reunited in Cleveland, even though Christian was still wanted for questioning in his father's murder.

They knew that Michael needed money for his daughter's care. And they knew that Michael had something *they* wanted.

Sarafina met Michael, gained his confidence, struck a deal. She offered him ten thousand dollars to steal the murder investigation file of Anthony del Blanco, the disappearance of which would all but eliminate any chance of Christian's future arrest.

That night at the Renaissance Hotel they got everything they wanted.

Including Michael Ryan's life.

When Sarafina committed suicide, Christian was distraught. He had worked as a prostitute in Mexico, and gained a reputation as a skilled lover, especially among the S & M and voyeur/exhibitionist crowd in Acapulco. He signed on with NeTrix, knowing he would meet the right woman for his "spell," if he could draw her in with his charms. Thus, Fayette Martin's fate had become sealed.

How Christian came to meet Mary is the mystery. In her statement, Mary had said they met in front of her building and it was after that he blackmailed her into helping him, threatening her daughter's life, a story the prosecutor's office seems very willing to buy.

Christian isn't talking.

Although Michael Ryan was posthumously cleared by Internal Affairs, anyone who looks closely at the evidence would never believe anything but the obvious.

Mike Ryan died in a pair of twenty-five-dollar shoes.

The money was never for him.

At the end of the first week in January, as Paris begins to box up the Ochosi files at his desk, it occurs to him how close it had all come to him once again, how close to Beth and Melissa. The man he had seen with Beth at Shaker Square—the guy with the shoulders—really *was* a guy Beth had met online at #christiansingles. The man's religious leanings, however, had not yet assuaged Paris's jealousy.

But Christian del Blanco did have his sights set on Beth. Paris has no doubt about that. Christian had found her e-mail address, had sent her the self-launching computer file of the velvet wing chair. Perhaps he meant to put her in it before it was all over. He just ran out of time.

As Paris marches the box of files to the elevator, it is that image that chills him more deeply than the winter storm raging outside.

* * *

Her hand is still in a splint. The doctors say she will, in time, regain most of its use, but the thick mound of scar tissue where the spike had penetrated will always remain.

She is being released from the hospital within the hour.

Paris stands at the foot of the bed. Mary sits, hands in her lap, a small suitcase at her feet. The only sounds are the hush of the heat register, the pellets of freezing rain on the window. Paris looks out at the confetti of ice-slicked cars in the University Hospital lot. He waits for the proper amount of silence to pass, then says: "Do you know why I'm here?"

Mary draws a deep breath. "Well, I've got it down to two things," she says, her voice shaky, hesitant. "I'm leaving here in either a cab or a police car. I've been up all night bouncing between the two."

"I came here to tell you that there won't be any charges filed against you," Paris says in a dry, emotionless monotone. He waits. Behind him, Mary begins to cry, softly. He doesn't look. He isn't interested in her tears.

After a few moments she says: "Thank you."

"I had nothing to do with it. Believe me."

"I am so sorry."

Paris turns around, surprised at how much older she looks. "What are you sorry about again?"

"Everything. For making it personal for you. For putting you in danger."

"I'm in danger by my second cup of coffee every day. You made a fool of me."

"I didn't mean to."

"Look, if the prosecutor's office didn't consider you a victim in all this, they might think you were trying to frame me for a capital crime. Maybe they need a little prodding in that direction. A little *character* reference." He drops a pair of black-and-white photos on the bed. Blurry photos of a woman running from the Dream-A-Dream Motel. "Maybe these would help."

"You don't understand."

"I understand *plenty*. I understand there's an active file in Robbery called the Kissing Bandit file. Romantic, huh? I understand how your prints led me right to a partial print in that file, a series of robberies about which no detective can ever seem to get a victim to stay on the record. It's all about a woman who dumps a couple roofies in the Cuervo and shakes down horny middle-aged businessmen."

Mary is silent for a moment, her heart quickening. "Everything I did, I did for my daughter. You have a little girl. Draw the line for me. What *wouldn't* you do?"

Paris has no answer to this question.

But it is just one of many he is certain will never be answered, especially about the Ochosi murders. And he knows why. The fact that such a high-profile monster as Christian del Blanco is now behind bars, and the fact that the Comeback City can now begin to pave over the nightmare, means that a lot of the loose ends are never going to be tied up.

Paris buttons his coat, pulls on his gloves.

"Is this where you tell me to leave town?" she asks, her eyes riveted on the photos on the bed.

Paris walks to the door. He glances at the picture of the beautiful, dark-haired little girl on the nightstand. "If you were anyone else, I'd probably have to."

"I understand."

Paris holds her gaze, recalling the last time he had looked so deeply into her eyes. He told himself he wouldn't, but does anyway. "Let me ask you something."

"Anything."

"None of it was real, right?"

Her face softens. She is young again. "*All* of it was real. We just met in hell."

Paris doesn't bother to respond.

Mary stands, takes a tentative step toward him, stops. "How do I prove it to you?"

Paris lingers for a moment, burnishing her silhouette deep into his memory, then turns and walks down the hall.

* * *

The packed courtroom is suffused with a jungle silence. Judge Eileen J. Corrigan presides. She finishes her decree. "You are to serve these terms consecutively, without the possibility of parole."

In the demeaning light of a room where justice is done, Christian del Blanco looks broken, small. Although Paris had aimed dead-center at his chest, fully prepared to blast him to hell, when Christian had leapt up from the floor the bullet tore into his right hip instead. The unfortunate prognosis is that he will one day walk again.

"Is there anything you wish to say to the court at this time?" Judge Corrigan asks.

"No, your honor," Christian says, head down, the perfect penitent.

"May God have mercy on your soul." Judge Corrigan bangs her gavel. She pauses briefly, then exits in a flurry of polished black cotton, an air of shunted revulsion.

Amid the melee of reporters leaving the courtroom, Jack Paris and Carla Davis wind their way to the defense table. Paris glances down at Christian del Blanco sitting in his wheelchair. He studies the man's sharp-hewn looks, thinking: He's going to have a *great* time in prison.

Suddenly, Christian looks up, acknowledging Paris's presence. The sheer blackness of his eyes chills Paris's blood. Paris had looked into these eyes once before.

Except, that time, they belonged to Sarah Weiss.

Christian says: "I have to know."

"Know?" Paris replies. "Know what?"

"How?"

Paris understands what Christian is talking about, just as he realizes that something like this would eat at a person like him. Christian the trickster, the man who had recruited a woman named Celeste Conroy to do his dirty work; Celeste who looked so much like Sarah Weiss that Paris had no trouble believing it really was her that night in his apartment. The magic mushroom helped a little, of course.

"You mean my little misdirection with the computer camera?" Paris asks.

"Yes."

"Actually, I got it out of a book. A hell of a good book. I think even you might get something out of it." Paris reaches into his briefcase. He drops a thin, softcover book on the table in front of Christian. *Internet for Idiots*. On top he drops a packet of ketchup and a paper clip.

Paris leans close to Christian's ear, and adds: "No *offense*."

❖ 79 ❖

A WEEK AFTER Christian del Blanco's sentencing, a January heat wave descends upon Cleveland. It is fifty degrees and portends an early spring, a lie that Clevelanders have bought into forever. It is Bobby Dietricht's third day back on the job; Greg Ebersole's first.

At noon, while looking out his window at the shirtsleeved men and the coatless women on the street, Paris hears Greg's knock on his doorjamb.

"Hey, Greg."

"Look at this. I can't bel*ieve* it," Greg says, entering. "I was just going through the backlog of mail and I got *this*."

He hands Paris a letter on a Mount Sinai Hospital letterhead.

"It's gotta be a joke, right?" Greg asks. "It's either a joke or a mistake, right?"

Paris reads:

Dear Mr. Ebersole: Please let the enclosed invoice serve as your paid-in-full statement regarding all medical bills for Maxim A. Ebersole, in the amount of forty-four thousand eight hundred sixty dollars, forwarded to us by The Becky's Angel Foundation, a non-profit organization.

"Wow," Paris says, reading it a second time, then handing the letter back. "And you didn't know anything about this?"

"Not a thing," Greg says.

"Amazing."

"Do you think I'll be allowed to keep it? I mean, job-wise?"

"I'm not sure," Paris says. "But if it's a foundation, I'm pretty sure you can."

Greg reads the letter again. "Have you ever heard of The Becky's Angel Foundation?"

Paris has to smile.

Rebecca D'Angelo.

"I may have run across the name," he says, his mind drifting to the old police report sitting on his dining room table, the one he had kept for so many years like a dirty secret, the one detailing how a then-assistant prosecutor was caught with a young girl in an alley behind the Hanna Theatre. An assistant prosecutor who now sits as a juvenile court judge.

Maybe I've found a use for that report after all, Paris thinks.

Greg shakes his head, smiles. "What a world, huh?"

"Yep," Paris says, clapping his friend on the shoulder. "Crazier by the minute."

"A fine specimen of dog," Paris says. "Beautiful *boy*, Declan." The Jack Russell terrier responds to Paris's encomium, its muscular haunches propelling him from the ground up to Paris's chest with one supple leap. "Is he a good ratter?"

"*Oh* yeah," Mercedes replies. "He's terrorized every squirrel for five blocks in every direction from my house. You'd think they'd have a contract out on him by now."

They are standing under a red cedar gazebo, waiting out a drizzle that has slightly delayed this year's Terrier Time Trials in Middlefield, a rural community near Cleveland. The time trials are a yearly event in which terriers of all types are tested in a wide variety of ways. The most popular, certainly among the dogs themselves, are the go-to-ground events, where a tunnel is buried in the ground, with a rat in a cage at the end, and the dogs are timed for how long it takes them to find and work their quarry. Dachshunds, Cairns, Westies, Dandie Dinmonts, and the undisputed king of the ratters, the Jack Russell, take part.

Manfred is a two-time champion.

Mercedes Cruz's article for *Mondo Latino* has turned into a feature for *Vanity Fair*, where it is currently slated for August publication. She had spent twenty-four hours or so in the trunk of her car, parked on East Eighty-fifth Street, surviving on Girl Scout cookies and a frozen bottle of Evian water she had found in her gym bag. Aside from having to be restrained by no fewer than three bailiffs on the day Christian del Blanco was arraigned, she seems to be over it.

The good news is that she has promised Paris a steak dinner at Morton's when the *Vanity Fair* check arrives. Manny and Declan have been promised the bones.

"Come *on*, Dad!" Melissa shouts. "They're *starting*."

Melissa stands at the edge of the split rail-fenced training field. Next to her stands her grandmother. Both are dressed in jeans and hooded parkas. Both are wearing rubber boots already caked with cold Ohio late-winter mud.

"Yeah, let's *go*," Gabriella says, echoing her granddaughter's plea. "Come on, Jackie. Bring your friend."

"Jackie?" Mercedes asks. She had lost a few pounds since her ordeal, had confessed to joining a karate class. Her braces are off, her hair is ponytailed for the day. She looks fit and agile and lithely sexy.

Before heading off to the trial field, Paris turns his attention to the two dogs before him.

Manny and Declan sit at his feet, considering each other carefully, nose to nose, brothers at heart, competitors for the moment. Manny looks up at Paris, knowing it is time to go, surely wondering if, in Declan Cruz, he may have finally met his match.

Paris glances at Mercedes, catches her smiling at him.

And begins to wonder the same thing.

❖ 80 ❖

THE DARK-HAIRED GIRL in seat 18A of the Greyhound bus heading west on Route 70 is making slow work of her Famous Amos chocolate chip cookie. Her mother, in 18B, holds an issue of *Vogue* in her hands, but isn't reading. Instead, she stares out the window at the flat Indiana landscape.

At the Indianapolis stop, the woman and the little girl exit the bus. They both freshen up in the ladies' room, buy a few more snacks, some tissues.

When they reboard and settle into their seats, the little girl's mother thinks about their future. They have just over two thousand dollars. They have nowhere to live. There are no job prospects. And yet, she thinks as she looks out the window to see the sun suddenly peer from behind a cloud, ever since that registered letter arrived, so crazily out of the blue, they suddenly have everything.

They have each other.

As the bus begins to pull out of the Indianapolis station, she glances up from her magazine to see a man of about thirty-five making his way to the back of the bus, a small duffel bag over his shoulder, a cute boy of six in tow. The only seats open are 18C and 18D.

The man smiles, stashes his bag in the overhead. Before sitting down, he ruffles the young boy's hair, then looks at the woman. "Hi," the man says. He has kind, blue-gray eyes, sandy hair. His son looks just like him.

"Hi," the woman answers.

"This is Andrew," the man says. "And my name is Paul. What's yours?"

The woman in 18B looks at the man, then at the boy, waiting for what she figures to be the proper amount of time. For a single mom. She reaches over and takes her daughter's gloriously sticky little hand in her own.

"Mary," she says. "My name is Mary."

❖ 81 ❖

THE WOMAN AT the USAir counter at Hopkins International Airport looks five years younger than the last time he had seen her.

The cop walking up behind her looks as fresh as yesterday's chili.

"Hey there," the cop says.

The woman spins around, as if expecting something . . . *what?* Terrible? For a moment, her expression is unreadable, then it fashions a smile, quickly and genuinely. "*Jack*," she says. "How sweet of you to come. How did you—"

"I'm a detective," Paris says. "It's a gift."

Dolores Ryan finishes her business at the counter, then turns back to Paris. "Is this an official city of Cleveland send-off?" she asks.

Paris smiles. "Yeah. Something like that."

The two of them step away from the counter. Dolores glances around the huge ticket lobby at the flurry of travelers. Her eyes find a familiar place; her heart, it seems, a secluded memory. "I remember, one time, I met Michael here when he was flying in from some cop seminar. Forensics, or ordnance, or something like that."

"Indianapolis."

"Right. He went twice a year. You were at those, too?"

"*Oh* yeah."

343

"Ever learn anything?"

"Well, I can tell you that it's precisely twenty steps from the bar to the men's room at the airport Ramada."

"That's what I thought."

Paris looks heavenward. "Sorry, Mikey."

"Anyway, Michael's flight was really late that time. Maybe two in the morning. And all I had on was this black plastic raincoat and spike heels."

Paris's eyebrows arch in unison. "Nothing else?"

"Not a stitch."

"I see."

"So, we're down in baggage claim, and it's deserted, and I give him this quick flash, right? Michael goes five shades of Irish red. Doesn't know what to do with himself." Dolores covers her mouth, keeping the laugh inside. "Do you remember that crooked smile he had when he was embarrassed?"

"I remember it well," Paris says. "Although, as I recall, it wasn't all that easy to embarrass Mike Ryan."

"Tell me about it."

"Let's get back to the black plastic raincoat," Paris says.

Dolores smiles, takes a moment, giving the remembrance its due. "We made love in the parking lot, Jack. Slow, sweet, married love. It wasn't all hot and crazy like you might imagine when a wife who thinks her looks are going south tries a stunt like that. I don't think Michael took his eyes from mine the whole time we walked from the baggage claim out to the parking lot. He was like a little kid in a toy store and the most sophisticated man in the world at the same time. And he was the best father I've ever known."

Dolores glances at the steward standing by the entrance ramp. Carrie Ryan, sitting in front of the man, looks at Paris, smiles, lifts a thin arm to wave. The little girl's smile squeezes Paris's heart, and, if there had been any doubt—and there had been many—he now knows he is doing the right thing.

Paris turns his attention back to Dolores. He reaches out,

takes her hands in his, searching for the right words. He had rehearsed them for a day and a half, but that didn't seem to matter at the moment. Finally, he says: "Look . . . Dolores, I . . . I just wanted you to know that it's over. All of it. That's what's important. You're going to have a whole new life in Florida. All of this is behind you now. Everything. Do you know what I mean?"

"Yes."

"Do you *really?*"

Dolores looks deeply into Paris's eyes. She holds him there for an instant, suspended, giving Paris hope that he will hear the words that will put his heart at ease. Instead, she offers him a sexy half-smile, nothing more. And, in that moment, Paris sees the twenty-four-year-old Dolores Alessio he had met so many years ago, the street-talking firebrand who had stolen Michael Ryan's heart.

"First call for boarding, USAir flight 188, nonstop to Tampa, Florida. . . ."

They both glance at the entrance ramp. The steward begins to roll Carrie Ryan's wheelchair onboard.

Dolores slides her hands around Paris's waist, hooking her thumbs through his belt loops. She regards him slowly, head to toe, and says: "You know, there's something I've always wanted to tell you, Detective Jack Paris."

"Uh-oh," Paris says. "An airport confession. I'm not sure I'm ready for this."

"It's a *good* thing."

"You sure?"

"Yes," Dolores says. "I'm sure."

"Okay. Let's hear it."

"I always thought you were the handsomest of Michael's cop-buddies."

Paris blushes a little. "I'm shocked."

"Shocked?" Dolores asks. "Why on earth would you be shocked?"

"Michael actually had other kinds of friends?"

Dolores laughs, pulls Paris into her arms, and the two of

them embrace for a full and solemn minute, holding each other with a passion forged of secrets, a bond of silence they both now realize, in their hearts, can never be broken.

Ten minutes later, as Paris watches the 727 make the final turn on the runway, readying for takeoff, he reaches into his coat pocket and removes the old crime-scene photo of Anthony del Blanco's mutilated body lying in the parking lot. He also removes the crumpled piece of paper, unfolds it, smooths it against his chest. He reads it for the fiftieth time.

Please leave the newspaper in the wooden box until Sunday. Thanks!

Paris isn't sure when the seed first took root within him. Maybe it was the moment he recalled seeing the red wig in the hatbox while rummaging around in bay number 202, the first time he visited My-Self Storage. Or perhaps it was when he had parked on Denison Avenue two days ago, binoculars in hand, the day Dolores Ryan sold her yellow Mazda to an elderly couple.

He looks at the back of the old photo, at the words written in the same blocky style, the same red ink as Dolores's note to the paperboy:

Evil is a breed, Fingers.

The jet engines roar.

Paris closes his eyes for a moment, imagining the madness of the final few hours of Sarafina del Blanco's life. Deep inside, where his own guilts live, he knows it just might have been Dolores Ryan, in her red wig, drinking at the Gamekeeper's Taverne with Sarafina that night. He knows it just might have been Dolores Ryan who sat with Sarafina in that car, on that hill in Russell Township, polishing off a bottle of whiskey. He knows it just might have been Dolores Ryan—a woman who had now lost both her father and her husband to a murderer's bullet—who had then splashed gasoline all over the interior of the car and, mad-eyed with rage and hatred and vengeance, tossed a match.

As the last of the exhaust from the 727 dissipates high

above the runway at Hopkins International Airport, as Detective John Salvatore Paris turns on his heels and heads for the parking lot, and the city beyond, there are two thoughts that track him, two thoughts he hopes will bring closure to the insanity that began on a hot July day twenty-six years ago, two thoughts that will be at his side, later that night, as he sits upon the rocks at the Seventy-second Street pier, as he makes a pile of photographs and negatives and yellowed police reports and handwritten notes, as he starts a small, purging fire of his own:

You square it with your God, Dusty.

I'll square it with mine.

❖ ❖

EPILOGUE

HE IS SIX-FIVE, two-seventy. A Goliath, even in here.

We are in the laundry, in the northwest corner, a spot furthest from the guard station at the southernmost end of C Block. We are both serving life terms at the Ohio State Penitentiary in Youngstown.

"My name is Antoine Walker," the big man says, blocking my path. "Ring a bell?"

I take a half-step back. The bullet with which Jack Paris had surprised me had shattered most of my right hip. The small stumble is not lost on the predator in front of me.

"The world is full of Walkers," I say.

"Not no more, see," Antoine says, inching closer. "One less now."

"Is that right?"

Movement behind me.

"Man name a *Willis* Walker. My daddy. Got his motherfuckin' *dick* cut off."

"I might have heard about it."

"Me too," Antoine says. "We *all* heard about it. Heard about that voodoo shit, too. They say you some kinda witch. That true?"

"No."

Antoine steps closer, towering over me. Hawk and rodent.

"The pain is coming," Antoine says. "You know that, right?"

351

I remain silent. I sense a presence behind me. I feel hot breath on my neck.

"The man ax you a question," the presence says. "He ax you a *question*."

"Yes," I say, without turning around. "I know the pain is coming."

"But you don't know when, do you?"

"No. I do not."

"I'm doin' life plus twenty," Antoine says. "You?"

This time, my silence suffices.

"See? We got *much* time," Antoine says as he unbuttons the fly on his prison scrubs. He does not take his eyes off me. "Much time in*deed*."

I feel a crowding of men behind me. The damp, ripe assemblage of a dozen or so bodies. When Antoine Walker places a heavy hand on my shoulder, I sink slowly to my knees, my mind and body and soul returning to another time, to a stifling room above a Tijuana bodega, thinking:

I am *nkisi*.

I am *brujo*.

I will survive.

Many thanks to Jennifer Sawyer Fisher and everyone
at HarperCollins; thanks also to my sister—handler
extraordinaire and keeper of the Certs; and thanks
especially to BQ and Bones for getting out
the coffee shop vote.

❖   ❖

Translation of the Dedication

*"Who starts with a spoon will finish with a ladle,
Who starts with a ladle will finish with a spoon."*

—ESTONIAN PROVERB